Behind the Green Curtain

Riley LaShea

Romance Books by Riley LaShea

Night Falls on the Piazza
Club Storyville

The Meddling Friends Trilogy
The Wish List
The Four Proposals
The Island Getaway

Other Books by Riley LaShea

Dr. Todson's Home for Incorrigible Women

The Black Forest Trilogy
Black Forest: Kingdoms Fall
Black Forest: Magicks Rise
Black Forest: Stories End

The Innocents
A Special Gift From Gram V

For everyone who asked if there would ever be a paperback.
Apparently, yes.

1

Halston & Company was like any office of its kind. The people at the top made all the money, while the work fell through the floors to pile on those at the bottom. It was an indisputable fact of life that insinuated itself into Caton's cubicle one random Tuesday morning in September when her supervisor appeared at her shoulder with the jolting abruptness of a Jack-in-the-box.

"Could you make copies of this?" the woman barked with more irritation than authority, as if she too had just been interrupted by the work of someone else.

"Yeah, sure," Caton replied, swiveling her chair in time to have a heavier-than-it-looked file dropped into her lap. Grunting as her supervisor walked off without a hint of thanks, Caton pushed up from the faux leather desk chair and headed for the copy room.

As far as she could tell from the snarky comments and water-cooler complaints that made up the background noise of the office, she was a minority of one, but she couldn't care less what she did each day as long as the checks kept coming, and she wasn't about to complain. She had lied to get the job, rounding down her education after the dozenth interviewer called her overqualified when she possessed minimal qualifications at best. A fancy degree and zero job experience qualified her for absolutely nothing, apparently, and if she had one regret in life it was that no one had asked, "You're getting a doctorate in Philosophy?" and then slapped sense into her when she responded "Yes" with the misplaced pride of youth.

The copy room door was barely ajar, but mind about as present as it was on any given workday, Caton failed to heed the warning, walking in on an event in progress that was completely inappropriate, but hardly unexpected. A mostly-closed door at Halston & Company was the equivalent of a sock on the doorknob of a college dorm room, and it wasn't the first time she had walked in on a similar scene in her eight months on the Halston & Company staff. The owner and CEO, Jack Halston, was a predator, a well-known and disregarded fact. Since the copy room was generally empty and provided the only privacy on the first floor, where entry-level fresh meat was kept on ice, it was one of his favorite hunting spots.

"I'm sorry," Caton uttered. That she had seen it, not that she had interrupted. "I'll come back."

"Don't be silly," Jack responded, removing only the hand from beneath the front hem of the transcriptionist's skirt, leaving the one blatantly on her ass. "The more the merrier."

As was their customary dance, Caton leveled her eyes at him in a way she hoped conveyed how much that wasn't going to happen and Jack grinned as if he thought himself the cleverest man on the planet.

"I should get back to work," the transcriptionist said uncomfortably, stepping out of Jack's groping hand and pushing her skirt back down her thighs.

"I didn't realize you'd stopped." Caton couldn't help herself as the woman walked by, and the transcriptionist paused long enough to give her a heated glare before continuing from the room.

"Looks like it's just the two of us," Jack said. "Come on in."

Making a deliberate show of pushing the door fully open, Caton walked to the copier, and Jack backed off, though not far enough for comfort. Placing the first stack of papers in the feed tray, Caton could feel his eyes on her. It took a distinct lack of imagination to know what he was thinking.

"You know..." Jack took a step closer, as if there was space to spare between them. "We still have room on the seventh floor, and I still think you should apply up there."

His hand running down the back of her arm, Caton shrugged it off. "I don't think I have the skills you look for up there, Sir," she responded, willing the gears in the copier to turn faster.

"Oh, I bet you do." Jack took another step until Caton could feel him just shy of brushing against her. It was the creep equivalent of a four-year-old holding his finger a half-inch from someone's face and saying 'I'm not touching you. I'm not touching you,' and she stopped herself just short of telling Jack as much as his eyes moved over her face. "I think you have all kinds of talents you're not telling anyone about."

Watching the number on the copier count down, Caton's finger hovered over the stop button, but she knew well that stopping the job mid-print would only result in a paper jam somewhere in the recesses of the machine. The last thing she wanted was to be bent over and preoccupied in Jack's presence.

"I know you do some of Jenna's work when she gets overwhelmed," Jack switched tactics.

Amusement overtaking her exasperation, Caton laughed. That was putting it mildly. In the six months since Jenna was promoted to Jack's personal assistant-cum-courtesan, Caton had done everything that crossed Jenna's desk, except for Jack, which was one part of her job Jenna was welcome to keep for herself.

"You shouldn't let all that talent go to waste," Jack added, sliding another step into her as the last sheet of paper shot into the catch tray.

Having to lean into him to fetch the copies, Caton took the move elbow-first and harder than necessary, gratified at the puff of air that expelled from Jack as she retrieved them. "I'm happy where I am," she declared, gathering the rest of the stack and heading for the door.

When Jack caught her arm, Caton's gaze turned deadly, and, releasing her at once, Jack put both hands in the air as if he was the victim of an unfair accusation.

"It's nice that you like your job." He brandished his laser-white teeth. Everyone thought Jack so charming. No one more so than Jack. "But that is a career-stalling attitude. You never get anywhere by being content with what you don't have. You've got everything you need to make it on the executive floor. You shouldn't be afraid of success."

Amazing. He almost made it sound like career advice.

"I'm not afraid of success," Caton replied. "I'm afraid of heights."

The sound of Jack's laughter crawling over her as she left the copy room, she wanted to keep walking, past her cubicle and out the front door. Or to call a lawyer. Jack really needed that kind of intervention. The eyes of her coworkers casting away a pair at a time as she took her walk of shame back to her desk, though, she knew no one in the office would back her up.

Power bought loyalty. That's why Jack had both.

2

Eyes locked on the plate before her, Caton didn't realize she had stopped seeing it until fingertips digging into the muscle at her shoulder stirred her back into awareness. Groaning appreciatively, she leaned into the touch, and it continued long enough to loosen the tension, before Laura dropped her hand to return to her dessert.

"You should quit," she declared, taking a bite.

"I can't quit," Caton responded, picking at the pie on her own plate, unable to stir up the desire to eat it. Pushing it away, she leaned back and stared across the room at Laura's bookshelf, wondering how anyone managed to align books with such precision. "Not until I find something else."

"Why does he keep coming after you?" Laura asked with palpable frustration, before sending a sidelong smile Caton's way. "I mean, aside from the obvious?"

"Because I keep saying no, I think," Caton returned.

"You can't be the only woman there who has said no to him," Laura insisted.

"I'm not so sure about that," Caton uttered. Thinking back on past encounters with Jack, she tried to remember the number of times she had seen him without a handful of office worker. They were rare to say the least. "I think he also thinks I'm younger than I am." She got that a lot, though she wasn't sure if it was due to her youthful appearance or her lack of real world accomplishment. "He probably has fantasies about deflowering a late-life virgin or something."

Head turning slowly, Laura licked her lip, smirk revealing her particular amusement at that notion. "Yeah, you're not that," she said.

"No, I'm not." Caton managed a laugh at Jack's expense as Laura leaned closer, mouth opening against Caton's just long enough to tease her with the taste of chocolate.

Watching Laura return to eating, Caton shifted in her chair, hand sliding up the wool fabric against Laura's thigh. "Is everything set for the weekend?"

"Mm hm," Laura responded, scraping chocolate off her fork as she pulled it from between her lips. "Now, we just have to be there at an ungodly hour Saturday morning to set up."

"Do you want some help?"

"Sure," Laura returned hesitantly. "You can help set up. You can bring us all breakfast. Then, you can come back here and sleep."

Eyes narrowing, Caton watched Laura fork the final bite into her mouth. "I know I'm no expert," she uttered, slightly jilted. "But I'm sure I can talk to a few kids."

"No." Laura shook her head. "It's too much."

"You do it all the time."

"I don't have to medicate afterwards," Laura softly countered, turning to maneuver her leg between Caton's, casually intertwining them, hands braced on either side of Caton's chair as she leaned closer. "Face it, your heart bleeds too easily to spend a day listening to other people's problems."

"You think I'm weak," Caton replied without real fight, wanting to defend herself with some little-known truth, far too aware Laura was already stating the truth.

"It's not weakness," Laura responded. "Besides, there are some areas in which you are..." Laura shook her head, gaze trailing down Caton's throat as she searched for the word. "Mighty."

"Mighty?" Even knowing it was praise as diversion, a grin tilted Caton's lips as she closed her hands around Laura's hips to draw her closer. "I've heard that about me."

"It's true," Laura breathlessly replied, arms snaking over Caton's shoulders.

On her feet in an instant, Caton pulled Laura up with her, and, leaning in to place a fleeting kiss against her lips, Laura dropped her hand into Caton's and tugged her toward the bedroom.

3

Spotlights cast the grandeur of the Halston residence against the black backdrop of night as Jack's car curved around the driveway and came to a stop on the gray cobblestone. All other lights were off, even the porch light, Jack noted, as he climbed out of the driver's seat and glanced toward the sky, trying to predict the chance of rain.

It would take only a few extra minutes to put the car in the garage, but, at the late hour, those minutes were precious, and he needed as much sleep as he could finagle out of the few hours left before morning. Every time they met, he swore Jenna discovered a new talent, each more tiring than the last. Usually by this point, Jack would be on the verge of boredom, would see the end of the affair in sight, but as long as Jenna kept up her level of enthusiasm, he could only picture a long-term position for her.

Angling awkwardly so as not to block the glow of the spotlight, he managed to get his key into the lock and let himself in. Toeing the door closed, he entered the key code for the alarm and was halfway out of his coat when a shadow fell over him. Arms bound by the fabric, he whirled around, barely able to make out the familiar form in the living room doorway. "Jesus Christ, Amelia," he muttered, pulling the coat free and yanking the door of the coat closet open.

"Did you forget something?" her clipped voice returned from the darkness, and Jack shook his head. If there was anything he hated more than being waited up on, it was his wife's female mindfucks.

Glancing past the closet door, he watched Amelia cross her arms over her long silk robe. To any other man, he knew she would be a sight to behold, furious but no less fuck-worthy, but no other man had been forced to behold her for as many years as he had.

"Was I supposed to pick up toilet paper or something?" he joked, refusing to let her ruin his rather satisfied mood, no matter how many dark porches and idiotic questions she threw at him.

"The benefit," Amelia stated.

"That was tonight?" He didn't even feign concern. "I forgot." He hadn't.

"I called you seven times. I left messages on your assistant's voice mail."

"We were busy," Jack returned, unable to keep the smile off his face. Not that he put forth a lot of effort.

"Oh, I'm sure you were," Amelia responded.

"What did you tell everyone?"

"I told them you were busy," Amelia answered. "Working."

"Good." Jack closed the door of the coat closet, removing the only barrier between them that was tangible. "So, how did it go?"

Scoffing, Amelia moved for the stairs, and he sidestepped into her path, bringing her up short, feeling an undeniable sense of enjoyment as her furious gaze rose to his. "What do you want me to say?"

"How about you're sorry?" Amelia suggested.

"I'm sorry." Jack said the words, but couldn't remember the last time he actually meant them.

When Amelia made another attempt to get around him, he grasped her arms with just enough force to keep her in place. Sincere or not, apology wasn't going to be the last thing she heard from him.

"What now?" he asked with a shrug. "I apologized."

"I spent three months putting this together for you," Amelia returned, eyes filling with traces of old fire Jack hadn't seen in some time. "These are your parents, your friends, your associates. I don't appreciate working on something for you that you can't even be bothered to attend."

"What else do you have to do?" Jack questioned, catching Amelia again as she tried to walk off. "You spend all day in this house with Sole to tend to your every waking need. I spend all day at the office to pay for it. And you're bitching about a little benefit?"

"You delegate work to a hundred people," Amelia shot back. "I can't delegate being your wife. When I do what you ask me to, I do it. Me. Every plan, every detail, every meeting. I don't want to do it, but I do. I know it's hard for you to believe, Jack, but I do have things I would rather be doing with my time."

"What are you saying?" he mocked. "You need an assistant?"

Sighing and deflating before him, Amelia seemed to come to the realization she cared as little about the conversation as he did. "What I am saying," she stated without inflection, "is that when I plan a benefit with your parents and your friends, the least you can do is show up. And when you don't show up, the least you can do is sound sincere when you apologize." Pulling out of his touch, she at last made it past him to the stairs. "You smell like cheap hotel soap," she added. "Don't come to my bed."

"Come on now," Jack called up after her. "You know this soap's not cheap."

Watching her ascend to the upper floors, he was rewarded a minute later with the muffled slam of their bedroom door, and followed its echo. It was almost endearing when Amelia thought she could tell him what to do.

4

As far as conversations went, the one he'd had with Amelia carried about as much weight as an argument with a cat, but Jack couldn't let it go. Over the past few months, he had let go of a lot - late-night tiffs, early-morning cold shoulders, over-the-phone discussions about things that didn't need discussing. Amelia was going through a rebellious stage, it seemed, and it was starting to show.

The first call he had gotten that morning was from his mother, informing him that Amelia had been less than gracious the night before, answering questions tersely and refusing to smile, even when a smile was the appropriate expression. Righteousness evident in every word, his mother had her own ideas about how to get Amelia back in line, but Jack knew his wife. He knew exactly how far he could and couldn't push Amelia to get what he wanted from her. His mother was demanding a shove where a nudge would prove more effective, and he wasn't about to destroy a system that had always worked well for him to appease her.

Lifting his eyes to the door, Jack knew there was a simple solution to his current dilemma.

"Jenna?" he called, and she appeared in the doorway like a centerfold, mini-skirt showing off a long expanse of leg.

"Yes, Sir," she purred.

"Would you please call Caton up here?"

"Caton?" Jenna's sensual pose faltered for only an instant, before she forced a megawatt smile. "Of course."

Watching her disappear to do as she was told, though it was obviously against her own interests, Jack thought maybe he should enlist Jenna's help in retraining Amelia. It would take a special sort to get through to his wife. Amelia wasn't like most people. She couldn't be influenced by deprivation. At least, not her own. Deprivation only ever seemed to increase her resolve, much in the way religious zealots found strength in fasting. It had always been overindulgence that weakened Amelia, reminding her where the power rested.

When the knock at the door came a few minutes later, it was not so much hesitant as lukewarm, as if Caton didn't want to be there but knew she couldn't outright refuse his invitation.

"Caton." Jack smiled, waving her inside and glancing over her shoulder. "Thank you, Jenna. Close the door."

"No, Jenna," Caton quickly interjected. "Don't close the door."

Eyes returning to her at the declaration, Jack realized Caton hadn't moved far enough inside his office to allow the door to close even if Jenna attempted it. Smiling at the prudence, he considered he might be making a mistake removing her from his team, instead of using the opportunity to try to coax her up the ladder.

"I guess don't close the door," he amended, and, with a dubious glance toward Caton, Jenna left them alone. "Take a seat." Jack motioned to one of the chairs across from his desk, and Caton sat in it with such rigidity, he knew she would be up in an instant if he made any sudden moves. "I have a position for you."

No hint of reaction in her unwavering stare, Caton's increasingly insolent posture tightened her shirt against her chest, and Jack could think of several additional positions he wanted to suggest. By the disinterested sigh that followed his statement, he knew that was the kind of offer she was expecting.

"My wife needs an assistant," he went on when he finished looking.

"Your wife?" Caton returned, gaze narrowing as if trying to figure out his gimmick. "Am I being fired?"

"No," Jack replied, engaging his best sales tone. "It's really more of a promotion, a chance to make a little extra money, get a little experience. You don't have to accept it."

He was overselling it, he realized, when Caton looked even more skeptical. "What would I be doing?" she asked.

"Amelia plans a lot of events, does some charity work," he answered. "Mostly you would help take care of things for me."

"That sounds like I'm working for you," Caton countered, as if she'd caught him at something she suspected since she first walked in.

"Then you're misinterpreting." Jack smiled at her unabashed distrust, which could have only been more apparent if it reached across the desk and slapped him in the face.

"What would my duties be, specifically?" Caton put ninety-percent of the question's emphasis on the last word.

"Whatever Amelia asks you to do."

"Not what you ask me to do?"

"She would be your boss," Jack asserted, and the response stalled Caton's rapid-fire comebacks.

"Why me?" she finally questioned, eyes attentive and suspicious.

"Well..." Jack settled forward in his chair, fingers threading before him. "You've made it clear you have no desire to climb on top here. So to speak." The unconcealed roll of Caton's eyes confirmed she was the perfect person for the position in question. "Since you're low level, the company won't miss you."

"Really?" Caton returned with a laugh. "Tell Jenna that."

"She'll make do," Jack replied.

Head shaking, Caton's humor faded quickly, and when her gaze returned to Jack, it was as if she could see right through him. "Why me really?" she asked.

He could tell he'd lost her, that he never really had her on the hook in the first place. She was smart. She didn't trust him at all. Despite his assurance that the position was optional, Jack felt a tickle of frustration. Maybe he wasn't as willing to accept her refusal as he thought he would be. Perhaps, he would find a reason to let her go after all, and replace her with someone more pliable.

"Because you're the only woman at this office who hasn't had my cock in her mouth," he replied, the disgusted look that appeared on her

13

face some consolation. "I think my wife would appreciate that. Unless, of course, you want to remedy that now."

As anticipated, Caton didn't last another second in the chair. He didn't even finish the thought before she was on her feet and halfway to the door.

"What do you make?" He directed the question at her back. "Fifteen dollars an hour? I'll pay you five-thousand dollars a month."

Coming to an abrupt stop in the doorway, Caton swayed precariously. Reaching out, she steadied herself on the frame, but not before Jack saw it, and when she looked back, he could tell the offer only amplified her reservations. "Why would you offer me that kind of money?" she questioned.

"My wife can be difficult to work with," Jack only half lied, though it was the difficulty Amelia would have working with Caton that was the appeal.

"Your wife?" Caton repeated, still not believing that truth from him.

"She's a hormonal cunt," Jack stated. "I wish someone would pay me to live with her."

"You could get a temp cheaper." There was finality in Caton's advice.

"I want you," Jack smiled, knowing it was the exact wrong thing to say to win her over. If the money alone didn't convince her, though, maybe she wasn't as smart as he thought.

"I'm going to have to pass," Caton declared, walking out the door.

"So, he wants to bring you home with him," Jenna taunted Caton outside the door of Jack's office.

Irritated enough by the conversation without unsolicited commentary on it, Caton continued to the elevator, punching the button to take her back downstairs, finding Jenna nearly as bad as Jack. As she waited, she could feel Jenna staring unrelentingly, as if the fact that Jack was aggressive in his pursuit of her was somehow Caton's fault.

When the silver doors at last opened, she rushed inside, hiding next to the panel until, to her great relief, the doors began to close. Before they fully shut, a hand wedged between them, forcing them apart, and Jenna's fake smile glared in at her. "I'll ride down with you," she declared, before carrying through on the threat and stepping aboard.

Two undesirable options available to her - the ride down with Jenna or waiting upstairs with Jack - Caton chose the lesser of the two evils, leaning her head against the silver wall and anticipating a long, excruciating return to the first floor.

5

Maybe she was more easily persuaded than she would like to believe. Hours after deciding with absolute certainty there was nothing that could get her to work in Jack's home, the pros and cons were still in balance enough for Caton to have accidentally brought it up.

"He wants you to work at his house?" Laura responded in a tone that left little question as to her immediate take on the situation.

"For his wife," Caton quickly added, watching Laura break off a piece of the soft pretzel between them and drop it back into the basket without eating it. "You think it's a bad idea?"

"What did you expect me to think?" Laura leaned across the table to be heard over the rising voices of two completely tanked businessmen debating politics two booths away. "You know he's just trying to get you there so he can -"

"I know," Caton cut her off. "I know what he'll try. But you know me, and that's not going to happen."

"He is a rich, powerful man," Laura reminded her. "You will be in his home. Do you really think he can't get away with anything he decides to do?"

"Nothing is going to happen to me," Caton assured her, refusing to let those concerns re-arise. She needed no reminder about the stickiness of the situation, or the fact that Jack would use it to his advantage given the slimmest of chances.

"You can't trust him," Laura exhaled worriedly.

Leaning across the table, Caton clasped Laura's fingers, which, for a full minute, had been worrying at the table like they were trying to rub the shellac from its surface. "I don't trust him," she said. "But I know what I'm walking into. It's not an ambush."

"Just because you see it coming doesn't mean you'll be able to stop it," Laura argued, and the veracity of the statement caused a lump to form in Caton's throat.

Laura wasn't wrong. All day, Caton had been debating the merits of taking Jack up on his offer, returning repeatedly to the possibility that the risk may well be greater than any potential reward. If she went to work for Jack, she put herself at stake, there was no denying that, but it could also change things.

"This is a good opportunity," she said, trying to think of something she could say to make Laura get it. Not that she could expect Laura to get something she hadn't fully wrapped her mind around herself. "Maybe a once-in-a-lifetime chance."

"What are you talking about?" Laura shook her head, looking rightly confused, and Caton wished she could better explain. "You will have other chances."

"Not like this," Caton countered. It was all she could say. She didn't expect Laura to understand. Even if the pay barely qualified as a living wage, and it did, Laura spent every day of her life doing something of value, while Caton spent her days doing grunt work for grunt pay. She didn't really need Laura to understand. She just needed Laura to accept her decision, to have one person who had her back as she prepared to enter the den of a legitimate and unapologetic lion.

"You're going to do this regardless of what I say, aren't you?" Laura questioned, though she sounded as if she already knew the answer.

"I think I have to," Caton suddenly realized, not sure at what point she had made a decision.

Unsurprised at the response, Laura nodded, eyes no less concerned as they regarded Caton. "Just be careful," she softly appealed to her.

"I will," Caton breathed in relief, squeezing the hand beneath hers, not sure whom she was trying to comfort more.

Jack was in the middle of numbers, a string of weighted averages to determine the cost-benefit of a venture he'd been considering for a while. It was the kind of thing he thought he would never do once he reached the top, only to discover some calculations were best kept to himself.

The commotion at the door breaking his concentration, he would have been angry if not for the unexpected vision of the two women hovering side-by-side, once again, in his doorway.

"She insists on talking to you now," Jenna huffed, sending Caton an irritated glance.

"Caton." Jack almost smiled at the intrusion.

"How long would the job last?" Caton returned without greeting. "I can't give this job up and be out of work in a month."

At that, Jack did smile. The money always won them over in the end, even when they tried to act as if it was inconsequential. People who spent their lives in gravel simply couldn't resist the allure of so much greenery. "I'll give you a six-month contract and pay you through it," he decided on the spot. "Unless, of course, you quit."

"And after that?" Caton questioned.

"You can have your job back here," he promised. "If it's still the job you want."

Stopping for a breath, Caton looked at him with even less trust than the day before, if that was possible. "I can get that in writing?" she asked.

"Of course," he returned, as certain he had Caton firmly in his net as he had been she was getting away from him the day before.

The beep of the phone in the outer office made Caton jump, and Jenna cast her a leery glance before retreating from the doorway to do one of the few parts of her job she couldn't put off on someone else.

"Along with my duties," Caton added when Jenna was gone. "All of them. I don't want any surprises."

"I'll have Jenna write it up."

"And I want more money," Caton declared suddenly.

That, Jack had to admit, did come as surprise. Resituating in his chair, he studied Caton with greater appreciation. As high as his estimations had been, it was possible he'd still underestimated her. "How much?"

"Seventy-five hundred," Caton returned.

"A month?" Jack sought verification, fingers squeezing the edge of the desk as he considered the offer.

"I did a risk-reward calculation," Caton spoke his language, and Jack couldn't help but laugh at being bested at his own game.

"And just what are you planning to do for that?" he questioned.

"Whatever your wife tells me to do," Caton countered. "That is the deal, right?"

Head angling up a little, it was clear she knew she was overreaching, but she had chosen to go for it anyway. Anyone else, Jack would have refused the counteroffer, or at least negotiated a rate more in his favor, but Caton was exactly the catch he needed - she proved it more and more every second - and he was going to net her, whatever the cost.

"I could get three temps," he argued anyway.

"You want me," Caton stated, and Jack felt the fact acutely beneath his desk.

"I didn't know how much until just now." He shook his head, eyes leaving Caton's to take her all in, imagining what she kept hidden beneath those concealing fits and fabrics.

"Jack, there's someone on the phone for you." Jenna reappeared in the doorway, shirt cut down to there, skirt barely giving cover, a perfect contrast to Caton's near-Puritan clothing choices.

"I'm busy," Jack pointed out.

"He's with the BRC," Jenna lowered her voice, as if Caton wouldn't hear her from six inches away.

"I'll take it," Jack uttered, looking to his phone with disdain. "I need you to write up a contract for Caton. She'll tell you what to put in it."

With an annoyed huff, Jenna accepted the task, pulling the door closed behind them, and Jack was left to field the unwelcome intrusion into his day.

"This is Jack Halston," he gruffly answered the phone.

"Mr. Halston," a deep voice responded. "My name is Marcus Slater. I'm with the Business Regulatory Commission. I'd like to ask you a few questions."

"Wouldn't be a Wednesday if you didn't," Jack replied. The fucking lot of them were like vultures, too scared to make their own kills, always looking for meat on bones picked clean.

Waiting to find out what they wanted this time, he cursed the piss-poor timing, wishing the universe would let him enjoy the moment he was about to turn his wife's life into a living hell.

6

Jack came home on time, in good humor. He insisted on eating dinner together and made conversation that was almost pleasant, complaining just enough about his day to make himself seem a common working man, and asking the details of hers as if they mattered to him. He had things that needed planning, end of the year parties and charity events to bring down the company's tax liability, and he requested Amelia's help, instead of telling her what to do.

Amelia played along, watching Jack the entire time for a tell, any indication as to why he was acting the part of the caring husband, but by the time Jack finally slid between the sheets on the other side of the bed, his "Goodnight, Darling" skidding over the line from patronizing into utterly absurd, Amelia still had no idea as to why he was setting the stage. She knew only that it was best to avoid him.

Climbing out of bed as soon as Jack disappeared into the shower, she descended the flights of stairs to the gym, working through her morning yoga with one eye on the clock, and finishing with more tension than with which she began. When the time finally ticked away, she made her way back up to the kitchen, walking through the doorway into the mid-morning sun and greeting Sole with the most genuine smile she could manage. "Good morning."

"Good morning," Sole returned. "Jack is in the dining room."

Offered casually, as if Amelia gave regular thought to the whereabouts of her husband, Amelia recognized the statement as warning. Sole never let her be surprised by Jack's presence when he should be somewhere else.

Sharing a long look with the other woman, who provided no further indication as to why Jack might be lingering at the house, Amelia realized she would have to address the subject or just wait for whatever unpleasantness was headed her way. Passing through the kitchen to the dining room door, she found Jack looking abnormally passive over eggs Benedict and his newspaper.

"What are you still doing here?" she asked him.

"Enjoying my morning," Jack answered with too broad a grin, and Amelia's throat tightened at the phantom sensation of a noose tightening around her neck.

"What about work?" She tried to sound unbothered, but the feeling of imminent doom stole her voice.

"I'll get there," Jack smirked, and Amelia thought it best to step off the platform before he kicked the stool out from under her.

Returning to the kitchen, her eyes went once again to Sole, who clearly shared her anxiety.

"Do you want breakfast?" Sole lightly offered.

"No," Amelia replied, more tersely than intended, the feeling of oncoming weakness the only thing keeping her in the room. Going to the fruit basket, she heard Sole pulling the blender out for her and gave her a tight smile of thanks as she slid the apparatus onto the counter.

A few minutes later, Amelia was knuckle-deep in peelings, juice dripping from her fingers, when the doorbell rang. Watching the doorway like it was a portal to misery, she was surprised when Sole returned moments after disappearing through it with a young woman who looked utterly harmless. Amiable even. Which was more than Amelia could say about herself at the moment.

"She said she's here to see you, Mrs. Halston." Sole used the formality in regard to the stranger, and it plucked the threads of Amelia's already frayed sense of normalcy.

Eyes locking on vibrant green as the stranger looked up, Amelia watched the youthful image come to a sudden stop across the kitchen and took in the demure business casual. The woman could have been there for a college admission interview or a visit with her grandmother, and Amelia wasn't sure why either would be directed to her.

"Hi," the woman quietly greeted.

"Hello," Amelia returned guardedly. "Who are you?"

"Caton," the woman replied.

"Should that mean something to me?" Amelia questioned, watching the green eyes darken to emerald, the face that housed them settling into a weary tension that made the woman look several years older.

"Caton." Jack suddenly appeared at Amelia's back. "Right on time."

Noting Jack's grin as he passed, Amelia wondered how long he had been waiting to make his timely entrance. Stopping next to Caton, Jack slid his hand onto her back as he turned to Amelia, and Amelia's dread was momentarily overridden by intrigue as Caton sidestepped Jack's touch and sent him an unmistakable glare.

"Well, here you are, Amelia," Jack announced with a smile.

"Here I am, what?" Amelia uttered, the thorny vines of vexation crawling down her back.

"You said you needed help," Jack returned. "I got you help."

"What?" The question came out a clipped syllable, and Jack grinned in response.

"Since the workload is too much for you to handle on your own, you clearly need an assistant." Jack managed to sound logical to the ear. It was the rest of Amelia that heard his demented truth, that he would pay someone for an unnecessary job just to make a point.

Withholding her retort, she let the irritation flow in a slow exhalation through her teeth as her eyes flashed to Caton, who stared unceasingly at the floor, face set so tight her cheekbones jutted unnaturally against her skin.

"I thought you would be pleased." Jack didn't even attempt to sound genuine, or hide his pleasure at the situation.

Dropping the knife on the counter before she was impelled by her desire to use it, Amelia grabbed a towel from the rack and moved for the dining room, the only escape route not blocked by Jack's nefarious intentions. She got only halfway down the length of the ridiculously-long table before Jack was at her side, mood not dampened in the least by his sprint to catch up to her.

"What's the matter?" he asked. "Isn't this what you wanted?"

"Why is she here?" Amelia turned on him.

"To help you," Jack maintained the lie.

"To help me what?" Amelia returned.

"I don't know," Jack responded, reaching out to pick what Amelia suspected was non-existent debris off her shoulder. "What does have you so overwhelmed in your life? What do you need to delegate?"

Nodding, Amelia remembered with sudden regret how she had earned the situation in which she found herself. "Get rid of her, Jack," she demanded.

"I can't," Jack countered with ease. "She has a contract."

"I didn't ask for help," Amelia argued pointlessly.

"No, but you got it. So, now you have nothing to complain about." Jack's smile finally lapsed. "I have to go to work."

With that, he continued through the dining room into the foyer, leaving Amelia to deal with what was left behind in the kitchen, a not-so-subtle reminder that he had the power to alter her world. Fabric of the towel sticking to her fingers and animosity sitting heavy in her chest, she turned back to the kitchen to deal with it.

Though the woman looked plenty uncomfortable as Jack revealed his scheme, it was nothing compared to how uncomfortable she looked when Amelia walked back in, despite the fact that Sole surely tried to make her feel more at ease. For a moment, Amelia didn't only sympathize, but felt kindred, as if they were on the same side.

"Caton, right?" she questioned, receiving a quick nod of confirmation.

Tension marring her features, the woman was still attractive in an unassuming way, as if she tried, but not too hard, aware enough of her looks that being regularly hit on couldn't come as surprise, but not so aware she expected to get perks out of it.

Going to the sink, Amelia washed her hands, taking the towel Sole offered and moving from behind the bar to approach Caton. The closer she got, the tenser Caton seemed to become, until her eyes skirted away from Amelia's and a muscle twitched in her jaw. "Listen," she stated, almost an order. "Is this some kind of weird couple thing? Because I really don't want to get in the middle of that."

Standing in her own kitchen, the question sounded brazen to Amelia, and she ceased her approach a few feet away. Up close, Caton was even more attractive, her face more sculpted, the hair that looked chestnut across the room showing traces of nuance with golden highlights flecking through it, but, eyes unflinching on Amelia, she also looked less innocuous.

"You work for the company?" Amelia questioned, all affinity dissolving in an instant when Caton admitted it with a nod.

Of course, she worked for the company. Of course, she was on Jack's payroll, Jack's team, brought in to do Jack's bidding, whatever Jack's bidding might be.

"What do you do for my husband exactly?" Amelia questioned.

"I don't," Caton answered. "I don't work upstairs."

"But you do work for him," Amelia asserted. "Everyone at the company works for him."

"I'm in the data department." Caton finally gave Amelia something with which she could work.

"Data," Amelia repeated, smiling at the easy solution. "Come with me."

Following Amelia back through the same spotless, high-end space through which she'd made her entrance, Caton had the distinct feeling she was being escorted from the premises, and wasn't sure she minded. It came as surprise when Amelia turned from the front door as they reached the foyer, marching instead to a door beneath the stairs, and pulled it open, touching the panel switch inside to illuminate another staircase.

Watching it sink before her, Caton realized she was being led into the depths of the house and glanced toward the ornately-carved front door, wondering if she should run while she still had the chance. The sound of Amelia's oddly light footsteps drawing her back to the moment at hand, she reluctantly abandoned daylight to trail Amelia down the stairs.

Darkened room after darkened room, the basement was like an underground bunker, spreading beneath the entire house. In another time, when royalty could get away with such things, Caton imagined it would have been where the dungeons and prisoners were kept. Unable to see much beyond the cloaked doorways, it occurred to her the prisoners could still be there, locked inside their cells, knowing silence was their best chance at survival.

Finally stopping before a door that, like the others, showed nothing but dim gray beyond, Amelia flipped on the light to reveal a labyrinth of file cabinets and boxes as far as Caton's eyes could see.

"Jack used to store company files here," she explained, "but those have been digitized. You know that. You probably typed up most of it." It sounded like an insult. "These boxes are from the city. They're old records they haven't gotten into the system yet. Jack did his civic duty by providing them storage space." That too sounded like an insult, so at least Caton knew she wasn't alone outside Amelia's goodwill, though she didn't particularly like being correlated with Jack.

"They were in a hurry to get them out, so they're in no type of order at all," Amelia continued. "They were supposed to send someone here to file them, but no one volunteers in this economy. So, now you can do it."

Turning her gaze from Amelia, who hadn't spared her a single glance during the explanation, Caton estimated five-thousand boxes, give or take an exaggeration. "This is what you want me to do?" she questioned. "File some papers?"

"Yes," Amelia replied, at last turning to Caton, her arms crossing over her chest. "It is your area of expertise, isn't it?"

The brown eyes were cutting, the stance almost confrontational, and Caton wondered what exactly she had done to fall so quickly into enemy territory with Jack's wife. Upstairs, she would have sworn the woman didn't hate her on sight. She was no longer so sure. Realizing Amelia was serious, it was hard not to laugh as she moved into the room, grabbing the first box from a cluttered table and lowering it to the floor.

For a moment, Amelia just stood there, and Caton did exactly as she was told, rearranging enough boxes to pop the first lid and pull out a stack of files. Satisfied, Caton assumed, Amelia finally walked off, and Caton glanced toward the doorway, grateful for its vacancy, everything suddenly making sense.

When she first walked into the kitchen, she had been rendered momentarily dumb, unable to fathom why in the hell Jack would ever cheat. Of all the women Caton had seen him seduce in her short time at Halston & Company, she hadn't once seen Jack with anyone who compared to his wife. Plus, they all wore the same blank expressions, as if the world needed to lead them around by the hand. From the moment Amelia's eyes met hers in the kitchen, they seemed infinitely mysterious, as if there was an entire world going on behind them.

That was hardly enticing, though, if that world was an empty, frost-encrusted bitch of a place where every step brought potential for frostbite, which, as far as Caton could tell, was Amelia's inner landscape.

Six months, she had to do what she had to do. She just hoped she didn't freeze to death in the process.

7

Whatever Jack's wife's faults, she was no liar. Caton spent the first few hours of her day in absolute chaos before figuring out a system that could potentially work to bring some order back to the city of Chicago. The haphazard dropping and cramming of files into boxes indicated someone was rushing to get them out, and she couldn't help but speculate as to what exactly she was helping hide in the vault beneath the Halston Palace.

It was quid pro quo, she was certain, Jack helping cover up some unnamed politician's crimes for a future favor.

In the first drawer of a file cabinet, Caton discovered what remained of some old business files. The logo on the label was for Fearful Clothing Company, one of Jack's early attempts at riches, she assumed, when he was actually trying to do something interesting. Flipping through it gave little insight into him or the fall of his business, and she turned to toss the file back onto a chair, coming eye to lens with the security camera mounted prominently at the top of the wall.

Once she made the initial discovery, it wasn't difficult to find the others. One shiny glass eye led to the next and the next, like a troop of Cyclops guardians watching over the indiscretions of the rich and powerful. And her, of course. Caton couldn't forget that.

Seeing the work spread out before her, she expected boredom and paper cuts. It never occurred to her she would be under constant surveillance, the character in someone's sick voyeur film. Though, she should have expected it. The downside of having everything was the fear of losing it, and, with the reception she had received from her, Caton should have known she'd be put someplace where Amelia could keep an eye on her.

Hours later, sleeves rolled to her elbows, Caton stretched her fingers against the ache of repetitive work and could no longer wait for a sign of life. Passing the same rooms she didn't dare peer into too hard with Amelia beside her, she was able to make out some detail. One sported a long table, designed for impromptu conferences, and another appeared to be an extensive home gym from what she could see before she climbed back up the stairs into anticipated hostility. Door closed before her, there was a moment of panic as she realized she could well be locked in, which only proved her paranoid as the handle turned with the ease of good upkeep and she emerged back into the foyer.

Not sure where to begin searching for Amelia, or that she wanted to find the other woman, Caton headed to the only other room known to her. As she stepped through the kitchen door, the maid, Sole, was cleaning the stove, seemingly unaware of her entrance.

"Excuse me?" Caton said, relaxing somewhat when Sole turned to her with a genuine smile.

"Yes?" Sole prompted her.

"I need to run out and get something to eat," Caton said. "Could you tell Mrs. Halston?"

"I can get you something," Sole offered at once.

"You don't have to do that," Caton returned.

"It's no problem. It's already done. And Amelia is out," Sole added, as if she could sense Caton's dread of her new boss' return. "Do you like salmon?"

Though she had been nice enough when Caton was waiting for Jack and Amelia to have whatever discussion they'd had in the next room, the ambiance of the palace still tilted more toward the unfriendly than the friendly and Sole's pleasant demeanor was difficult to trust.

"Yeah, sure," Caton nodded lightly, glancing uncomfortably through the doorway, before finally going to the bar that split the kitchen. When Sole placed a plate in front of her, asking what she wanted to drink, and went to the refrigerator to get it for her, Caton accepted the possibility that there might be unexpected benefits to the job.

"Thanks," she said, watching Sole move back across the floor to lean against the counter, wondering if they were breaking some kind of fraternization rule. Remembering the unpleasant surprise in the basement, she cast her eyes to the corner of the room, not entirely satisfied at finding it empty.

"Did you lose something?" Sole asked with amusement, and Caton glanced to her plate, picking up the fork beside it and tapping the edge nervously.

"Are there cameras everywhere?" She tried to make the question sound casual.

Glancing up, it came as great relief when Sole smiled sympathetically. "No," she responded. "Outside, in Jack's office, and in the storage room. I know they can be uncomfortable. Sorry you got cast down there."

Smiling hesitantly, Caton finally took a bite, realizing just how hungry she was. Had she known there would be so much drama and physical labor, she would have eaten a bigger breakfast. "This is really good. Thank you."

Again, Sole's smile looked sincere, and Caton thought she might have an ally. Though, rich people did know how to set their traps. Or so she'd been told. In her way, Sole could have been just another camera, monitoring Caton's moves, ready to turn her in at any moment for putting her feet on the furniture or using the wrong fork.

"How big is this place?" Caton asked between bites.

"Big," Sole responded. "Eat, and I'll show you around."

The rooms and hallways of the Halston Palace went on forever. Sole led Caton through the dining room, past paintings that were undoubtedly originals, into a room with a baby grand piano that must have cost tens of thousands of dollars and that Caton doubted anyone could actually play. On a table near the piano was a photo of a teenage girl, and she picked it up automatically, amazed at the similarity between mother and daughter.

"Selene," Sole informed her, and Caton attempted to return the frame to its original position on the table. In most homes, one could expect to find traces of dust to use for guidance, but, in the Halston Palace, there wasn't a speck of dust anywhere.

Up the imposing, intricately-carved wood staircase that greeted Caton upon her entrance, Sole led Caton past Amelia's office and the spillover room next to it, filled with pieces of unused computer equipment. There were three average-sized bedrooms, and a massive one at the end of the hall that could only have been that of a teenage girl, though no teenage girl Caton had ever met. The entire room looked as if it was lifted out of a furniture store catalog and dropped into the space from the stained wood flooring to the locker-style storage units to the pile of pillows stacked perfectly against the headboard.

Coming to the foot of stairs that indicated yet another floor, Sole motioned to the master suite and Jack's office, but didn't lead Caton up, letting her know without verbal warning that the top floor was off-limits, before leading her back down the stairs to the basement where she pointed out the gym, the conference room, and an oddly relaxed rec room that looked almost like the living room of a normal home and grated against everything in the house that came before it.

At last returning Caton to her place of exile, Sole glanced toward the cameras, softly informing Caton they were virtually-controlled with a stream up to Jack's computer. The fact that she sounded as disturbed by the fact as Caton brought some measure of comfort, if not relief from the ever-watchful Cyclops.

After that, Sole left her, and Caton went back to the files, which, much to her dismay, hadn't miraculously vanished in her absence. A few hours later, fingertips just starting to crack from the continuous contact with dusty files, she was finally free to go and she headed back up to the kitchen to thank Sole, who seemed honestly happy when she told Caton she would see her in the morning and provided the unsolicited information that Amelia was upstairs in her office.

Not particularly wanting to approach the other woman, but not particularly wanting to spend the entire six months afraid of running into her boss either, Caton slow-stepped up the stairs and hesitated outside the door of Amelia's office. Finally sliding into the doorway, she discovered Amelia with her head bowed over a piece of paper, hand moving across it, and waited for a break. When Amelia at last dropped the pen on the desk and leaned back, Caton watched her pull her bottom lip between her teeth in concentration, trying not to notice the way the buttons on her shirt strained as Amelia stretched, revealing a hint of red silk against skin.

"Same time tomorrow?" she asked, and Amelia jostled to attention as if she had no clue Caton was standing there. "Sorry," Caton uttered, and it sounded as insincere as it felt.

"Did Sole say you could come up here?" Amelia questioned in a tone that reminded Caton just how deceiving looks could be.

"No," Caton replied. "I didn't realize I needed permission."

For a moment, Amelia said nothing, her chest expanding and contracting as she stared across the office. Fleetingly, it occurred to Caton she should try being less confrontational, though she doubted it would change anything.

"I don't like to be surprised," Amelia stated at last.

"It won't happen again," Caton uttered. "Since this filing is going to take months, can I wear casual clothes?"

"I don't care what you wear," Amelia countered with such indifference, Caton bristled instantly.

"Okay." She couldn't stop the irritated sigh from leaving her lips. "I don't know what's going on, but Jack said you needed help. That is the only reason I am here. Now, I'm helping the city, and as long as I get paid I'm fine with that, but I could help you."

"I don't need your help," Amelia calmly asserted. "I don't know why Jack brought you here. I just need to keep you busy until I figure that out."

She seemed more annoyed than concerned by the situation, and did appear to be telling the truth. So, neither of them knew what was going on, and they were enemies for no other reason than they had been pitted against each other in some weird power play Caton probably should have seen coming, but didn't. Now that it was in motion, all she could do was let it play out. She couldn't win. Amelia couldn't win. It was Jack's game, that was clear, and only he knew what he expected to get out of it.

"Goodnight," she said, surrendering to the situation as it was and getting no response from Amelia.

She didn't expect one.

8

Each day, Sole greeted Caton with a smile and the offer of coffee. By the third day, Caton gave into her hospitality, figuring it was going to be a long six months regardless, but would be considerably less painful adequately caffeinated.

On the rare occasion their paths crossed, Amelia eyed Caton warily, her expression revealing nothing. She said "good morning" if it was morning, "goodnight" if Caton was on her way out, but that was the extent of the conversation, and she never went out of her way, not even to check on Caton's progress. Though, it wasn't too hard for Caton to imagine the impenetrable woman walking down to the dungeons each night to go through the day's work, making sure her commands were being followed and that Caton knew the alphabet.

It was a blessing, Caton decided, the easy work, being left alone, a comfortable routine, both mindless and painless. The storage room was a haven from Amelia's persistent suspicion and the plague of her own thoughts, because apparently "good morning" and "goodnight" were all it took.

Amelia was beautiful, that was an undeniable fact, but Caton had been around plenty of beautiful women. She'd even dated her share. Physical attraction simply didn't explain the way, every time she happened upon Amelia unexpectedly, Caton felt her mouth go dry, her heart race and the immediate desire to find something to say that would make Amelia see her as less of a burden. She really thought she had grown out of being intensely attracted to people who treated her like a nuisance. By her thirtieth birthday, she thought she had grown out of senseless attractions period, and it was rather irritating to discover she could still be dominated by her hormones at the worst possible time.

Given a say, Caton would have opted for the path of least resistance, would have been content to persist with her routine of hiding in the basement for the entirety of her contract. As was the way of life, though, there was always something waiting to intervene. In this case, it was Jack, standing next to the bar in the kitchen when Caton walked in one morning a couple of weeks into her sentence expecting to find Sole alone. There had been no warning, no sign of his presence in the house. Suddenly, he was just there, bombarding Caton with the uneasiness she always felt in his presence, compounded by the fact that he had a home field advantage.

"Good morning." Sole's greeting was slightly more subdued.

"Good morning," Caton returned with equal caution.

"Coffee?"

"Yes, please," Caton said, stepping up to the bar, discomfort acute as she watched Jack from the corner of her eye. It wasn't just that Jack was staring at her - she was rather accustomed to his unrelenting leering - but the way Jack was staring at her that made Caton desperate to flee the kitchen. Beneath the blatant intention, there was an underlying aggression she could feel like pin pricks against her skin.

"Good morning, Caton," Jack uttered.

"Morning." Caton glanced his way, giving him no more, and managed a distressed smile at Sole as she sat a mug before her on the counter.

"Sole, go see if Amelia needs you," Jack ordered.

Eyes locking with Caton's, Sole looked on the verge of disobedience, as if she knew it was a bad idea to go, and knew it was a bad idea not to go. Vacillating between the two conflicting paths, she finally chose the path of least resistance herself and walked out of the room.

Left to the wolf, Caton turned to face him, showing no concern about being alone in his presence, but readiness for his boorish behavior, as if she'd been trained from birth in the art of evading creeper Lotharios.

"How's it going here?" Jack asked, taking a step closer that he probably thought Caton didn't notice.

"I really don't think your wife wants me here," Caton stated.

Where a person with a conscience might have shown concern, Jack seemed oddly pleased. "I've told her many times to be careful what she wishes for," he responded. "There are very few things I can't provide. Still, I don't think I deserve all the hostility." Jack took another step, and Caton's hand tightened on the handle of her mug. "After all, I was just trying to help."

So, that was it then. Jack and Amelia had a fight, and Jack wanted to spread the ill will.

"You look nice like this." His hand rose between them. "Young."

"Don't touch me," Caton warned him.

"What is your thing with touch?" Jack asked, hand stilling, but hovering, as if it might land at its leisure.

"I don't have a thing with touch," Caton protested. "I have a thing with people thinking they can touch me when they can't."

Taking another step toward her, Jack smiled, fingers testing their luck.

"Don't touch me, Jack. I mean it," Caton firmly stated.

"I like you calling me by my first name," he responded. "Makes it sound like we're on intimate terms."

He spoke in a tempering tone, like he saw Caton as a wild animal he could tame and pet freely. Little did Jack know, he was about to be on intimate terms with a scalding cup of coffee, and potentially the knife Sole had abandoned on the bar, if he went too far. Jack's fingertips brushing her collarbone, Caton cocked the mug back for dispersal.

"Jesus Christ, Jack," Amelia's voice cut in before she could fire, and, for the first time, Caton was truly happy to hear it. "Could you at least not try to fuck her while I'm in the room?"

Smiling at being caught in the act, which was probably his intention the entire time, Jack turned to face his wife. "I have to go to work," he smirked, leaving Caton and Amelia alone, once again, in the aftermath of his choices.

More shaken than she wanted to admit, Caton turned to the bar to put her coffee down, grimacing as the ceramic hit the granite too hard and a small crack appeared along the bottom ring of the mug. Hearing Amelia's approach, she circled back around, meeting a molasses-thick gaze. The dark eyes raking up and down her, Caton couldn't even see the judgment in them, though she could certainly feel it was there.

"Well, it all makes sense now," Amelia uttered. "What are you, his favorite? Or maybe his least favorite, since he did send you here."

Caton suspected it was Amelia's idea of a joke, but neither of them was the tiniest bit humored.

"I'm not sleeping with Jack," she recovered from the encounter, and subsequent accusation, to assert.

With a derisive laugh, Amelia started off, leaving a hollow vibration in her wake.

It didn't matter, Caton tried to remind herself. What Amelia thought of her had little impact on the course of events. It wasn't her job to soothe Amelia's pain or embarrassment, if the woman was capable of either emotion. Watching her walk away, though, she couldn't let Amelia put her into bed with Jack either, even if it was only in her mind.

Rushing after her, Caton caught Amelia's arm by the doorway, and Amelia whirled on her, more shocked than angry, as if she didn't expect Caton to make any bold moves to defend herself. Hanging on to that tiny spark of surprise, one of the few real reactions she had seen from Amelia, Caton took a step closer without conscious thought.

"I am not sleeping with Jack," she stated. "I have never slept with your husband."

With every syllable, with each finger that felt Amelia's bicep flex beneath it, Caton willed Amelia to believe her, and there was a flicker. For an instant, Amelia's icy expression thawed and Caton could see beyond the deep gray haze into the depths and shadows of dark brown eyes. Maybe whatever world lay inside Amelia wasn't as desolate and unwelcoming as it first appeared.

Gaze falling to Amelia's lips, Caton watched them part and eased closer. It wasn't until the back of Amelia's hand brushed against her thigh that she jolted into awareness. Two minutes before, she was lecturing Jack about thinking he had the right to touch her, and now she was practically pouring herself onto his wife.

Letting Amelia go at once, Caton took several desperately-needed steps backward, too scared to look up. When she finally gathered the courage, it was clear it didn't matter. Internally, she was berating herself for her inability to keep a check on something completely primal, though it had come out of nowhere and surprised her more than Amelia, and Amelia looked as unfazed as ever, the steely gaze back in place as if it had never slipped.

Maybe it hadn't. Maybe Caton had imagined it.

That piercing, unaffected stare lingered on her a moment longer before Amelia disappeared through the doorway, and Caton closed her eyes, hoping it would all be a dream when she opened them. When Sole came in and asked if she was okay, Caton had no idea how long she had been standing there, but her coffee was cold by the time she retrieved it from the bar and retreated to her lair.

At least solitary was free of conflict.

How she had managed to make avoidance of both Jack and Amelia vital to her survival in a single morning was a feat that could have taken gold medals at the Stupidity Olympics. In one fell swoop, she had taken her self-imposed situation from scarcely tolerable to completely fucking impossible, and the fact that the dungeon was her only place of safety in the house was just punishment.

'Place of safety,' of course, was a relative term, and solitary was only solitary if the warden decided it so.

Hours after Caton had confined herself to the basement, "What the fuck were you thinking?" running through her head in an agonizing loop, she heard a noise at the door that was easy to ignore. With the rows and rows of file cabinets and shadowed corners, she had already discovered the storage room was the kind of place conducive to seeing and hearing things that weren't really there.

As she turned to grab another box of files, though, Caton found it wasn't her overactive imagination, but Amelia who stood in the doorway, impeccably-dressed and completely put-together. Leave it to Amelia, and her enduring grudge, to finally show up the afternoon Caton least wanted her around. Absently wondering how long she had been standing there, Caton rested the box on the table and pulled off the lid.

"Do you need something?" she asked.

"No." Amelia made no move either in or out of the room, choosing instead to just stand there silently watching as Caton pulled folders from the box. From the side of her eye, Caton could see her like a hazy vision, a cruel memory of a terrible mistake.

The room was as chilly as always, but heat infused Caton's face. Sweat formed on her chest, cooling when the air hit it, causing her to shiver. She hated that she let the woman get under her skin, but Amelia was clearly embedded in it, whether the sensation was welcome or not.

"Are you just going to stand there and watch me?" Caton's gaze snapped in Amelia's direction.

"For now," Amelia responded, settling herself more deliberately in the doorway because she could.

A sigh rushing past her lips, Caton laid the files on the corner of the box, too aware of Amelia. Struggling to remember what letter came after 'D,' she fought the urge to wipe her forehead with her sleeve, assuming further signs of weakness were exactly what Amelia was hoping to see.

Though, there could have been a more aristocratic basis to Amelia's unexpected appearance. Maybe it was the thrill of command. A blue collar peepshow. Entertainment for a wealthy woman who never had to dirty or dry out her hands.

Under-utilized and pampered, Amelia's hands had to be incredibly soft, the thought hit Caton without warning, and the folders tipped on the edge of the box. She tried to catch them in a display that must have looked comical from Amelia's vantage point, but they spilled to the floor anyway, scattering in every direction. Dropping her head, Caton stared at the paper stuck to the top of her shoe, before masochistically shifting her gaze to the doorway and Amelia.

To her surprise, Amelia seemed to take no joy in the blunder. Or, if she did, it didn't show. She just continued to stand there looking gorgeous and unapproachable, and Caton focused on the latter, letting Amelia blur into a monster before her eyes.

"My mom drives a school bus," Caton stated, picking up the file that landed on the chair in front of her. "My father, he's a janitor. So, if you think I am somehow humbled or humiliated by getting paid over seven-thousand dollars a month to file, you should know I am not that proud."

She was painfully uncomfortable, though, and, as Amelia held her ground in the doorway, Caton felt as if nothing she could say would make a difference. Amelia was going to do what she was going to do, and it was her domain, so there was nothing Caton could do about it, other than prove herself utterly uncoordinated in the other woman's presence.

Dropping to retrieve the files from the floor, she let the table serve as her shield, blocking her from Amelia's view as she gathered slowly and lingered behind the barrier.

When at last she rose, Caton was alone.

9

Caton wasn't sure if she was avoiding Amelia, or if Amelia was avoiding her, but whoever was making the most effort, she was doing a damn fine job of it. Caton never saw Amelia in the mornings when she came in, and never when she left in the evenings. It was hard to tell the woman even lived there, which, Caton suspected, was exactly how Amelia wanted it.

Whether she desired the title or not, though, she was still technically Caton's employer, and, though they didn't have to play nice, there were certain permissions Caton was required to ask from her, and that couldn't be avoided.

Taking the steps to the second floor with vigor, she made sure Amelia knew she was coming, but Amelia's head still popped up in surprise as Caton's knuckles rapped the open door, her gaze leveling Caton and not letting go. She said nothing, either in greeting or contempt, and Caton looked for signs of anything in her gaze, finding nothing behind the dark veil Amelia always wore.

She was apathetic, Caton reminded herself. She was unaffected by Amelia. Still, eyes held captive by Amelia's gaze, she lost her mission for a moment, looking away in an effort to recover it, remembering at last she had come up the stairs to say something. "I, uh..." she tried, stopping to clear her throat and head. "I have a... a friend... who's getting an award on Thursday. Can I take the afternoon off?"

Behind Amelia's facade, Caton knew there were gears in motion, but she couldn't see them and had no idea what they would churn out. "I don't care," Amelia responded, dropping her gaze back to her desk.

"I'll work in the morning," Caton added. "I wouldn't have to leave until like two."

"What part of 'I don't care' was confusing for you?" Amelia looked up solely to pierce Caton with her indifference.

Feet angling at once toward the top of the stairs, Caton's instantaneous physical reaction was flight, but a surprising flash of rage held her in place against her body's good sense. She had no reason to fight with Amelia, no real need to defend herself. She had gotten what she wanted, and could serve out the remainder of her sentence in relative peace. The way she had been brushed off, though, as if she wasn't even worth a minute-long conversation was enough to provoke her ego, which she, frankly, had never been good at keeping in check.

"You know what," she said, and Amelia seemed almost surprised to still find her there. "I'm confused. I was under the impression you needed someone here."

"And I already told you you were under the wrong impression." Amelia spoke very slowly, like she was explaining the situation to a certified idiot, and, once again, Caton could have gone. She had been dismissed from the moment she appeared in the doorway.

Smoldering anger working its way up her throat until her teeth pressed together and she felt the burning behind her eyes, though, she abandoned the unrewarding path of civility. "Why are you such a cold bitch?" she questioned, knowing as the question left her lips she was heading to a place from which there was no return, but unable to care. That was the real question, the one to which she wanted an answer.

The sudden outrage that appeared on Amelia's face was so unprecedented, it was deeply gratifying, and Caton felt the smoking embers inside her spark into flame.

"Excuse me?" Amelia returned, the two words laced with so much honest anger, they sounded like an explosion, despite how quietly Amelia uttered them.

"Your heart must be hypothermic." Caton couldn't stop the assessment after seeing how effective her first words had been against Amelia's seemingly-impenetrable exterior.

When Amelia stood, it was in a deliberate manner that made Caton swallow nervously at its intent. It was as if she had spoken the catch phrase that triggered an assassin, and Amelia looked decidedly deadly as she approached the doorway. Trying to stand more erect, Caton was determined to withstand whatever was coming at her, but Amelia's presence was imposing as she moved closer, mere inches left between them.

"You don't know anything about me," Amelia declared, her always-shielded gaze filled with barely-restrained fury.

Caton had hoped to get a rise out of her. She didn't expect the amount of anger, or the underlying passion, that radiated off the other woman, scorching the air between them.

"Oh, please," she countered, too far in the swamp to return to solid terrain. "You are not a mystery. You married too young and you did it for money. Your husband is aware of this fact and that's why he prefers to fuck outside of your marriage, which is just fine with you, because you don't want anyone touching you anyway."

Amelia appeared stunned, whether by the fact Caton had the nerve to say it or by the accuracy of the statement, Caton wasn't sure, but when Amelia's anger subsided enough for other emotions to rise to the surface, Caton looked away to avoid them. Thinking Amelia had the capacity to feel was what had gotten her into trouble before.

"You're fired." Amelia's voice wavered for the first time.

"I figured," Caton countered, only realizing how much she was shaking as she turned to the stairs and rushed unsteadily down them, the consequence hitting her square in the chest and making even the downward trek arduous. All the things she could have done, and she had done the one thing she absolutely couldn't. But she couldn't take it back. She wouldn't if she could.

Stepping off the bottom stair in the foyer, the insults she didn't get the chance to lob bounded so wildly in her head, Caton didn't hear Amelia behind her until a vice tightened on her arm and she was yanked around like a rag doll. Amelia's fingers on her almost violent, Caton could feel her heart pound against them.

"You think that's all that I am," Amelia harshly whispered, mask further slipping. "But you do not know me."

In the thick of it, Caton didn't have time to contemplate the fact that Amelia had followed her for the sole purpose of continuing to fight.

"I know how you treat people," she returned, though it wasn't true. If anything, it was selfish. She knew only how Amelia treated her, and she was tired of being made to feel like a commodity that could be put to use and then disregarded. "I know it has no effect on you. Nothing has any effect on you."

"That is not true," Amelia countered, blistering gaze forcing Caton to avert her eyes. "Just because I am not screaming at the top of my lungs or bursting into tears every five seconds doesn't mean I don't feel. I don't... I am not..." She couldn't seem to find the words, or to admit them.

"What?" Caton returned her gaze to Amelia's. "Frigid? Dead inside?" The descriptions proved themselves on target when Amelia flinched in response. "Please. I have never met anyone so completely devoid of emotion," she continued, not sure why it mattered so much. "You could hit a kid and drive over the body. I could walk around here naked and you wouldn't even be embarrassed. You would probably just ask why I didn't have a banker box in my hands."

Her shock at the scenario silenced Amelia for only an instant. "Let's see," she uttered. "Take your clothes off."

With a heartfelt scoff, Caton turned to leave, tired of the game and Amelia's quiet malice, which always felt on the verge of becoming a real knife in her back. When Amelia's touch softened, though, simultaneously pulling her back, Caton crashed against her, feeling the give of the fabric between them, instantly aware that Amelia's body at least had contour, despite the sharp planes and lines of her perfectly-pressed apparel.

"Take your clothes off," Amelia said again, the request little more than a breath against Caton's cheek. Half-plea, half-demand, Caton couldn't tell which part was more sincere.

Words shivering through her, she knew she could - that she should - leave, but, meeting Amelia's eyes, she also knew she wouldn't.

Cold. It was the term she had most associated with Amelia since she first met her. But the heat of Amelia's body, in her gaze, contradicted Caton's initial classification with a vengeance, turning everything Caton was sure she knew on its head, so that Caton knew nothing except what she felt, and it prompted her to act without consulting her rational mind.

Strap falling from her shoulder, she dropped her bag to the floor. It was easy to pretend she was testing Amelia, calling her bluff. Somewhere on the edges of her consciousness, though, Caton knew she had lost all will to protect herself, that, in that instant, she would acquiesce to anything Amelia asked of her.

As her hands moved to the hem of her shirt, Amelia backed away, just far enough to allow Caton to pull the fabric over her head and let it fall on top of her bag. It was cold in the foyer, Caton had felt it when she first came down, but she could no longer tell, skin immunized against the room's chill by Amelia's eyes sliding over her, warming everything in their path.

Hands moving to the button of her jeans, Caton popped it open without hesitation, breath ceasing as Amelia's gaze trailed back up to hers. Without so much as a blink, Amelia turned and walked away, and Caton froze in place, hands grasping tightly to the denim at her waist as she realized Amelia may have been the one calling a bluff.

To her surprise and relief, Amelia's next move wasn't to leave her standing half-dressed in the middle of the foyer. It was to climb three stairs and turn to sink down on the fourth, gaze returning expectantly to the skin of Caton's abdomen.

Still inscrutable, Amelia's stare was powerful enough to control Caton's hands from a distance, making one move to the zipper of her jeans, tugging it down, before they worked in tandem to push the denim down her thighs. Slipping free of her shoes, she pushed the jeans aside with her foot and stood like a showpiece in the home of someone wealthy enough to get away with asking for such a piece of art.

"Did I tell you to stop?" Amelia questioned quietly, and it too was request.

Any hesitation Caton had gave way under the enchantment of Amelia's gaze, and her hands curved up her back, slipping the satin closure free to let her bra slide from her arms and fall to the floor.

So, Amelia wasn't lying, she realized. She could be affected. Gaze easing down Caton's body, she shifted on the stair, an involuntary reaction that made Caton abandon fear. Utterly vulnerable, more than she could recall being in her life, Caton felt more powerful than she ever thought she could.

Fingers smoothing down her stomach, she watched Amelia's lips tremble, her own body tightening in response to the ragged breath she heard escape them. Wanting nothing more than to give Amelia full access, to see what other unexpected reactions she could pull from her, Caton slipped her thumbs beneath the fabric of her panties, seizing painfully at the intruding voice.

"I am so sorry." Sole sounded as mortified as Caton felt, and Caton spun from the living room door, arms crossing for cover. Shame hitting her all at once, she thought she might cry, or throw up all over the imported wood flooring.

"It's all right, Sole," Amelia responded calmly, heightening Caton's humiliation. Amelia did feel something, she couldn't have imagined that, but the woman's ability to sound completely blasé about the whole thing made Caton feel like she was the instigator and Amelia had just happened upon her striptease by accident. "What is it?"

"Mr. Reynolds is on the phone," Sole replied, struggling to match Amelia's composure. "You told me to find you if he called."

"Yes, I did," Amelia returned. "Tell him I'll be a minute."

"Yes, ma'am." Sole sounded happy to flee.

Even in her absence, Caton found she couldn't move, muscles so tense she knew she would be sore for days to come.

Amelia got up, her shoes clicking softly down the stairs and over the wood floor, but Caton refused to look at her. She could picture the victorious expression, the look of entitlement and arrogance she knew Amelia must be wearing.

The soft fabric of Amelia's tailored jacket brushing her bare arm, Amelia's breaths fell mercilessly against her shoulder, and her hand rose between them, hovering an inch from Caton's stomach, but Caton felt the touch as surely as if it had landed. Then, Amelia's hand moved quickly upward, fingers as soft as expected curving around Caton's chin, forcing Caton to meet her gaze, ready or not.

There was nothing cavalier in the way Amelia looked at her. If anything, Amelia looked more human than Caton had ever seen her, and it stole Caton's breath. For a moment, she thought she might be rewarded for her submission. Amelia's fingers abandoning her chin to slide down her throat, Caton willed Amelia's lips to hers, for just one taste.

"You can quit if you want to," Amelia declared, releasing Caton and walking off, the steady click of her heels echoing her departure.

When she was certain she was alone, Caton dove for her clothes, pulling them on with sloppy haste, recognizing as she dressed that she couldn't undo or explain away anything. It wasn't some drunken mistake, with a built-in excuse and no repercussions, forgotten in a night. There was a witness, and she and Amelia were both stone-cold sober.

Fully-dressed, Caton felt no less naked. Amelia had stripped away her power, if she had any to begin with, and, in the trench as she was, Caton had only two choices left to her. Retreat, or surrender.

Driving home was an out-of-body experience. Caton watched her hands perform the necessary functions, but she couldn't feel the steering wheel beneath them, her body against the seat, or the cool metal of the gear shift when she finally pulled into her parking space, somehow without incident.

Though she could feel her uncontrollable trembling, she couldn't grasp the cause, couldn't get a handle on her own emotions. Was she angry, or was she gratified? Disgusted, or thrilled? Everything she could feel, she felt, until it all jumbled together into a singular sensation.

Turbulence.

Climbing the stairs to her apartment, her steps grew short when she saw the visitor waiting outside her door.

"Hey." Laura looked up at her with a relieved smile. "Where've you been?"

"I..." Caton glanced back at the stairs, helplessly realizing it was too late not to make her presence known, and remembering in shameful detail why she didn't want to face Laura at the moment.

"You're late," Laura stated gently.

"For what?" Caton returned in confusion.

"Movie," Laura returned. "Remember?"

"Oh, yeah," Caton breathed, shaking her head, trying to shake some semblance of balance into place. "Sorry. I got held up at work."

"Files desperately in need of permanent placement?" Laura quipped, stepping out of the way to give Caton enough space to unlock the door, though it wasn't space enough for Caton to breathe.

"Something like that," she uttered. "What time is it?"

"We'll make it," Laura replied. "We'll just eat after."

She wasn't angry. She didn't even sound reasonably perturbed. Laura was possibly the most easygoing human being on the planet, a model of compassion and understanding. She was kind, she was warm, and, as Caton turned to face her inside the door, she gave a dazzling smile just before pressing her lips to Caton's.

At the sudden sensation, the turbulence inside Caton didn't stop, but it did find focus. Maybe she knew how she felt after all.

Hand curving around the back of Laura's neck, Caton deepened the kiss, feeling Laura's arms slide around her waist as she pressed closer. Tugging Laura inside, they barely got the door closed behind them as they staggered toward the bedroom like overanxious teenagers.

It was never like this with them. It never had been. There was always time to take. Urgency was never required.

Through the bedroom door, Caton tore at Laura's clothes, ridding her of the majority of them before pushing her onto the bed to mark her body with her lips and teeth and tongue, and Laura arched against her, pulling her closer, wordlessly capitulating to the frenzy.

Fingers sinking into warmth, Caton closed her eyes. It was Laura who moaned and moved against her, but Caton was back in the foyer. The heat she felt was Amelia's, each touch, the veritable caress of Amelia's gaze. She was victim to the power Amelia wielded so effortlessly over her with only a request. It was disconcerting, terrifying, but there was euphoria to be found within the fear, like a free fall into a black hole. She couldn't know what was at the bottom, but the path down felt like flying.

10

In all outward appearances, morning in the Halston household was as
quiet and unaffected as ever. Standing at the bar, Amelia dropped fruit
into the blender as Sole moved around behind her, providing assistance
without being invasive. An illusion of perfect calm.

Inside, Amelia whirred with nearly the same intensity as the blades
that spun before her. Not once all night had her mind stopped working,
and her body was even more keyed up, reacting to everything as if
waking from a long, deep sleep. The world she inhabited was full of
beautiful people and casual flirtations, but sitting on the steps in the
foyer, watching Caton bare herself before her, something was different.
Something had been different. Caton was different. And the series of
orgasms to which Amelia had treated herself in the time between Sole
retiring to the guest house and Jack arriving home spoke for themselves.

When Jack entered the kitchen, expression smug as if he was anxious
to see what pleasures awaited him in the day, Amelia barely glanced up
in acknowledgment.

"Is Caton downstairs already?" he asked, stopping across the bar.

Glancing toward the clock on the convection oven, Amelia realized
morning had gotten away from her. 8:50. Jack was there. Caton wasn't.
Both of those things were off, and the realization pushed the abnormally
relaxed bend of Amelia's shoulders back into their regular posture.
"Caton's not here," she said, words echoing hollowly in her head as she
wondered how she had failed to notice Caton's arrival time roll by
without her appearance.

"Where is..."

Amelia punched the blender on harder than was necessary, and the room filled with the loud groan of metal blades whipping against solid chunks of fruit. Taking her finger from the button, she looked back up at Jack, who studied her with a look somewhere between annoyance and amusement. "Where is she?" he finished his question.

"I don't know," Amelia shrugged. "I guess she's not coming."

It didn't matter. It couldn't possibly matter. There was no reason for it to matter. Knowing there could be no good reason for her to be there, she'd wanted Caton gone, and Caton was gone. Yet, she could hear the traces of disappointment in her own voice, and was grateful for the fact that Jack didn't care enough to notice.

"Why?" he returned. "What did you do?"

Staring across the bar at him, Amelia felt the antagonism set in, eradicating any residual pleasure. "I guess I made it impossible for her to work here," she replied.

"Why? What did you do?" Jack posed the question again, and Amelia was on the verge of answering him in graphic detail when Caton walked through the doorway.

"Did someone quit?" she asked, and Amelia wasn't sure if it was fear of Jack or of her that slowed Caton's steps and sent her eyes skittering away from both of them. "Sorry I'm late. There was an accident."

As Caton's eyes at last flitted to hers, albeit fleetingly, Amelia felt more than one emotion she hadn't felt in some time lurch within her. Fear, desire, and something she couldn't identify beyond the disturbing sensation that it was more.

"Well, good morning." Jack made even the simple greeting sound like a pickup line.

"Good morning, Caton," Sole added.

"Good morning," Caton responded, doing an impressive job of ignoring Jack and keeping an eye on him at the same time.

"Do you want some coffee?"

"It's a little crowded in here. I'll come back for it," Caton responded, sending another brief glance Amelia's way. "If you need me, you know where to find me."

Then, Caton retraced her steps out of the room, and Amelia heard the door to the basement open and close softly from the foyer. Feeling oddly unbalanced, she put her hand on the bar and took several deep breaths that did little more than fill her head with thin air.

After watching Caton, or, more likely, certain parts of Caton, depart from the room, Jack turned back to Amelia with a gleeful expression. "Whatever you did," he prodded, "I guess it wasn't enough to scare her away."

Not sure if she was relieved at the fact, or if scaring Caton away was exactly what she had intended, Amelia returned her gaze to the blender. "So, it would seem," she conceded, pressing the button again and watching the tornado of color spin inside the glass.

11

Triumph had come with so little effort, Jack had to question it.

With few weapons in her arsenal, Amelia didn't win many battles between them, but she didn't forfeit them either. He had expected more fight out of her, another proclamation about what an inconvenience it was to have Caton imposed upon her life.

Clearly, there was conflict, though, if Amelia believed she had run Caton off, and conflict was exactly what Jack was counting on. Caton being as disagreeable and sharp of tongue with Amelia as she had always been with him would teach his wife a lesson she wouldn't soon forget about asking for things she didn't really want.

That thought, above all, was what put the smile on Jack's face as he walked into the more casual of the club's two restaurants. Looking through the sea of sport coats and plaid golf pants, he spotted Mr. Taylor at a table at the far end of the room, engaged in what appeared to be a lively conversation with a man Jack had never met.

Exchanging greetings with other club members as he passed them, Jack made it to the edge of the table before Mr. Taylor's amused eyes caught on him. "Jack, I'm sorry. I didn't see you come in." Mr. Taylor rose to his feet to give Jack a firm handshake. "This is Mark."

Upon his introduction, the stranger stood too, standing inches taller and broader than Jack, his muscles pushing against the fabric of a long-sleeved polo, looking so much the part that Jack took his offered hand without second thought.

"Slater," the man added. "Marcus Slater."

Recognizing the voice before the name, Jack pulled out of the handshake, watching Slater try to cut an imposing figure on another man's turf.

"We were just talking about you," Slater continued, and Jack's eyes moved to Mr. Taylor as he sat back down. He tried not to think about the kinds of things his old friend and collaborator might have said that he shouldn't. "What? You've had fourteen companies?" Slater questioned. "Only two successful. And now you're this big shot. That is a heart-warming story. Truly. Amazing, how you managed to turn things around like you did."

"Some people just have a sense for business," Jack returned, hoping for a quick end to the conversation.

"Well, I'm sure it helped that you had your parents' money to bail you out," Slater uttered. "You know, until you found your true calling."

Leaning forward in his chair, Mr. Taylor seemed to suddenly realize the man who had happened by his table didn't end up there by chance. "Whoa, I didn't tell him that," Mr. Taylor stated, though it sounded as if he agreed with Slater's assessment.

"How did you know where to find me?" Jack asked, need for pretense gone.

"Your assistant," Slater responded. "But don't be too hard on her. I'm pretty free with the obstruction and abetting threats."

"I can have you removed," Jack declared.

"Is that really what you want to do?" Slater asked, stepping closer to slap Jack on the shoulder as if they were old friends. "Make a scene?"

"I'll, uh... I'll get another drink," Mr. Taylor said in a rush, hurrying from his chair and maneuvering off through the tables, as Jack stepped out of Slater's false affection.

Well aware that the best way to handle a rat was to deal with it as expeditiously as possible, he took a vacant seat at the table, watching Slater return to the seat he'd made his own, looking pleased to have scored an impromptu conference.

"What do you want?" Jack asked.

"I want you to tell me what you've done," Slater returned without hesitation, just enough edge to his voice that he probably thought he was menacing.

"I haven't done anything," Jack responded.

"You have an awfully thick file at the BRC, Mr. Halston."

"And, yet, nothing has ever come of it," Jack replied. "So, I guess this may be the one time size really doesn't matter."

"Agent after agent has believed there is something not right about your business," Slater stated, anger more palpable, though his surface remained unruffled.

"I'm allowed to make money," Jack countered. "That is perfectly legal."

"If you do it by the books," Slater returned, hand moving to the table to drum a loud, repetitive beat Jack suspected was a part of his training. Glancing at the hand, he smiled in good humor, though the noise did seem an annoyance to those at nearby tables.

"I do it by the books," Jack returned.

"In this country," Slater quasi-agreed. "You do most of your international work off-book, though, don't you?"

Jack wasn't expecting the question. No one had ever gone beyond the borders before. But, still, he barely wavered. They had no jurisdiction - not Slater, not the BRC - and he was used to these hero-complex types, boy scouts charging in thinking they were going to save a day that didn't need saving. "What I do outside this country isn't your problem."

"Actually, it is." Slater smiled slowly. "When I called you, I was just testing the waters. I wanted to see what you would say. We're not the ones on you this time, Mr. Halston. Interpol has requested our assistance, and, personally, I'm not interested in jurisdictional disputes. I just want to see a really bad guy get what he's got coming to him."

Jacket suddenly too tight, Jack unbuttoned it, leaning forward on the table, gaze steeled. He couldn't manage to completely discount Slater's words, but he could appear to do so. "Well, thanks for the warning, and for stopping by," he said. "Next time you want to talk to me, let me know in advance. I'll make sure my lawyers are present."

Smile never wavering, Slater got up from his seat, appearing even more hulking from Jack's lowered perspective. "You sound like a guilty man, Mr. Halston," he declared. "Or at least a man who isn't entirely sure he's innocent." Though Slater left room for response, Jack had nothing to say. "Tell Mr. Taylor I'd love to get in that game of squash sometime." Slater smiled.

Following the path of his self-assured exit, Jack knew he would never fall to whatever allegations the cocksure agent tried to turn into charges, but it was the first time he had ever been worried about the inquisition.

12

If you need me, you know where to find me. Jesus Christ. She may as well have said, 'I'll be waiting in the basement to strip on command.'

Since the work she'd been given to keep her busy, as Amelia had freely admitted, was the most mindless on the planet, Caton had nothing but time to think. So, she thought about what would have happened if she hadn't given in to Amelia's request, if she had never gone up to Amelia's office in the first place. It was what she needed to be thinking, how to avoid further entanglements. She couldn't undo what she had done, but she could certainly make her time left at the Halston Palace less complicated.

Mostly, though, as desperately as she tried to force her mind in the other direction, she thought about what would have happened if Sole hadn't made her untimely entrance, and it was that inner musing that drew Caton's eyes to the doorway every few minutes.

Of course, Amelia never came. If she was paying any attention to Caton at all, it could only be through the one-way street of the security system, on which she could watch her subject without having to engage.

Caton left without seeing Amelia again. The next day came, and she left early to keep her promise to Laura. Friday came, and Amelia was nowhere to be found.

It was as if nothing had happened.

Over the weekend, Caton tried to forget about it, but those few moments in the foyer entered her thoughts more often than she would have liked, especially when Laura was right in front of her and Caton knew how unfair she was being.

Monday, Tuesday, Wednesday, Caton fluctuated between relief that Amelia wasn't using what had happened against her and the overwhelming desire to track Amelia down and ask her who the fuck tells someone to take her clothes off and then returns to ignoring her as if she's never seen her naked.

Then, maybe it just wasn't all that memorable for Amelia.

Though Sole had made her usual efforts, Caton avoided their small talk and any unnecessary interaction, keeping to her crypt, where she could suffer her thoughts in relative peace. Every morning, she stopped in to say hello, and each night she said goodnight on the fly as Sole was preparing dinner with the precision of someone who did it every day and could handle the task without conscious thought.

Leaning into the delightful-smelling kitchen after a full week of civil avoidance, Caton did exactly that, saying her goodnight in a rush and turning to go.

"Caton," Sole called, and Caton paused in her fleeing, hand tightening on the strap of her bag as she glanced back. "Do you want a cookie?"

When Sole gestured to the racks on the counter with a smile, Caton instantly shook her head, self-preservation compelling her to flee in a hurry. "No, thank you."

"Amelia is out," Sole added, before Caton could make her escape. "Are you ever going to talk to me again?"

The powerful desire to save herself superseded by an unexpected flood of guilt, Caton sighed. Feeling called out, which she had definitely earned, she stepped into the kitchen, stopping across the bar from Sole, slowly meeting her gaze. "I'm sorry," she uttered, but Sole looked more sympathetic than upset.

"Do you want a cookie?" she offered again.

"Yeah, kinda," Caton admitted, and Sole grinned at her, grabbing a cookie from a rack and sliding it across the bar top on a napkin. Settling onto her usual stool, Caton dropped her bag to the stool next to her and took a bite, marveling again at Sole's culinary talents and glad for how much she got to indulge in them when the boss wasn't home. "This doesn't really strike me as a cookie household," Caton said, taking another bite.

"Amelia does work with a women's shelter," Sole explained. "She took most of them there. A little Halloween treat."

Forgetting her lingering discomfort, Caton ceased to chew, moist cookie bits going suddenly dry on her tongue. Licking her lips, she swallowed with substantial effort, and Sole brought her a glass of water, as if she had taken a clairvoyant reading of the humidity level in Caton's mouth.

Taking a drink, the guilt amplified. She hated the way things had been with Sole. Before the incident in the foyer, talking to Sole had been the only enjoyable part of Caton's day. She was so afraid, though, of any topics that would point to the huge elephant hovering just over her shoulder. As it turned out, Amelia was, indeed, the first topic of conversation, and, as if to emphasize how absolutely self-centered Caton had been over the past few days, it had absolutely nothing to do with her at all.

"I know she does good work," Caton said, voice weak, but it was all in theory. She knew Amelia handled Jack's charity work, he had told her so himself, and she knew Halston & Company had ties to multiple charities. It never crossed her mind that Amelia might ask someone to bake up homemade desserts and hand-deliver them. The information was so incongruous with everything she had experienced with Amelia firsthand, she couldn't even begin to process it.

She couldn't completely ignore the mention either, or the warmth that spread through her in reaction, moving up to her face where she was certain Sole could see. The elephant put its foot on her shoulder and pressed. "About the other day..."

"Hey, you don't have to explain anything to me," Sole cut in at once. "It's my job not to see anything that happens in this house."

With a flimsy laugh that brought no real relief, Caton watched Sole snag a cookie and bite into it. She could have left it alone. She probably should have left it alone. Sole was giving her a pass it would undoubtedly have been wisest to use. The not knowing, though, it was killing her.

"Does she, um..." She tried to keep the question light, glancing away as Sole looked up. "Does she do that with everyone?"

"What?" Sole returned with such shocked haste she had to catch cookie crumbs that tumbled from her lip. "Watch them take their clothes off?"

"Yeah," Caton responded with a shrug, hoping it looked more casual than it felt and realizing how ridiculous she had to sound. "Is it like a power trip for her or something, making someone do something just to prove she can?"

Wide eyes narrowing to a point, one of Sole's eyebrows quirked up, and Caton knew she had been made. "I can say I have never walked in on Amelia watching anyone strip in the middle of the foyer before," Sole stated. "And she's certainly never asked me. Whatever that was, it's between you and Amelia."

Eyes dropping to her water glass, Caton closed her hands around it, the cold against her skin doing little to alleviate the increasing warmth of her blush. Rolling the glass back and forth, she tried and failed to make sense of it. Maybe it was better if she didn't make sense of it. Maybe it was better if she just never emerged from the basement again.

"So," Sole said, letting the small utterance linger until Caton at last met her gaze. Though, for the most part, Sole held her game face, Caton could see the smirk restrained only by years of hiding her true feelings from rich people in order to keep her job. "Is that what you wanted to hear?"

Feeling read like pop fiction, all her secrets quickly and easily uncovered, Caton tried not to let anything else show. "I should go," she said quickly, standing up and pulling the strap of her bag over her arm. "Thank you for the cookie. Goodnight."

"Goodnight," Sole returned, and Caton could almost hear the smirk break free as she rushed from the room.

Whatever Caton wanted, the dungeon was what she had. Boxes and boxes of files, and drawers upon drawers into which to shove them. Nothing more. Just a ridiculous amount of money for mindless, seemingly never-ending work and the silence in which to drive herself crazy.

That was what she had for another day and a half, at least, until Amelia suddenly alighted in the doorway like she owned the place, which, of course, she did. The house, the room, and everything in it. Caton wondered if that included her, for the bargain price of seventy-five-hundred dollars a month.

Unlike the time Amelia had been there before, the sound didn't blend, and there was no mistaking who stood at her back. Caton made no false attributions to the creaking of the house or to her own imagination, sensing Amelia as surely as if she had her eyes plastered to the doorway, just awaiting her arrival.

She was supposed to turn around and acknowledge Amelia's presence, she was certain, with a curtsy, perhaps, or something equally deferential. Days before, in the wake of the undeniable feelings Amelia had stirred, Caton might have done just that. Days before, she might have been more delighted than she let on to see Amelia. Having been kept waiting, though, intentionally ignored, without explanation or justification, Caton wasn't exactly feeling the loyal subject.

With scarcely a glance toward the doorway, she grabbed more files from a box and flipped through them, coming away with the fleeting image of Amelia's casually-dressed outline and confident stance. It must have been a powerful feeling for Amelia, she thought bitterly, to know she couldn't be completely ignored, but, still, Caton did her best.

Entering the room when she decided, at the pace of her choosing, Amelia's footsteps were different than normal. Softer. Less pronounced. Caton could feel her drawing quietly closer, a pressing threat, almost predatory. Trying to ignore the sensation, she flipped a folder, shoving it into the metal cabinet with such vigor, the tab bent beneath her hand.

In the instant it took Caton to glance back down at the pile she held, Amelia flattened against her, out of sight and without sound at her back, and that Caton couldn't ignore. The rush of Amelia's breath stirring the hair at the back of her neck, her smell was invasive, the faded remnants of expensive shampoo and soap, masked by the earthy smell of sweat. It should have been a turnoff, but goddamn if Amelia's sweat couldn't have been its own high-dollar fragrance.

Caton tried not to drown in it, the feel of Amelia's body, her smell, the sound of her breath, but she was only treading water. With the paralyzing sensation of Amelia against her, she couldn't swim away if she wanted to, but, of all the desires racing through her veins, getting away was least amongst them.

Amelia pressed closer, fingers grasping Caton's hips to pull her more tightly into her, and the folders in Caton's hands fell to the floor in a mess. Whenever Amelia came into the room, it seemed, she brought disarray along with her.

Overwhelmed by the heat engulfing her, Caton didn't move, didn't breathe. She didn't try. Not until Amelia's hands slid across her stomach and forced the breath from her lips. She had been waiting. She could tell herself it was for an explanation, for clarity, for apology, but this was what Caton had been waiting for, Amelia to finish what she had started.

Hand sliding up Caton's body, Amelia's fingers splayed across her breast, branding Caton through the thin fabric of her shirt, palm teasing the nipple that had hardened the instant she entered the room, before her hands dropped lower to grasp the bottom of Caton's shirt and yank it over her head. Then, Amelia was back against her, and Caton swore the soft moan she heard wasn't hers.

Not lingering or hesitating, Amelia's hands went for the button of Caton's dusty jeans, flicking it open and working the zipper down in what felt like one seamless motion.

Caton lurched as the tips of Amelia's fingers slid over her panties, stroking and pressing, forcing her to react, and Caton could do nothing but react. Eyes closing, she reached out, seeking the edge of the file cabinet, trying to hold onto reality, but when Amelia's hand retracted just long enough to bypass the barrier of her panties and find her wet and open, Caton gave up on the real world and gave in to the fantasy.

Gasping at useless air, she lost herself in the sensation of Amelia's fingers moving against her, reaching back to snake her hand through tangled dark hair, clasping the back of Amelia's neck. It was a surprise, maybe even pleasant, when a groan sounded in her ear and Amelia's hand quickened its pace.

Caton wanted more. She felt as if Amelia was only skimming the surface. Still, it was more than enough, and Caton came apart under skilled hands, a technique perfected through practice. Maybe Amelia wasn't frigid after all, she realized, and the idea of Amelia lying in bed touching herself like this was enough to send Caton toppling into the abyss she'd been standing on the edge of for what felt like forever. The free fall was every bit the flight she imagined.

When Caton's knees gave out, Amelia's body provided support enough to keep her standing, and when the world finally came back into focus, Caton collapsed back against her, upright but depleted. She could feel her sweat sinking into Amelia's shirt, could hear Amelia's softly discharged breaths over her own labored breathing.

Then, without warning, Amelia suddenly pulled away, and Caton did find the file cabinet, pitching forward to catch herself on the edge of it before she fell to the floor like the jumbled folders at her feet. The same silent steps that brought her into the room signaled Amelia's departure, and, as they faded, Caton gave up her effort to remain standing. Letting go of the cabinet, she slid to her knees on the cold floor, hand finding her shirt beside her and holding it to her chest, shielding her too late from cameras that had already seen more than enough.

When Amelia came in, Caton was in no mood to acquiesce, or to even be polite. She meant to stand up for herself, demand some decency. For the amount of pride and anger she managed to retain at Amelia's touch, though, she may as well have signed herself over to Amelia for the duration of her employment, because as tall as she tried to stand, she still ended up on her knees.

13

When you come in Monday, you'll be upstairs.

That was the declaration that haunted Caton all weekend. Along with the guilt, which plagued her each time Laura smiled at her, and the memory of Amelia's touch each time she was alone.

Workday only half through, following Amelia's hasty retreat from the storage room, Caton had no choice but to pick herself up and try to readjust to reality. When she had emerged from the dungeon at the end of the day, the late afternoon sun streamed through the stained-glass windows of the foyer, and she had been drawn in the wrong direction.

Finding herself at the foot of the stairs, knowing Amelia was up there somewhere, she wanted to climb, to find Amelia and see what she had to say for herself. Or what she might do given another chance. Those stairs led to the unknown, though, and Caton couldn't work up the nerve to face any more surprises.

Apparently no place was safe from surprise, though, she had discovered in the kitchen when she'd gone in to say goodnight and Sole hit her with the news.

"When you come in Monday, you'll be upstairs."

"Oh, okay," Caton responded, glancing away, feeling the panic of not knowing rear up. "Why?"

With a shrug that indicated she had no idea what had happened on the floor below, Sole walked to the bar to start dicing. "Amelia needs your help with some project." She glanced up just long enough to toss Caton a smile. "Congratulations. Sounds like you've been promoted."

The situation was not without irony, Caton acknowledged, as she'd made her way to her car. Refusal to play the games at Halston & Company had led her to her current career placement, and, somehow, she had still managed to fuck her way to the upper floors.

With a change in position came a necessary change in attire. That was Caton's internal excuse for ditching the casual wear and the conservative clothing choices she wore largely to keep Jack at bay for something more presentable and flattering. She knew she had overdone both when she walked through the kitchen door and Sole did a double-take, her brief glance turning into a lingering gaze that made Caton shift in place.

"Good morning," Sole smiled.

"Good morning," Caton replied, uneasily. "Do you know where she wants me?"

Smirk flashing over Sole's lips, Caton wished she had chosen any other phrasing. "She'll be down for you," Sole assured her. "Just relax." As if that was possible. "Do you want some coffee?"

Managing no more than a nod, Caton walked to the bar and steadied herself on the edge, trying to ignore the erratic excitement and gnawing trepidation threatening to combine into hysteria inside of her. Glancing over her shoulder as Sole poured the steaming liquid, she watched her back, both anticipating and fearing Amelia's entrance, not sure she could endure too sudden an appearance. Hearing the thud of the mug hitting the bar, she turned back, picking up the offering Sole pushed toward her and watching the coffee slosh dangerously close to the rim before returning it to the flat surface in an effort to prevent second degree burns.

"What are you afraid she's going to do to you?" Sole questioned.

Eyes flashing upward, Caton forced a laugh that was meant to sound casual, but came out more demented than anything. "Nothing," she croaked. "I'm not afraid."

"You shouldn't be," Sole countered gently. "You know, Amelia's really not who she seems."

Caton was fairly certain she knew that better than just about anyone, but it was easier to pick up her coffee and sip mindlessly than let her mind wander down that track. "No?" she tossed out absently.

"When I came to this country," Sole continued. "I spoke hardly any English. Amelia made sure I still got this job. She made it so I could move into the guesthouse, so I would have more money to send home. She even got me an English tutor, and every day she would take time to talk to me so I could practice. She's kinder than she wants people to know."

Amelia was definitely not the public portrait she painted, Caton silently agreed, coming in straight from a workout to fuck her in the middle of a dusty basement. Leaving her utterly undone without any remorse wasn't exactly what Caton would call kind, though. "I'll keep that in mind," she uttered.

The sound at her back drawing her attention instantly, she watched Amelia walk in with her usual self-assured perfection. If the Amelia from Friday was a hot mess, Monday-morning-Amelia was a perfectly-coifed aristocrat, in a pencil skirt and tailored blouse, unbuttoned just enough to divert Caton's attention. It was hard to believe the two were one in the same, and Caton wondered if the event of the previous week had actually taken place at all.

"Good morning," Amelia greeted, and the instantaneous reaction of Caton's body assured her it had. Apparently, she couldn't even hear Amelia's voice without feeling those hands on her, abnormally soft, with more skill than she could have imagined.

Opening her mouth to return the greeting, air wisped pointlessly across Caton's lips as Sole poured another cup of coffee without missing a beat and slid it across the bar. Stepping up next to Caton without hesitation, Amelia was seemingly unbothered by their proximity.

"Thank you." Amelia smiled at Sole.

"You're welcome," Sole replied, and Caton wondered how they were being so normal when the entire room was whirling like a vortex.

When Amelia's attention turned to her, Caton firmed her shoulders, meeting her gaze in a manner that would have been challenging in the animal kingdom. Those eyes were as unreadable as ever, justifying

Caton's anxiety that she would have no clue about anything from that moment on. Whatever Amelia chose to do, whenever she chose to do it, Caton would never see it coming.

"Caton," Amelia stated, voice low and commanding, and every muscle in Caton's body went weak. "Come with me."

Looking for anywhere to avert her eyes, Caton landed on Sole, and wasn't sure if she felt better or worse when Sole winked her support, though she did manage to fake enough poise to follow Amelia out of the kitchen.

Walking the familiar path through the front room and into the foyer - 'the scene of the crime,' as Caton now thought of it - they made their way up the stairs, past Amelia's office. Having been beyond Amelia's office door only once before, when Sole had showed her around in the absence of the house's masters, Caton felt as if she was being granted further liberties. To what, she wasn't entirely sure.

The room next to Amelia's office had undergone a transformation, the storage space turned into a high-end office, unneeded equipment carried off someplace unknown.

"This is quite the set-up." Caton tried to inject a modicum of normalcy back into the situation.

"There's a lot to do," Amelia replied.

"So, you do need help." Caton made no effort to withhold the reply, and something slipped in Amelia's gaze, as if a reaction might actually leak out.

It could have been a good thing, Caton considered, returning them to a place of mutual distrust, where Amelia would order her back to the dungeons and Caton might survive by distance alone. Whatever Amelia was thinking, though, she never revealed it, and distrust was hardly the overwhelming sensation in the room.

"What do you need?" Caton asked, voice barely above a whisper.

For a moment, she wasn't asking a work-related question, and she was convinced Amelia wanted more than her assistance. When Amelia looked away, though, the spell ended before it could truly take hold, leaving Caton unsteady in its wake.

"I have to organize an event for investors," Amelia said, moving toward the computer and powering it on. "It's one of Jack's pet projects, an organization that designs clean water devices."

"Shining Life," Caton stated, and Amelia glanced back, eyes dipping down Caton's body for an instant, before returning to Caton's.

"You know about Shining Life?" She sounded impressed.

"Yes."

"Good," Amelia replied. "That will make things easier." Picking up a pile of papers from the desk top, she tugged the chair from beneath the desk. "Here. Sit."

Gaze locking on Amelia's hand on the back of the expensive office chair, Caton was slow in following the directive. As she at last dropped into the seat, Amelia's fingers brushed the back of her shirt, and Caton closed her eyes against the rush of memory of where those fingers last touched her.

Leaning over her shoulder, Amelia laid the papers back on the desk, her hand spreading out next to them, long, skilled fingers on flagrant display.

"Here," she whispered, lips so close to Caton's ear any other manner of speaking would have sounded like yelling. "This is a list of potential investors. I need to talk to all of these people, but ninety-five percent of them will insist on scheduling those conversations. So, I need you to make appointments for me."

"Okay," Caton said quickly, hoping to back Amelia off for the sake of her sanity.

Amelia only leaned closer, though, breasts pressing against Caton's upper back, hair falling forward to cast shadow on Caton's face, her free hand moving to Caton's shoulder as if it was the type of work that required physical direction. "If, by some chance, you do get one of them directly," Amelia softly continued, "just put him or her on hold and come get me. I'll show you how to transfer it."

It was intentional, that Caton knew. She just wished she knew why. Refusing to be played by desire, she glanced toward Amelia with some sense of indignation, finding the thin column of Amelia's neck too close. Any determined glare she might have produced to ward Amelia off was eclipsed by the immediate impulse to thread her fingers through the dark fall of hair and pull Amelia's lips to her own. "Okay," she breathed.

Eyes finding Caton's for an instant, Amelia finally moved away. Her hand abandoning Caton's shoulder, the touch lingered.

"I'll be right next door," Amelia said, turning and disappearing into the hall, and Caton released the breath lodged in her throat.

She didn't need any reminding. She knew well where Amelia would be. It was what worried her the most.

14

Maybe it wouldn't happen again. That was the thought that tormented and comforted Caton in the days to come. Perhaps, it was a one-time error in Amelia's judgment, and Caton doubted she made many such errors.

Not that Amelia wasn't seductive, accidentally brushing against her, dropping innuendos in the guise of workplace conversation, looking more and more appealing each day.

Not that Caton didn't have it coming. Every morning, she rushed to work. She leaned into Amelia's casual touches, she held Amelia's long glances, hopelessly wondering where they might lead. The more time she spent around Amelia, the more Amelia enveloped her, and the more Caton craved the tease turning into something substantial that didn't leave her utterly pent-up and dissatisfied at the end of each achingly long work day.

Days turning to weeks, though, Amelia seemed content to toy with Caton, never approaching with the same possessive intent she had in the basement, and it occurred to Caton it could have been a fluke, an isolated event that would never happen again.

Maybe torture was Amelia's true pleasure.

Or, maybe, Amelia was simply too busy.

From a distance, Amelia's life looked like one of leisure. From a closer perspective, Caton could see that Amelia's position as Jack's wife was, in fact, work. What Amelia did for her husband would have earned her an executive-level salary at any company. How good she was at the job would have earned her multi-million-dollar bonuses and respect in the field.

Over the weeks they had worked together, Caton watched Amelia talk people into donations, future alliances and volunteering armed with nothing but charm and sincerity. When Amelia opened the door between their offices, creating an express pathway between them that felt like a particularly cruel tease, Caton could hear the other woman's throaty voice captivating her distant audiences and extracting promises from them in one way or another. It was the kind of passionate dedication that came only from true belief.

Those whom she couldn't convince over the phone, Amelia talked into letting her have another shot at them. She invited diplomats and businessmen to dinners and parties, agreeing to attend as many. She met potential donors at hockey games and concerts. Caton entered event after event, watching Amelia's calendar fill up like the squares on a bingo card, and wondered how much of her life Amelia had spent being Jack's full-time employee and whether she ever left the house on her own time.

It was as Caton was packing up to leave one evening, having seen Amelia little throughout the day, that Amelia came through the shared door, her unexpected presence enough to send a jolt through Caton's body. Far from resistant, Caton had grown used to the sensation of Amelia. Being near her was a constant state of arousal, nothing tempered it, so she had learned to live with it much as she learned to endure her sixth-grade crush on her English teacher.

Brushing Caton's arm unnecessarily as she passed, Amelia turned to lean against the edge of the desk, skirt riding up as her legs crossed next to Caton. "Do you like the opera?" she asked.

"I don't know." Caton sighed at her own juvenile libido, which simply refused to be tempered in Amelia's presence. "I can't say I've had a lot of exposure."

"You're going to find out," Amelia declared.

"Okay," Caton drawled uncertainly. Hand resting an inch from Amelia's hip, she sent every ounce of willpower to the appendage to keep it from reaching for the silky fabric of Amelia's skirt.

"I have to meet with some potential donors," Amelia went on. "I know absolutely nothing about them beyond the fact that they like to be around beautiful women. That means you. So, I expect you to come with me."

Feeling the flush crawl instantly over her face, Caton dropped her head, feeling every bit the hormonal teenager, hoping Amelia didn't see. It wasn't just a bad idea. It was perhaps the worst idea. Getting involved in Amelia's dealings outside of her agreed-upon work schedule was the last thing she needed.

"Please." Amelia's hand moved from its resting place against her thigh to the back of Caton's hand, fingertips stroking gentle paths over her skin.

Even knowing Amelia was doing it to get what she wanted, any objections Caton might have made disappeared into the realm of unspoken reservations. "All right," she whispered.

Pulling her hand slowly away, Amelia's fingertips trailed against skin so sensitive, Caton feared it would catch fire beneath her touch.

When Amelia at last pushed off the edge of the desk, the same hand alighted on Caton's shoulder. "Goodnight, Caton," she murmured, fingertips tickling down Caton's shoulder blade, before trailing away.

15

Amelia didn't go in half-prepared. For her, there was no strategy too well-formulated. Everything was down to the last detail.

When the limo rolled up outside Caton's apartment, it was stocked with imported Indian fare, from the wine to the appetizers. The music was tailored, the driver was tailored, even the interior of the limo was tailored. Caton knew this, because she had been told very specifically what Amelia expected out of the evening's transportation, a list that involved many long conversations and deep sighs of frustration on the other end of the phone as the sales rep at the limo company tried to decide if jumping through hoops was worth the additional fee Amelia was willing to pay.

Amelia hadn't, however, told Caton what she expected of her. So, looking out at the black car against the curb, windows dark and concealing, Caton feared what awaited her beyond the glass. Bracing herself, she abandoned the safety of her building, pulling her cape tighter around her shoulders, asking herself in no kind terms why she hadn't bought a dress with more fabric. From ribcage to toe, she was warm enough, but as the wind whipped through the cape, despite its lining, to sink into her largely-exposed upper half, she realized she was a fucking moron for trying so hard to impress someone who had given her nothing but confusion in return.

With a small nod, the limo driver opened the door for her, and Caton hustled inside, sliding against the plush leather seat with a shiver as the door closed behind her. Turning to Amelia, she warmed again instantly.

The deep red dress Amelia wore contrasted against her skin where a shawl in deeper red lay open at her shoulders, but it was Amelia's eyes that made the expansive space of the limo feel uncomfortably intimate.

"Let me see," she requested, and a burst of laughter escaped Caton's lips. She should have known she would be subject to Amelia's approval. She didn't exactly have Amelia's wardrobe or sense of style, and the dress she'd bought for the occasion cost more than she should have paid, but still came off a rack. Pinching free the loop enclosures that held the cape together, she pulled the sides apart, turning full-on to Amelia in a poor imitation of a flasher, and awaited Amelia's assessment.

Confident gaze stroking down Caton's body, Amelia's eyes lingered everywhere the dress was designed to draw attention. Then, lingered some more, before they finally made it back to Caton's. "You look perfect," she said at last, in such a way that Caton considered the request may have been less in line with the trimmings she had demanded for the limo and more in line with her request the day in the foyer.

Either way, it had the same effect, and Caton turned in the seat, refastening the cape's enclosures with trembling fingers, as she realized not looking at Amelia was her safest option. "Thank you," she replied, trying to sound more mannerly than affected. "So do you."

Amelia's subsequent silence made Caton think she had succeeded in sounding merely polite, but the false sense of security was waylaid seconds after the limo began moving as Amelia's fingers pushed through her hair, tucking the loose locks behind Caton's ear, effectively eliminating the only barrier Caton had available to her. Glancing to Amelia again, she watched the slow curve of lips as Amelia smiled.

"You don't happen to speak Bengali, do you?" Amelia asked, voice quiet in the vast space of the cabin.

The question was unexpected enough that Caton was able to laugh through her discomfort. "No."

"We'll wing it," Amelia countered.

"They don't speak English?"

"They do..." Amelia paused long in her explanation. "But some things have gotten lost in translation. I wouldn't want anyone to misinterpret anything."

Gaze held by Amelia's, Caton felt all traces of humor or civility evaporate at once, amazed at how quickly Amelia could go from cordial to cutting. "No," Caton uttered. "You wouldn't want that."

Turning away, she stared out the window, hoping to deter further discussion, but her cold-shoulder was of little use, because Amelia had said all she needed to say.

Taking the final turns in silence, the limo pulled up outside the lighted facade of a hotel that could have been a still life in a museum exhibit of the wealthy. As she waited for the driver to open her door, Amelia glanced her way, and Caton anticipated the next vaguely-concealed rejection.

"Come with me," Amelia ordered, before stepping out of the car, and, withholding her instantaneous response, Caton slid across the seat to follow.

Taking the driver's hand as she emerged from the car, she somehow landed in Amelia's waiting touch, which slid inside the fabric of her cape to clutch her arm. From any other perspective, they must have looked like two people closer than they were, but, not wanting to misinterpret anything, Caton focused on the distance between them.

Led into the warm interior of the hotel lobby, which spilled over with such opulence it bordered on obscene, Caton expected Amelia to release her. Anger simmering, she wanted Amelia to release her. Instead, Amelia directed Caton by the arm until they reached a group of men, who stood at their approach, ogling freely.

"Mr. Argo." Amelia picked the correct man from the group, indicating she had done her research. "I'm Amelia."

"Well, you are each bit as lovely in life as you sound on the phone," Mr. Argo responded, taking Amelia's offered hand to press his lips to her knuckles.

"Thank you," Amelia smiled, and Caton's arm was moved for her, pushed through the fabric of the cape and offered to Mr. Argo as sacrifice. "This is Caton."

"And you are as lovely in life as I was told you would be," Mr. Argo said, lifting Caton's hand to his lips.

Anticipating the compliment, but not the revelation of its original source, Caton manufactured a smile that felt fake, but looked real enough to satisfy Mr. Argo. Not once had she heard Amelia exuding her loveliness to anyone. But that was probably for the best. If she had, she might have misinterpreted it.

Mr. Argo released her hand, and Caton pulled it back inside the cape for safety, but Amelia returned to her place as well. It was hardly fair that Caton felt such a rush of longing at the simple touch, when, to Amelia, the connection was nothing more than a rudder by which to guide Caton through the dangerous waters of high-dollar fundraising.

"Shall we go?" Amelia asked, and Mr. Argo agreed with a nod. The men at his back pulled on their coats, and Caton could hear their shoes thudding against the floor behind them as Amelia led the formal parade back to the limo.

When the driver opened the door, Amelia pushed Caton inside, following her into the seat. With each man who climbed in after them, the space grew smaller and Amelia inched closer, until she finally sat flush against Caton's side. Unhooking the closures of her cape once again, Caton hoped her sudden overheating and the low cut of her dress went unnoticed in the dark interior of the cabin.

The kind of casual conversation that Caton had learned came effortlessly to Amelia filled the car as it curved through the streets, and Caton felt Amelia's throaty laugh against her, turning to watch the man who told the funny story smile with the elation of impressing such an alluring woman.

Amelia had enchanted them already, Caton could tell, just by appearing before them and being everything she had promised over the phone. Whatever she was asking of them, whatever dollar amount she had in mind, Amelia had virtually in hand. The rest of the night was for show, and Caton had been drawn into her act. She shouldn't be a part of it, she was well aware of the fact, but she was just like the men currently hanging on Amelia's every word, an adherent to the woman's unrelenting appeal. Amelia said jump, and Caton had done so in a dress she couldn't afford and three-and-a-half-inch heels.

When the limo took a hard right that tested everyone's balance, Caton found herself suddenly pinned between the door and Amelia. The sound of the men's laughter masked the gasp that slipped from her throat as Amelia placed her hand on an exposed knee to right herself. Returning to her original position, Amelia laughed along, perfectly at ease. Her slightly chilled fingers, satin against Caton's skin, fluttered inward, one finger dipping toward the cleft in her knee, and remained, as if it had every right to be there.

Glancing down at Amelia's hand, Caton felt as if the limo was still careening. She turned her gaze to the window, watching the city roll past and trying to calm the sudden surge of desire that Amelia stoked with the soft touch. She wished she could tell herself it was the last time she would give into Amelia's clear lust for control, but she knew if she told herself that, she would be lying.

16

From the limo to the box at the theater, Amelia didn't miss a beat. Nothing could get her off her game. Not a botched punch line. Nor an aggressively suggestive comment. Not even the unexpected accident that had them sitting in traffic for forty minutes and arriving at the theater at the last moment. Ushering the men inside, Amelia still managed to check their coats in an orderly manner, and Caton wondered if anything could fluster the woman.

Of course, it already had, and Caton had borne witness to it. This woman, the one in control of every step and word, would have let Caton walk out of her job and her life the day she fired her without a second thought. She would have stayed behind her desk, completely unresponsive. The other Amelia had gotten hurt. She had gotten up. She had chased Caton down the stairs.

That Amelia was so rare, though, Caton had seen only glimpses of her in the time since, and was starting to wonder if those ephemeral moments even belonged to reality. The Amelia who had greeted her in the limo was almost too stalwart, too at-ease, too trained. It wasn't even natural to be so untouchable.

Even the usher recognized that Amelia was in charge. Trying to hustle them into their seats before the curtain went up, the tuxedo-clad man finally admitted defeat, realizing Amelia's guests would take their seats when they were good and ready to do so and not a moment before.

"Please, sit," Amelia said, motioning to the seats that lined the front of the box, as the opening chords started below them, and Caton cast her gaze toward the overdressed patrons in the orchestra seats below.

"It's your compartment," Mr. Argo argued.

"I insist," Amelia stated, somehow commanding and demurring at the same time, and succeeded in getting the men seated without pressure or demand.

Nodding toward one of the chairs at the back of the box, Amelia dictated Caton's position as well, and Caton sunk into the velvet cushioning, a pawn moved onto her square. Warmed by their haste to the box, she removed her cape, letting it slink down her back as Amelia took the seat beside her with such an abundance of grace, she may as well have floated into her chair. Not for the first time, Caton wondered if Amelia had the capacity to just be human.

Watching Amelia hold the usher in her sights until he finally left the box and pulled the curtain shut at their backs, Caton's eyes drifted downward as Amelia shrugged her shawl from her shoulders and exposed just how low the red fabric dipped between her breasts.

Before Amelia, she had never thought herself a lecherous person, but, whatever Amelia showed, Caton always felt instantly drawn to it, like Amelia's skin was a magnetic field and her eyes were crafted of nickel. Of course, to be fair, her desire to look at anything Amelia chose to reveal could have been due to the fact that Amelia kept so much of herself concealed. The more important parts of Amelia felt permanently vaulted, like they were locked behind a steel door Caton would never figure out how to access.

As the curtain rose, Caton dragged her gaze to the stage. From the side of her eye, she could see Amelia silently situating herself, smoothing her dress down her legs, adjusting the shawl behind her back, crossing her legs in front of her. It wasn't until Amelia settled back fully into her seat, arm pressing against Caton's, that Caton became aware of just how close Amelia was sitting, how much of the lingering warmth she felt in the cold darkness was owed, not to their sprint through the theater at all, but to Amelia.

She tried to ignore it, but, as always, Amelia was impossible to ignore. Just knowing her skin was so close made Caton yearn to touch. As she spent her days yearning. As she suspected she would spend the length of her employment yearning. Though, she still couldn't understand why. She had better judgment, she had Laura, but, whenever she was around Amelia, she forgot she had either of those things.

Sometime later, Amelia shifted, legs uncrossing and recrossing to angle closer. That was all it took to hasten the beat of Caton's heart, to make her mouth go dry, to draw her body instantly in Amelia's direction. When she felt the back of Amelia's bare foot slide down her calf, Caton wanted more than anything to give into the sensation. Still raw from Amelia's warning, though, she knew it was contrived, as everything was with her, a cat-and-mouse game where Amelia cornered and toyed with her until she chose to set Caton free just so she could come after her again when she got bored.

Loath to misinterpret anything, Caton shifted away, crossing her own legs to remove herself from Amelia's range, as distant as she could make herself in the limited space. When Amelia looked over at her in the darkness, Caton could feel it, the amusement in the eyes sliding over her face, before Amelia's fingers reached out to feather her hair out of the way.

Arm sliding across her shoulders, Caton was torn by equal urges to lean into Amelia and away from her, to settle comfortably into the embrace and tense within it. Her body decided for her, suddenly so rigid against the back of the chair, she had a better view of the stage. If she went through life more aware of her posture, she suddenly realized, she would have a completely different perspective on the world.

Undeterred, perhaps even encouraged, by the attempt at defiance, Amelia's hand curved around Caton's arm, sliding up and down the exposed skin in a calculated caress. The goose bumps formed against her will, but what Caton could control, she did. Eyes locked on the stage, she saw nothing, felt everything, and pretended the opposite.

Amelia's hand trailing over her shoulder to the sensitive skin of her neck, Caton's eyes closed on instinct, and, when Amelia's fingers moved up a vein, it throbbed wildly in response, belying where Caton's real attention lied. It was futile trying to resist Amelia when her body offered nothing but encouragement, so she decided to surrender, head falling to the side, giving Amelia more skin to explore.

The featherlight touch traced Caton's jawline to her ear, skimming around its shell and pressing into the hollow behind it, a spot Caton didn't know was that erogenous for her until her breath turned choppy in response.

Slowly retracing the path, Amelia started again and again, sometimes with the soft pads of her fingertips, sometimes scratching Caton's skin with her nails, until Caton couldn't remember where she was or why she was supposed to be refusing to let Amelia touch her.

It might have been minutes or hours later that the curtain fell on the first act, and by the time the lights came up, Amelia had already moved away, shawl back in place to cover the most revealing parts of her dress, at the ready before Mr. Argo and his colleagues got to their feet in the front of the box to stretch.

Turning around, Mr. Argo smiled widely at the sight of her, as if he'd forgotten how stunning Amelia was in the short time he'd been turned toward the stage.

"You let me buy you a drink," he said.

"Of course." Amelia flirted like a professional.

"Both of you," Mr. Argo added, glancing Caton's way.

"Caton," Amelia coaxed, holding her hand out, expecting obedience.

Staring at the hand as if it was loaded, Caton refused the offering, steadying herself on the back of her chair as she got to her feet. "I have to go to the restroom," she responded. "I'm sorry."

Moving around the outside of her chair, despite the limited space next to the railing, she succeeded in avoiding Amelia's spellbinding touch as she fled the box. Behind her, she could hear Amelia giving an undoubtedly perfect explanation, and imagined her sliding her hand into the crook of Mr. Argo's waiting arm and being escorted to the lobby by the same man who would later donate millions of dollars for the privilege of having had exactly this moment with her.

The long line at the restroom gave Caton time to partially recover, to mentally prepare for more of Amelia's special brand of torture. This Amelia, Caton knew well though, and she didn't doubt her little display would be long forgotten by the time they returned to their seats. Waiting for Amelia's next touch without answer was a familiar feeling, much like praying to a god who didn't exist.

The need to relieve herself of the pressure Amelia built inside of her was also painfully familiar, and, while she convinced herself that compassion for those at the end of the line was what stopped her from masturbating in the bathroom stall, it was really more logistics and the quarter-inch gap at one side of the old wooden stall door.

Still, as she returned to the lobby, Caton had nearly found her way back to the relative normalcy of being in Amelia's presence. Then, she spotted Amelia, standing like a beacon in the center of the room, holding not only the entire group of potential investors captivated, but a few passersby who had been drawn into her orbit as well.

As she finished her story, the group went up in raucous laughter, gaining Amelia even more attention from the room's patrons, and Amelia's eyes rose to the crowd, scanning her admirers with haste, stopping only when they got to Caton. She didn't smile, but Amelia's gaze was oddly unguarded, burning with desire as blatant as Caton had ever seen it. Desire for her, though, or for the power she held over her? Realizing the two may be one and the same for Amelia, Caton turned from the temptation and burrowed into the crowd, leaving Amelia to her flock.

The clutch in her hand felt solid, and it occurred to Caton she could escape. She wouldn't want to risk the run-in with Amelia to retrieve her cape from the box, so she would run cold if she ran, but she would be liberated, free of Amelia's strange power over her. Unready to make that kind of commitment, apparently, Caton found herself back in the loge, watching the crowd below, considering how she ended up in her current position, knowing she had only herself to blame.

As the lights blinked in warning, Amelia returned with her arm in Mr. Argo's. Watching the men strut back toward their seats with expensive wine in cheap plastic stemware, Caton put on her best fake smile for them. If this was what Amelia wanted from her, reinforcement in her seduction of complete strangers for profit, then that's what Caton would give her. But it was all Caton would give her. Amelia had no right to ask for more.

Mr. Argo and his slightly-inebriated friends settling back in, Caton glanced at Amelia, knowing Amelia only responded to strength and facing her was the best way to regain some element of control. Staring back with her usual indecipherable look, Amelia held out a bottle of water, and Caton blinked at it, searching for the skull and crossbones on the label.

Thrown from her intended course, she couldn't remember what stand she was trying to make. "Thank you," she said on automatic, taking the water and discovering how thirsty she was when she twisted the cap off and took a drink.

The darkness sinking back over the theater, civilized applause rising toward the rafters, Caton settled back into her seat, capping the water and setting it on the floor beside her. Remnants of Amelia's touches still on her skin, she feared a reenactment, and longed for it, two contradictory poles that always seemed to balance each other and exist harmoniously when she was around Amelia.

On stage, an aria swelled and, beside her, Amelia nudged slightly closer, her hand breaching the slit in Caton's dress to settle above her knee. There was almost affection in it, and Caton sighed, partly in irritation, partly in delight, and folded her hands primly in her lap, as if feigning purity would make Amelia abstain.

For a while, it seemed to work. The hand just sat there, perfectly still, making an impression on Caton's leg like an iron held on the same sleeve for too long. Then, there was the slightest movement of Amelia's fingers, a barely-there brush easing over skin already branded, turning into an explorative up-and-down slide along Caton's thigh. Easing inward, the touch traveled further with each pass, ceasing its advancement only when it reached the point where Caton pressed her thighs solidly together beneath the fabric of her dress.

Swallowing at nothing, Caton managed not to squirm in her seat. Weeks ago, it would have been impossible, but, evidently, Amelia's bouts of torture had been good training.

Amelia's touch wasn't insistent, it was persuasive, her fingers moving at leisure over Caton's rapidly-heating skin to test the boundaries of Caton's resolve, and Caton struggled to hold her ground, not against Amelia, but within herself. With each sweep of Amelia's hand, she wanted nothing more than to open up and let her in. It was only the very public venue and immediate company that made her clutch the seat of her chair until her hand ached in resistance, knowing even as she did that it was only a matter of time before she gave into her.

"Let me." Amelia's words ghosting over Caton's ear were more sensation than sound. Like the movement of her hand, they were far from an order. Two words, barely spoken, they were almost plea, almost apology, and Caton wanted so much to believe they were both, that if she let Amelia in, it would be fruitful and not the same painful longing she had been plagued with for weeks.

The simple request wedging into Caton's rational mind, ceasing its operation, at the slight nudge of Amelia's hand, her legs fell open. Holding her breath, she still couldn't stop the gasp that slipped free as Amelia's hand penetrated her resistance to brush against her panties. Eyes focused on a spot on the stage, she tried to maintain an iota of control, but she had no control. All she had wanted for weeks was for Amelia to fuck her again, and, as she was discovering, it didn't matter when or where that took place.

Eyes closing, Caton submitted to the hand moving in unhurried strokes, the pounding of her heart so forceful it seemed to add an extra beat to the music, the lightheaded sensation threatening to carry her away. Even in the darkness, Amelia exposed her, made her vulnerable. Someone with wandering opera glasses was sure to get the show of a lifetime, but Caton simply had to trust that Amelia wouldn't be doing it if she weren't in control, if they didn't have privacy enough not to be seen.

Edging upward, Amelia's fingers breached the barrier of Caton's panties, and the notion that she should try to stop her from going too far flitted through Caton's mind with the staying power of a snow flake. As Amelia's touch moved against slick skin, she only opened to her more.

There was no rush, no haste to finish, just a precise, determined touch that sent Caton soaring instantly and kept her hovering over Eden. It could go on all night that way, as far as Caton was concerned. All the days that had passed, she thought it was release she so desperately needed, but it wasn't. It was Amelia's touch she had craved. She realized it the moment she gave herself over to it. Her tension melted away instantly, a form of release all its own.

Choruses went by, sweeping melodies filled with grand, impassioned voices singing words Caton didn't need to understand. They swept up around her in a wave, taking her higher, until the music was all that surrounded her. With the low rumble of a kettle drum, Caton's tension returned. Body straining, she exhaled a desperate cry for mercy.

"Shhh." Amelia's breath was on her cheek, and Caton turned into it, inhaling sharply as the warm air licked the corner of her mouth, the sweet smell of red wine filling her head.

Amelia's hand maintaining the same unhurried pace, Caton knew she couldn't endure it, couldn't possibly sit still and silent while Amelia made her come apart. Reaching blindly for Amelia's forearm, Caton felt it flex beneath her hand. "Don't," Amelia stated, and that did sound like a command.

Opening her eyes, Caton found Amelia's so close, she could see flecks of silver shining in them. Across the small space, she could feel Amelia's lips, and craved her kiss as she had craved nothing before it. The muscles in Amelia's arm jumped as her touch grew firmer, faster, and Caton's mouth opened to protest. Or to encourage.

"Shhh," Amelia whispered again, before she could do either, and Caton's eyes closed as Amelia's breath slipped into her mouth and mixed with her own. Clasping tighter to Amelia's arm, Caton reached out with her free hand, looking for anything to give her traction, and, finding the silken fabric of Amelia's dress, she clutched the tense thigh beneath it.

The sound from the orchestra pit grew louder, bolder. It overtook the hall, and Caton felt Amelia's head rest against her own, heard Amelia's breath in her ear. It was as if Amelia was all over her, and Caton gave in to the crescendo, body rupturing pleasure, shuddering in time to the rich sounds of cello and violin. Riding out the notes with Amelia close at her side, it was as if they were on a wave together to some unknown destination.

As unexpectedly as the sentiment came on, it receded. Amelia pulled her hand away, wiping it without discretion on the inside of Caton's expensive dress, and Caton felt Amelia's arm slip through her fingers as Amelia pried her other hand from her dress like it was a parasite.

When Amelia stood up, Caton was sure she had been discarded, used and tossed away. Then, the clapping started, staggered over the last notes of the opera, and Amelia's guests were on their feet too. Caton righted herself to a nearly-presentable state just in time to see Mr. Argo turn back to them with a smile.

The only person in the theater not standing in ovation, Caton knew she should get up. Pushing up from the chair, she lost her legs, staggering forward, but miraculously didn't fall. Reaching out instantly, her hand cradling Caton's elbow, Amelia was there to catch her.

Amelia engaged in the same easygoing banter with her guests on the way out as she had on the way in, and Caton marveled at her ability to act as if she hadn't just brought her assistant to climax behind them in a crowded theater.

Back at the hotel, where Amelia again dragged Caton around by the elbow, Mr. Argo asked them in for a nightcap, but Amelia was quick with a believable excuse and bid them goodnight. Leaning in for a kiss, Mr. Argo made a last ditch effort for Amelia's lips, and she dodged even that with such grace, Argo probably convinced himself he had been aiming for her cheek the entire time.

Sending the men off with a smile, Amelia slid her arm through Caton's once more and led her back to the limo, and, for the first time since the ride to the hotel, they were truly alone again. Divider up, the driver was a nonentity, and, though there was plenty of empty space, only inches divided them on the seat.

"Did you like the opera?" Amelia asked casually, and Caton wondered if it was meant to be a joke. If there was one thing Amelia had to know very well, it was that Caton had been aware of very little that took place onstage.

Sending Amelia a look that said as much, Caton didn't know whether she should be angry or ashamed, so she settled on being strangely amused by the absurdity of the situation. Amelia had coaxed every voyeuristic quality Caton never knew she had out of her. Humor fading slightly, she wondered what she wouldn't do if Amelia asked her, frightened when she couldn't come up with an immediate answer.

As the limo pulled up outside her building, Caton glanced toward the stone facade, imagining how Amelia must feel about having to pick her up and drop her off in her working-class neighborhood. She tried to think of something to say, but, by the time the door opened for her, she still had nothing. "Goodnight," she settled for saying as she glanced back at Amelia.

"Goodnight," Amelia returned, those unreadable eyes giving nothing away.

Gaze dropping to Amelia's lips, Caton shivered at the mere idea of them against her own, and moved away from Amelia to take the driver's offered hand before she could act on impulse. Outside the car, she paused, words pouring into her head, instantly aware it was a mistake to voice them. So, it was as much a surprise to her as anyone when she released the driver's hand and turned back, hand clutching the top of the door in support as she leaned down to look in at Amelia.

"Don't you need those papers?" She invented a plausible excuse on the fly. "You could come in and get them." It was a fool's request, Caton knew as she proposed it, but, apparently, she couldn't resist the fractional possibility of the answer she wanted.

When Amelia's eyes changed, no longer unreadable, but unamused, ice-filled even, Caton wished she had heeded her reservations. "I'm sure they can wait," Amelia uttered, voice unforgiving.

It was everything Caton had expected, but she still felt the sting. Casting her eyes from Amelia, she backed away quickly, letting the driver close the door of the limo, before he hurried to the door of Caton's building to let her inside. Caton produced the key and the driver took it, unlocking the door for her and placing the key ring back in her hand as she stepped into the warmth of the lobby that did nothing to ease the cold running through her.

"Goodnight." The driver nodded.

"Goodnight," Caton returned. "Thank you."

Letting the door close before her, she watched him hurry around the car and climb back into the limo, and the limo drive off into the night. Though, she couldn't see Amelia through the tinted glass, Caton somehow knew she wasn't looking back.

17

Amelia was dismissive. She was cold. She was cruel. She was impossible.

Maybe Caton liked being mistreated. Maybe it suited her. There was simply no other explanation as to why, in the presence of Laura, a genuine human being who was attentive and communicative and open, she could think of nothing but a woman who was conceited and detached and did the majority of her communicating through stares and poisonous remarks.

Flawless on the outside, there was simply no consistency in what lay beneath Amelia's perfect facade. Laura was beautiful both inside and out. She never wavered. She laid all her cards face-up on the table. With Amelia, one could never guess what was in her hand, and she bluffed better than anyone Caton had ever known.

Over the weekend, spent recuperating in Laura's presence, where Caton knew each touch meant what it seemed, Caton was well aware of those truths. By Monday morning, though, when her irritation with Amelia should have been at a peak, it refused to arise. It was only excitement, the eager desire to see Amelia again, that carried Caton through the morning and the gate that led onto the driveway of the Halston Palace.

Inside the front door, her eyes went immediately to the stairs. Trying to bend her gaze around the landing, she wondered if Amelia was in her office, but couldn't rush to find out. Overanxious, she had arrived early, and suspected Amelia would have a field day if she knew she was already there. If she could only kill enough time, she might actually be able to pull off nonchalant.

Walking into the kitchen, Caton returned Sole's warm smile. "Good morning."

"Good morning," Sole responded. "How was the opera?"

"It was fine." Caton struggled to hold Sole's gaze.

"So, Amelia wasn't too rough with you?" Sole's temperate expression indicated the innuendo was accidental, and Caton was fairly certain she didn't need to worry about Amelia telling anyone. More likely, the event that took place in Loge Box 22 would never be mentioned again, relegated to the deep, hidden pit of secrecy with their other savage tryst.

"No." Caton dropped Sole's eyes. "She was fine."

"Good." Sole turned and poured coffee without asking.

At the unspoken invitation, Caton wandered over to the bar. "Thanks," she said, as Sole slid the mug to her. "Is Amelia upstairs?" For once, the question sounded amazingly casual, and Caton lifted her coffee smugly to her lips.

She didn't know what she expected, but it certainly wasn't the confused expression that appeared instantly on Sole's face. "She's not here," Sole replied. "She's visiting her parents in Venezuela. She didn't tell you?"

Coffee suddenly burning her throat, Caton forced it the rest of the way down. "No."

"Oh," Sole replied, playing the slight off with a shrug. "I guess she forgot. She left Saturday morning. She left work for you, though. She said she'd call later."

Nodding on autopilot, Caton wondered why she felt surprise at the news. She should have been expecting it. Amelia never did anything without a plan. "Great," she uttered dully, unable to hide her disbelief, which rose up and left her deadened in its wake. "How long will she be gone?"

"Two weeks," Sole gently answered, seeming to realize it was a blow that needed softening. "So, easy days for you. You can relax."

Maybe Sole was right. After all, if Amelia wasn't around, Amelia couldn't fuck with her. She couldn't put on her little displays of power. She couldn't make Caton do anything she would later regret.

Dropping her bag on the floor, Caton took her seat at the bar, feeling no motivation to go upstairs to work, and Sole smiled. "That's the spirit. Do you want anything else?"

Trapping her tongue in her cheek, Caton wanted to tell Sole everything, the entire chain of events as they unfolded on Friday night, from Amelia's order not to read into things to Amelia fingering her to the refrains of Don Giovanni and then acting as if the invitation into Caton's apartment was an affront to her character. She wanted to ask Sole if that was what she meant when she referred to Amelia's "kindness".

"I assume you have liquor." Caton clamped down on the urge, pushing her mug back across the counter, hoping Sole would take the request as professional rebellion instead of a pathetic attempt at cauterizing the pain of Amelia's most recent slap to her face.

With passing hesitation, Sole went to a cabinet and pulled out a bottle of amaretto, brandishing it in the air for Caton's approval. "Tell me when," she said, starting to pour, but when never came.

Pre-drunkenness was a preferable state in which to speak to Amelia, Caton discovered when the phone rang less than an hour after she finally made it up the stairs.

"This is Caton," she answered, voice as relaxed as she felt.

When silence reigned for a moment, she glanced at the caller ID again, making sure she'd read it right. Amelia's cell number glared back at her in hazy gray until the sound of Amelia clearing her throat finally floated across the line. "It's Amelia," she stated unnecessarily.

"Is it?" Caton responded lightly. "I heard she's in Venezuela."

"I am in Venezuela," Amelia returned, and Caton grinned at the palpable confusion in her voice.

"Hmm," she hummed, lifting her empty mug to her lips and pouting as she dropped it back to the desk. "Phones work all the way down there?"

"Why are you acting so bizarre?" Amelia asked.

"I'm a little bit drunk," Caton responded matter-of-factly.

"Are you serious?"

"No," Caton countered quickly, pushing more upright in the chair as she realized she wasn't, in fact, drunk enough for the conversation. "I'm not serious. I'm barely tipsy. What do you want?"

More silence following the terse response, Caton expected Amelia's next words to be angrier, to be as cold and unforgiving as she was, to scold her mercilessly for her utter stupidity. Her stupidity for giving into Amelia at the opera. For inviting Amelia in, as if Amelia had any interest in spending time with her that wasn't pre-calculated. For feeling rejected, when she knew rejection was all she could ever really expect from Amelia. Maybe she even expected Amelia to fire her again, because, why the hell not? Amelia loved her power, and why shouldn't she toss it around every chance she got?

"Did you get the information I left for you?" Amelia said carefully instead.

"You did put it on my desk," Caton responded. "It was hard to miss."

"Jack throws this dinner party every year," Amelia expounded as if Caton cared. "It's an early Thanksgiving for casual friends, mostly business acquaintances. It's all just a big show, but it's got to be done. Everything was taken care of, but the caterer fell through."

"So now you want me to take care of it," Caton countered.

"It is your job, Caton," Amelia stated deliberately.

Again, Caton thought there would be more. She had never spoken to anyone who was paying her with such unrestrained license. She actually had it coming if Amelia chose the re-firing bit.

"I'm not complaining," Caton replied when Amelia didn't take the prime opportunity afforded her. "I'm just confirming. Dinner party for sixteen. Typical holiday themery. Got it."

"You are drunk, aren't you?" Amelia asked.

"Just a little," Caton admitted.

"Were you drunk when you got to work?" Amelia's voice softened, almost caring. It sounded like a lie.

"Why?" Caton's jaw went tight, and she felt the sudden need to protect herself. "Do you want to reprimand me for getting into your stash?"

"No."

"Then I guess it doesn't matter, does it?" Caton tossed out, but the question went unanswered for both of them.

"So, do you think you can handle it?" Amelia returned to the topic at hand.

"It's a fucking dinner party, Amelia," Caton snapped, snatching at the words as they left her mouth, but failing to reel them back in.

Closing her eyes, Caton waited, convinced Amelia would finally rise to the challenge. But there was nothing. Only a return to silence so long, Caton wasn't sure it would ever end.

"I'm sorry," she whispered to break it. She knew she was angry. She had felt it all morning. She had no idea how angry, though, until she heard Amelia's voice, and, instead of wishing it away, wished it were closer. "Yes, I can handle it."

"I'm sure you can," Amelia returned calmly. "I'll call you tomorrow to see how it's going."

"Okay," Caton said weakly.

"And Caton?" Amelia's voice eased up again. If it were anyone else, Caton might have thought it concern, but, with Amelia, she knew it was a ploy. Everything was a ploy with Amelia. "Don't be drinking."

A rush of shame effectively killed what little buzz Caton had left. "I won't be," she murmured.

"I'll call you," Amelia reiterated, hanging up before Caton had a chance to say anything, which, in the moment, was probably the most decent thing Amelia could have done.

18

Amelia woke at the curve of the driveway. Lethargic gaze trailing up to the home in which she'd spent the largest part of her adult life, the tinted glass turned the white pillars gray, giving them the appearance of giant prison bars against the night.

Righting herself in the seat, she rubbed the corners of her eyes as she waited for the door to open and the steady, familiar hand to help her from the car. Her bags already waiting by the door, Antonio carried them the rest of the way in and set them in the foyer while Amelia punched in the alarm code.

"Would you like me to carry these upstairs for you?" he offered.

"This is fine," Amelia softly replied. "Thank you, Antonio." She pulled out a bill large enough to make the driver smile, which he did without even looking at it. He had no need to look. All animosity toward Amelia came from within the walls of her household. Outside, she was far more loved than she was within.

"Thank you," Antonio said, stepping back out onto the porch and pulling the door closed behind him.

Door locked and alarm reset, Amelia grabbed her smallest bag and started up the stairs. At the third floor, her steps gentled, and she approached the bedroom warily. Inside, Jack slept, tucked on one side of the bed, head angled away from her. She could get into the bed without waking him, she knew. Sleeping through security alarms, a false fire alarm, and the cries of their daughter as an infant, Jack had always slept like a man who had no worries at all.

The empty space beside him looked emptier than ever, and, though she was tired, Amelia wasn't tired enough. Placing her bag inside the door, she retraced her steps, back down the stairs past her office and into the front room. Clicking on the small lamp by the window, she curled up at the end of the couch, knowing she would fall asleep there. She often did on nights when she was too tired not to think too much. She should have taken an earlier flight, gotten home in time to sleep before her subconscious kicked in. The middle of the night was no time to refrain from thinking.

Not that she could claim much to think about, free as she was from the worries of people who weren't her. Her parents were well. Her father had grown stronger as he had grown older, a blessing Amelia couldn't ignore. Her mother had always been strong, for all of them. Her daughter was in one of the best schools in the world, exposed to opportunity Amelia never could have dreamed of at her age. Her husband was successful. Her home was, for most people, a castle in the sky.

From nearly any vantage point outside her own, Amelia always ended up admitting to herself in these moments when gloom turned her pristine world into a dystopia, she had no right to sleepless nights.

It was Sole who found her in the morning as she entered the room to crack the wood blinds. Opening her eyes into the sunlight, Amelia knew Jack must be awake. Jack never slept in late. There was too much life for him to live. Or so was his mantra.

"You stayed down here?" Sole asked, moving to the end of the sofa.

"I fell asleep," Amelia replied.

It was the answer she always gave, less taxing than the truth, but she wasn't keeping anything from Sole. Sole was well aware why Amelia ended up on the uncomfortable sofa the times that she did. She knew the transition from her parents' home, where affection lived and breathed, to the house she lived in, where affection came to die, was always a difficult one for Amelia.

"You look like you could use some more," Sole softly prodded. "Why don't you go upstairs for a while?"

"I'm fine," Amelia said, sitting up as if to verify the statement. "Is everything ready for tonight?"

"Yes," Sole nodded. "Caton and I took care of it."

Though the mention was expected, Amelia's reaction to it wasn't. Surging through her unbidden, warmth filled the hollows, and she took a steadying breath, trying to adjust to the sensation. "Good. I'm glad I was worried for nothing."

"Were you really worried?" Sole questioned, and Amelia shrugged noncommittally as Sole perched on the end of the sofa to study her. "You know, she thinks you don't like her."

That was a ludicrous notion, Amelia thought instantly, though she didn't share why it was so absurd with Sole. She suspected Sole knew more than she let on anyway. Walking in on her watching Caton strip didn't leave much to the imagination. "Why would she think that?"

"I don't know," Sole shrugged. "She's scared of you."

"Scared?" Amelia almost laughed.

"You make her nervous," Sole returned carefully.

Watching Sole glance toward the corner of the rug Amelia had accidentally flipped up on her walk to the sofa the night before, and hadn't bothered to fix, a light smile broke through on Amelia's face. Sole walked the line with the precision of a tightrope walker. Not once had she given Amelia advice straight out, even when Amelia had asked for it. Sole knew it was beyond her role. She had a way, though, of saying just enough to make Amelia take a second look at things, forcing her to reevaluate on her own.

"Do I?" Amelia posed with no expectation of response. "Let me see what you've done."

Gaze returning to Amelia's, Sole looked awfully satisfied for someone who had said so little, and, with a nod, she stood to lead Amelia from the room.

At the very least, Caton's party-planning was complete. The room was decorated, the food plentiful and agreeable, and there was enough drink to go around, which, Amelia thought, looking down into the swirling liquid, was all that was really necessary.

Raising her eyes to the guests in her home, she maintained her pleasant disposition without effort. It was easy to fake interest in others, she had realized years before, by not being entirely present. She was an expert at hearing just enough to respond if called upon, even as her mind drifted to places she would rather be.

It was where her mind kept drifting that was proving problematic. She had charged Caton with putting the event together, and Caton had done so with minimal direction, so her touch was on everything, from the slightly eclectic food selections to the place settings. That visible presence, and the fact that Sole had brought her up earlier in the day, were surely to blame for the invasive thoughts in Amelia's head that left her restless and picking at her main course.

Watching Sole lead the small serving crew into the room, Amelia waited for Sole's eyes to land on her. When they did, she waved Sole over, taking little time to consider, and Sole responded like someone accustomed to following her every command. There was some injustice in that, Amelia thought, when Sole was the only person in her life who seemed to truly know her at all.

"Yes, Ma'am." Sole approached her formally.

Waving her into confidence, Amelia drew Sole near enough no one would overhear. "Call Caton and tell her I need to see her."

"Now?" Sole asked in surprise.

"Yes, now," Amelia replied, returning her eyes to the table as if she was making a sensible request, knowing Sole would do as she was asked, even if it was a mistake on both their parts.

It felt like hours later, after the dinner plates were cleared and dessert was on the table, and the constant flow of alcohol had turned business bragging into bawdy tales of after-work activities, that the doorbell finally rang. Turning from the far end of the table, Jack appeared concerned at the interruption, and Amelia felt a peculiar sense of expectation roll through her as Sole walked into the dining room with Caton at her back.

Though she looked decidedly uncomfortable entering the crowded dining room, Caton was surprisingly fitted to the formal occasion.

"Caton, Ma'am," Sole announced, moving aside to give Amelia an unobstructed view.

Flowing emerald dress turning Caton's eyes to chlorophyll, they locked intensely on Amelia, and she knew she was wrong to have called Caton. And right to have called her.

"Caton, what are you doing here?" Jack uttered, and a surprising wave of anger rolled through Amelia at the question he had no right to ask.

"I asked her to come," Amelia declared, standing from the table, but it failed to ease the panic that darkened Caton's gaze. "I apologize. I'll be only a minute."

Grabbing her half-full glass from the table, she walked past the curious dinner guests and turned Caton by the arm, pressing her out of the room. By touch alone, she led Caton up the stairs and into her office, shutting the door behind them. The moon full outside, it provided light enough to illuminate both the room's surfaces and Caton as she turned back to her, so Amelia didn't bother to turn on the light.

"What did I do?" Caton questioned, arms crossing over her chest, marring the perfect image she presented when she walked in. "Bad cider? Wrong place cards?"

Amelia didn't know what exactly she intended when she told Sole to call Caton. She knew only that she wanted to see her, whether or not it made sense. Watching Caton dig in for an argument they weren't even having, though, Amelia was struck by exactly what she wanted to do with her. Hand going to the lock, she turned it, her intent suddenly clear to both of them.

Any further questions appeared to die in Caton's throat as she took small backward steps at Amelia's approach. Perhaps Caton truly was afraid of her, Amelia considered, watching her retreat.

Backing between the two leather visitor chairs, Caton reached the desk's edge and had nowhere left to go, and Amelia closed in on her gingerly, realizing, if Caton feared her, it was by her own actions and only she could erase the lines she had drawn.

One step at a time carrying her ever closer, she pushed the chairs apart, not stopping until she was practically on top of Caton, Caton's lips hovering an inch from hers. In either fear or expectation, Caton closed her eyes, and Amelia fought the urge to rush forward with abandon and cover Caton's lips with her own.

"You didn't have to dress for the occasion." She busied her mouth with words, sucking in Caton's uneven exhalation as her lips parted.

"I was on a date," Caton responded, opening her eyes, something almost angry flashing in them, and Amelia took a startled step back, inexplicably bothered by the statement.

Glancing down at Caton's dress, at her guarded stance, Amelia let the words work themselves out in her head, smirking as she came to the result. "You were on a date," she stated. "But you left to come here."

"Sole said you needed me," Caton returned weakly.

"I do," Amelia replied, stepping forward again with satisfaction and sliding her wine glass onto the corner of the desk.

Body bumping into Caton's crossed arms, Amelia circled her hands around Caton's wrists, easing them out of the way, and Caton's eyes fluttered shut again, resistance melting along with her defenses. Every breath that left Caton's body felt and sounded like surrender, and, heart thumping in response, it was Amelia who was suddenly afraid.

Ignoring the pressing temptation of Caton's lips, Amelia dropped down before her, hands running up Caton's legs until they reached fabric and edged it upward. When she glanced up, Caton's eyes were open wide, but she made no effort to impede her, and Amelia certainly had no power to stop herself.

Her fingers slipping beneath the edges of Caton's panties, she pulled downward, and Caton stepped free of them without protest, allowing Amelia to push the fabric back up her legs, complying without hesitation when Amelia urged her onto the edge of the desk.

Bunching Caton's dress in her hands, Amelia nudged Caton's thigh with her chin and Caton opened herself up with surprisingly little inhibition. The acquiescence was more than enough to alleviate any reservations Amelia had, and she gave in to the craving she'd been fighting all night, laving a wet line up impossibly soft flesh. As Caton moaned in response, Amelia felt no need to quiet her. Unless someone was standing right outside the door, there was no one who would hear.

Insinuating herself deeper, Amelia closed her eyes at Caton's flavor flooding her tongue, and with a groan, her body gave in, pressing closer to Caton of its own accord. Releasing one side of Caton's dress, Amelia felt the fabric fall over her shoulder as she wrapped her arm around Caton's thigh, hand clutching Caton's hip to draw her closer.

As her tongue moved upward to circle Caton's clit, Caton's staggered breaths fell over Amelia like rain. A soft flick, and Amelia succeeded in pulling a strangled cry from Caton, before she closed her mouth around the spot, sucking with gentle pressure.

Caton moaned again, and Amelia opened her eyes, raising them to Caton's face. Moonlight hitting her from the back, Caton was cast largely in shadow, the yellow light bordering her like a halo, basking her in an ethereal glow, and, instantly, Caton's pleasure became Amelia's sole intent.

Seconds ticking by much too quickly, the chance of being interrupted ever-increasing, she traced a rapid pattern against Caton's flesh until Caton began to rock against her and her head arched back, casting light over her features. Amelia watched her go still, a portrait of beauty frozen in time, one leg so taut against her side, Amelia knew it would ache in the morning, until finally, with a ragged exhalation, Caton's pleasure pulsed against her mouth.

Amelia finished at her own pace, long, leisurely strokes catching the nectar that dripped from Caton's body. It was only when Caton pushed her away, trying to close her legs against her continuing exploration that Amelia retreated far enough to open her lips against the creamy skin of Caton's thigh in a near-kiss.

For a moment, Amelia simply existed there, where there were no rules, no expectations, no duties she had to return to fulfill. Fleetingly, she wondered if Caton could tell she was no expert, that the single time she had done this before was so long ago it was from another life altogether.

Knowing more time had to have passed than it seemed, Amelia at last gave in to the inevitable, settling back on her heels and looking up as Caton's eyes opened. She let the dress fall back into place, grabbing the edge of the desk on either side of Caton to pull herself up, fabric warm and soft against her legs as she reached for her wine glass and lifted it to her lips.

On shaky arms, Caton pushed herself up, sliding off the edge of the desk, and Amelia didn't move as their bodies lightly brushed. When Caton's hand slid over her hip, pulling her closer, Amelia allowed it, the intimate press of their bodies, for only a moment.

"I have to get back," she said, watching disappointment flash and turn quickly to resignation on Caton's face.

It was almost enough to change Amelia's mind, to make her step closer to Caton instead of away, but Caton released her immediately, as if she expected nothing more, so without further explanation to herself or to Caton, Amelia moved for the door before she lost her will.

"Could I have my panties?" Caton asked as she turned the lock.

Glancing back, Amelia watched Caton uselessly attempt to brush the wrinkles out of her dress, before glancing down into her hand. Surprised to find Caton's panties clutched in her fingers, picked up from the floor and carried off with her like some kind of trophy, she realized there would have been no explaining it away if she had walked back into the dinner party with Caton's panties firmly in hand. Not that she would attempt to go back without a few touch-ups. If there was anything Amelia knew about the crowd in her dining room, it was that they were trained to look for imperfections.

Almost smiling at the realization of what she had done, Amelia glanced to Caton again. "No," she replied, thumb stroking over soft cotton as she walked out the door.

19

Slipping out of the house while Amelia returned to the dining room, and the holiday festivities within, felt much like Caton suspected it would feel to escape through a window while a lover distracted her unexpected spouse in the living room. Amelia's spouse had been present the entire time, though, a fact conveniently ignored by Caton's desperate mind in its quest for exactly what Amelia had given her.

Caton didn't know what the hell to call whatever it was she was doing with Amelia, aside from disconcerting and invasive, but she was actually starting to understand, much to her repugnance, the rules by which they were playing. Even when Amelia changed them without warning.

It was a symptom of insanity, she acknowledged, accepting such a pivotal role in her own downfall. Whatever Amelia was trying to do, Caton was a willing accomplice, and she knew she would continue to be willing the moment she walked into the kitchen Monday morning to find Amelia standing behind the counter, juice from a mango dripping from her fingers as she looked up with a rather proud smile. Averting her eyes, Caton wondered when exactly she'd become that easy to turn on.

"Good morning." She aimed the words at Sole, who moved about behind Amelia doing her own morning's work.

"Good morning." Sole stopped to smile at her. "How was your drive?"

"Not that bad," Caton responded, glancing out the window toward the falling snow. White and sparkling against the sky, she wondered if it could somehow purify her thoughts.

"Do you want some coffee?" Sole asked.

Eyes flicking back into the kitchen, they caught again on Amelia. The grin had faded from Amelia's lips, but Caton could still see subtle traces as Amelia carefully observed her. "No." She struggled to draw breath. "I'm going to head upstairs."

Ducking back through the doorway, she paused on the other side, legs oddly numb. Nothing had changed, she tried to remind herself. Amelia would continue to be exactly as Amelia had been. Seeing her standing there, though, looking unusually natural with her hair pulled back and the morning light streaming in through the window, Caton had a momentary lapse. Despite how well she was adapting to the rules, and how adamant she knew Amelia would be in their enforcement, for a split second, she wanted nothing more than to lunge across the counter and invent a few of her own.

When she finally made it up the stairs, Caton settled at her desk and waited for work to come. When it didn't, she spent the morning staring into space, head too full to do anything else. She saw Amelia pass the door on her way upstairs and again, fully-dressed, on her way back down. Amelia never stopped, though, and by the time lunch came, Caton was almost afraid to leave her office.

At last giving into her body's needs, despite the fact that it was that very thing that had caused her plight in the first place, she passed Amelia's empty office on her way downstairs, and found Sole alone in the kitchen. "Hey."

"Hey," Sole returned. "Are you all right?"

"Yeah," Caton responded, frowning slightly at the notion that her precarious emotional state was clearly on display, and glanced over her shoulder as she walked up to the bar.

"She's not here." Sole picked up on the gesture, and Caton realized it was her own fault if Sole could see everything. She wasn't exactly being subtle. Relief and disappointment warring within her, she turned sheepishly back to Sole.

"Pumpkin bisque?" Sole offered.

"Please," Caton said, more grateful for the change of subject than the free food.

Dishing out two bowls, Sole brought them to the bar and settled on the stool next to Caton. Half of the time spent sipping bisque, they spent the other half talking about nothing of consequence, and Caton tried not to consider how long Amelia might stay gone this time.

Much to her surprise, it was only late afternoon when Amelia returned to the palace. Regardless of her attempts to think about other things, Caton had spent the entire day with one eye on the clock before she finally heard Amelia's footsteps on the stairs, followed by the familiar sounds of her moving around in her office. Amelia took her time in making her presence officially known, alighting in the doorway in pressed slacks and a fitted button-up just as it was time for Caton to go home.

"Come into my office for a minute." Amelia tilted her head in that direction, not waiting for Caton's response before walking off again, seeming to know without doubt that Caton would follow. It was like being called into the office in a wealthy school district where the extremely hot principal could afford to drop a year's salary on her wardrobe.

Trying to ground herself before following, Caton realized that was impossible. She knew the rules, and the first rule was that she never knew what was coming next.

Inside the door of Amelia's office, Amelia waited to press the door closed at Caton's back. She gestured to one of the chairs, returned perfectly to its position since their last encounter, and Caton took the seat offered her, accepting the fact that things went more smoothly in her life when she did as Amelia requested.

The rewards were greater too.

Hovering at the side of her desk, fingertips clutched on the edge, Amelia looked strangely ill at ease, and Caton rolled her shoulders, feeling the conversation they were about to have was going to be a decidedly uncomfortable one.

"How are you?" Amelia finally asked, the socially-courteous question entirely unexpected.

"How am I?" Caton returned as if was the most bizarre thing she'd ever been asked. Coming from Amelia's mouth, it may very well have been.

Sighing, Amelia seemed to know the question was ridiculous, and her aberrant unease made instant sense. With all Caton had witnessed the other woman excel in, genuine conversation wasn't one of them.

"I'm fine," she responded. The last thing she needed or wanted was to give Amelia insight into what she was thinking, and, without her help, Amelia didn't seem to know where to go next.

Eyes trailing over Caton, she gave up the effort of coming up with something else to say, making a sudden approach, and Caton felt every nerve-ending fire in anticipation as Amelia curved out of sight behind her. Hands landing upon her shoulders, her body responded a dozen ways at once as Amelia's fingers started gently kneading the flesh at her neck, finally relaxing into the touch when she determined it meant her no harm.

This made it easier for Amelia, Caton realized, knowing she was in control, that she had the power to bewitch in her fingertips, and that Caton was helpless to resist it.

"Thank you for taking care of everything," Amelia said in a hushed voice that added to the quiet more than disturbed it. "Jack wasn't completely thrilled, but I thought it turned out well."

"I'm sorry," Caton responded, only half conscious of why she was saying it. Thumbs stroking up the muscles in her back, they slid to the base of her neck, edging inside the fabric of her shirt to meet bare skin, and she was only half conscious of anything beyond Amelia's touch.

"I'm not asking you to apologize." Amelia's voice surrounded her. "You did nothing wrong. This is what Jack does. He demands and he complains. Personally, I thought you made some interesting choices."

"That doesn't sound positive," Caton replied, shakily exhaling as one of Amelia's hands slipped over her shoulder, smoothing along her clavicle before dipping beneath the fabric of her shirt.

"It is," Amelia replied quietly. "I like people who think differently than I do."

Caton wasn't sure if it was a compliment or a challenge, and found it difficult to care. She was far more concerned with the way Amelia's voice kept catching over her responses, panting breaths falling between the words.

"Stand up," Amelia said, the breathless whisper right at Caton's ear, and the air fled Caton's lungs in a rush.

Following the command without delay, Caton arched into Amelia's hands as they moved down either side of her back, until one hand fell away and the sound of the chair being tossed aside filled the office. Amelia's other hand propelled her forward with enough force that Caton had to catch herself on the desk, sending a pile of papers to the floor, but Amelia showed no concern for the mess they were making.

Foot wedging between Caton's, she nudged Caton's legs apart, and Caton pressed back as the heat of Amelia's thigh slid between her own. Hands skating around Caton's sides to slip beneath the hem of her shirt, they exposed Caton to the room's chill for only an instant, before those hands warmed the skin they uncovered. Caton's muscles clenched at the thought of where Amelia's touch would move next as her hands continued upward to cup her breasts.

Strength faltering as Amelia teased through her bra, Caton's arms shook as Amelia pinched her nipples and they grew firmer at the touch. It was when one hand disentangled itself to sweep Caton's hair aside and Amelia's lips attached themselves to her skin, though, that Caton was sure she would topple them both.

Mouth hot against her, Amelia's tongue trailed the throbbing vein in Caton's neck, and Caton wanted to turn, to force her way around to face Amelia, see if she could coax Amelia's mouth to her own. When Amelia's hands dropped suddenly to her waistband, though, it was enough to distract Caton from any rogue thoughts.

She felt her pants go slack at her waist, and then Amelia was sliding away, moving down her back, hands dragging her pants and panties down her legs until they sat like shackles at her ankles. A blast of cold air hitting her, it occurred to Caton how exposed she was, but when Amelia wrenched her shoe from her foot, Caton lifted her leg to free it from her binds, as if she felt no shame at all.

Amelia paused on her way back up to sink her teeth into the flesh of Caton's left buttock, hard enough that Caton knew she would have a mark, soft enough that she wanted Amelia to do it again. Then, Amelia was back in place at Caton's back, hand slipping between Caton's thighs from behind without preamble, finding the indisputable evidence that Caton had been thinking about her all day, and Caton's hands skidded over the desktop as she tried to find center.

"I probably should have asked if this was okay," Amelia whispered.

"You've never asked before," Caton reasoned, voice catching. "I don't know what we'd do about it at this point if it weren't."

"Good point," Amelia acknowledged, voice as seductive as ever, but touch turning hesitant. With no choice but to prove her consent, as if she hadn't proven it a hundred times already, Caton pressed back into Amelia's hand, demonstrating her acquiescence.

Reassured, Caton could only assume - though it was difficult to imagine the woman who just pushed her down on a desk and yanked her clothes to her ankles needed any type of reassurance - Amelia's touch returned with its usual assurance, circling around, over, against Caton, skimming up and down, teasing at more without giving it to her.

Amelia's fingers gliding back, Caton's breath held, desperate need gripping at her, before Amelia returned to the same excruciating caress, unceasing, always effective, but never as much as Caton wanted. The fingers sliding back again, Caton strained toward them in invitation. Or maybe she was begging. She simply couldn't tell anymore.

"Please," she whispered.

"Please what?" Amelia breathed.

She knew. Caton could tell by the way Amelia's hand danced away every time she moved toward it, intentionally refusing her what she wanted, holding tight to the control she never let slip.

Fingers clutching at the desktop, Caton pressed toward Amelia's hand again, but Amelia avoided her with just as much intent. Eyes squeezing shut, Caton felt tears form at their corners, the sound escaping her lips almost a sob.

"What do you want?" The breathless command at Caton's ear was just another caress, working against her last bastion of dignity. "Tell me."

The only power that remained to her was that Amelia didn't know how much she wanted her, how much she thought about her, how much she craved these moments, how much she craved her touch. How deeply she craved her touch.

Amelia's fingers moved back again, circling desperate flesh, and Caton thrust against them, groaning when Amelia moved away from her in perfect time.

"Amelia." The name sounded undeniably needy on Caton's lips.

"What, Caton?" Amelia's voice turned unnaturally soft. "What do you want?"

"Fuck," Caton hissed, trying desperately to do without, to be content with enough, instead of pleading for more. "I want you inside me." The confession, a rush of broken syllables. Her breaths, no longer her own, but the notes of Amelia's conducting.

Amelia's ragged exhalation filled Caton's ear, but her touch still refused Caton. "That's a little intimate, don't you think," she husked. "For a cold bitch?"

"I don't..." The words caught on a sob. "I don't... think... you're a cold bitch." Forcing the words out, she strained toward Amelia, perspiration rolling down her hairline as she grasped at what was so close.

"Yes, you do," Amelia replied, lips brushing Caton's ear, the small intimacy almost painful. "Remember this."

How Amelia thought she would ever forget it was the question. The instant Amelia's touch moved inside of her, a pervasive sense of release eased through Caton's entire body, calm so profound she went utterly still, letting the euphoria wash over her in waves. For a moment, she was without thought, without fear, every heightened sense aware only of Amelia.

Arms finally giving out, she dropped to the surface of the desk with nearly enough grace for it to have been intentional, and Amelia fell with her, warm weight pressing Caton down against the cool wood.

Painstakingly slowly, their bodies moved together, Amelia's touch expanding, pressing deeper, invading every inch of Caton's body, and, for the first time since Amelia stared at her across the foyer, her gaze promising things Caton was convinced she was never going to deliver, Caton felt truly and wholly fulfilled.

Amelia's touch directed her to paradise, and held Caton captive there, hovering on the verge of that familiar abyss, the one that threatened each time to pull her down into a darkness she couldn't fully see. Amelia's lips on the back of her neck, unbelievably gentle against her skin, and Caton leapt into it, quaking between the unforgiving surface of the desk and the soft, warm curves of Amelia's body.

Amelia was right there with her, keeping Caton from falling alone, the one thing that sent her soaring and the one thing that kept her grounded. Wings and anchor. There was an instant, a single pinpoint of ecstasy so acute, Caton thought she may cease to exist, simply blink out like a dying star, but at last she fell free, heart restarting with a desperate tremor as she returned to her body.

Bereft of breath and fight, she remained there, unwilling to move even if she could, realizing she had survived Amelia yet again as the big picture began to return to its individual parts - Amelia flush at her back, Amelia's smell, her uneven breaths, her hand finally where Caton had needed it for so long.

When that hand retreated in haste, Caton forced her eyes open, staring across the surface of the desk at the pieces of an expensive desk set, neatly arranged and in sharp focus. Half of Amelia's body still weighting her down, Caton heard the zipper of Amelia's pants before she felt the frenzied movements against the back of her thigh.

Energy she thought utterly depleted returning in an instant, she tried to push herself up, to turn, but Amelia's body kept her trapped against the desk. Forcing one sluggish arm to move, Caton reached back, finding the curve of Amelia's thigh, pressing her fingers into impossibly soft skin, and, with a sudden hitch of breath, Amelia moaned softly in her ear, sending a satisfying aftershock through Caton's body, though she wasn't sure if was an offshoot of Amelia's climax or the remnants of her own.

As Amelia collapsed against her, there was stillness, a moment of near serenity, but it lasted only as long as Amelia allowed it. Too soon, she pulled away and Caton's warmth dissipated into the biting reality of being face-down, ass-up on Amelia's desk.

The image she must present sinking in, Caton attempted to stand, but her loose limbs made messy work of it, and she felt her face flaming for all the wrong reasons as she turned her back to Amelia and unsteadily thrust her foot into the leg holes of her panties and pants to pull them back into place. Stopping to readjust each piece of clothing, as if it would somehow alter the fact that she had just been in an extremely awkward position, she turned to find Amelia sitting on the edge of her desk, legs crossed, looking almost untouched. The only sign she'd had any part in what just transpired was the open closure of her expensive slacks, and glistening fingers that hovered at her lips before Amelia sucked her middle finger between them.

As calculated as it was, it had the same effect. Feeling a fresh flush of desire that was hard to believe considering the undeniable fucking she was just given by the woman sitting before her, Caton knew she would let herself be pulled into the same moment again, embarrassingly as it had ended, for the few moments those fingers were inside of her.

Amelia held her hand out in offering, and Caton tried to channel the confidence of someone who hadn't just been bent over a desk and made to beg for her pleasure. Palm settling on Amelia's thigh as she stepped nearer, she closed her lips around Amelia's index finger, tongue wrapping around it, rewarded by Amelia's jagged breath. Teeth raking the flesh of Amelia's finger as she released it, Caton battled the urge to close in on Amelia and find out how determined she really was to be in control.

"So, not a prude then," Amelia stated.

"Did you really think I was?" Caton returned in amused disbelief.

"I don't know," Amelia responded, eyes dropping to Caton's lips just long enough to make Caton yearn for something she knew Amelia wasn't going to give her. "I don't know you."

"Do you want to?" she heard herself ask before she could think to quash the question.

It was so unexpected and so quickly masked by her usual assuredness, Caton couldn't be sure what flashed in Amelia's eyes, but, for a split second, she would have sworn it looked like fear.

Pushing Caton's hand from her thigh, Amelia stood suddenly, forcing Caton to take a step back. "I want to wash my hand," Amelia said, all hints of intimacy, real or fake, gone as she walked toward the door. "And I'm sure you want to go home."

Well aware it would come whenever Amelia decided, and that she would have no say, Caton leaned against the desk, watching Amelia's departure with little emotion. For a while, she loitered, wondering if it was a good time to reevaluate her life choices, but she didn't bother sticking around for long, because she knew Amelia wasn't coming back.

20

All week, Caton waited to be summoned. That was what she had been reduced to - half assistant, half slave to her own body and Amelia's sexual whims. Amelia was in need of neither of her services, it seemed, because she came to Caton for nothing, gave her nothing, and whenever Caton stopped in at Amelia's office looking for some sense of direction, she was greeted and dismissed in less than a minute. Amelia wasn't as off-putting as she had been in the past, but she was neither inviting nor repentant, and, each day, Caton left feeling more baffled than the day before.

Sole told her it happened, the lulls in work. It was the perk of working for people who could afford everything, but needed nothing, she said.

As well-intended as the explanation was, it only served to remind Caton that she was among those things Amelia didn't need. Which Amelia had made clear from the beginning, and had proven many times since.

Caton didn't need Amelia either. It didn't change the fact that every time she saw Amelia across the room, or listened to her throaty laugh through the door that separated them, she was back on that desk with Amelia on top of her and inside of her, and yearned to feel her that way again.

Walking into the Halston Palace Friday morning, after an entire week of checking her words and expressions, Caton was already on edge, more than ready to be through with the week and free of Amelia's crippling presence. Then, she saw Jack's briefcase on the table, keys resting on top, and the feeling amplified. "Jack's still here?" she asked quietly, moving to the bar to accept the coffee Sole wordlessly poured for her.

"Yes." Sole abruptly nodded. "There's some benefit at his parents' house today. They should already be gone."

Feeling a tinge of something she refused to accept at the idea of Amelia playing the happy family with her husband, Caton attempted to shrug it off, ignoring the weight that seemed to only grow heavier as she stared at the bar top. Having Amelia out of range for a day would be a blessing, she reminded herself, no matter how it came to pass.

At the noise behind her, Caton turned to see Jack walking into the room alone, free, for once, of his tailored suit in khakis and a polo that made him look almost tame.

"Is *Amelia's* famous flan ready?" Jack emphasized the name in a way that indicated Amelia had never made flan in her life, letting his eyes drag over Caton without an ounce of restraint. "Morning, Caton."

Recognizing the man she knew him to be, even in the sheep's clothing, Caton looked away without response, in no mood to exchange niceties.

"Everything's packed up," Sole responded dutifully. "Do you want coffee for your drive?"

"Sure," Jack answered, moving in on Caton, and, though Caton kept her gaze averted, she could feel Jack's all over her like an infestation.

"Is Amelia coming?" Sole asked as she poured coffee into a travel mug.

"She claims to be ill," Jack replied, tone somewhat amused.

"That's too bad. I'll make her tea," Sole responded without hesitation, tightening the lid on the mug and setting it next to the other prepared items on the bar.

"Nice outfit." Jack ignored Sole's response completely, words coming from too close, and Caton turned a discouraging look his way. "It's a compliment."

Remembering too well the last time he gave her a similar compliment in his kitchen, Caton considered telling him she had picked it out special for his wife, hoping Amelia might find her irresistible enough to give her one of those uncontrollable orgasms she seemed to specialize in.

"Thank you." Caton uttered to appease him, eyes never leaving Jack's as he took another step, though he seemed to know better than to try to touch her.

"Why don't you come with me?" Jack asked casually. "You could be Amelia's surrogate. Everyone will probably like you better anyway."

Hardly a fan of Amelia's past behavior, Caton found herself considerably less tolerant of Jack trash-talking his wife while she was right upstairs. Especially when she had seen Amelia bend over backward to make the perfect impression on a group, and suspected there was no crowd Amelia couldn't win over with her smile alone, whether it was sincere or just for show.

"I don't think Amelia would approve of that," Caton replied.

"It's not up to her," Jack said, finally testing his luck and drawing the backs of his fingers down Caton's arm.

Not bothering to shrug out of the touch, Caton's hand tightened into a fist, and it was only her father's constant advice to "choose her battles" that kept her from swinging. "It is, actually," she declared. "I don't work for you, remember?"

For a moment, Jack looked stunned. Angry even. Then, with a laugh, as if no one of her lowly caliber could truly bother him, he shook his head, gathering the items from the counter, and grabbed his keys on the way to the French doors. Glancing toward the abandoned briefcase, Caton wondered for a moment what secrets might be hiding inside it, before realizing Jack would never leave his secrets so easy to access.

"I cannot believe you said that to him," Sole marveled, watching out the window as Jack walked along the back path to the garage.

"I don't work for him," Caton stated. "That was our deal."

"Still, you're braver than I am," Sole declared, generally upbeat demeanor darkening for a moment. As she went back to the task of turning fresh oranges into juice, something in her voice made Caton afraid to ask for more detail. She had been around Jack long enough to know that Sole couldn't have possibly gotten through her years of service without Jack trying his luck with her, and she really didn't want to know how successful those efforts had been.

Finishing her coffee in silence as Sole poured hot water over a tea bag, Caton wondered if Sole actually believed Amelia was sick, or if she was protecting Amelia's privacy and right to lie to her husband from the prying eyes of an outsider.

"I'll take it up," Caton declared, wondering where the words had come from, as Sole added the mug to the tray.

"Are you sure you want to do that?" Sole asked.

Though it wasn't the singular cause of Caton's hesitation, Sole's question did prolong it. She wasn't sure about anything. She never was anymore, and she doubted she would be until she was free of the contract, the situation, and Amelia's hold over her. "Yes, I'll take it," she said at last, dropping her bag onto the closest stool, tugging the tray across the bar, and turning to head out of the kitchen before she could talk herself out of it.

Up the stairs, Caton forced her feet to climb until she breached the barrier of the third floor for the first time. Glancing down the hallway, she noted the door that could only belong to Jack's office, before knocking softly on the closed door that had to belong to the master suite and taking a deep breath, wondering what in Satan's dominion had motivated her to volunteer for the fool's errand.

"Come in," Amelia said, voice too muted to determine the state of its health, and Caton pushed the door open enough to skim several pieces of a high-end bedroom suit before her eyes alighted on Amelia sitting up against the headboard, a book bent open in her hands. The deep purple silk of the nightgown Amelia wore hugged everything, and Caton's eyes struggled to focus anywhere else.

"Are you really sick?" she asked, knowing the answer before she posed the question. Even Amelia couldn't look so insanely desirable ill.

Staring at her for a moment, as if debating whether she wanted to answer, Amelia finally closed the book and slid it onto the bedside table. "No."

"Then you're not going to want this," Caton declared, walking into the room without waiting for invitation and pushing the door closed at her back. Turning away from Amelia to set the tray atop the dark wood dresser, she grabbed the glass of freshly-squeezed juice she had been eyeing ever since Sole set it down and took a defiant drink. Seduced by the sweet, fresh flavor, she took another sip as she walked over to Amelia. "Well, you may want this," she amended, offering her the glass.

Much to her surprise, Amelia took it without comment, staring up at Caton from the luxurious pile of pillows and high-thread-count sheets as she took a drink. Amelia's eyes unguarded, her expression achingly familiar and tempting, Caton made a valiant effort not to see it. It was always this way. On Amelia's whims. On Amelia's desires.

"I was going to come find you," Amelia breathed, voice so enchanting Caton sighed at her instantly crumbling resolve.

"Were you really?" she asked, focusing on the only flaw in the headboard, a nick that showed the raw wood hiding inside the perfectly-finished surface. "You've known where I've been all week."

"Strip for me," Amelia commanded, feeling no need to apologize or explain herself, or even to act as if Caton had spoken.

On Amelia's whims.

On Amelia's desires.

Scoffing less at the request than her immediate urge to obey it, Caton returned her gaze to Amelia. "Why?"

"Because I want you to," Amelia replied instantly, and it wasn't what Caton wanted to hear. It left too much question as to what Amelia truly desired - her or the power she held over her.

Shaking her head, Caton walked away, hand wrapping around the bed post to pull her back to Earth.

"Caton." Amelia's voice drew her to a stop, and Caton tried to hold onto Sole's sage insight that there was nothing the Halstons needed, because Amelia had managed to sound very needy indeed. "I want to look at you."

Even with the admission, it would have been more dignified for Caton to leave, to prove to Amelia, and to herself, that she was not under Amelia's complete control. It would have also been counterproductive. Forcing Amelia's hand was, after all, why she had made the journey upstairs in the first place, to remind Amelia she was waiting whenever Amelia decided she wanted her.

Shrinking an inch as she stepped out of her shoes, Caton turned to meet Amelia's gaze. Half the time she spent with Amelia was spent faking confidence she didn't possess. When Amelia looked at her like that, though, blistering gaze penetrating Caton's skin until Caton would swear Amelia could see inside her, she felt like a different person, a person who was comfortable taking her clothes off at a moment's notice just because she was asked.

Loosing the pinstriped pants at her waist, she eased the fabric down her legs, and Amelia slid the glass in her hand onto the table to push more upright in the bed.

Maybe she did have some power, it occurred to Caton, some element of control. As much as she craved Amelia, she hadn't asked for what was happening. She hadn't started it. Amelia was the one who had followed her, who had come to her, who had touched her.

At the realization, something relaxed inside of Caton, and it was enough to make her remove the rest of her clothing without delay and stand in front of Amelia, naked and waiting. One hand sliding up to her breast, her fingertips teased at her nipple, but it was Amelia who reacted, arching slightly against the pillows at her back, eyes flicking from the hand at Caton's breast to the one traveling over the sensitive skin of Caton's abdomen.

"Touch yourself," Amelia whispered, slumping slightly in the bed, hair rucking up against the pillow, a blight on her picture-perfect image, and even if Caton wanted to make Amelia wait, or beg, or suffer, her body was nothing but willing. Fingers pulling at the nipple that hardened more at Amelia's gaze than her own touch, Caton's other hand dipped between her legs, fingers moving through thick warmth.

It wasn't Amelia's power, she realized, or her own. Amelia wanted her. She wanted Amelia to want her. Their powers were shared, intimately linked. They worked in tandem. What Amelia wanted from her, Caton wanted to give her, and the more Caton gave her, the more Amelia seemed to want. Maybe the confidence wasn't all fake. Amelia watching her, reacting to her, Caton's inhibitions seemed to fall away as easily as her clothing.

Amelia's gaze focused, Caton dared think even hypnotized, one hand curved around the top of the headboard, the other disappearing beneath the covers, and Caton followed its path with envy. She did have power, but power wasn't what she wanted. Maybe that satisfied Amelia, but it didn't satisfy her. Amelia had followed her, had come to her, had touched her, but she had never once felt free to touch Amelia.

Dropping her hands instantly, Caton stalked to the bed, and Amelia's gaze followed her, the movement beneath the covers never ceasing. As soon as she was in range, Amelia reached out, transferring the hand from the headboard to Caton's hip, thumb dipping inward, her eyes never leaving Caton's, as if she could just continue on as she was, as if Caton would stand for that.

Wrenching back the covers that shielded Amelia from her view, Caton lowered herself to the edge of the bed, bare hip bumping Amelia's silk-clad one, breaking the rhythm of Amelia's hand where it disappeared beneath her nightgown. Hand tightening around the smooth skin of Amelia's wrist, she pulled it away without resistance. When she tried to replace Amelia's hand with her own, though, Amelia's reflex was lighting fast, fingers latching onto Caton's forearm. "No," she said, voice rasping between uneven breaths.

After everything Caton had allowed Amelia to do to her, the rejection was caustic, crawling over her exposed skin, deadening every nerve ending one-by-one, threatening to extinguish all of her unexplainable feelings for Amelia.

"I'm paying you," Amelia added. She tried to look formidable, but failed, apprehension and need rising to the surface, two emotions Caton never thought she would see Amelia display independently, let alone as one.

Unbalanced by the unexpected honesty, Caton's heart pounded an almost tribal rhythm against her chest. "You think I would do this for the money?" she asked, any offense she felt overshadowed by relief. If that was the reason Amelia never let Caton touch her, it was nothing. Amelia wanting her touch was everything.

"I don't know," Amelia tried and failed to conjure some indignation. "Would you?"

Flicking her wrist in Amelia's hand, Caton broke free to press Amelia's arm to the mattress beside her. "I want to touch you," she stated, vulnerability shivering down her spine, despite the fact that Amelia couldn't possibly know how much.

Releasing Amelia's arm, grateful when it stayed in place, Caton brushed her fingers against Amelia's thigh, relishing the soft canvas of Amelia's skin, painfully aware that Amelia could backpedal at any time. Almost expecting it. When Amelia offered no resistance, Caton's hand edged beneath the silk boundary bunched at her thighs, drawn by the heat emanating from beneath. Skin meeting skin, she inhaled sharply at the realization that Amelia wasn't wearing anything beneath the nightgown.

The discovery drawing her eyes once again over Amelia's form, it occurred to her that Amelia looked awfully flawless for someone who had feigned illness a short time before, and that she hadn't seemed all that surprised to see Caton walking through her bedroom door instead of Sole. If Amelia really was planning to come find her, maybe Amelia had an objective. Despite her feeble attempt at protest, maybe this was exactly what Amelia was hoping for all along, and the possibility alone was enough to cast off Caton's lingering doubts.

Fingers sinking between inflamed flesh, she watched Amelia's eyes fall closed, captivated at the way Amelia's cheeks flushed redder, by the rapid movement of Amelia's eyes beneath their lids, by the pulsing of Amelia's anxious, responsive skin against her fingers. Irrefutable proof of Amelia's desire coating her skin, Caton struggled to keep her eyes open, not wanting to miss anything, knowing it might be the only time she ever got to see Amelia so unguarded.

Finding the perfect rhythm, she pulled Amelia's hand to her breast, expelling pent-up air as Amelia squeezed softly and opened her eyes. What Caton saw in them, swirling whirlpools of unchecked emotion, was so real, she could hardly endure it. An instant later, when Amelia's hand abandoned her breast to slide upward, palm warming Caton's chest before moving onto her neck and brushing against her cheek, Caton stilled, feeling the vortex yawning wide, threatening to suck her in. There was more, she could feel it in Amelia's touch, and, if this was the inevitable progression, things were progressing far too slowly.

Withdrawing her hand from beneath Amelia's nightgown, Caton fisted the hem in both hands, not sure if she yanked her upward or if Amelia surged from the bed to tug it over her head and toss it carelessly aside.

It was far from elegant as she twisted onto the bed, but when Amelia's arms closed around her, their bodies pressing together, warm and intimate, Caton didn't care what it looked like. Groaning, she slipped her hand between them, fingers sinking back into position, surprised when Amelia opened up to her. Without hesitation, Caton pressed inside, and, with a restrained moan, Amelia arched against her hand, pulling her deeper.

Head falling to the pillow, Amelia was utter perfection, and Caton was torn between the urge to never stop looking at her and the craving for more. More, while Amelia was under her spell for once. More, while Amelia would allow her to have it.

Lips fastening to Amelia's neck, Caton tongued tangy skin, nipping at flesh until Amelia moaned in pleasure or pain. Downward, she dragged her teeth over Amelia's bare skin, up the slope of one breast to suck Amelia's nipple into her mouth. The frantic breaths from above and Amelia's fingers tangling in her hair provided encouragement, and Caton crossed to the other breast, fingers thrusting deeper as her thumb teased against Amelia's clit.

She wanted more time, but time barely passed, or Caton lost all track of it, before Amelia's body seized against her, contracting around her fingers, a series of suppressed moans and gasps pouring from full red lips. Wanting to prolong, as much for herself as for Amelia, Caton slowed her movements to a crawl, and when Amelia's fingernails dug sharply into her back in response, she felt as if she was wielding whatever power she had to its fullest potential.

When Amelia at last fell back against the mattress, panting for air, Caton couldn't stop. Where she could have relented, withdrawn, she only pressed deeper, demanding response. Convulsing slightly at the touch, Amelia opened her eyes. They held Caton's for a moment that seemed to stretch into eternity, before drifting closed as Amelia's body tensed again, her open hands clutching Caton's back. The softened caress felt like affection. Or was affection.

It was always more than it seemed.

When Amelia flinched at every touch, Caton relented, running coated fingertips along the inside of Amelia's thigh. Amelia looked completely unraveled and unconcealed as her eyes opened, and Caton wanted to fall into their depths and find bottom. The potent desire luring her closer, she watched Amelia's eyes go wide, the cluster of emotion in them displaced by one unmistakable one. Panic.

Shoving Caton off with an astonishing amount of force, Amelia swung her legs to the edge of the bed, reaching blindly for the sheet and jerking it up against her body.

Stunned by the sudden change in the atmosphere, Caton could only stare at the smooth curve of Amelia's back, realizing how little chance she'd had to admire Amelia in their haste to be closer, and grudgingly acknowledging how fitting it was that her first memory of Amelia naked would be of her cold shoulder.

"Are you okay?" Caton asked carefully.

"I'm fine," Amelia returned, and if her actions hadn't already done so, the shaking of her voice would have given her away.

"You don't seem fine," Caton argued.

"Well, I am," Amelia snapped.

Caton knew she should go, try to minimize the damage. She could tell it wasn't wanted, wouldn't be accepted, but the urge to reach out to Amelia was as instinctive as the urge to breathe. Her fingers barely brushed Amelia's back before Amelia flinched away as if her touch was lethal.

Knowing no attempt would prove effective, and that she was no longer wanted in Amelia's bedroom, Caton chose to cut her losses. It wasn't the first time she had been sent away at Amelia's command before she was ready to go, and she doubted it would be the last.

Crawling out of the bed, she retrieved her clothes from the floor, glancing up at Amelia as she redressed, but Amelia refused to look at her.

She didn't speak. She didn't move. She sat as still and silent as a statue as Caton finished dressing and left her to the silence.

Back down the stairs, Caton didn't stop, following the well-beaten path all the way back to the kitchen.

"How is she?" Sole asked as Caton entered the room, heading directly for her bag and throwing it over her shoulder.

"Contagious," she responded on her way back out the door. "I'm sick too."

21

Watching the last splash of Jack Daniels hit the bottom of her glass, Caton absently wondered how many fifths she would go through in her remaining time as Amelia's assistant. She wasn't a total lush yet, but one glance at her recycle bin was proof alone that her desire for mind-numbing drink had increased exponentially with the unwritten functions of her job.

Further inspection would reveal the liquors had gotten harder and the proofs higher. The way Caton figured it, she was about three days away from opening the dusty, factory-sealed bottle of Absinthe given to her as a joke on her twenty-first birthday with the assurance it would "shred her insides" and joining several members of her extended family in functional alcoholism.

Halfway through her first sip of her second glass of the night, the knock on the door caught her off-guard, and Caton glanced toward it with irritation. As more of the building's residents had come to recognize Laura, she had been getting in more frequently without buzzing up, a habit that was becoming increasingly annoying as the rest of Caton's life spiraled further out of her control.

Capping the bottle, Caton added it to the bin and dropped the lid that didn't quite close, before walking to the door and peering through the peephole, breath catching at the sight of the woman on the other side of the door.

Head tilted down, Amelia's eyes were unreadable - not that Caton would expect to see anything legible in them even if they were staring straight at her - so she could only imagine why Amelia had shown up at her apartment without warning.

To fire her probably, properly to her face. Amelia would surely want it no other way.

To scold her, perhaps, for leaving without telling her, just because it was within her power to do so.

Then, maybe Amelia had just come to heckle, to interrupt Caton's routine on an even grander scale. Caton, and every god she had silently praised every time Amelia was fucking her, and blasphemed every time Amelia treated her like dirt, knew that was within Amelia's power.

Unless she had trolled the parking garage before somehow letting herself into the building, though, Amelia couldn't know she was inside, and Caton considered not opening the door. Twenty minutes earlier, she could just as easily have been in the shower. Ten minutes later, she could just as easily have not been home. If she couldn't brood in her own apartment without Amelia interrupting her, where could she be safe from the other woman?

When Amelia finally looked up, she looked neither vengeful nor mocking, but Caton had a hard time believing what she did see. If she were to put a name to Amelia's expression, she would call it defeat. Through the peephole, she watched Amelia's eyes trail over the surface of the door and Amelia raise her hand once again to knock, before she pulled it back against her chest and turned to go.

It was the sight of Amelia leaving that spurred Caton to action, driving one hand to the deadbolt and the other to the doorknob. Turning the locks simultaneously, she yanked the door open, and her instantaneous relief upon discovering that the Amelia she saw through the peephole wasn't a hallucination turned to dread as Amelia looked back at her and she realized she still didn't know why Amelia was there.

Amelia looked so surprised to find Caton standing there, she too seemed unaware of why she had come. Tempering the expression, she turned around fully, and Caton dropped her gaze. The alcohol fueling both her temper and her libido, she didn't know if she wanted to bruise Amelia or please her. Though, with them, the two seemed to overlap, or so testified the unmistakable handprint Caton discovered on her chest after her shower and had been trying to come up with a good explanation for ever since.

Eyes falling over faded jeans and a leather jacket that looked like it was off the rack of a vintage store, Caton deemed Amelia's attire decidedly un-Amelia-like. Were rich people even allowed to buy clothes sans designer tags? The question sounded fearless in her head, and Caton was about to pose it defensively when Amelia suddenly eliminated the space between them in a series of rapid steps, and abnormally gentle hands grasped either side of Caton's face, pulling her head up and killing her sarcasm.

Amelia's lips meeting her own, Caton ceased to function. Mind going blank and knees giving out, her mouth surrendered to Amelia as every other part of her had. Instincts returning as Amelia's tongue brushed against her bottom lip, Caton's lips parted on moan, hands clutching at the soft leather of Amelia's jacket to keep her on her feet.

Amelia's tongue coiled around Caton's like silk, or like a serpent, as she stepped flush against her, and Caton felt herself moving, scarcely aware of the door clicking closed at Amelia's back. Somewhere on the edge of her mind, there was something Caton needed to remember, some reason they shouldn't be doing this, but Amelia's tongue drew back just enough to flick against the tip of Caton's, and Caton could find no objections.

Whatever else there was, whatever else existed, the only thing that mattered were Amelia's lips against hers, quenching a longing so deep-seated, it was as if Caton had been born with it.

Hands sliding inside the barrier of Amelia's jacket, Caton pushed it from her shoulders, letting it drop to the floor by the sofa as she pushed Amelia down on one flat, faded cushion. Kiss broken, Caton feared it would break the spell. One look around, and she was sure Amelia would realize she was on a hand-me-down couch in a rent-controlled apartment. Surprisingly, though, Amelia's gaze made no attempt to roam. Her eyes stayed on Caton, wide, exposed and anticipating, as Caton slid into her lap, legs straddling Amelia's thighs, hands pressing her against the back of the couch.

She was afraid to go further, she realized, to try for what she wanted, for fear that Amelia would pull away again, would change her mind at the last second and send her hurtling backward into the secondhand coffee table. In the end, though, the fear was weak in the face of her desire, and there was nothing else Caton could do but press forward. All she had wanted for longer than she would ever admit was for Amelia to kiss her, and all she wanted was to feel Amelia's lips on hers again.

Lowering her head, Caton watched for any indication Amelia was going to retract her offering, but when Amelia's hands fell to her hips, pulling her tighter against her and causing a pleasant throbbing outward from Caton's center, she closed her eyes and covered Amelia's lips with her own. Purring at the taste between them, she breathed Amelia's breath, lost in the feel of Amelia's body beneath hers, for once not fighting for dominance.

Hand on the back of the couch next to Amelia's head, Caton knew she shouldn't pull away, that she should take what she had been handed as it had been handed to her without question. The desire to look at Amelia, though, to really look, was too compelling to resist, and she pushed back just enough. Eyes moving over Amelia's face, the fingertips of Caton's free hand ghosted along Amelia's jaw, brushed against one lightly-reddened cheek.

Fingertips moving across kiss-reddened lips she longed to feel everywhere, Caton watched Amelia falter, saw the tinge of doubt pass through her eyes, before a hand tickled up Caton's back and Amelia's fingers slipped beneath her hair to pull Caton back down. Bringing their lips together again, the slow, firm press pulled a sigh from deep within Caton. Opening her lips, she felt Amelia's part in response, and their tongues rushed to tangle.

Amelia's hands moving under her shirt, trailing up overheated skin, brought immediate insistence to Caton's body. Rocking against her, Caton felt as if she would come apart, fully-clothed and hardly-touched, just from the overwhelming sensation of Amelia's lips against hers.

Drumming, rhythmic and loud, intruded upon the wordless chorus of their breathing, and Amelia pushed Caton away, palm pressing unknowingly into the bruise she'd made earlier, ripping a hiss from

Caton's throat. Staring down at Amelia, who looked more than a little undone herself, Caton felt the sting of rejection she always seemed to suffer at Amelia's hands.

Then, the drumming came again, more recognizable, and Caton's eyes shot toward the door. "Shit," she whispered. Suddenly remembering why she shouldn't be doing what she was doing with Amelia at the moment, she made no move to get up, wondering if Laura would leave.

"Aren't you going to get that?" Amelia asked, and Caton looked down to see Amelia's stare shuttering, every visible emotion disappearing behind her usual veil of mystery. She knew then it didn't matter if she did or didn't answer the door. Whatever Amelia had open when she stepped into the apartment had just closed before her very eyes.

Sliding off Amelia, Caton felt the cold rush in as she watched her sit upright on the couch, running her fingers around the edges of her mouth to wipe away evidence they had ever kissed, and could only imagine the image she had to present. Stopping at the mirror by the door, she grimaced at lips too pink and skin too flushed, and switched off the light in the entryway, hoping Laura wouldn't notice the change from the other side of the door.

Another knock falling right beside her, Caton at last opened the barrier between them, and Laura's hand pulled back in surprise. "Hey," she greeted, leaning forward to press a kiss against Caton's swollen lips.

"Hey," Caton returned, dropping Laura's gaze and fighting the urge to glance back to see if Amelia had seen.

"I was starting to think you'd stood me up," Laura said, eyes trailing over Caton's shoulder at the sound of Amelia getting up from the couch. Smile fading slightly, Laura didn't ask. Her eyes returning to Caton's, they silently demanded explanation.

"Sorry," Caton mumbled, turning around and gesturing toward Amelia, belatedly inspecting her hand for any signs of what she'd just been doing with it. "This is Amelia, my boss."

"Oh." Laura smiled in obvious relief, stepping over the threshold. "I'm Laura."

Closing her eyes on what felt like the traces of a lie, Caton pushed the door closed and turned to watch Laura step around the sofa.

"Laura." Amelia pronounced the name like it was up for debate, inspecting her unabashedly, as if everyone was subject to her appraisal. Her eyes returning to Laura's, she made it clear she'd made her assessment, but gave no indication as to what opinion she might have formed.

Shifting uncomfortably, Laura glanced to Caton for help, and Amelia turned her gaze on Caton too, her expression revealing nothing. Not sure how exactly she had ended up in such a decidedly unpleasant position, Caton rounded the sofa to step between them, feeling a desperate compulsion to keep them apart a little too late.

"Laura works at a non-profit that helps kids living on the street." She attempted to mitigate any unfair estimation Amelia had undoubtedly made on Laura's character. "Amelia handles a lot of Jack's charity work."

Glancing to Amelia's jacket, draped neatly over the arm of the couch, Caton was amazed at how innocent Amelia's visit appeared.

"Oh." Laura smiled at Amelia. "Cool."

With a tight laugh that was nothing short of belittling, Amelia smirked. "Indeed. It sounds like we have our hands in a lot of the same things," she declared, and Caton tried not to choke on air.

"Laura, I'm sorry." She rushed to put an end to the conversation before it took any more unexpected turns. "I didn't know I would have to work tonight, but -"

"She doesn't," Amelia cut off her explanation, reaching for the jacket and pulling it on, and Caton felt her chest constrict as her eyes met Amelia's.

Trying to find a speck of what was there before, she found only the gaping void of nothingness that most often stared back at her. "I thought you needed me," she said, the words coming out amazingly calm amidst the tempest that kicked up inside of her.

"I don't," Amelia declared with callous conviction, and Caton dropped her gaze, wishing she had the same veiled defenses as Amelia, certain Amelia had to have seen that the words stung. "Have fun," Amelia added on her way out.

Eyes locked on the floor, Caton refused to see, refused to feel. At the sound of the door closing with a quiet click, she left Laura standing in the middle of her living room and moved toward the abandoned glass on the kitchen counter.

"Wow," Laura casually exclaimed once Amelia was gone. "She is gorgeous."

"Is she?" Caton returned, picking up the glass.

"Don't pretend you haven't noticed," Laura chided good-naturedly. "She is kind of a bitch, though," she added, almost as an afterthought.

"Yes, she is." Caton couldn't have agreed more. Tipping back the last of the whiskey, she cast a futile look toward the cabinet that housed deeper, darker spirits within.

She could hear Laura moving behind her, drawing closer, and took a breath that failed to soothe. The anger was unexpected and unfair, she knew that well, but she still tensed as Laura's arms slid around her waist.

"Come on," Laura whispered. "Don't let her ruin your night. Please."

Amelia wasn't the one who ruined her night, Caton thought bitterly. Or maybe she was. Maybe it was a blessing that Laura showed up when she did, to save Caton from herself, to keep her from digging a deeper grave from which she would never claw free. Regardless, none of it was Laura's fault. If there was one victim in the situation, it was the person who had no clue what was going on.

Setting the glass on the counter, Caton turned in Laura's arms and looked into her tentatively smiling face, realizing, with no small amount of guilt, that she didn't deserve what was standing in front of her. "She hasn't," she assured Laura, and tried to mean it. "What do you want to do?"

"Dinner, movie." Laura shrugged, hands sliding to Caton's back as she stepped closer. "Or we could stay here."

When Laura leaned in, lips teasing Caton's cheek, it was tempting. Because it was easy. Laura wanted her. She was good to her. She may have even had feelings for her that she hadn't yet declared. Sometimes it felt that way. No matter how Caton tried to force it, though, in the moment, easy wasn't enough.

"Dinner sounds good," she responded, hoping it sounded more like hunger than a brush-off.

It wasn't rejection, though, it was only postponement. After dinner, Caton felt more like herself, Laura felt less like a substitute, and, when she woke up the next morning with someone lying next to her, it was easy for Caton to pretend it was who she wanted it to be.

22

Apparently saying she didn't need Caton wasn't enough. Amelia felt the need to drive the point home with every action. When Caton returned to work Monday morning, Amelia avoided the places Caton would be, barely acknowledged her greetings, and when Caton finally went into Amelia's office, against all hope of self-preservation, to ask if she could talk to Amelia, she saw the frost reform right before her eyes when Amelia looked up and said, "What do we have to talk about?"

Caton wanted to rail, to scream, to demand an explanation for Amelia showing up at her apartment and kissing her the way she had, deeply, as if she meant it. She doubted Amelia would hear anything said to her inside the armor of ice, though, which, as far as Caton could tell, had zero points of vulnerability.

Not that she tried particularly hard to find one. Remembering her reactions to Amelia, the rush of elation, the immediacy with which she had yielded her very will, Caton wasn't sure it was in her best interest to restore the balance between them. Before Amelia, she'd always had a very rational understanding of romantic relationships. She really didn't need some clandestine fling messing with her head.

In the wake of Amelia's most recent lapse in judgment, work was left on Caton's desk without commentary, and Caton did it. That was all there needed to be between them. Anything else had repercussions, and repercussions Caton couldn't afford.

"Are you coming to the Halston & Company holiday party?" Amelia's voice came out of nowhere, surprising enough after two weeks of silence that Caton jerked forward and smashed her hip into the edge of the desk. Grunting, her hand went to the point of pain as she remembered with dismay what happened when she showed Amelia weakness.

"Sorry," Amelia had the surprising good grace to say, and Caton glanced back at her.

One hand holding on at the doorframe, Amelia's other hung loosely beside her, and Caton was annoyed to see that she didn't look the least bit uncomfortable. She looked like an employer coming to talk to an employee. Nothing more.

"I wasn't planning on it," Caton responded. "I don't really work there."

"Well, Jack said you could come," Amelia replied, tacking on more carefully, "I want you to come."

For a moment, it almost sounded like concession, like it had leaked through a crack in that armor, and Caton damn near fell for it. "I'm busy that night," she finally responded, turning back toward her desk.

"Then cancel." Amelia's response was less conciliatory, and Caton knew it wasn't a request. She just didn't know which Amelia she was being ordered by, the one who controlled her with managerial authority or the one who controlled her by carnal influence.

Either way, it didn't matter. She would do as she was told.

Caton knew Laura had plans the night of the Halston & Company holiday party. The only reason she told Laura about it at all was to explain why she couldn't come to the get-together Laura was having before she left town for a few weeks.

Caton never expected Laura to volunteer to change her plans, or to look so anxious for an invitation when she asked if the party was employee-only. That was how she ended up walking through the door with Laura's hand in hers, as if they were a couple outside their circles of friends and acquaintances and the casual mentions of Laura that Caton had made to her parents to appease their persistent parental curiosity.

Not seeing Amelia would have been the ideal, so, of course, Amelia was the first thing Caton saw when she walked through the door. Standing next to Jack as if they were the queen and king of a wealthy kingdom, Amelia smiled at the employees of Halston & Company, clasping their hands with false joy, like she remembered and was glad to see each one. Or maybe Amelia did remember them. Maybe she truly was glad. It was such a rare phenomenon, Caton still had difficulty telling when Amelia was being sincere.

Hired right after New Year's, she had just missed the party the year before, had just missed meeting this Amelia first, the one who made everyone feel acknowledged and at-ease. It was for the best, she knew. She would have fallen for the boss' wife in a single night. Even knowing Amelia's many flaws hadn't kept her from giving in to Amelia's more appealing traits.

As expected, Amelia was dressed at a level of designer luxury that was almost absurd in the room. The dress alone probably cost more than Jack paid five of the mid-level employees who mingled around them in a week. Where Caton would have anticipated some perfectly-pinned updo, though, one that made her look more expensive and less approachable, there was the familiar dark fall of Amelia's hair, dipping just past her shoulders to brush the bare skin exposed by the off-shoulder dress. Remembering the feel of that hair against the side of her face, brushing the inside of her thighs, Caton swallowed an upswell of longing she hoped didn't show.

When Amelia's gaze at last found her, the smile that came to her lips might have been real too. Then, Amelia's eyes tracked to Laura and the smile slipped, replaced near-instantly by a look that Caton tried not to let worry her. Often, Amelia did nothing but her worst, and she hadn't broken Caton yet. Sometimes, it seemed the only part of Amelia that wasn't completely noxious was her facade, but there were times when Caton hated it the most. Because it was unfairly misleading. Perhaps if Amelia's outside matched her inside, she would be easier to resist.

"Do you want to say hi to your boss?" Laura asked, and Caton realized she'd been caught staring at Amelia. She only wished she knew for how long.

"Let's get a drink," she responded, pulling Laura by the hand to escape Amelia's penetrating gaze.

Beelining for the bar, she picked up two glasses of champagne, handing one to Laura and sipping the other even as she tried to decide what she wanted from the open bar. A liberal application of alcohol was the only way she would get through the night, she could tell already, and she trusted Laura to keep her from making a fool of herself. Which was more than she could say for Amelia.

"This place is incredible," Laura said, looking past Caton at the food spread and candlelit tables, before glancing up at the lights falling like icicles from the ceiling. "Maybe working for this company isn't so bad."

"I don't work for this company," Caton reminded her sullenly.

"Wow," Laura returned, eyes affixing to Caton's face with surprise and concern. Both clearly readable, because Laura didn't try to hide anything. "You're really not appreciating any of this, are you?"

"I didn't want to come," Caton admitted, sighing. "You shouldn't have let me bring you. I am going to be a miserable date."

"Why?" Laura asked, taking a step closer, lips turned softly upward, coaxing Caton into relaxing without forcing her. "Look at this place. They dropped a lot of money on this. It doesn't matter why you're here. Just eat and drink and enjoy it."

Smile slowly breaking through, Caton was reminded of every reason she was attracted to Laura in an instant. Eyes trailing down the black dress, her fingers reached out to skim the smooth surface of Laura's arm. "You look really beautiful," she whispered.

"You already said that," Laura responded, smile expanding as she took a drink.

"It deserves to be repeated," Caton declared, sliding her arm around Laura's waist to lead her to a nearby table.

It wasn't her plan to come to the party. It wasn't her plan to bring Laura. All of Caton's plans had fallen through, so she needed a new plan. She had come with Laura, and Laura was more than beautiful. She was funny, she was optimistic, she was willing to sit close enough to Caton that it was obvious they were together and to make small talk with Caton's past coworkers who joined them at their table.

Laura was a good person. Laura was a good date. Laura was the kind of woman anyone would want to spend time with and introduce to her family. She had no secrets. She had no desire to control or manipulate. She was exactly the kind of woman Caton should have been giving her all to keep. Laura deserved that, and Caton knew if she didn't start doing it, someone else would.

"Do you want another drink?" she asked with a laugh a few hours later, as Laura finally succeeded in getting it through to a guy from advertising that she was not about to try the hotter-than-hell salsa that had turned the faces of everyone else at the table red and had them reaching for their glasses, wishing they had chosen water over alcohol.

"I probably shouldn't," Laura responded, glancing at the sip left in the bottom of her glass. "But yeah, sure."

"We can call a cab," Caton assured her. Slight intoxication spurring her to affection, she leaned in to kiss Laura's warm cheek before getting up from the table. Amazingly enough, in spite of herself, she had been in a good mood for most of the night. The open bar didn't hurt, but neither did the people at her table. The workers of Halston & Company weren't total bores, and Laura had been far more perfect than Caton deserved.

Perhaps the real secret wasn't in who was present, though, but in who was missing. Since they had made their entrance, Caton hadn't seen Amelia, and not having Amelia around, not thinking about her, not longing for her, was welcome relief.

In the past, it was always when Caton trained her thoughts away from Amelia, when she was certain the other woman wouldn't come, that Amelia seemed to appear, so she should have been expecting it. She should have seen it coming. Regardless, the body that checked her through the slit in one set of red velvet curtains that hung over the windows around the room took her totally by surprise, as did the cold blast of air that came with being on the wrong side of the fabric.

The only thing that stopped Caton from screaming was the knowledge that only one person in the room felt she had the right to manhandle her in such as fashion, and she turned toward Amelia with a glare, finding the space behind the curtain surprisingly accommodating. Standing fully sideways in the floor to ceiling window frame, she had room to spare. When she glanced toward the glass at the street some thirty floors below, though, she had to put her hand on the cool surface to steady herself.

"What in the hell are you doing?" she hissed to Amelia.

The sliver of light that leaked between the towering curtains at her back casting her face into shadow, Amelia's features darkened as she stepped closer. "Are you having fun?" she asked.

"I was," Caton returned.

"With the little people?"

"Yes," Caton countered with a smile only half-forced. "One guy even works in the mailroom."

"You're really not proud, are you?" Amelia tossed back.

Smile dropping from her lips, Caton tried to push past Amelia, but Amelia's hand, light on her arm, was all it took to hold her in place. The only escape would be a scene and explaining that to Laura was the last thing she wanted to do. Not when she'd just realized she needed to be better for Laura, to focus on what she should want, instead of what seized her and made her lose her senses.

Even standing with Amelia now, Caton felt outside of herself. Amelia had too much power over her. She was dangerous.

"You've been ignoring me," Amelia said, as if she had made any effort to talk to Caton or be near her. Of course, that wasn't what Amelia meant. She meant Caton was supposed to come to the party and stare longingly at her from across the room, to make Amelia feel beautiful and powerful and desired, while she got nothing in return.

With a contemptuous laugh, Caton glanced out the window, no longer bothered by the precipitous drop. If the glass weren't there, she would have stepped off the ledge rather than continue the conversation. "I've been ignoring you?" she snapped. "You have been ignoring me for days."

Smiling a little, Amelia eased toward Caton, fingers trailing up and down her arm. "Did that bother you?" she asked.

Climbing quickly to a point where she didn't care what kind of scene she had to explain, Caton wanted nothing more than to shove Amelia out of her way and escape. And nothing more than to stay where she was and let Amelia's touch move where it would.

"Let me go," she said weakly.

Hand moving up the slope of Caton's shoulder, Amelia stepped closer instead, her long fingers smoothing down the side of Caton's throat, dipping into the hollow at its base, before flicking at the neckline of her dress.

As much as she needed to be Amelia's opponent, Caton was always her accomplice, always more willing than she wanted to be. Fingers trailing back up her throat to spread across her jawline, she let Amelia conduct her, not even noticing Amelia's free hand gathering the fabric of her dress, hitching it upward little by little, until the cold air blew across her ankles.

Realizing her intent, Caton grabbed Amelia's hand in a grip that she could tell hurt. Amelia could hide almost anything, but she couldn't hide pain, and Caton gentled her touch just enough to ease the look. "You came to my apartment," she uttered. "You kissed me. Then, you ignored me. Again. And now, you really think I'm going to let you fuck me behind a curtain in a room full of people?"

Amelia's reply was concise and brutal. Hand returning to Caton's shoulder, she pushed hard enough that Caton grunted as she hit the flat surface of the window frame behind her. Pressing closer, pinning her in place, she gave Caton no chance to respond, to flee, to fight, if that had been Caton's instinct. Caton wished it could have been her instinct. She knew it should have been her instinct.

Amelia's lips covering hers, though, all of Caton's protests were swallowed by the veracity of her kiss. Giving in instantly, she inhaled Amelia's fire, tasted the wine on her tongue. Even her hands were traitors, burying themselves in Amelia's silken hair. And when Amelia's hand moved to her dress again, working its way beneath it, Caton only half-heartedly tried to stop her, batting her away with little more than minor discouragement.

Finding its target, Amelia's hand pressed against her panties, and Caton arched into her touch, heels slipping on the wooden frame so that Amelia had to press closer to hold her up. She didn't want to believe any of it - Amelia's kiss, the warm press of her body. Amelia's apology was always insincere, Amelia's emotion was always false, but it never felt false in the moment, when Amelia's hands and eyes were on her, when Amelia's lips were caressing hers.

Pulling away to catch panting breaths, Amelia's fingers slipped beneath the fabric of Caton's panties, starting a rhythm that assured Caton wouldn't dare try to stop her.

"Do you golf?" The random words cut behind the curtain, and Caton tensed in Amelia's embrace.

Only pulling back enough to glance over her shoulder at the shadows hovering just outside the curtain, Amelia's body still trapped Caton against the window frame, her hand continuing to move in perfect rhythm.

"Nah, not really," a second voice returned.

"That's too bad. That's the excuse I use when I want to get away for a while. You know, it's a good long one, gives you plenty of time to shoot eighteen and still spend two hours at the bar with her none-the-wiser."

The second voice laughed. "I'll have to think about that. I think my old man had some clubs. They're probably in the attic or something."

The tedious conversation should have been enough to douse the flame that threatened to consume Caton, but, instead, it prolonged it. The material of her dress suddenly too thick, Caton sweat beneath it, breaths coming in shallow pants as she tried to swallow enough oxygen.

"Uh, there she is now," the first guy moaned. "I got to go."

"I should get back too," the second voice responded.

Then, the shadows were gone. Amelia watched them go and turned back with a look Caton couldn't make out in the darkness, before pressing her lips to Caton's again. It was almost like relief, almost as if, for once, they were in it together.

Amelia's fingers thrusting suddenly into her, climax seized Caton without warning. Foot slipping from the edge of the window frame, her shoe dropped to the floor beneath the curtain, but Amelia caught her, held her, covering Caton's mouth with her own so the sounds Caton couldn't help but make were sent into the depths of Amelia's body.

Clutching at Amelia's face, fingers digging into the soft skin of Amelia's neck, dark hair caressing the backs of her hands, a flood of ecstasy engulfed Caton. Lips trembling against Amelia's, she forgot everything that was wrong with what they were doing and could feel only what was right.

When some sense returned, she half-expected Amelia to drop her, to call it a job well done and take her leave. Instead, Caton felt the soft press of Amelia's hands helping her stand more upright, until her foot returned to the window ledge and she could hold herself in place, before finally releasing her. Dropping to a crouch before her, Amelia retrieved the shoe from the floor, coaxing Caton's leg up with a hand on the back of her ankle, and slipped it back onto her foot.

Watching Amelia stand in awe, Caton wondered if she was drunk enough to imagine it, because it was damn near reverential.

Hands on Caton again, Amelia straightened her dress, skilled fingers moving with precision to make everything exactly as it had been before her attack. Then, with a final glance, though Caton couldn't tell what lay behind her eyes in the darkness, Amelia turned to go.

Reaching out on impulse, Caton caught Amelia's wrist and held her in place. Missing the feel of Amelia against her the second she moved away, she took unsteady steps from the wood frame of the window and bumped against Amelia's side.

Her free hand sliding instantly to Caton's neck, Amelia pressed her lips to Caton's in a kiss that was meant more to comfort than arouse. Then, almost reluctantly, it seemed, she twisted her arm out of Caton's grasp and disappeared back through the curtains.

23

If taking the job had done one thing for Caton, it had made her a better liar. Returning to Laura with another drink in hand, because God knew in the end they were both going to need it, the excuses she had for her were almost the truth. She had gotten cornered by Amelia, she told her, who wouldn't let her go. The rest of the story Caton could simply call detail, and convince herself was unimportant.

Like the detail that she wasn't merely relieved to discover Amelia still wanted her, but, when she stepped out from behind the curtain a minute after Amelia disappeared through its soft contours, she felt inexplicably content. It wasn't exactly her idea of romance, but Amelia had turned something that could have been condescending and bordering on vicious into near perfection, and Caton swore she had felt something shift between them.

She knew Amelia would play it off, that she would return to her ways, given the chance, but it had been there, both acknowledged and unacknowledged, and Caton had felt it, not just within herself, but in Amelia's hands, in Amelia's kiss. There was more than the power and lust and greed that seemed to fuel their uneven relationship. Caton wanted the more. It grasped at her and wouldn't let go. It didn't matter why. It didn't need to make sense.

Walking nervously into the Halston Palace Monday morning, she was met almost immediately by Amelia's presence. Standing in the kitchen with Sole, Amelia looked up as Caton entered. Eyes meeting, for once Caton felt no pressure to avert hers.

"Hello, Caton," Amelia greeted, voice low and seductive.

Tamping down on the smile that threatened in response, too telling, she knew, for Amelia and for Sole, Caton failed to stop the rush of desire that came from nowhere and everywhere at once. "Hi," she husked.

"Good morning." Sole turned from her work at Amelia's back to smile.

"Good morning," Caton returned, wrenching her eyes from Amelia's.

"Coffee?" Sole offered.

"Sure," Caton nodded, approaching the bar slowly, afraid of what she might do if she got too close to Amelia, already feeling any control she had around the other woman slipping. She wondered if she would let Amelia take her right there on the bar, with the curtains wide open and Sole as witness.

Gaze lowering, Caton watched Amelia's hand tap nervously at the counter, and when she risked looking up, Amelia's gaze was on her, warm and curious. Resisting the urge to reach across the barrier and touch Amelia's hand, or climb across the barrier and show Amelia exactly what was in her head, Caton managed to turn her attention once again to Sole as her coffee was delivered to its usual perfection.

"Thank you," she said, voice coming out little more than a whisper.

"Of course." Sole smiled again.

"I'm going to head upstairs," Caton said, needing the space to breathe, silently hoping Amelia would follow.

Settling at her desk, thumb stroking the smooth ceramic of her mug, warmed by the liquid within, Caton's thoughts led back to Amelia, just as they had every waking moment the day before. After what happened at the party, after Amelia's greeting downstairs, she actually believed the feeling might be shared, but all morning Caton waited for Amelia and Amelia didn't come.

When Caton went to look for her under the guise of a coffee refill, Sole said she wasn't sure where Amelia might be hiding. Realizing, if Amelia didn't want to be found, she would never find her in the vast recesses of the house, Caton went back to her workless office to wait some more.

An hour passed like a day as she bided the time between her morning exchange with Amelia and the moment she finally heard Amelia next door in her office. The warm tones of persuasion Amelia always used on the phone with potential donors carried through the barrier of the door between them and Caton felt her body respond to her sheer proximity, felt herself pulled in the direction of Amelia's office. She could be waiting the rest of her life, it suddenly hit her, if she waited for Amelia to come to her.

It was always on Amelia's whims, on Amelia's desires, but Caton couldn't discount her part of the blame. For weeks, she had been letting Amelia control her, manipulate their time together, call every play and act between them. Why wouldn't Amelia use the power handed over so willingly to her?

When Amelia's voice went silent, Caton gathered the fragmented bits of her courage and traveled the abbreviated distance from her office into Amelia's. Looking up from where she was leaned over her desk, digging through a pile of files, Amelia looked much too dignified in a pant suit that was official, yet chic.

"Caton," she proclaimed, voice slightly surprised and carrying an underlying trace of something that sent a wave of desperation through Caton's body. "Do you need something?"

Caton needed her. Amelia was all she needed. It had been true for weeks, but she couldn't imagine admitting it to the other woman. In her current state, Amelia didn't look like the type one could convince or rattle, and Caton's bravery flickered, threatening to extinguish.

But then, only two days before, she had to remind herself, Amelia had looked like royalty, but had proven herself the kind of royal who would drag a subject into a hidden alcove at the ball and disrupt the monotony of her position. The same kind of royal who would call a subject to her castle for a secret tryst and then return to the feast as if nothing had happened.

As Sole once told her, Amelia simply wasn't who she seemed.

"I want to talk to you," Caton returned diplomatically.

"Well, it'll have to wait," Amelia responded, finally locating the folder she was looking for and grabbing it as she moved around her desk. "I have a meeting."

It was clear how much Amelia expected Caton to simply move aside at the words by the way she had to come to an abrupt stop to keep from running right into her. Staring defiantly into Amelia's eyes, Caton tried to maintain her backbone in the face of Amelia's overwhelming sense of entitlement to be where she wanted to be when she wanted to be there.

"Caton, I have to go," Amelia declared, but it was softer than usual, gentler than the orders she normally gave. It was almost overly-kind, and Caton was in no mood to have her feelings coddled when they could be fulfilled.

"Is it about your daughter?" she questioned, and confusion passed over Amelia's face, though Caton wasn't sure if it was the question or the fact that she was being questioned that came as such surprise to her.

"Selene is in London," Amelia reminded her, though Caton needed no reminder.

"Then, there is nothing more important than me," she declared, plucking the folder from Amelia's hand and flinging it to the floor.

Watching its contents scatter, Amelia didn't look angry or even irritated. Her gaze returning to Caton, the emotions weren't that easily identified. Not that it mattered. Caton had kept her mouth shut and catered to Amelia's whims for as long as she could stand it.

"You," she began, sliding her fingers inside the loop of Amelia's belt to pull her closer, "can have me whenever you want me. A point you have gone out of your way to prove on several occasions." Bodies bumping together, Caton reveled in the gasp she forced from Amelia's lips. "But you need to accept the fact that I want you too." Her hands came together at Amelia's waist. "And I am tired of waiting for space in your schedule."

Making fast work of the expensive leather belt, she took more satisfaction than she should have in crushing the perfectly pressed fabric of five-hundred-dollar slacks beneath her hands in her search for all their hidden buttons. Without asking for or awaiting permission, because

Amelia never did, her hand slipped inside the fabric, past soft panties and over softer skin.

When Amelia exhaled unsteadily in reaction, hands flying to Caton's shoulders to steady herself, Caton's entire body, coiled all morning, unwound. Stepping closer to Amelia, her cheek slid against the smooth skin of Amelia's, as her fingers teased inside warm flesh, finding Amelia impossibly wet and open. "I want you now," she confessed, and, to her great surprise, Amelia sagged against her, instantly acquiescent.

"The door is open," Amelia breathed.

"I don't care." Caton's words were muffled against the smooth surface of Amelia's neck. Darting her tongue out, she tasted the moisture springing up on Amelia's throat, and it acted as aperitif, only making her craving more pronounced.

"And there are beds in this house," Amelia added, succeeding in stilling Caton's hand and mouth.

Grasping Amelia's collar with her free hand, unwilling to let go until she was sure she wasn't being played, Caton pulled back enough to study Amelia's face. It might have been a trick, but, if it was, it didn't show. Nothing seemed hidden or below the surface where Amelia kept her emotions. She looked exposed, raw, as if she never expected Caton to come to her, and now that she had, she had no idea what to do about it.

Taking a chance on Amelia's sincerity, Caton extricated her hand from its intimate entanglement with Amelia's body, watching dark eyes flutter, and wanted to return her hand instantly, do it again, just to prove that she could, that she could make Amelia react, make her feel something, that she could penetrate those walls even if only for brief moments and through sex.

Holding her slacks together with one hand, Amelia grabbed Caton's arm with the other, tugging her into the hallway. The path was clear in either direction. Amelia could have just as easily pulled her down the stairs to the front door and kicked her out for the final time as led her into a guest bedroom as exquisitely-furnished and impeccably-decorated as the rest of the house.

When Amelia chose the bedroom, turning to face Caton inside the doorway, Caton knew she wasn't wrong. It wasn't all wishful thinking.

Something *had* changed. Something *was* there. Beyond their previous encounters, past the distance Amelia had tried so hard to maintain, there was something worth seeking.

Pushing the door closed, Caton stepped into Amelia, arms encircling her waist, hands splaying over a lightly muscled lower back. Her lips met Amelia's without protest, and the alien sensation of Amelia's arms wrapping around her shoulders, one hand cradling the back of her head in a dizzyingly tender fashion, nearly stole Caton's ability to stand.

Mouth opening on a sigh, her breath mingled with Amelia's, her hands skimming the soft fabric of Amelia's shirt. Finding the top button, she worked it apart. Another button undone and, with some effort, Caton pulled her lips from Amelia's to lower them to the patch of exposed skin, feeling Amelia's heart beat faster against her fingertips where they lingered at the slope of her breast.

Sliding each button slowly free, mouth trailing behind, she tasted Amelia as she revealed her. Before, she couldn't have pinpointed it, but this was what she had been longing for, Caton realized, what she had been craving, time to do as she wanted with Amelia, as slowly as she wanted to do it. Pulling the tail of Amelia's shirt from her waistband, Caton slipped the final button free and dropped down to press her lips to the skin above Amelia's silk panties.

A shuddering exhalation from above drew her gaze, and her breath caught at the sight of Amelia so utterly exposed to her. Transfixed, she stared at Amelia's expressive features until Amelia's eyes opened and dropped to meet her own. Suddenly too distant, Caton stood at the same time Amelia's fingers thrust into her hair, pulling her up, and their lips came together in an almost painful crush.

Hands finding their way between fabric and skin, Caton pushed Amelia's shirt from her shoulders, catching it with one hand and tossing it haphazardly toward the chair by the wall, doubting it would make it there, but knowing, for once, that Amelia wouldn't care. Moving to the loose waistband of Amelia's slacks, she pushed them down, and felt Amelia move against her as she kicked them off along with her shoes, not bothering to retrieve them from the pile at her feet.

When Amelia's hands slipped beneath her shirt, inching the fabric upward, Caton grabbed her wrists, removing the seeking hands from her body, and Amelia pulled back to look at her, eyes darkly intrigued. Nudging Amelia to the bed, Caton reached past her to pull down the quilt and coaxed Amelia back onto soft sheets.

It was surprisingly easy. Amelia was surprisingly accommodating. Watching her settle herself against one thick pillow, Caton's eyes trailed over light olive skin, fragmented only by the navy patches of Amelia's bra and panties, and felt her desire to take her time go head to head with her urge to take everything Amelia was offering as quickly as humanly possible. Devil and angel, Jekyll and Hyde. Caton moved her gaze back to Amelia's, and knew Amelia could read her mind by the smile that spread slowly over her lips, not quite a smirk but far from unaware of the effect she had.

That's when Caton decided she would take her time, even if killed her, if only because Amelia didn't think she had the willpower.

Climbing onto the bed next to Amelia, close but not quite touching, when Amelia's hand reached for her, Caton impeded its path.

Free hand moving to Amelia's throat, Caton was nervous. She was overwhelmed. Courage shaken by the acute awareness of just how much she wanted Amelia, how much she had wanted it to be like this with her, her fingertips trailed the rise of Amelia's chest, down Amelia's sternum. Pressing softly between the sides of Amelia's rib cage, her hand passed over the slight swell of Amelia's stomach to skim along the top of her panties, and there was some relief when Amelia jerked toward her hand.

"Impatient?" Caton murmured, glancing up at Amelia's face and feeling rather satisfied at the flush she'd put there.

"No." Amelia tried to appear unmoved, and there was only the slightest tremor to her voice.

"Good," Caton said, returning her eyes to her hand, which retraced its path, past Amelia's belly button, between her breasts and over her chest to her shoulder. Trailing down Amelia's sculpted bicep, over her elbow, along her forearm, Caton watched goose bumps form. "Cold?" she asked, hand curving around Amelia's, fingertips teasing lightly against her palm.

"No," Amelia whispered, and the honesty was almost shocking.

Hand sliding back up Amelia's arm to her jaw, Caton turned Amelia's head enough to capture her lips, and Amelia turned into her, body shifting closer. One knee captured between Amelia's legs, Caton pressed her back against the mattress, releasing her restrained arm and dragging her lips along a soft cheek until she could suck gently at the skin beneath Amelia's jaw. Her hand closing over silk as she licked and nipped at the expanse of Amelia's throat, she finally drew a moan out of Amelia, though she didn't know if she owed it to the bite or her fingers circling Amelia's nipple through the blue fabric.

Unhooking the bra with a trained hand, Caton tugged the barrier from Amelia's body and tossed it toward the other cast-off pieces. Hands curving around Amelia's back, she felt the muscles tense as she took one hard nipple into her mouth.

With a surprised moan, Amelia arched from the bed, hand thrusting into Caton's hair to hold her in place, and Caton circled the nipple with her tongue, sucking harder until Amelia had no choice but to cry out. Moving slowly across Amelia's chest, she repeated the actions, determined to take her time, to make it last, to make it more. But, tongue flicking against Amelia's nipple, she felt Hyde taking over as her need to taste more of Amelia rose to a point of near madness.

Of their own volition, Caton's hands trailed the toned muscles of Amelia's sides, catching the fabric of her panties and sending them soaring to the floor. Glancing over the contours of Amelia's body, she settled between Amelia's thighs, watching need swirl dangerously behind dark eyes.

For someone who didn't need anything, Amelia's need was on flagrant display, and Caton understood that danger well. Dropping the gaze, she opened her mouth at the bottom of Amelia's rib cage, tongue trailing flawless skin, lips closing against it in gentle caress. The firm pressure of Amelia's hands on her shoulders prodded her downward, and Caton resisted, lips trailing the twitching muscles of Amelia's lower abdomen. It was a power play, Amelia's determination to get what she needed versus Caton's determination to take what she wanted.

"Caton," Amelia pled, and Caton gave up the fight in an instant.

Hands slipping beneath sweat-slickened thighs, she pulled Amelia toward her, dropping her lips beneath a perfectly-waxed patch of hair to trace a long, wet path in uncharted territory. Groaning at the deeply satisfying flavor of Amelia, she forced her eyes to stay open, watching Amelia's head press back against the pillow, hands flexing beside her on the mattress.

Days before, even minutes before, Caton couldn't have imagined it, Amelia completely exposed and utterly compliant, trusting Caton with her body. Pushing deeper, Caton wanted to invade Amelia, to take over as Amelia had taken possession of her, to be inside Amelia, to consume her mind, to insinuate herself into Amelia's very soul.

Tasting, teasing, Caton listened to the sounds above her, each gasping breath, each long moan Amelia probably didn't know she was producing. The idea that she could make Amelia do something against her will went to Caton's head and she felt drunk on the sheer power.

She was in no hurry. She was content where she was, a place she had yearned to be welcome for weeks. When Amelia's moans turned into near whimpers, though, when she rocked against Caton, leg bending and foot pressing into the mattress in desperation, Caton sacrificed her contentment for Amelia's, concentrating fully on Amelia's need, moving to Amelia's rhythm, giving Amelia exactly what she yearned for until that pleasure broke over her in electric waves.

Riding the current with her, Caton closed her mouth around Amelia again as it began to subside, Amelia's clit firm beneath her tongue. Feeling a hand at her shoulder, as if it might try to stop her, Caton thrust her fingers into Amelia in a seamless motion that made the hand dig in instead. With a moan, Amelia pushed down against her hand, and Caton reveled in each hitch of Amelia's breath as she pressed deeper inside of her.

At a stroke of Caton's tongue, Amelia arched from the bed, the hand on Caton's shoulder moving to her hair, holding painfully tight as she tugged her upward. Caton's free arm circled Amelia's waist, and she held her up, lips finding Amelia's and drinking in her uneven exhalations as her fingers continued to move inside of her, unwilling to relinquish their claim.

Without warning, Amelia jerked her mouth from Caton's, struggling for breath, arms tightening around Caton's shoulders as a maelstrom of sensations, not all identifiable, seized them both. Amelia throbbing around her fingers, Caton felt Amelia's climax echoed in her own body, a barrage of inexplicable vibrations that left her nearly as anemic as Amelia.

Trembling in the aftermath, Caton lowered Amelia to the bed and panted above her, fingers still enveloped in her velvet warmth. When Amelia moved, her fingers wrapping around Caton's wrist to force her hand away, Caton realized it was the moment she had feared, the moment when Amelia realized what just happened, how much she had given, how much she had revealed, and closed herself off, kicking Caton out of bed, and possibly her life, forever.

Amelia's eyes slowly unshuttering, Caton awaited the fallout. Where it should have been, though, there was only Amelia's hand, moving from Caton's upper back to her face, thumb stroking gently over skin that tried to meld into her touch, and Amelia's eyes searching for something Caton was certain she would find without effort.

When Amelia's eyes at last fell closed, her hand dropping from Caton's cheek to her shoulder, it was invitation enough that Caton lowered herself next to Amelia, pressing her lips to Amelia's neck as she listened to her struggle to catch her breath. Arm slipping tentatively over Amelia's waist, Caton sighed in relief when Amelia's hand came to rest on her back, not pulling her closer, but not pushing her away.

24

Time was fading on the day when they at last rose from the bed. From the cryptic clues Jack had dropped that morning, Amelia suspected he would be home earlier than usual. Though, she wasn't sure when that might be, she did know they were pushing the limits of the time allotted them.

It had been so long since she felt anything like it that Amelia scarcely recognized the feeling sweeping over her as shyness as she pulled her clothes on across the bed from Caton, trying to regain her traction. They had been moving quickly, picking up momentum even, she would concede that - she'd been shifting most of the gears herself - but they had been on a closed course where everything was within her control. Now, it was as if Caton had flung the gate open and sent them reeling into unbounded territory. It was far more dangerous, but also more exhilarating, Amelia had to admit, as Caton looked up and smiled at her, and she felt the same thing that flared in her the night she went to Caton's apartment, and again at the company party when she watched Caton enter with Laura and wanted to stake a claim that wasn't hers to stake.

Jack could sleep with all the women he wanted, and it had little impact beyond her pride. Seeing Caton with someone else, though no one even knew it was an affront to her, had gutted her in an instant, leaving her hollow in a way she finally realized only Caton could undo. Punishing Caton for having someone else, despite her own very-married situation, was reflex, but forcing her way back into Caton's arms was even more impulsive and far more effective at filling those empty spaces.

Of course, she would never tell Caton that.

Dressed and mostly presentable, they walked downstairs in silence, little to discuss after they had spent most of the day making nonverbal declarations that it would be difficult to take back. Amelia wondered if it was fair for her to feel without restraint, to be honest with her touch. If Caton wanted more from her, Amelia wanted to give it to her, but each time she let Caton step closer, she felt as if she was making promises she could never keep.

"Hungry?" Sole asked as they entered the kitchen, giving no allusion to anything other than a burning curiosity as to the state of their stomachs.

"Starving," Amelia returned, and Sole spun instantly, but not before Amelia caught the traces of the smirk that appeared on her face.

"I made empanadas," Sole announced, retrieving them from the warming drawer and sliding them onto the counter.

Cocking her head, Amelia lifted an eyebrow that Sole pretended not to see. So, she did know. Amelia suspected she had known for some time, though she never expected Sole to tip her hand, or her hat, by commemorating their afternoon in bed with Amelia's favorite special-occasion dish.

"Are you eating together?" Sole asked, smirk replaced by an impeccable smile that even a priest would have bought as innocent.

Faltering, Amelia realized she didn't know. She could feel Caton beside her. She knew Caton hadn't eaten all day and had done more than her share of calorie-burning. She was sure Caton needed sustenance. She just wasn't sure if Caton wanted to get it with her. Unable to recall a time when uncertainty had benefited her, Amelia nodded without so much as a glance at Caton. "Yes. We'll take it to the dining room."

As Sole readied their plates, the thought that Caton may have somewhere else to be entered Amelia's mind, but Caton didn't make it known if she couldn't stay and Amelia decided to take Caton's silence as acceptance. As she always had.

"While we're eating, could you call Mrs. Dreese?" Amelia requested. "I was supposed to meet -"

"I already did," Sole cut in, sliding their plates across the bar. "When you were running late and I didn't find you in your office, I knew you had something more pressing." Innocent intent slipping, she glanced toward Caton. "She never misses meetings."

Giving Sole a look that promised retribution for the unnecessary addendum, Amelia picked up her plate and headed toward the dining room.

"I'll bring you some drinks," Sole said, and Amelia heard Caton mumble her thanks before following.

Pulling out her usual chair at the nearest corner, Amelia watched Caton sink down at the head of the table. As they awaited Sole, they had an acceptable reason for their silence, but, once she came and went, there was simply no excuse for two people who had spent the day as they had being unable to talk to each other. Searching her repertoire of conversation pieces, though, Amelia found none satisfactory and had no idea what to say.

Sinking her fork into the pastry instead, she watched it split open and took her first bite, delighting in the decadence, as she had in so many things that day.

"Sole said you were born in Venezuela," Caton began softly, glancing at Amelia through shielded eyes.

Not sure whether to be flattered or concerned that Caton and Sole had talked about her, Amelia swallowed and nodded. "Caracas," she responded. "You?"

"Toledo... Ohio," Caton answered, taking a small bite and chewing thoughtfully, before glancing to Amelia again. "So, how did you end up here?"

The question was too much too soon, and Amelia felt her defenses engage at once, the strange serenity she felt slipping through her fingers. It was hardly Caton's fault. She couldn't possibly know what not to ask, but, still, Caton backpedaled instantly. "I mean," she qualified, "did you go to college here or something?"

"No," Amelia replied, feeling her heart slow in response to Caton's reversal. "I never went to college. I assume you did."

Nodding quickly, Caton tucked a somewhat larger bite into her mouth without elaborating, and minor amusement put a grin on Amelia's lips. "Are you going to tell me where?"

The way Caton looked at her, Amelia suspected Caton didn't think she would care, and the knowledge snaked through Amelia with a surprising twinge.

"The University of Michigan and Northwestern," Caton returned at last.

"What did you study?" Amelia encouraged.

"Philosophy, but I minored in sociology."

Nodding at the information, Amelia glanced toward her plate. "Explains the attraction to the social worker."

When Caton's eyes jumped to her, Amelia realized how jealous the words sounded. Even more surprising was that she felt it again, the jealousy. It rose out of nowhere, totally uninvited. Irritated, she cut a bite from the empanada and occupied her mouth. Stealing a glance at Caton, she watched the tines of Caton's fork move against her plate without purpose. "You don't like it?" she asked, pulling the cloth napkin from her lap to wipe her mouth.

"No, I do," Caton responded, but still didn't take a bite. Finally, she lowered the fork to the edge of the plate and sat back in the chair, looking Amelia full-on. "What's going to happen tomorrow?"

With the force of a shove, the question pressed Amelia back against the seat. She hadn't been expecting the day she'd just had. She couldn't begin to imagine the next. Picking up her glass, she took a drink, trying to decide on the proper response. "What do you mean?" she finally asked, taking the easy route of playing dumb.

"I mean, are you going to treat me like you have been treating me?" Caton asked with amazing calm. "Or are you going to treat me like this?"

Fair as the question was, it still made Amelia flinch. It was her chance to renege. Caton was expecting it. If she said, 'I think it's best if we keep things savage and bitter between us,' Caton would agree. Watching

Caton's gaze fall away, Amelia knew she would accept whatever response she was given.

"You don't have to answer that," Caton whispered at last, her hands clutching the tabletop as if she was trying to steady herself.

Caton was right. She didn't have to answer. It was one of the best things about Amelia's status in the world. She rarely had to answers questions she didn't want to, and most people let her get away with it.

Looking at Caton's fingertips, so delicate and attentive all day, turning to stone against the African mahogany, Amelia couldn't let the question go unanswered either. The need to atone for past behavior overriding her reservations, she slid her hand over Caton's, feeling the tension crackle beneath her palm. When Caton looked up at her, though, Amelia still didn't know what to say. This hadn't been her intent. She wasn't sure what her intent had been, but she knew the bolts that shot up her wrist and into her arm at barely touching Caton's hand wasn't it.

"Sole!" Jack's voice suddenly called from somewhere beyond the dining room, shattering the moment in an instant.

Looking to the door that led through the piano room and into the foyer, Caton ripped her hand from under Amelia's, dropping it to her lap, and Amelia sat back in her chair, eyes not leaving Caton until Sole led Jack into the dining room from the kitchen.

"What are you doing here?" Amelia asked, as Jack stepped up behind Caton, hand alighting on the back of her chair.

"I live here," he reminded her, leaning over Caton. "What are you doing here?"

"Sole made empanadas," Amelia replied quickly. "Caton wanted to try them."

"Hope you didn't eat my share," Jack said with a grin, hand moving from the back of Caton's chair to her shoulder.

"I'm sure there are plenty." Amelia gave her husband a glare that made him release Caton.

"Good," Jack said, turning to where Sole waited in the doorway. "Get me a plate. I'll join them."

Moving around the table to pull out the chair opposite Amelia, he made himself comfortable in an intimate moment that didn't belong to him, and Sole sent Amelia an apologetic glance before following the command.

"Actually..." Caton rushed to stand. "I have to go. Thank you for..." She glanced fleetingly in Amelia's direction, and Amelia leaned forward unconsciously, but, like Caton, could think of no appropriate way to finish the thought.

Whirling around, Caton escaped through the kitchen door, and Amelia stared after her, not entirely sure she wanted to stop her.

"Just you and me, Darling," Jack said, looking across the table with amusement bordering contempt. Pulling Caton's plate in front of him, he picked up the remainder of the empanada and stuffed it into his mouth, and, discovering she had no appetite after all, Amelia pushed her plate away.

25

For a moment, weak and unwise, Caton let herself believe.

She had been so good at discerning what was real and what wasn't, what she could and couldn't have from Amelia. Sitting at the table, though, away from the sexual intimacy, Amelia seemed almost... interested... in her.

Nothing had changed, though, nothing really could. Jack was a painful reminder of that. Amelia was still married, Caton was still the third party, and, when all was said and done, there would be nothing for her. It was an unwinnable game she never should have been playing in the first place.

Yet, when Caton walked into the kitchen the next day to find Amelia sitting at the bar, reading a newspaper and drinking her coffee in a relaxed fashion Caton had never seen on her, it looked as if everything had changed.

Amelia lifted her head, looking at Caton in a way Caton couldn't shake off even if she wanted to, as if she had been waiting for her, as if she was happy to see her.

"Good morning," Sole greeted, pouring Caton coffee without asking, and Caton didn't know whether to meet or avoid Amelia's eyes, so she chose a combination, glancing toward her and looking away before she could stare.

Taking the coffee that Sole slid across the bar, she tried to think of something to say that sounded normal, but couldn't find any normalcy in the room. "I guess I'll go on up," she mumbled, spinning toward the door. Though she was certain she looked ridiculous, it was safer to back away than walk straight into the patch of thorns so clearly visible.

Putting the mug down on the desk in her office, Caton noted the light tremble in it. She had just enough time to drop her bag into her chair and punch the computer on with more vigor than was necessary before the noise came at her back. She didn't need to turn to know it was Amelia, but felt compelled to turn anyway.

Leaning in the doorway, Amelia stared at her with a question she didn't bother to voice, stepping into the room instead, and, as unsteady as Caton felt on them, her feet took automatic steps to meet Amelia. Amelia's arms sliding around her waist, Caton tilted her head up, finding Amelia's seeking lips and sighing into the welcome sensation. Hands coming to rest on Amelia's upper arms, she was almost surprised to find her tangible.

Caton wondered if it was exactly the kind of thing from which she should have been running, to which she should have been putting her foot down and holding her ground. Letting herself believe that she could be any more than Amelia's few-month work fling was a wayward, impossible fantasy she couldn't afford to entertain. No matter how she felt in Amelia's arms.

Relaxing into the other woman's embrace, it was as if she had been waiting for it since she woke up. Maybe she had.

Composure Caton once thought was unshakable faltering for just an instant, Amelia glanced away, pulling Caton's mouth into a hesitant smile. She had seen Amelia surprised, flushed, wanton, but she had never seen Amelia genuinely flustered. "I have some work that I need you to help me with," Amelia finally said. "But maybe later we could do something else?"

Warm eyes returning to Caton's, they left little to the imagination, and Caton's entire body jumpstarted at the look alone. 'Now would be better,' she thought, staring at Amelia's lips, wondering how she had developed such a rapid addiction. Again, it occurred to her that she should try to resist, that what she was doing was unwise, that nothing good could come of it in the end.

"Okay," she breathed, despite all her logical reservations. Apparently no amount of reality could shake her from the feel of Amelia's arms around her by choice, or from her kiss that felt sincere.

It was the kind of path one could only veer from at the beginning. Once committed, the only available stops were the slow deceleration at the bottom or a painful one along the way.

When Caton followed Amelia into the same bedroom that afternoon, she knew it was her final chance to escape, her last opportunity to abandon the ride before there were only those two ends in sight. Amelia looked at Caton as if she wanted to be there with her, though, as if she was the only thing on Earth that mattered at that moment, and, if it was an illusion, it was an illusion that broke Caton's will.

Things weren't comfortable, they weren't easy, but over the following days, things were at least different enough that when she heard the sound of the piano floating up the stairway, Caton felt the freedom to get up from her desk to investigate. The logical part of her knew it must be Amelia, but she didn't believe it until she turned the corner into the piano room and saw her perched on the bench, fingers moving tentatively over the keys.

Amelia looked uncertain for a moment as she glanced up, missing several notes before she dropped her eyes back to her hands and regained her place, and Caton was almost afraid to approach, afraid Amelia would stop, that the surprising new information about Amelia would shrivel before her eyes.

Sliding over on the bench, though, Amelia didn't miss a beat, and Caton sat down in the space beside her, feeling the vibration through the body next to her every time Amelia hit a powerful chord. It was far from perfect, the song, but Caton heard only the right notes as she watched Amelia's fingers crawl the keys in front of her, reaching across her to hit the last high note, before Amelia pulled her hands away and glanced over.

"You play the piano." Caton saved the data to memory.

"Not very well." Amelia's gentle laugh was like a note left behind. "Not for a long time."

Her hands returning to the keys, they moved across them with obvious affection, and Caton wondered how many things Amelia had given up along the way to being the person she had become, a woman seemingly devoid of interests outside her desire to fulfill her proper place in society.

"It sounded good to me," Caton declared.

Eyes never leaving the piano, there was a sad tilt to Amelia's smile. "You would say that," she returned.

"Why?" Caton questioned in mock offense. "You think I have no musical talent?"

"I think you're..." Amelia breathed instantly, stopping herself, and Caton wished she knew what she was really going to say. "You're careful about what you say to people. You try to be tactful."

With a light laugh, Caton leaned into Amelia's shoulder, the desire to touch her too strong to resist. "Not with everyone," she reminded her. "Not with you two months ago."

"Well, that didn't turn out that bad," Amelia replied, finger pressing a key to send a single tone through the room. "And you could have been worse. God knows I was. But things have changed, haven't they?"

The question felt overwhelmingly intimate, and when Amelia looked over at her, Caton didn't know if she should answer. If she could. These moments between them, increasing in frequency, always felt so authentic, but they were always so fleeting.

Hand rising to Amelia's face, Caton allowed herself an indulgence, savoring the feel of Amelia's heat and skin beneath her fingertips, before brushing her lips against Amelia's, scarcely believing she had gained such standing that she could do so without question, still somewhat afraid Amelia would pull rank.

Sighing, Amelia turned into her, mouth opening, tongue sliding between Caton's lips, and Caton responded the only way she knew how, by giving Amelia exactly what she wanted. It had been only hours since they last left the bedroom, but she knew they would end up there again.

Fully invested in the feel of Amelia's tongue dueling with her own, Caton hardly registered Amelia's hand grasping hers and guiding it down her body until it came to rest against the heated fabric between Amelia's thighs. Pulling her lips from Amelia's, she dropped her gaze to the hand, fingertips teasing ever so lightly against the seam of Amelia's pants, and smiled when Amelia shifted against them.

Hands going to her waist, Amelia unfastened her pants with dexterous fingers, urging Caton's hand inside, and Caton's fingers slipped beneath the fabric of her panties, her free hand going to Amelia's back when it looked as if she might keel backward off the bench.

Caton was well aware of where they sat, of the uncovered windows that would provide a perfect view from the right vantage point, but Amelia didn't seem to care how exposed they were, or that Sole could walk in at any moment.

Rising enough to throw one leg across the bench, Caton turned Amelia without ceasing the touch, drawing a gasp from Amelia as she pulled her closer, hissing at the upswell of sensation as Amelia's body pressed back between her legs.

Amelia relaxed against her, arching from the bench to give Caton more access, and, free hand slipping beneath the soft cashmere of Amelia's sweater, Caton felt Amelia's stomach muscles tighten with need, tension fluttering against her fingertips, as Amelia reached back, hand threading through Caton's hair to pull her closer.

Breathing in the hair at her face, Caton latched onto an exposed patch of skin on Amelia's neck, drawing from the spot until Amelia moaned in response, the sound reverberating through both of them, as Amelia's thrusts grew more desperate against Caton's hand.

The sound of the front door invading on their intimacy, they froze as one, both sets of eyes going to the open pocket doors to the foyer as footsteps fell against the marble floor. Extracting her hands hastily from Amelia's body, Caton watched Amelia scramble to her feet, struggling to find her footing and refasten her pants. She had just straightened her sweater when a teenage girl, whom Caton would have recognized at once as Amelia's offspring even if there wasn't a photo of her sitting two feet away, walked into the room.

Turning toward the doorway, Amelia's face froze upon seeing her daughter, before her shock broke into a sincere, surprised smile. "Selene."

"Yeah." Selene shrugged as if her mother wasn't staring at her as if she was the most amazing thing ever created.

"You're home." Amelia's voice held a touch of wonder.

"I told Dad I was coming," Selene stated. "He didn't tell you?"

Anger tightening her smile, Amelia shook her head. "No," she uttered, shaking it off as quickly as it appeared. "But I am so happy you're here."

Amelia sounded happy, she looked happy, but, moving slowly toward her daughter, she also appeared overly-cautious, as if she thought Selene might slip away from her. Watching from the corner of her eye, Caton knew she too was infringing on a private moment, but she still watched as Amelia pulled Selene into an awkward embrace, the cashmere at her neck slipping slightly, revealing the deep red mark Caton had just left on her skin.

Pulling away before Amelia was ready to let her go, Selene didn't seem interested enough in her mother to notice. Staring blankly at Amelia, her expression was disturbingly familiar to Caton. It was the same look Amelia had worn like a mask when she first met her.

"Where's Dad?" Selene asked.

"He's at work," Amelia returned.

"Who's that?" Selene finally cast her eyes in Caton's direction, and Caton tried not to be intimidated by the glare of a teenager.

When Amelia glanced toward her, eyes warming as a small smile curved her lips, it eased Caton's growing discomfort. "This is Caton. She works here."

"What happened to Sole?" Selene questioned at once, finally showing some emotion.

"She's still here," Amelia assured her with a smile, laying a hesitant hand on her daughter's arm. "Caton is my assistant."

"Oh, okay." Selene shrugged out of Amelia's touch. "I'm going up to my room."

"Okay, but..." Amelia stepped forward as Selene turned and walked from the room. "Do you need anything?" she called into the hall.

"No," Selene's dull voice returned, and, no reason left to fake it, Amelia's smile fell from her lips.

Staring at the space where her daughter had just been, it took Amelia a moment to remember she wasn't alone. "That was Selene," she stated, turning back to Caton at the piano.

"I gathered," Caton said softly, sliding off the bench and approaching her cautiously, afraid of breaking the other woman with a wrong word, because, as unbelievable as the sight was, Amelia looked that fragile.

"I didn't know she was coming," Amelia uttered, more to herself than to Caton. "She was supposed to be in Germany with friends. I wonder what happened."

"You could go ask her," Caton suggested, observing Amelia carefully for reaction.

"What?" Amelia returned absently, glancing to Caton before returning her gaze to the empty doorway. "Oh, no. No. She'll come down when she's ready."

Nodding without comprehension, Caton could think of nothing consoling to say "Do you want me to leave?" she asked, dreading Amelia's response.

Eyes whirling toward her, Amelia frowned. "No, of course not," she returned. "But we probably shouldn't..."

"No," Caton agreed, stepping closer to Amelia anyway, the heat radiating between them serving as momentary consolation.

"I'm sorry," Amelia whispered.

"Don't be sorry," Caton returned. "Your daughter is home. I know that makes you happy." Recalling the few things Amelia had said about Selene in the quiet, unguarded moments when they had to catch their breath, she watched Amelia find her smile again. "I'm here to work, so I'll work. If nothing else, I know where there's plenty of filing."

Laughing softly, Amelia's eyes roamed her face, and Caton wanted to know how, in all their recent conversations that sounded like honesty, she never picked up on the fact that Amelia's relationship with Selene was fractured.

"I'm going to go up to my office," she stated, backing away before the desire to ask such questions became impossible to deny.

Amelia nodded her agreement, adding to the silence, and Caton stepped through the doorway with no idea how she would survive the days to come. It wasn't long ago that pining for Amelia from a distance was her only option, and the last thing she wanted was to be reduced to that sorry state again. At the very least, she wished she could be happy for Amelia, but, as far as Caton could see, there had been little happiness in the reunion between mother and daughter.

Halfway up the stairs, the blaring sound of bass-heavy club music cut into Caton's thoughts. Rounding the banister and turning into her office, she watched the frames on the wall rattle and knew it would be one very long holiday.

26

By the third day of Selene's homecoming, Amelia was already tired of the constant battle. All she had wanted was Selene home, but now that she was there, Amelia couldn't help but wonder if it would have been better for their relationship if Selene had stayed on the other side of the Atlantic.

Her daughter still had nothing but contempt for her. It was clear with every action, with every word, with every irritated look Selene turned her way when Amelia attempted to talk to her. It was most clear, though, in the way Selene jumped up from the table as Jack walked in the first night and hugged him as if he was her knight in shining armor, after saying no more than ten words to Amelia throughout dinner.

Casting her eyes away, Amelia let it go as she always had, allowing Selene to use Jack to get back at her without comment. If Amelia had any belief at all in equitability, she might have deemed it unfair, but she had long given up the idealistic notion that people were judged as they deserved to be judged. Jack's good fortune was tied to Amelia's misfortune. But, then, it had been that way for many years.

Truth, in their family, was a complicated thing. She and her daughter, they weren't enemies. They were on the same side. That was the reality of the situation. When the other side held all the power, though, it was sometimes hard to see where the lines were drawn. Laying out the facts might have given Selene more sympathy for her, but there were some things her daughter simply would never need to know.

Every day Amelia tried, and every day she got the same lackluster responses. There were moments when she wanted nothing more than to say 'fuck it,' call Caton to her, and spend her days as she had before Selene's arrival. As it was, each moment she'd had with Caton was fleeting, each kiss stolen, and it occurred to Amelia how much she missed their afternoons in bed. How much she missed Caton.

Ephemeral escape wasn't going to fix what was broken, though, if anything could, so Amelia chose to overlook Selene's attitude. Every snarky response, every angry glare, every time her daughter ignored her, Amelia only tried harder, believing each time that they could return to the place they were at only a few years before, but that seemed like a foreign land now.

It was when she made the most effort that Selene fought against her the hardest, so Amelia knew waking Selene to announce she had planned a full day for them - shopping, which Selene loved, lunch, a ride through the park, which Selene once loved - would end in a fight. The same announcement that would have made her daughter giddy not that long ago was taken like punishment of the highest order.

After sitting up with an abundance of drama to complain about it from the pile of covers for five minutes, Selene finally got out of bed, slamming the door of her bathroom on the way to shower, and Amelia thought it had dawned on her daughter that it was a done deal and she would simply have to endure her mother's presence for an entire day.

She was in her office, writing a note to Caton, when Selene reappeared. Why she felt the need to explain her presence or lack thereof to Caton, Amelia wasn't entirely sure, but it felt wrong somehow to be gone without explanation.

"How close are you?" Selene was asking someone, as she breezed by the doorway without even a glance, and Amelia hurried out of her chair.

"Selene." She stepped into the hall behind her, and, though she was sure she had been heard, Selene didn't look back.

"Yeah, I'll see you soon," Selene stated, pulling her phone from her ear and shoving it into her pocket.

"Who was that?" Amelia asked, trailing her daughter down the stairs.

"Kaley."

"Why did you tell her you would see her?" Amelia tried to keep calm as Selene came to a stop at the mirror in the foyer to push her hair from her eyes. It had been hanging that way since she woke up, the same untamable lock Selene had from birth, and Amelia had fought the urge to reach out to her daughter and push it back multiple times during the morning's debate.

"They're going to the mall," Selene returned. "And since somebody woke me up, I'm going too."

"No, you're not," Amelia declared, the tremor in her voice turning to anger as Selene rolled her eyes in the mirror and walked off. Rushing into her path, Amelia halted her progress. "Call her back and tell her you can't go."

"No."

"We are going shopping," Amelia stated, knowing she was much too wound up about a day at some damn boutiques. "We are going to the park."

"A carriage ride in the park?" Selene countered, looking at her with disdain that Amelia couldn't help but feel. "You are so fucking lame! That is so fucking stupid!"

"You didn't used to think that," Amelia replied softly, though she knew it was a flimsy response. Selene used to love sitting on her lap on those rides too. These days, Amelia wondered if her daughter would wrap her arms around her to save her life if she were choking.

"I already told her I would go," Selene countered, walking past her as if the fact determined the outcome.

Amelia considered letting it. At least with Selene gone she would have a few hours when she didn't have to be on edge. She could probably send Selene off every day of her visit. After that, Selene could return to school, and things could go right back to the way they had been. The same, but from a distance.

The thought of sending Selene away again with the same walls between them spurred Amelia back into action, and she trailed her daughter through the living room. "Well, call her back and tell her you can't." She felt as if she had been doing nothing but repeating herself since Selene's arrival.

"But I can," Selene tossed back. "It's not like you planned anything monumental. We can do your stupid day later."

"I want to do it today."

"Well, then do it alone," Selene uttered, disappearing through the doorway.

Stopping for a breath, Amelia felt the sting of her nails digging into her palms, and tried to loosen the tension, already halfway to a headache, as she followed her daughter into the kitchen.

She expected Sole to be there, pretending, as usual, not to hear a word being screamed in the next room. She didn't, however, expect Caton, and it was clear Caton didn't expect to be a spectator. Sitting at the bar, she kept her eyes on her mug as Amelia pulled up short at her presence, before returning her eyes to Selene, who dropped her purse on the end of the bar to start yanking open cabinet doors.

"What are you doing?" Amelia asked as calmly as possible.

"I'm looking for something to eat," Selene returned.

"I can make you something." Sole found her opportunity to intervene, and Selene stopped her invasion of the kitchen, leaving the cabinets hanging open, knowing they would be closed for her. It was a very Jack behavior that made Amelia even more livid than usual.

"I'll take toast," Selene said, not bothering with 'please' or 'thank you' as she went to the fridge and pulled open the door. "Wrap it up for me, okay?"

"No, Sole," Amelia corrected. "She isn't going anywhere."

"Yes, I am." Selene sent a glare her way.

"No, you're not," Amelia declared. "You are going to eat, and then you are getting in the car and we are going out. Together."

"Jesus Christ!" Selene shouted. "You already didn't want me to go to Germany with my friends. Thank God Daddy was going to let me."

"That's because I wanted you to come home," Amelia couldn't stop her voice from breaking. She wished, just once, she could make Selene understand.

"And now that Lisa's parents said she could only bring one person and I got dropped like a loser and stuck here, you won't even let me see my friends?"

"I want to spend time with you," Amelia pleaded.

"Well, I don't want to spend time with you! I hate you!" Selene returned, and Amelia lapsed into silence.

She was well aware. It was impossible to be unaware of the fact, but somehow hearing Selene say it with such conviction made it more real. Throat tightening, she refused to let the tears that formed in her eyes, despite her lifetime of training, fall. Tossing her head back and blinking them away, she turned her gaze to the snow lightly covering the back yard.

When Selene's phone rang, she pulled it from her pocket, glancing at the screen and looking up as if she was ready to further argue her position, but Amelia had heard more than enough. "Go," she said, looking across the room at her daughter, and Selene hesitated, but not long enough that it didn't hurt when she left and her retreating footsteps echoed through the kitchen.

With nowhere to go, Amelia didn't bother to move. Looking up as a hand gently grasped her side, she wondered how she hadn't heard Caton's approach.

"Are you all right?" Caton softly questioned, stepping closer until her thigh brushed against Amelia's, but Amelia's body felt numb and the touch brought no comfort.

"Of course." Amelia returned to her game face, the one that always convinced everyone her house was perpetually full of fresh flowers when it was overrun by weeds. "I'm fine."

Glancing toward the doorway, Caton frowned. "Does she always talk to you that way?"

"That's none of your business," Amelia snapped, and Caton's hand retracted instantly. She'd been wrong, she realized at once. Caton's touch had brought comfort.

When Caton tried to leave by the same exit through which she just watched her daughter walk out, Amelia thrust her arm in front of her to impede her departure. "I'm sorry," she breathed. "I didn't mean that." Hand falling to a warm hip, she drew a dubious Caton back toward her.

"I'm going to make sure they got over that patch of ice in the driveway," Sole said, heading toward the dining room door.

"Thank you, Sole," Amelia responded as she left them, returning her attention to Caton, who didn't particularly look as if she wanted to be alone with her.

"You're right," Caton rasped. "It is none of my business."

Fingers spreading up Caton's back to persuade her closer, despite some resistance, Amelia sighed as Caton's body gave in to her own. "It is if you want it to be," she whispered.

With a shake of her head, Caton looked away, and Amelia thought she had said too much. It was true, and, yet, she wasn't even sure what she meant by it.

"Is it?" Caton asked. "Is anything about you my business?"

"I have told you things about me," Amelia argued, the accusation striking her as incredibly unfair. Over the past days, she had told Caton more than 99.9 percent of the people in her life would ever know about her.

"Have you, Amelia?" The soft question broke through Amelia's certainty. "What do I know about you? What do you know about me?"

Pausing to consider - really consider - the question, Amelia knew what Caton meant, as much as she wanted to pretend she didn't. Caton did know more than 99.9 percent of the people in Amelia's life, but that didn't take much. And though it felt as if she knew Caton, when she tried to recall the things she knew, she realized they were in short supply.

"What do you want to know?" she uttered, hands clutching tighter to Caton, afraid of what she would ask, but more afraid that Caton would decide her not worth knowing.

"What about Selene?" Caton returned at once.

"I did tell you about Selene," Amelia stated. Selene was the one thing she knew she would never fail to mention.

"That she was in boarding school and you wished she was home, and about her love of photography and swimming and telenovelas. Not..." Caton threw her hand toward the doorway, making her point.

"She's a teenager." Amelia attempted to play it off on instinct.

"Really?" Caton questioned, anger, or pain, tightening her face. "That's what you want to say right now?"

"What do you want me to say?" Amelia countered.

"Nothing," Caton shook her head, her eyes on Amelia dejected, as if she knew there was no point to the conversation "I will only get half the truth anyway, right?" she asked. "The story you've edited for the masses."

There was truth in that too. Caton had gotten more from her, whether she believed it or not, but the stories were edited. They had to be.

Feeling the tension in Caton's body where there could have been something so much better, Amelia silently cursed her timing. If Caton had come only a few minutes later, she wouldn't have to know any of this, and they could be spending their time alone together as they should be.

"It's complicated, Caton," she uttered.

"Do you think this is not complicated for me?!" Caton's sudden outburst surprised Amelia. It sounded like anger, but when Caton took a deep breath before looking up, tears threatened behind her eyes, and Amelia knew the anger was tempered by something more profound.

Hand winding into Caton's hair, Amelia gently fisted it, and Caton allowed her. Tilting Caton's head back until she could capture her lips, Amelia reveled in the feel of Caton's arms sliding around her waist, of Caton's body pressing closer. She hadn't been deprived of Caton long enough to be desperate, but, as she relinquished everything, both bad and good, to the sensation of Caton's lips, to the feel of their bodies pressing against each other, Amelia felt undeniably needy.

"No, Selene, wait..." Sole's voice came from the doorway an instant too late, and, reluctantly breaking away from the sweet haven of Caton's lips, Amelia opened her eyes to discover her daughter staring at her with a thunderstruck expression.

"Mom," Selene uttered, eyes flicking briefly to Caton before returning to stare at Amelia. "What in the hell are you doing?"

Too in shock to do anything, Amelia felt the chill as Caton backed away from her. Trying to figure out what she should and shouldn't say, she glanced to Caton and found a reserve of calm. "What did it look like?" she asked, and Selene's mouth dropped open, as if she had been expecting some kind of explanation that would negate what she had seen with her own eyes.

A scoffing smile coming to her face, Selene marched back across the kitchen, grabbing her purse from the counter and throwing it onto her shoulder, before returning to the doorway with a sneer and something disturbingly like satisfaction in her voice. "I'm telling Daddy," she proclaimed, whirling on her heel and pushing past Sole into the living room.

Filled suddenly with every ounce of rage she hadn't let herself feel in three years of her daughter's unfair incivility, Amelia followed Selene from the room. "Go ahead," she prodded, stopping at the back of the sofa as Selene turned to look back at her. "Tell your father."

"I will," Selene shot back, conviction, or something else, shaking in her voice.

"Well, at least I will finally know where we stand," Amelia bit out angrily. "If you want to pretend that what I am doing is somehow worse than the way your father has treated me for the past two decades, then you go right ahead and tell him. I tried to protect you, but I know I couldn't have done that good a job of it."

Staring back at her for a moment, more in shock at the unforgiving response than at walking into the kitchen to find her mother kissing another woman, Selene finally turned and fled. Whether it was to try to stop Selene from leaving that way or to give Amelia privacy, Sole trailed Selene back to the foyer, and, suddenly exhausted, Amelia leaned on the back of the sofa, her arms barely holding her upright.

In the residual silence, she wished she hadn't said it, and was glad that she did. She didn't want Selene to hate her father, she had always tried to uphold Jack in the eyes of his daughter, but she was tired of being the target of her daughter's hatred when Jack was the one who had earned it.

"I'm sorry." Amelia heard Caton's hesitant voice at her back, and realized she preferred it when Caton was telling her exactly what she was going to do in no uncertain terms. Most of her life, Amelia had fought to keep things under her control, when what she really needed was guidance.

Pushing off the sofa, she turned to Caton, who looked achingly bright against the dark backdrop of Amelia's life. Weeks ago, even days ago, she might have blamed her. It would have been the simplest emotion to find.

Against the tide of her other feelings, though, Amelia couldn't find any rage left. "You can make it up to me," she murmured, reaching out for Caton's hand and tugging her against her, finding a streak of serenity in the intimate press of their bodies.

"That's not...," Caton shook her head, hand rising to Amelia's chest to keep her gently at bay. "Amelia." Caton searched her eyes, and, unable to endure the close examination, Amelia glanced away, though she couldn't quite bring herself to step out of Caton's touch. "You have to fix this. I don't know what this is between the two of you, but if there is one thing I do know, it is how much you love your daughter. You can't let it go like this."

Feeling the tears forming again, Amelia couldn't contain them. Perhaps, without realizing it, she didn't feel the need to try. "She really does hate me," she whispered, returning her eyes to Caton and feeling the first hot tear drip onto her cheek. It felt almost unnatural, and she tried to remember the last time she had actually let one fall.

"Why?" Caton watched the drop with fascination, and Amelia brushed it quickly away.

"Oh, I'm sure you can think of at least a hundred reasons she should," she attempted to lighten the conversation, but Caton neither laughed nor retreated.

Pressing closer instead, Caton's arm curved around Amelia's waist, and Amelia sagged against her, not sure how she had been standing on her own. "Don't you even want to try to fix it?" Caton gently questioned.

"I can't," Amelia admitted, more tears slipping free to run down her cheeks. "I have been trying."

"Then, try again," Caton whispered, and when her hand slipped beneath the back of Amelia's shirt to rest against skin, her warmth infused Amelia, pushing out the rest of the cold. "When will she leave?"

Surprised at the question, and distracted by the patterns Caton's warm fingers drew against her back, Amelia took a moment to find her thoughts. "The first week of January, I suppose," she answered. "Nobody really tells me anything."

Nodding, Caton's other hand slid onto her side, and Amelia couldn't decide which touch to lean into.

"I'm going to take off until then," Caton announced.

"No." Amelia's awareness focused immediately. Hands clutching Caton's shoulders, she tried to hang on. "I need you here."

"I am the last thing you need here," Caton softly countered.

Meeting Caton's eyes, Amelia knew she was going to do it regardless. Even if she wanted Caton to be wrong, to retract it, to say she couldn't go, she wouldn't go, Amelia knew that Caton leaving, temporarily, was the right thing for all of them.

"What if I do need you?" The words sounded desperate, but even her pride didn't stop her arms from closing around Caton in a last ditch effort to change both their minds.

"You know how to find me," Caton returned, leaning in to kiss Amelia so fleetingly Amelia wondered if their lips touched at all, and stepping away before Amelia could protest.

Caton's steps across the kitchen and through the opposite side of the house were so quiet, she may as well have been gone the instant she left the room. Amelia knew when she was truly gone, though. The entire mood of the house seemed to change, and she felt alone, abandoned, though she knew she had no right to feel either of those things.

Caton wasn't her keeper. She hadn't signed up for any of this. She had been recruited in all areas, and no one could ask her for more than she wanted to give.

27

With no worthy means of distraction, all day Amelia wondered how she could explain something to Selene she didn't fully understand herself. She thought she knew what she was doing with Caton when it started, but she could control only some of the turns taken, and, as she was discovering with trepidation, only so much of what she felt.

The more time that ticked away without Selene coming home or even bothering to call her, though, the less Amelia felt the need to explain herself. Not for the last few months. Not for Caton. She had spent Selene's entire life making poor decisions based on necessity, and had never once bothered to justify those to her daughter. Bad or good, she wasn't about to explain one of the few choices she'd made that had brought her any pleasure at all.

By the time Amelia finally heard footsteps outside Selene's bedroom door, it was well after midnight. Jack had already come home and gone to bed. When he asked the whereabouts of Selene, Amelia told him she was out with friends, feeling no need to elaborate on how it came about and bring an undeserved smile to his face.

Knob turning silently, the door creaked open, and Amelia watched Selene jump in the doorway. "Jesus, Mom," she snapped, and Amelia calmly slid the bookmark back into her book. "What are you doing in here?"

"Waiting for you." Amelia pushed up from the chair in the corner and tugged at the comforter on the mattress, smoothing it to perfection.

"I'm tired," Selene said. "Can we do this later?"

"It won't take long," Amelia stated, inspecting Selene and trying to determine what she might have been doing all day. She appeared sober, sounded her usual irritable self, so Amelia was sure it was nothing unseemly. More likely, it was of the most wholesome variety, making cookies and singing carols and drinking cider with someone else's family. Losing nerve at the notion, she tightened her fingers around the edge of the book until they made imprints on the cover. "You're grounded for the rest of your break," she finally said.

"What?" Selene fired back. "*I'm* grounded because I saw *you* making out with that slut?"

"She's not a slut." Amelia didn't even realize how prickly she was about the subject until it was broached, and she trained warning eyes on her daughter. "Don't call her that again."

Selene seemed to realize she had overstepped one of the few boundaries she'd ever been given, swallowing as her gaze fell to the floor.

"That is not why you're grounded," Amelia went on. "You are grounded for talking to me like I am one of the students you don't like at your school. Even if you don't want me to be your mother, you will treat me with the same respect with which you treat other adults."

"You can't ground me," Selene muttered.

"Actually, I can," Amelia corrected her. "I'm your mother."

"I'll tell Daddy what I saw," Selene threatened instantly.

"Yes, you already said that," Amelia reminded her, moving around the end of the bed. Walking past her daughter without another word, she expected to leave things that way. Far from good, they were also no worse than they had been for the past few years, which was good enough for one night.

And one night was all Amelia really had. The situation would rectify itself for Selene in the morning. As soon as she told Jack she was grounded, he would pardon her from both the offense and the punishment, with or without knowing what she had done. Selene wouldn't even have to ply him with her intel. Jack always overruled Amelia's attempts at discipline for the sole purpose of reminding her of his authority.

"Who is she?" Selene's quiet voice halted Amelia's retreat, and she turned to find her daughter looking far more confused than angry.

Heart pounding in a way it hadn't during the familiar routine of the fight, Amelia wasn't sure she was ready for that particular conversation. "I told you, she's my assistant," she answered simply.

"Yeah, but, I mean...," Selene started uneasily. "So, you're sleeping with her?"

Taking a breath that did nothing to soothe her nerves, Amelia realized she should have prepared for the line of questioning. It was just such a past trait of Selene's, the kind of in-depth curiosity her daughter hadn't shown in some time, at least not toward her. "Yes," Amelia responded, not wanting to lie.

Selene dropped her gaze, and Amelia almost used the opportunity to flee, to leave as she had intended and spare herself any further flailing. At the door, though, she realized she didn't want to go anywhere. She wanted Selene to ask whatever she wanted to ask, just glad Selene wanted to ask her anything.

As Selene at last looked up, she struggled with the anxiety behind her eyes, biting her lip like she was withholding something she was afraid to say out loud, and, chest instantly tight, Amelia took an encouraging step back into the room.

"Have you ever done anything like this before?" The move drew the question from Selene, so quietly Amelia could just make out the words. "I know Daddy has, but you... you haven't, have you?"

The pain prevalent in the question, it occurred to Amelia how much Selene might worry about turning out like either one of her parents. Neither of them had been particularly good role models, and God knew Amelia wanted Selene to follow in neither of their footsteps. She could hardly blame her daughter for fearing which of their horrible personality traits she might inherit. Even if it hurt.

"No," Amelia assured her. "I have never had an affair with anyone else."

"Then, why are you doing it now?" Selene questioned weakly.

Breath rushing from Amelia in an unsteady exhalation, she searched for the answer on the light purple accent wall of Selene's bedroom, finding it creeping up inside her instead, sending a shiver through her as she tried to reject her own thoughts.

She couldn't explain to her daughter that she had watched Caton and found her mesmerizing, that she had challenged her and found her reactions exhilarating. Selene surely understood by now that her elevated status in society made people defer to her, that money made them blind, made them hold their tongues, that power made them fear and submit. Caton wasn't blind, she wasn't afraid, and God knew she couldn't hold her tongue, Amelia thought with a smile. And when Caton submitted, she did so by choice. At least, Amelia could believe that, and Caton's behavior since seemed to prove it. Whatever else Amelia was feeling had no explanation in reality. Not in hers.

"Are you in love with her?" The question came as such a shock, Amelia put her hand on the doorframe to steady herself.

She hadn't thought about it. Not in those words. Nor did she particularly want to think about it in those words. Opening her mouth, her instinct was to say 'no,' to push the suggestion away without deeper consideration, but, realizing outright denial felt like a lie, she clutched the frame more firmly to keep from sinking to her knees. "I don't know," she breathed, looking to Selene for reaction, surprised when Selene only nodded in response.

"Is she nice?" Selene asked, and Amelia watched the look of interrogation fall from her face, leaving behind a more neutral expression as Selene let her purse drop from her shoulder and tossed it onto the bed.

"She's nice to me," Amelia replied, and Selene's mouth twitched up, only for an instant, but Amelia chose to hold it as the only truth.

"That's good," Selene said.

Managing a shaky smile, Amelia took the momentary peace as the right time to leave, not sure whether it was a real truce or the calm before the storm. "You should get some sleep," she said.

"Okay," Selene nodded, glancing at her impeccably-made bed before looking back at Amelia in the doorway. "Am I still grounded?"

"Yes," Amelia stated firmly. "Goodnight."

When Selene didn't return the sentiment, Amelia worried it was all just a show to have her sentence revoked. It seemed genuine, but a lot of things that appeared real in Amelia's world turned out to be illusion, and she wondered if things would ever be right between them again as she turned to the hallway.

"Mom." Selene's fragile voice pulled her to a stop once more. Looking back, Amelia saw a different girl standing there, one who was more open, one who still trusted her. "I just want to come home."

Tears pooling in Selene's eyes, Amelia closed her own eyes for a moment against the pain she saw reflected back at her. She always hoped she could protect Selene from it, but it was clear that, even with her own daughter, her power was limited. "I know," she said. "I'm sorry." It did nothing, it had no real use, but apology was all she could give her. "Do you want to talk about it?"

"No." Selene shook her head. "I really am tired. I just want to go to bed."

Nodding in reluctant acceptance, Amelia backed out of the room.

"But, maybe tomorrow?" Selene added.

Of the many unexpected twists the day had taken, the simple request was most surprising of all. "I'm free all day," Amelia uttered, and the smile Selene produced was weak, but real.

"Night, Mom," she whispered.

"Goodnight, Mija." Amelia returned the smile, pulling the door closed behind her.

Alone in the hall, she placed her hand against the cool wood and released a stale breath, not even attempting to figure out where things had gone so right. Feeling the tears rise to the surface, she moved away from Selene's door, making it down the first few stairs, before finally sinking onto them. Hand wrapping around a carved post, Amelia leaned her head against it, letting the tears fall, the steady stream impeded by broken laughter, as she realized, for the first time in what felt like forever, they were happy.

28

Caton didn't expect Amelia to call. Though she had looked the picture of vulnerability when Caton left her standing in her front room, Caton knew Amelia was far from helpless. She didn't need reinforcements to handle her own family. She didn't truly need Caton for anything.

Despite knowing that well, when the gift basket arrived at her door, Caton still felt like she'd been jilted. There was no identifying information, but the courier knew her name, was adamant in telling her he had already been tipped, and there was only one place from which it could have come. Overflowing with the type of luxury holiday fare Caton assumed they would be dining on in the Halston Palace, it seemed to say, 'Since you're alone and will be spending the holiday season outside our magical realm, here are some items you can't afford to buy yourself.'

It was also more food than she could eat in a year, so Caton lumbered the over-sized basket down the stairs and into her car Christmas Eve morning, trying to find some gratitude that Amelia had acknowledged her at all and trying not to think about how slowly time had been going without the prospect of Amelia suddenly appearing to drag her away for a few hours of libidinous delight.

Moving the monstrosity from one place to the other was difficult enough without obstacles, so she didn't even attempt to maneuver the basket into the backseat. Plopping it down in the passenger side, she pulled the seatbelt across it, and it rode next to her like a stand-in for something she didn't have.

The second she pulled into the driveway, it seemed, her dad was yanking her door open and dragging her from the driver's seat to wrap her up in a giant bear hug Caton made no attempt to escape. When he asked what he could carry, Caton pointed him to the basket and spared herself the shame and wound-licking of having to haul the sufficiently jumbled gift inside.

Walking through the front door of the house in which she grew up, the smells of the holidays assaulted her senses before she stepped around the half wall into the living room to discover that her father's enthusiasm for the season had spilled over into his decorating again. The tree, two times too big for the space, sported twice as many lights as it needed, and barely a pine needle was to be seen beneath the garland and icicles. The train chugging through the Christmas town on the nearby table played a carol as it went, and every Christmas-themed stuffed animal Caton or her two brothers had ever owned had found its way out of the closet and into her dad's motif.

It was almost ridiculous, the wonderland of hope and cheer, glaring against the melancholy in which Caton had let her thoughts hold her prisoner over the past few days. Laura was out of town being a saint, Amelia was busy with her family, Caton missed one considerably more than the other, and she knew it was the wrong one to miss. By her own choice, she was heading straight into a mess of heartache. Yet, in her childhood home, life went on, so joyful and festive, it was almost mocking.

"Caton!" her mother shouted, rushing into the room to capture Caton in the iron vice of her embrace.

Smiling automatically, Caton hugged her back, before a flash of memory transported her to Selene's unexpected homecoming and the uncomfortable steps with which Amelia approached her daughter. Wondering what it must be like to have such distant family relations, she frowned slightly as she pulled away.

"Are you okay?" her mom asked in concern.

"Yeah." Caton forced the thought of Amelia from her mind. "Just a long drive."

"Well, come into the kitchen," her mom ordered. "Come on. I've got all kinds of fresh cookies, and we'll make coffee."

Taking her coat off, Caton tossed it at the couch and allowed herself to be bustled into the kitchen, sending the gift basket a small glare when she saw it sitting on the table.

"Where'd that come from?" her mother asked, busying herself making the coffee.

"I got it from someone," Caton said, with all the casualness she could muster. "It's yours now."

Coffee finally dripping, her mom positively shined with excitement as she stalked toward the massive variety gift and the unknown treasures within, like an explorer on a hunt. "You haven't even opened it?" she asked.

"No," Caton returned dismissively, wishing she could share in her mother's good humor. "I won't eat it."

Getting up from the table as her mom pulled the ribbon and let the cellophane fall with childlike glee around the edges of the basket, Caton grabbed two mugs from the cabinet and filled them, listening to the oohs and ahhs at her mom's findings. "Are you sure you don't want any of this?" she asked.

"I'll have some of it while I'm here. I'm sure there will be nothing left by the time I leave," Caton said, finally smiling as she imagined her brothers making short work of the massive quantity of food in one late-night holiday face-stuffing.

"Hmm." Her mom hummed thoughtfully, and Caton froze at the unexpected tone. She knew that hum. It was the same one her mother used whenever she caught her at something punishable as a kid. "I think you'll want this. It has your name on it."

Looking over her shoulder at once, Caton's eyes fell to the silver box, held together at the edges with red silk, a small envelope tucked behind the ribbon at the corner. Given a look that was far too inquisitive as she stepped back to take it from her mother's hand, Caton ignored it, watching her mom return to the basket and pretend to focus her attention elsewhere.

Turning back to the counter, Caton slid the envelope from the ribbon, thumb swiping beneath the metallic sticker that held the flap in place, and pulled the small white rectangle from inside, watching the words appear little by little, like an oasis rising on a barren landscape.

Thinking of you.

That was all, penned in red ink in Amelia's unmistakable handwriting, half severe angles and half large, flowing curves, a personal calligraphy, as much a contradiction as the woman herself. Just seeing the scrawl, Caton was hit by the same undeniable sense of longing that had plagued her for days. She shouldn't miss Amelia. After all that had happened between them, with so few days that could have been considered civil, there was no place for such a visceral reaction to knowing what she was without. She wasn't even sure if she ever really had it.

Pressing the card back into the envelope, Caton closed the flap against prying eyes and her own uncomfortable thoughts and placed it name-down on the counter. For a moment, she considered seeking privacy, but knew it would only result in a barrage of questions that she would eventually answer anyway. To spare herself the foreseen interrogation, she slipped the ribbon from one corner of the box. It fell in a slack pile of red as she moved her hand to the lid, almost afraid to open it.

Trembling fingers at last easing it off, Caton dropped the lid to the counter and pulled back the light swath of fabric inside, biting her lip to suppress a gasp or an expletive, not sure which would escape her mouth if she let it open. The moon and star pendant might have been mistaken for highest-quality silver if Caton didn't know the giver so well. Intimately-acquainted as she had become with Amelia, she could only guess how much those four small diamonds set in platinum and sapphire had to cost.

"Is that real?" Her mother didn't bother to stifle her gasp, leaning in over Caton's shoulder, mouth slightly agape.

"No." Caton forced a laugh. "I'm certain it isn't." She was certain it was, and Caton could see the disbelieving look her mother wore from the side of her eye.

"It looks real to me," she declared, a hint of accusation in the tone that Caton chose not to hear. "Who did you say this was from again?"

She hadn't, and with her mother hovering at her shoulder awaiting explanation, Caton wasn't sure if that was a good or bad thing. "Why? Do you want it too?" she joked, moving the fabric back into place to hide the proof of her less-than-pristine love life.

"No," her mom replied. "It wasn't my name on that card."

That sounded accusatory too, but, then, maybe Caton was just waiting to be burned at the stake. She tried to imagine the look on her mother's face if she told her she'd not only been sleeping with someone behind the back of the sweet, sincere woman she had been dating for months, but that someone was a married woman. Able to imagine the disappointment with painful clarity, Caton lifted the card from the counter before her mother's curiosity could get the better of her and carried the gift back to the table, sliding into her chair and dropping the box into her lap, hoping the barrier of the tabletop would make her mother forget what she had seen.

Distracted by the rampant thoughts in her head, the sentiments of the card, and the question of whether or not she should call Amelia, Caton was surprised when the coffee she'd left on the counter was put in front of her, and she smiled up at her mom gratefully.

"All right." Caton's dad entered the room with his usual bluster, and Caton was even more grateful to have someone else to occupy her mom's attention. "I've got you all stowed away upstairs."

"You didn't have to do that," Caton said, watching him approach the fresh pecan pie on the counter. "I was going to get it later."

"Too late," he announced. "Already done."

As he reached for the pie, Caton's mother turned instantly, just waiting for her moment to intervene. "Don't touch that pie," she scolded. "There are all kinds of cookies and other things you can eat."

"I was just going to get a little piece of the crust," he said.

"Don't," Caton's mom warned as her dad reached for the pie again. "Don't," she repeated. "Don't."

Her dad's fingers barely brushed the crust, and Caton swore her mother pulled a spatula out of thin air. Dodging the flying utensil, her dad laughed at every swat. "All I do around here, and I can't even have a piece of pie?"

"I didn't spend all day on these so you can have them half-gone before everyone gets here."

"I tried to help." Caton's dad looked to her for support. "She didn't want me in here."

"You eat more than you help."

"Well, every job has its rewards," he countered.

"If you want something, get it out of that basket over there," her mom finally ordered. "There's all kinds of expensive stuff in there, both of the edible and non-edible variety."

Risking a glance at her mom's inquisitive expression, Caton knew she wouldn't say another word without her permission, though she did wish her mom would just forget about it completely.

Going to the basket as directed, Caton's dad found plenty of acceptable options. Gathering three boxes in his arms, he sat down at the table across from her and started popping them open. "How's your job?" he asked. "Do you like it?"

"It's temporary," Caton returned, realizing she'd made even neutral topics uncomfortable, and wondering, with remorse, how she was going to get through the visit without a constant stream of lies.

"Does that mean you don't like it?" he prodded.

"No," Caton uttered. Hand going to the box in her lap, her fingers tangled in the silk ribbon, and she tried to shake off the reminder of Amelia's skin beneath her fingertips. "It's just best not to get too attached."

"What are you doing there exactly?"

"Charity stuff," Caton responded distractedly. "Fundraising and planning."

"Sounds like worthwhile work." Her dad smiled.

"It may be the most important thing I've ever done," Caton declared instantly. She had repeated it to herself at least a thousand times over the course of the last three months. Like a pep talk. Eyes dropping to Amelia's gift, she only wished it could be less complicated. "No matter what happens."

It was the abnormal silence in the kitchen that alerted Caton to the fact she'd said too much, and she tried not to look stricken as she raised her eyes to meet her dad's.

"What's going to happen?" he asked.

"Nothing." Caton forced casualness. "I'm just being dramatic."

When her dad glanced to her mom, in a silent communication she hadn't seen since she lived under their roof, Caton knew she hadn't sold it. "Is something wrong?" her dad asked, turning the concerned gaze back on her.

"No." Caton lied for the first time. "Everything's fine."

Every recent decision she had made only heightening the demands for secrecy, there were no truths in her current life she could share with them. She had made her own bed, she was lying in it with Amelia, and having to face her parents with a muddied conscience was the price she had to pay.

29

Glancing toward the passenger seat, Amelia wanted to turn the car around and take her daughter home in accordance with both of their wishes. Of course, she knew what the outcome would be. Jack would come in, see a piece of his life out of place, hear nothing said to him, and put Selene in a car with a chaperone who would make sure she got where she was supposed to go.

That was the reality of the situation. Amelia wasn't consistently overruled. Her voice went completely unheard. Most of the time, it wasn't even worth the effort to speak.

Pulling into the first available parking space, she killed the engine and tried to remain stoic as she looked fully at Selene for the first time since they had left the house. The accord they had was genuine, but delicate, and if there was anything that could destroy it in an instant, it was sending Selene back to the place of her greatest misery. Both grateful and troubled when Selene forced a sad smile, resigned to the circumstances, and got out of the car, Amelia listened to the door close with a hollow thunk and couldn't stand the sound of her own life.

Before she could disintegrate, she followed her daughter from the car, helping Selene retrieve her bags from the trunk and carry them as far as airport security allowed. When she held her arms out to her daughter, she did so without hesitation, but with the lingering fear of rejection, feeling tears gather as Selene stepped into them without a fight.

"Call me when you get there," Amelia requested. It was a poor substitute for all the things she wanted to say, for what she truly wanted to do. She wanted to keep Selene home, to continue rebuilding the fragile relationship they had. She knew well how it felt to struggle with the same torments day after day, and knew she had been compliant in her daughter's suffering.

For many years, Selene blamed her alone for it, and maybe she was right to blame her. After all, Amelia thought, standing on the other side of the barricades with a forced smile as Selene waved and disappeared amongst the passengers in the terminal, what kind of mother sent her own child away?

When she got back to the house, Sole was out, and the void inside the walls felt deeper than Amelia had anticipated. Her breakdown had come in the airport parking garage, a veritable spectacle, she suspected, for anyone who happened by, and she was utterly cried out. Not knowing what else to do with herself, she walked the empty recesses of a house too big to be useful. More maintenance than living.

She had given into the most morose form of self-indulgence, and was sitting on the edge of Selene's bed, when the intercom shook her from her despondency. "Amelia, I'm home." Sole's calm voice sounded throughout the house.

It was pity, Amelia knew, but she was nonetheless thankful for the disruption of her thoughts, which were leading to all kinds of worrisome places. Trying not to let her desperation show, she waited as long as she could take her own company before finally making her way down to the kitchen. Sole smiled at her entrance, and Amelia sat on the bar stool that Caton seemed to favor, trying to appear reasonably pleasant.

"Are you okay?" Sole asked.

"Yes," Amelia returned automatically, unable to remember the last time she'd taken the time to consider or respond truthfully to that question.

"I'll make you coffee," Sole stated, and Amelia nodded numbly. "Do you want something to eat?"

"No," Amelia replied, the emptiness of her stomach feeling perfectly in line with her mood.

"Have you eaten anything?" Sole questioned, but didn't wait for response. "I'm making you something. Do you want an omelet?"

"Okay," Amelia uttered, and Sole went instantly to work, starting the kettle and pulling expensive kitchenware from drawers and cabinets.

Examining the tools as Sole put them on the counter, it occurred to Amelia she didn't know the use of half the things in her kitchen. Growing up, she didn't have those things. Everything she helped her mother make was by hand, the kind of time-consuming work that made you stronger and wearier at the same time. It was no kind of life, she knew, but not knowing the purpose of the contents of her own kitchen, maybe that was no kind of life either.

Sighing, Amelia reached for the pile of magazines at the edge of the counter, smiling at Sole's fondness for Spanish-language tabloids. Pulling one from the pile, she flipped to an embarrassing picture of a celebrity she didn't recognize as Sole slid a steaming mug of freshly-pressed coffee in front of her.

"You could call her, you know?" Sole said quietly, and Amelia glanced up.

"She's on the plane," she returned, rolling her shoulders at the intense way Sole was studying her.

"I meant Caton," Sole returned.

Read with too much precision by the inquiring eyes that stared over the bar, Amelia tried to act as if Caton hadn't crossed her mind numerous times since she dropped Selene off, as if she hadn't wanted to go straight to Caton, take solace in her arms. Absolute certainty she would find it there was enough to frighten Amelia back to her own home instead of to Caton's apartment.

"I will," she uttered, dropping her eyes to the magazine, feigning interest in the words on the page. "I have to tell her she can come back."

"Or you could tell her you want her to come back," Sole suggested.

Gaze rising once more, Amelia knew she could stare all day and she wasn't going to intimidate Sole out of the conversation. It was the kind of thing Amelia would have once argued, whether it was true or not. "I think it's fair to say I've made that clear," she stated instead.

"Mm," Sole countered lightly. "Because all these material things have always made you feel so appreciated?"

Sitting back on the stool with deliberate calmness, Amelia closed the magazine and dropped it back into the pile. Clearly, Caton's gall had rubbed off on Sole, and she wondered if she should expect the spread of any of Caton's other bad habits. "You have a lot of thoughts on things you claim not to see," she said.

"I never claimed not to see this." Sole shook her head, finally walking off to start gathering ingredients, giving Amelia some space in which to get her bearings. "I can ignore almost anything, but there are some things I can't help but see."

"And what do you see?" Amelia asked in a near-whisper, knowing she should put an end to the discussion, but unable to channel anything but curiosity.

Turning back to her, Sole's eyes pierced her skin and Amelia knew that she could, in fact, see everything. "Ever since I have been with you, there has been exactly one thing that has made you genuinely happy."

"Selene," Amelia responded instantly, and Sole nodded her agreement.

"Now, there are two," she surprised Amelia by declaring.

The defensive urge to assert her authority was immediate. Clamping down on it, Amelia cast her eyes toward the floor and took steadying breaths. Sole was her friend, perhaps her only true friend, but that hadn't stopped Amelia from treating her like a servant in the past when it suited her interests. If she told Sole to mind her own business, Sole would mind. It was her job to mind.

"I wouldn't characterize my... relationship... with Caton as happy," Amelia finally uttered.

"It isn't," Sole acknowledged. "Given the circumstances, it probably won't be. But for the past few weeks, every so often, for the briefest of moments, you have been. I can't help but have seen that."

Aware that any argument would be false and futile, Amelia didn't deny it. Still, she couldn't shake the doubt that had haunted her for days, the uncertainty that had stayed her hands each time she'd thought about calling Caton, that had brought her back home when she left the airport, that made her fear Caton's return.

"She didn't even acknowledge my gift." Amelia knew she sounded pathetic, petty even, but she had spent the entire morning pretending to be together as she fell apart. She didn't have it left in her to pretend Caton's silence hadn't hurt.

"Maybe she didn't know if you wanted her to," Sole returned, opening her mouth again and closing it a beat later, as if she decided the rest of her thought best withheld.

"Go ahead. We've come this far," Amelia prodded, not sure what could be more out of line than the things Sole had already said, and more curious about the rest of Sole's observations than she dared admit.

When Sole stepped forward to lean against the bar, though, gaze unwavering, Amelia wasn't sure she wanted to hear the rest after all.

"If you want more, Amelia," Sole carefully stated. "You're going to have to give more."

The honest assessment stealing her breath, it also took her voice, Amelia discovered, when her words came out barely a wisp. "You know it's not that simple."

"Yes," Sole acknowledged. "I also know Jack never has to know."

It was both advice and assurance, and, swallowing against the fear that crawled its way up her throat, Amelia wondered how many times in one morning the woman could be right.

Selene texted when her plane landed, and called when she made it back to school. Though she tempered the distress in her tone, Amelia could hear it, pronounced and aching in her daughter's voice, and regretted not taking the risk of bringing Selene back home with her. It was late in London, so she told Selene to try to get some sleep, but she imagined her lying awake dreading the coming days, just as Amelia always did when Selene went back to school.

Hanging up the phone, it felt like a lifeline in Amelia's hand. She knew the call could wait, that, in her emotional state, it would probably be best, but her hand dialed the number automatically and she found herself waiting impatiently for Caton to take her call.

"Hello." Caton's voice was tentative.

"Hello, Caton," Amelia returned, not sure where to look in the room, what to do with her body, or which words should come next. The things Sole had said made it harder, not easier, she realized. Maybe she did want more, but with Caton, nothing ever felt certain. It was like grasping at something before her, finding it solid half the time, and the other half an apparition. "Selene left this morning."

"I'm sorry," Caton replied with such sincerity Amelia thought she might dissolve back into tears.

"So am I," she admitted, blinking them back.

"How did it go?" Caton sounded scared to ask.

"Surprisingly well," Amelia returned.

"Really?"

"Yes," Amelia said simply, still amazed at the fact herself.

"What about, you know..." Caton questioned. "What she saw?"

Settling deeper into the sofa, Amelia let her head fall back, oddly soothed by the sound of Caton's voice. "She had a lot of questions," she responded. "It was the best conversation we've had in three years."

"Good. I'm glad." Caton sounded truly relieved.

Silence descending, thick and heavy, it didn't feel threatening or overbearing. She could live within that silence, Amelia realized, shivering at the knowledge that she would gladly spend the whole night listening to Caton breathe.

"You can come back whenever you're ready." She cut the silence short, scared of her own thoughts.

"Okay," Caton returned uncertainly. "I guess I'll see you on Monday then."

Suddenly despising the two-day weekend like the owner of a sweatshop, Amelia glanced toward the darkness outside the window, watching time stagnate. "Mm hm," she breathed.

In the lull that followed, Amelia started to wonder if Caton was still on the other end of the line, before Caton finally spoke again. "Or you could come over now."

Feeling something she couldn't define and wasn't sure she should feel, Amelia knew it was unwise to give into it. "I could," she hedged, filtering through all the valid reasons she should decline, feeling them edged aside by all the reasons she wanted to accept. "Give me an hour."

"Okay," Caton returned softly. "I'll see you then."

As the call ended, Amelia wondered what it would look like to others if they could see her. What she was feeling, it had to be a noticeable blight, a soft spot in the steel she had worked so hard to forge. She should have been working to repair it, to fortify herself against potential destruction. So long she had been hiding, though, fighting from behind the safety of shields and mirrors. For just one night, all she wanted was to let down her guard.

30

Amelia said an hour, but it was more like forty-eight minutes between the time Caton hung up the phone and the knock came at the door. In the slow-moving time, she had managed to make herself and her apartment presentable, and to get just enough alcohol flowing through her system to take the edge off her nerves.

Unless Amelia had called to fire her earlier, it was an inevitable meeting. She would have to see Amelia at some point. The closer that point came, though, the more Caton feared it. Things weren't exactly how they had left them when they last saw each other, she was largely to blame for that, and, as she awaited Amelia's arrival, she considered the possibility that their rendezvous may be more of a confrontation.

Refilling her wine glass, Caton swallowed a large mouthful on her way to the door, pulling it open to find Amelia standing there, utterly appealing in jeans and no makeup, an instant reminder of why the desperate craving she had suffered for the past two weeks had been so debilitating.

"Hi," Amelia quietly greeted her.

"Hi," Caton returned, stepping aside to allow Amelia to enter, trying to calm her overstimulated senses as she closed the door.

Turning at the sound of Amelia's bag dropping onto a cushion, she watched Amelia slide her wool coat down her arms and drop it over the back of the couch. Waiting for the slightest indication of one, Caton took the action as invitation and gravitated toward Amelia, arm wrapping around Amelia's waist to pull her close.

Amelia's head dipped to capture her lips, hands winding into Caton's hair, and Caton thought maybe things were as they'd left them after all. Body responding to Amelia as it always did, with instantaneous submission, it would have been easy to give into it, to let things transpire as they did between them. Knowing it would only postpone the inevitable conversation, though, Caton utilized every ounce of willpower she had to pull away.

Dark eyes regarding Caton thoughtfully, Amelia slid the wine glass out of her hand, eyeing her over the top of it as she took a sip and drifted away. Walking around the room, she inspected everything in-depth as if she was looking at displays in an art museum.

If she weren't preoccupied herself, Caton might have worried about what potentially embarrassing mementos she had on display. Gaze trailing over Amelia, though, the realization of how much she had missed her weighed heavily as she tried to fathom how someone could look so perfect in faded jeans and a plain, dark t-shirt.

"You are so fucking beautiful," she stated, warmth infusing her as Amelia glanced back, seemingly surprised by the statement, which was interesting, since Amelia was clearly aware of the fact.

"You don't have to say that," she said, returning her gaze to Caton's bookshelf.

"I don't have to?" Caton questioned. "Or I'm not allowed?" Eyes turning to her once again, Caton shrugged. "There seem to be a lot of unspoken rules I don't know about until I've broken one."

Amelia's eyes narrowing slightly, she turned away again, and Caton watched the tiniest trace of a smile appear on her lips before she raised the glass to take another drink.

"How long have you lived here?" Amelia asked.

"Three years," Caton said, looking around her apartment and realizing how proletariat it must look. Amelia hadn't been all that interested in her surroundings the last time she was there, but now she was practically gawking at Caton's middle-income living.

"It's nice," Amelia said.

"You don't have to say that," Caton stole Amelia's reply, moving back to the counter to replace the glass of wine Amelia had taken from her.

"It is nice," Amelia repeated.

"For what it is," Caton tacked on.

No longer interested in the mishmash of inexpensive, stylistically-challenged decor around her, Amelia turned completely. "Is that how you think I look at the world?" she challenged, watching Caton carefully.

"Isn't it?" Caton returned.

"You really don't know me at all," Amelia uttered, and, the defiance in her stance melting, she simply looked hurt.

"I know," Caton acknowledged grudgingly. "You don't exactly make it easy."

The statement lingering, Amelia finished the contents of her glass, lowering it to the coffee table and shoving her hands into her back pockets as if she didn't know what else to do with them. Taking a drink from her own glass, Caton was suddenly reminded why she'd felt the need to start drinking in the first place. For a moment, she was certain Amelia was going to decide it was all too much trouble and walk right back out the door.

"Where did you spend Christmas?" she asked at last instead.

"With my family," Caton replied.

"The bus driver and the janitor?" Amelia interjected, a cocky smirk coming to her face, as if remembering the details of Caton's life proved something.

Maybe it did.

"Otherwise known as Dan and Reese," Caton countered. "My brothers and their families were there too."

Smirk leveling back out, Amelia's face fell to a near-grim expression. "I didn't know you had brothers."

"You never asked," Caton responded. She could hardly be upset about it. She'd never asked either. Amelia could have an entire trove of siblings she didn't know about. In the few moments they had spent together that lended to personal conversation, they avoided future and past, keeping it surface and in the present, as if they both knew it was all they really had.

The fact clearly bothered Amelia, though. Even across the room, Caton could see her face tighten, hands clenching in her pockets.

The reminder of her family, and the holiday spent in their presence, reminded Caton of the other unacknowledged subjects between them, the number of which only seemed to multiply the closer they got to each other. If they were getting closer to each other. Sometimes it seemed as if she and Amelia were on completely separate planes, side-by-side but completely isolated.

"I did get the necklace," Caton said carefully.

"Oh?" Amelia gave her nothing in return, no indication she'd even noticed the change in topic.

"It's gorgeous," Caton stated, eyes dropping to the glass in her hand. "But I can't keep it."

The same wounded expression that had come and gone so quickly returned to Amelia's face as Caton glanced up, and she wondered if she could ruin the entire night through her seeming inability to keep her mouth shut. Maybe they should have just started fucking the moment Amelia walked through the door. They never seemed to have any problems when they didn't talk.

"Why?" Amelia asked.

"Because it's too much," Caton returned.

"It's not too much for me," Amelia declared, and the line between financial statement and profound confession was so hazy, Caton didn't know whether to feel insulted or enchanted. Both came remarkably easily with Amelia, and they were often helplessly interconnected.

"I'm sorry I didn't call you." Caton shook her head, knowing there was no real excuse. At the very least, it was rude, and she couldn't explain that away. "I didn't know if I should. I didn't want to intrude."

She also didn't want to encourage, she admitted in her head. She was already in deeper than she needed to be. Yet, when the idea of waiting another two days to see Amelia had been posed earlier, offering a highly-encouraging invitation was all Caton could do, and, with Amelia standing there before her, she wasn't sorry. Even if the conversation felt like walking a narrow path with drop-offs straight to hell.

"I'm sorry I didn't call you," Amelia returned quietly. "I had to put Selene first."

"I know," Caton returned.

Nodding slowly, Amelia's eyes dropped to the floor. It was too difficult for them, this part. It took far too much effort. It took more wine than Caton had on hand, and, at the rate they were going, it could take the rest of their lives just to get past the surface.

When Amelia said nothing else, Caton assumed they had reached an agreement that there'd been enough talking. Probably too much. Abandoning the safety of the counter, she moved toward Amelia, slowly but deliberately, and Amelia pulled her hands from her pockets, so that when they came together next to the coffee table, her arms were free to circle Caton without hesitation, pulling her closer as their lips met.

Caton moaned as Amelia's tongue insinuated itself into her mouth, feeling all the pent-up need flooding through her, making every nerve hyperaware of Amelia, leaving no doubt as to the proper course of action. This, they had always done well. It was everything else that clouded the waters around them.

Making their way into the bedroom over shuffling, tripping feet, they fell into the tangle of blankets on Caton's bed. Pulling her shirt over her head, Caton tossed it to the floor, latching onto Amelia's neck and sucking at the warm skin as if it was sustenance. Maybe, for her, it was. Amelia's body was like a reservoir of pleasure, and, without access to it, Caton had to endure the incessant pain of her own thirst.

Yanked and torn, clothing flew in a frenzy, and Caton fell back against Amelia's body, pressing into the feel of intimacy - even if it wasn't real, even if they couldn't translate it into any other part of their lives.

Amelia's legs coiling around her thigh, Caton wrenched it away, earning a growl of frustration from Amelia, before her hand slipped between their bodies, fingertips skimming Amelia's slick flesh as the world closed in around them. Amelia arched into her hand, and Caton obliged them both, sliding lower to drag her teeth over the inviting skin of Amelia's chest as she pressed inside Amelia, so deep she feared the warmth Amelia kept so well-hidden would consume her.

When Amelia's hand alighted on her head, gentle fingers working into her hair, and she raised her eyes to meet Amelia's in the dim light filtering in from the street and the living room, Caton knew it already had.

Hand moving to Caton's cheek, Amelia's palm was soft and enticing. Tongue darting out to taste the thumb that traced her bottom lip, Caton pressed down on the firm thigh between her legs, eyes closing at the instant friction, and Amelia pushed up, bracing herself with one surprisingly sturdy arm, tongue sweeping up Caton's neck as her other arm wrapped around Caton's waist to steady her.

Working with and against her, Amelia drove Caton's fingers deeper. Firm nipple brushing her breast, breaths sharp and desperate in her ear, Caton could feel the need shuddering through every fiber of Amelia's body, and, her own breaths coming in uneven bursts, light bursting behind her eyelids, Caton feared she would pass out. It was more than it seemed, more than the sum of its parts, more than either of them would ever say out loud.

"Come with me," Amelia panted, and Caton wasn't sure if it was a sexual command or an all-encompassing request, but, as usual, she was helpless but to follow.

The sound of Amelia's breath hitching, and Caton was seized by the other woman's pleasure, ripples of ecstasy passing through and around her, piercing sensation in every spot where her body came into contact with Amelia's. Fingers digging into Amelia's back, Caton clung for traction, but skidded into the ether, losing herself entirely to the rhythm of Amelia's body.

It was what possession must feel like, she would think later, once her body had disengaged from its union with Amelia's and her mind was once again her own. It would take some time, though, before Caton could recognize herself as anything other than an extension of Amelia.

Lying atop Amelia's cooling skin, eyes blinking slowly open, she wasn't sure how she ended up there and thought maybe she actually had blacked out for a moment. Trying to lift herself off Amelia, her arms would scarcely hold her, and Amelia further impeded the effort, pulling Caton back down as she attempted to break free.

Sinking back into Amelia's body, head lowering to the thudding flesh above Amelia's breast, she was exactly where she wanted to be. Suppressing her flight instinct at the terrifying realization, Caton pulled the mussed blankets up around them and pretended it could last.

How long it did last, she wasn't sure. Every moment with Amelia went either too fast or too slow. Often, both at once. Amelia's heartbeat slowing, her breaths growing deeper and longer, it was only the feel of her fingers running through Caton's hair, lightly tickling the skin of her upper back, that indicated Amelia hadn't fallen asleep.

"I should go," she whispered, and Caton opened her eyes, almost like waking from a dream. One day, she suspected she would remember the moment as fantasy instead of reality.

When she rolled off Amelia, Amelia made no effort to stop her, and, without further explanation, Amelia slid from the bed, picking pieces of clothing off the floor and pulling them on.

Head propped on her hand, Caton watched every movement, refusing all thoughts that tried to enter her mind. There was no other way the night was going to end, and acting as if there could be was a child's game. Knowing exactly what she'd gotten herself into, Caton had no right to imagine anything different.

Finally clothed, Amelia turned around, feeling her pockets as if she lost something she never had with her in the first place, proving she was at least uncomfortable, which was better than her feeling nothing at all. "Thank you for inviting me over," she said at last, apparently satisfied she was leaving with everything with which she'd arrived.

With a humorless laugh, Caton looked away, not particularly surprised that the night had been reduced to social propriety. "Sure," she shrugged. "Any place we can have sex, right?"

Failing to keep the dejection from her voice, she lowered her eyes to the bed, noticing a snag in the sheet, and wondered if it had been there before, or if it had been put there by Amelia's clipped but uncommonly sharp nails, which seemed to leave marks on everything.

Bed dipping, Caton glanced up as Amelia sat down, and, an instant later, Amelia's hand was on her chin and Amelia's mouth was on hers, kissing her with such ferocity, Caton was certain she didn't want to leave. It didn't stop Amelia from pulling away, though, from pushing up from the bed and walking out on Caton without another word.

Listening to the door quietly click shut in the next room, Caton rolled to her back in the cold space left behind her, the emptiness that sank in on her nothing less than she deserved.

31

At the sound of her phone, Caton rolled out of bed so quickly, she forgot to breathe. Rushing light-headed into the living room, the air pricked her bare skin as she followed the sound to the counter, disappointment stabbing her, followed by a jab of guilt, as she read the name on the screen. She considered not picking up, turning around and walking right back to the bed to wallow, but decided that would be worse than the sentiment she had unfairly attached to the caller for no other reason than she wasn't Amelia.

"Laura, hi," she answered, moving back toward her bedroom as the cold settled painfully in.

"Hi." Laura sounded too happy to be talking to her, and Caton grimaced as the pang of guilt reared back up. "I'm home."

Pausing, Caton looked around for a calendar, knowing there were none in the room. For weeks, she had known when Laura was returning, but, somehow, in a single night with Amelia, she had forgotten. "That's good." Caton hoped she sounded more pleased than she felt as she climbed back into bed and pulled the covers around her. "How was your trip?"

"It was fantastic," Laura exclaimed. "I want to tell you about it. Are you busy tonight?"

Glaring toward the rumpled sheets beside her, it occurred to Caton she would never be as busy as she wanted to be as long as she was fucking someone else's wife. "No, I'm not busy," she responded, not sure whom the reply was the most unfair to, Laura, Amelia, or herself.

"So, should I come over?" Laura had to ask, though Caton knew she should have extended the invitation.

Leaning back against her pillow, she no longer knew how to answer. She couldn't keep doing this, knowing and then not knowing what she wanted. "Sure, come over," she finally responded, deciding that avoiding Laura until she figured it out was the most selfish possible course of action, and she was already spending enough time running circles on that particular track. "What time?"

"Seven?"

"Sounds good," Caton returned, wishing it did.

"Okay, I'll see you tonight," Laura replied. "And Caton?" The words stopped Caton's hand just as she was ready to hang up.

"Yeah?"

"I missed you."

Eyes closing at the declaration, Caton wondered at what point she had become a truly horrible person, completely corrupt and irredeemable. "I missed you too," she whispered.

Her goodbye robotic, Caton dropped her cell to the bed beside her, fingers moving to the suddenly throbbing vein in her forehead. It was true, at least. She didn't have to lie. And she didn't have to compare. Missing Laura may have been a blip on the radar next to the desperate need that consumed her in the absence of Amelia, but she had thought about her. Just not as much as she should have thought about her, considering how much time they had invested in each other.

Deciding those thoughts pointless, Caton veered from them enough to climb out of bed and find her clothes on the floor. Each piece eliciting the memory of its removal the night before, she scowled at her inability to control her brain when it came to Amelia.

It was late, almost lunch time for most normal people, she realized, looking toward the clock. Not that she had anything particularly pressing to do. Pulling the sheets from the bed as if to hide the evidence of a crime, she couldn't help but wonder if she had alienated herself from normal life forever.

Having made her cleaning rounds the night before, there was little that needed doing in the apartment, so, despite her best efforts, Caton kept getting dragged back into thought, overtaken by recent memory, and ended up rushing to get herself ready before Laura's arrival. When the call box buzzed a few minutes after seven, she started at the sound, surprised by the formality of it, and buzzed Laura in, answering the door with a sincere smile seconds after Laura knocked.

"Hey." Laura smiled.

"Hey," Caton returned.

Stepping through the doorway, Laura balanced herself with a hand on Caton's side to kiss her hello, and Caton relished the ease with which everything happened with Laura.

"It's good to see you," Laura said.

That was easy too, how Laura said what she was thinking, without the need for translation and examination of every syllable to determine what she really meant. Caton didn't need to compare, but the memory of the almost painful conversation with Amelia the night before fresh on her mind, it was difficult not to note the difference.

"You too," Caton replied.

Smiling brightly, Laura looked revitalized by life as she walked past Caton into the living room, shedding her jacket and tossing it on the nearby chair, before sinking down on the couch.

"Do you want a drink?" Caton offered, watching Laura kick her shoes off and settle in as if she belonged there.

"Sure," Laura returned. "Whatever you're having."

Going to the refrigerator, Caton retrieved two pumpkin ales and uncapped them, walking to the sofa and handing one to Laura as she dropped down next to her. "'Tis the season," she uttered, and, with a laugh, Laura pressed the bottle to her lips.

It was so easy.

"So, tell me about your trip," Caton coaxed, sinking into the cushion, arm resting along the back of the couch to give Laura her undivided attention. As undivided as it could be.

Laura's hair was slightly longer, her skin slightly darker, but everything else was the same. Scooting across the inches between them to settle against Caton's side, Laura's hand fell to her thigh without reservation, and Caton felt herself relax into the familiarity as she lifted the bottle to her lips.

After Laura launched into her holiday tale, all the things she did overseas, the projects she helped work on, the kids who told her about the everyday horrors of their lives, Caton got up only once, for a box of tissues and more drinks, before returning to her position at Laura's side. Watching Laura soldier through the more difficult parts, tears falling openly, she was struck again by what an incredible person she had sitting beside her on the couch in her living room.

"I'm here overeating with my family and you're off saving the world," Caton declared when it was clear Laura was finished.

Laughing lightly, Laura leaned forward to set her bottle on the table, sliding Caton's out of her hand to put beside it. "Well, you can't save the world all the time," she said, turning to Caton with a look that was clearly readable, because Laura had nothing to hide. "Sometimes you have to do something that makes you happy."

"Yeah, of course," Caton murmured, watching Laura move closer.

When Laura kissed her, deeply and slowly, it was with such sweetness, it was as if her lips were made of honey. Nice, as always, but only nice. Not amazing. Not consuming. Not intoxicating or overwhelming. None of those things were sustainable anyway, Caton knew, not with anyone. Eventually, they would fade, and it was what would be left behind that mattered.

Pulling back, Caton studied Laura, watched the easy smile come to her face. She should love Laura by now, she realized. Laura was the kind of woman who was easy to love. She wondered if she would love Laura if their relationship hadn't been disrupted in its early stages. She wondered if it was possible to love her still, once she got away from Amelia and had time to get the other woman out of her head.

"Are you okay?" Laura softly asked.

"I'm fine," Caton lied, hands sliding onto Laura's cheeks, letting out a desperate breath as their lips met again. Wanting nothing more, she tried to find the feeling, and, when she couldn't find it, she tried to force it. Laura was incredible and open and available. Laura wanted to be with her. Laura should have been the one for whom she spent the holidays pining, the one she couldn't wait to see again. It was so easy with Laura. If only she could find something to feel.

Breaking away on a frustrated exhalation, Caton couldn't look at Laura as she stood from the couch. Taking a few steps away, she tried to sort through her thoughts. She needed some time, time to think before she made a huge mistake and threw away something she knew she didn't really deserve anymore.

"Caton?" The worry in Laura's voice prompted Caton to face her before she was ready. "Did I do something?"

"No," Caton said more sharply than she intended. Laura even thinking that was so unfair, she couldn't even begin to wrap her head around it. "It's not you."

"Yeah." Laura looked suddenly nervous as she tossed her head to one side, hand moving anxiously through her hair. "When people say that, they usually mean it is you."

"Not this time," Caton uttered quietly, acknowledging to herself that she couldn't possibly be more to blame for her own tangled life.

Wishing she could get over it in an instant, that she could shake Amelia's hold on her, or lie until she found a way, Caton cursed beneath her breath, knowing she couldn't stop the conversation now that it had started. Truth had been elusive for her of late, and it was starting to eat away at every part of her. With every lie, she was becoming a worse person, she was becoming less worthy of Laura. She was becoming less worthy of anyone.

Taking a deep breath, Caton crossed her arms over her chest in preemptive defense, knowing whatever came back at her, she had coming. "I... I've been sleeping with someone," she confessed, eyes dropping to the floor, unwilling to witness Laura's reaction.

It was the disbelieving laugh that drew her eyes back up, and Caton watched Laura try to formulate a response to the unexpected proclamation. "I didn't think I'd been gone that long." Her attempt at a joke fell flat, and Caton flinched at the pain the words failed to obscure, watching Laura push to her feet and put more distance between them. "We never..." Laura shook her head. "We never actually said we weren't going to see anyone else. I just assumed."

"I wasn't seeing anyone else," Caton replied instantly.

Staring across the room at her, Laura didn't move, and Caton tried to guess what she must be thinking. "Who is it?" she finally asked.

"Does that matter?" Caton replied, careening at the question she should have seen coming.

"Yes," Laura replied, voice hardening slightly. "Oddly enough, it does."

It wasn't exactly the kind of question one could refuse to answer. Laura had a right to know with whom she'd vicariously shared a bed. Still, Caton searched for a reason Laura didn't need to know, unsure whom exactly she was trying to protect.

"My boss," she admitted when she couldn't come up with one.

The revulsion that appeared on Laura's face was surprising, instantly kicking in Caton's defenses. "I knew why he wanted you there," Laura began. "But why would you -"

"Not Jack," Caton interjected on a sigh.

Disgust evaporating at once, Laura's eyes went wide. "The wife?" she questioned. "You're sleeping with the wife?"

Cringing internally at the designation Laura chose to give Amelia, Caton merely nodded, wanting nothing more than to just get the conversation over as quickly as possible.

For a moment, Laura looked almost as if she wanted to laugh, as if the surprise and irony were enough to make her forgive everything. Caton knew when Laura remembered everything, though. She could see the change on Laura's face, the sudden indignation as she nodded. "So, that night she was here..." Laura started to ask, but didn't need Caton to answer. "Well, that makes more sense now. I'm sure she had a great laugh at my expense."

"No," Caton breathed. "It wasn't like that. It was never about..." Laura. It was never about Laura. When she was with Amelia, Laura was the last thing Caton thought about, but she doubted seriously that was what Laura wanted to hear. "It just happened." She wished she could retract the flimsy excuse the moment it left her lips. It made no difference, and it was mostly a lie. The first time just happened. That hardly explained the times since, or how Caton had felt when Amelia left her bed the night before.

Taking up the same defensive stance as Caton, Laura finally seemed to realize she too needed protection. "I thought we were..." She shook her head, eyes dulled as she returned them to Caton's. "I thought we were headed somewhere."

"We were," Caton responded honestly, the cold of the room seeping fully in until she went numb from the inside out.

"So, is this what you want?" Laura asked with a helpless shrug. "An open relationship?"

Staring blankly at Laura, Caton tried to work her mind around the question. She hadn't even considered it an option, and it was with some dismay that she realized she could discard it without any real thought. "No." She shook her head, and the answer led Laura directly to the right conclusion.

Channeling some real anger, it showed in Laura's eyes, before moving into her shoulders, which Caton had never seen so firmed. "What do you think is going to happen?" she asked. "Do you think she's going to leave her rich husband and her mansion and her life to be with you?"

"No," Caton returned, the truth of it sinking in on her. There was no happy ending with Amelia. She had known it the whole time. With Amelia, she was always riding slipshod into heartbreak. She was already halfway there.

"But that's what you want," Laura surmised.

"I don't know what I want," Caton whispered, telling herself it was a lie to spare Laura's feelings, instead of to protect herself.

"But you know it's not me," Laura stated, and Caton couldn't deny it.

She wanted to make Laura see that she was better off, that she was too good for her anyway, that she deserved to be with someone who wouldn't even look at another woman when they were together. She wanted to be that woman. She had let Amelia take too much, though, and she knew she would never be right for Laura again.

Returning to the couch, Laura pulled on her shoes, reaching for the camera she'd taken out to show Caton the photos from her trip only an hour ago when they were still on speaking terms. Dropping the camera into her bag, she slid it onto her shoulder and grabbed her jacket on the way to the door.

"Laura," Caton said as Laura's hand turned the knob. It was her last chance to stop her, to tell Laura how wrong she had been, that Amelia was a mistake, that she would quit her job and be the kind of person she could count on. "I'm sorry," was all she managed.

When Laura looked back, it was the only time Caton would ever see her look as cold and emotionless as Amelia. "You should be," she said, walking out, the door slamming at her back.

Alone in the silence, Caton realized she had nothing left. Even if she could win Laura back, she couldn't change her own feelings. Letting Laura go was one of the few decent things she had done in weeks. She just wasn't sure if it was the noblest or stupidest decision she had ever made.

32

Pulling up outside the Halston Palace Monday morning, Caton looked at the soaring beams, a grand entrance designed for important people, or for those who thought they were. It wasn't her life. She had never wanted it to be. Throughout her youth, she had seen people like the ones who lived in these houses look down on her parents because they worked hard for what they had, and she had never wanted any part of it. There was nothing in the world of excess Caton ever thought she would need, until she found the one thing she did.

Laura was right, though. This was what she was up against. Her opposition wasn't just a sleazy, rich husband. It was perfectly-manicured lawns, and extra rooms no one ever used, and gourmet meals served without ever lifting a finger, and diamond-and-platinum pendants like the one around her neck that felt suddenly like an albatross.

Making her way through the empty spaces into the kitchen, Caton tried to smile as Sole greeted her with the usual enthusiasm.

"Hey, how was your weekend?" The question was casual enough, but Caton could tell by the look Sole directed toward her that she knew how'd she'd spent at least part of it.

"It was... eventful," Caton said, lacking the wherewithal to lie.

"Good or bad?" Sole asked.

"Some good, some bad," Caton admitted. Lately, they had fused together so much, they were almost one and the same.

Delivering her coffee to the bar, Sole gave her a sympathetic smile, and Caton returned it gratefully. "Thanks."

At the sound behind her, Caton could admit to herself that she had just been waiting for Amelia's entrance. Moving into the room, Amelia appeared the picture of confidence and perfection in a suit just formal enough for business and just fitted enough to make anyone who saw her forget about business entirely.

"Good morning, Caton," she murmured, a barely-there smile lifting one corner of her mouth.

"Good morning," Caton returned carefully, wondering if she could trust it.

"Can I get you anything?" Sole asked.

"No, I'm already running late," Amelia replied, sidling up at Caton's side, so close it would have been inappropriate if Sole weren't already clearly aware of everything. "I have a lunch meeting at eleven-thirty. The information is in my datebook. Could you call Ms. Laurence and ask if we can move it to noon?"

"Yeah, of course." Caton nodded nervously.

Stepping closer, Amelia's body pressed against hers, and Caton lifted her eyes to Amelia's, overwhelmed with the desire to make her abandon her lunch date and whomever it was she was running late to meet. "I have meetings all day," Amelia said quietly, smile genuine as she reached up to toy with the pendant at Caton's throat. "I don't know what time I'll be back. Will you wait for me?"

It felt like all Caton had been doing, waiting for Amelia, but she didn't have it in her to say no to the request. Nodding slowly, she watched Amelia glance toward Sole, who had already busied herself on the other side of the kitchen, but made an extra show of paying no attention to them.

Amelia's head dipped to capture her lips and Caton melted against her mouth, savoring the unique flavor of Amelia, as the backs of Amelia's fingers brushed the skin of her chest. Pulling away, Amelia gently squeezed Caton's arm on her departure, and Caton turned shakily back to her coffee. These were the moments of danger, she knew, the ones that seemed normal, but couldn't possibly be. There was nothing normal about the situation, and she needed to keep that in perspective.

When Sole turned back around, Caton's hands clenched the mug tighter between them. She always anticipated judgment now, knowing she had it coming. But, smiling, Sole turned the conversation to neutral subjects, no mention of Amelia, until she reminded Caton on her way from the kitchen to move Amelia's lunch meeting, as if she could tell Caton lost all retention the moment Amelia laid lips on her.

After making the call, Caton found a few things on Amelia's desk with which to busy herself, needing something to keep her from fixating on Amelia's return. Afternoon came, and, as Caton dined on Sole's lunch offering in the kitchen, she thought about Amelia sharing lunch with some potential investor, undoubtedly talking the woman into adding an extra zero to whatever she intended to donate.

How many of them fell for Amelia? Surely, the night of the opera wasn't the first time a donor had tried to get more from her. They were probably all in love with her, or at least with the persona Amelia projected. As far as believing it could be more than the spell of a seductress, though, Caton thought she might be alone in her delusion.

Regardless, Amelia told her to wait, so Caton waited, and when Amelia alighted in the doorway with the grace of a dancer, Caton swiveled to face her with the most neutral expression she could muster. It would do no good for Amelia to know how anxious she always was to see her.

"I've been asked to plan an event for one of Jack's associates," Amelia announced, walking into the room and leaning against the edge of the desk. "It's going to be a pain, and I'm going to need your help."

Caton nodded, eyes trailing down Amelia's tailored suit, marred now with a few wrinkles from her busy day. "Is that why you wanted me to wait?"

An irresistible smile coming to her lips, Amelia wrapped her hand around the arm of Caton's chair, turning it toward her. The hand dropping to Caton's knee to uncross her legs, she slid from the edge of the desk, sinking into Caton's lap, hands slipping beneath Caton's hips and tugging her forward when the arms of the chair proved an impediment.

Whatever sense Caton managed to maintain dissipated at the feel of Amelia's body pressing her into the chair. Hands smoothing up Amelia's slacks, they settled at the bend of her hips, and Caton groaned as Amelia's hands wound into her hair to tug her head back.

"Not exactly," Amelia whispered and seized Caton's mouth in a long, slow caress that weakened Caton's body and resolve instantly. "Can you stay?" Amelia asked.

Distracted brain trying to make sense of the question, Caton shook her head. "No," she reasoned. "Jack will be home."

"Not until at least midnight," Amelia replied, lips hovering so close Caton could still taste her breath.

"How do you know that?" Caton asked.

"Because if there is one thing I know, whether I want to or not, it's Jack" Amelia stated, pulling back to meet Caton's eyes.

Despite the reality check, Caton's body strained toward Amelia. What she knew she should do and what she wanted to do were in opposite directions, but Amelia was always the stronger pull, her gravity undeniable.

"I'll make you dinner," Amelia tempted, and Caton smiled in spite of herself.

"You mean, you'll have Sole make me dinner."

Looking almost pleasantly offended, Amelia abandoned Caton's lap, leaving a red aura of desire in her wake, and walked to the intercom inside the door, fitted slacks hugging every curve.

"Sole?" she said, holding down the talk button and releasing it.

"Yes, Amelia?" Sole's voice returned several seconds later from somewhere inside the house, creeping Caton out as much as usual.

"Why don't you take the night off?" Amelia commanded.

"Okay," Sole returned, as if she was expecting it. "Is there anything you need before I go?"

Glancing back, Amelia's eyes ignited, and Caton was sure she would catch fire. "I have everything I need," Amelia returned, and Caton knew she wouldn't deny Amelia, couldn't deny Amelia.

"All right." Sole's voice filtered into the room. "Goodnight."

"Goodnight." Amelia released the button, turning to lean against the door frame with a smirk. "Do you believe me now?"

"What choice do I have?" Caton asked. What choice did she ever have? "How can I resist that?"

"You can't." Amelia's smile was victorious as she pushed off the frame. "I'm going to go change. Don't run off anywhere."

Eyes following Amelia's retreat, Caton swallowed roughly, thinking it was exactly what she should do. Running was her only real option. Every time she thought about running from Amelia, though, she ended up running toward her, so Caton thought it best to just not move at all.

Stepping out of her shoes, Amelia put them in their proper place, arranged by color and heel, and wished everything in her life was so easily organized. For the first time in what felt like a lifetime, she had no idea what she was doing, no idea how to get what she wanted. She had no idea what she wanted.

However she felt about her life, she did know her role in it, how she was supposed to act, what she was supposed to say. She was used to the script. With Caton, everything felt like improvisation, and Amelia was often as surprised by the things coming out of her own mouth, by her own actions, as she was by the things Caton said and did.

Slipping out of her suit, she hung each piece carefully, wondering if it was too late to come up with an excuse, something effective, but believable, as to why Caton had to leave after all. She could have forgotten a meeting. Jack could have called and said he was on his way home. It wouldn't be difficult to invent a reason, and Amelia knew Caton would go whether she believed the excuse or not.

If she wanted Caton to go, which, Amelia admitted to herself as she reached into her bottom drawer for her favorite jeans and a long-sleeve t-shirt, she didn't. If she didn't want Caton to stay, she wouldn't have asked, but, now that Caton had agreed, Amelia had no idea what to do with her.

Padding down the stairs after delaying as long as she could, Amelia landed in the doorway of Caton's office, and Caton's eyes rose silently to her. Taking her in, they paused on Amelia's slipper boots, and a small smile tugged at Caton's mouth. "Want a pair?" Amelia offered, only half-kidding. "I have more."

"I'm fine." Caton laughed lightly, standing and stretching, and Amelia was struck by the simplicity of it, the ease of the exchange. It was almost normal, almost mundane. She wondered if it could be like that with them, if she wanted it to be that way.

"Come on." She turned from the doorway and headed down the stairs, Caton's footsteps behind her inordinately nerve-racking.

Through the kitchen doorway, she felt even less at ease as she realized Sole had already taken her leave and she had no one on whom to fall back if she needed reinforcements. Yet, somehow more comfortable at the same time. In this room, she knew what to do, granted to a minimal extent, but at least it was a step-by-step process. She would have paid top-dollar for a recipe for Caton.

"Sit down," she invited, but realized it might have sounded like an order when Caton did it promptly, as if afraid of repercussion. It was surprisingly subordinate, and Amelia wondered how Caton could still feel that way with her. After the way things had been before she left, after she invited Amelia to her apartment, Caton had seemed more sure in her place.

But then, maybe Caton was sure. Maybe she was just as nervous as Amelia.

Pulling the perfect Chianti from the wine cooler without thought, it was a grating reminder of how fluent Amelia was in so many insignificant things, and how ignorant she was in subjects of value. The cork popping with ease, she pulled two glasses from the rack beside the cooler, filling them on the way to the bar. Offering one to Caton, Amelia's breath caught as Caton's fingers brushed over her own, a perfect demonstration of her profound ignorance. After everywhere those fingers had been on and in her, she simply couldn't wrap her head around the science of how it was still possible to so keenly feel the fleeting contact.

"Thank you." Caton took the touch away and raised the glass to her lips.

Head nodding in response, Amelia sat the bottle on the bar and gulped half her wine, before turning to face her objective. Trying to remember where everything was so she didn't look like a stranger in her own kitchen, she gathered what she needed and dropped the items on a counter, pressing the button to start the electric kettle before washing her hands. Every move she made, Caton's eyes followed, gaze so focused, Amelia could only imagine what she saw.

Opening the flour as if Caton's observation wasn't distracting, she dipped her hand inside, pulling out a handful and then another. It felt natural, though she never did it anymore. This was how she had been taught to cook, by hand, by feel, and the return to the basics helped Amelia relax into Caton's gaze, the silence between them less uncomfortable than she feared it would be.

"What are you making?" Caton asked at last, and Amelia swore she heard a trace of suspicion in the question.

"Pizza," she responded.

"Pizza?" Caton seemed amused by the response.

"I haven't spent a lot of my adult life in the kitchen, as you know," Amelia explained. "I think it's best to keep it simple. I don't want to give you food poisoning."

"I appreciate that," Caton replied, and Amelia risked a glance over her shoulder, watching Caton smile against the rim of her glass.

Only realizing her glance had turned into a stare when Caton tilted her glass and obstructed her view, Amelia turned back to the counter, pressing the dough through her fingers one last time, before covering it and washing the debris from her hands. After setting the timer and returning everything to its rightful place, she had no further excuse to avoid Caton's presence, and it was with great effort that she didn't shrink under Caton's forceful gaze as she walked to the bar. "That will take a while," she said, retrieving her glass and swallowing most of what was left.

Bobbing her head lightly, Caton said nothing. For a moment that stretched toward eternity, she simply continued her silent examination. "So," she drawled at last, taking her last drink and setting her glass on the bar. "What now?"

The sense of calm Amelia had stumbled upon by chance began to dissipate around her, indicating it had been illusion from the start.

It sounded so simple, but that was the question, the one that lingered over every moment they were together.

What now?

They could attempt to talk, but Amelia suspected that would only result in both of them losing their appetites. In heat and silence and desire, they were perfectly in-sync. As far as everything else, they barely knew how to coexist. Sighing, Amelia knew she had no right to be disheartened at the dichotomy when it was mostly her own doing.

Returning her glass to the bar, she curved around the end of it, and Caton slid off her stool, spinning to her with an expression somewhere between amusement and resignation. "Best to keep it simple?" she reasoned.

"For now," Amelia responded, too aware that every step toward Caton made everything more complex.

Nod barely perceptible, Caton's gaze fell away, catching on a minor flaw, and the brush of Caton's hand sent electricity arcing through Amelia's abdomen. "Flour," she stated, fingers gently coaxing it from the fabric of Amelia's shirt.

When she glanced back up, it was no longer resignation, but the constant, simmering yearning that drew them together. Hands sliding over Caton's shoulders, lips meeting Caton's, Amelia felt the tension recede, replaced by a familiar, far more pleasant sensation. Maybe this was the only place she and Caton could truly connect, but at least they connected somewhere without effort.

Caton's hands spreading over her back, they warmed her, not quite setting fire, and the urge to take away the guesswork, to return to the same place was strong. Once they became ingrained, patterns were hard to break, though - Amelia knew from experience - and she was already dangerously close to a pattern with Caton that failed to fully satisfy.

Pulling away, she combed her fingers through Caton's hair, reveling in the softness that enveloped them, and Caton buffered her look of concern with a smile. It occurred to Amelia that avoiding the easy pattern would require giving more, just as Sole had said, no matter how terrifying the prospect. Hand trailing Caton's arm to wrap around her hand, she tugged Caton from the room.

In the front room, around the end of the sofa, Amelia dropped Caton onto the sofa with a soft push, fingertips on Caton's chest leading her gently backward. Knee sinking into the cushion next to Caton's hip, Amelia's other leg situated between Caton's as she dropped down with her, and as Caton turned into her, trapping her against the back of the sofa, Amelia felt strangely liberated as Caton's lips seized her own.

Burrowing into the heat of Caton's body, into the play of Caton's tongue against hers, Amelia swore it lasted only minutes, but when the beeping from the kitchen pulled her from her haze, it had to have been more than an hour since they landed on the sofa.

Lifting her head, she had no clue what was going on behind the green eyes that stared back up at her. Everything was unknown, everything was improvisation, and that scared Amelia more than she would ever admit. Pushing back slowly, she rose from the couch, pulling her eyes from Caton and trailing her fingers up Caton's arm to her shoulder before returning to the kitchen.

She had no idea what she was doing, beyond the irrefutable fact that she was making a huge mistake, but it was a mistake Amelia simply couldn't convince herself not to make.

33

Adhered to the sofa, Caton listened to the soft footfalls that carried Amelia back through the kitchen doorway. Remnants of Amelia lingering on her skin, the muted sounds of Amelia echoing in her head, she tried to wrap her mind around the fact that they had just spent time together in which they didn't have sex and didn't completely repel each other.

Things were different. Again. For once, it felt as if Amelia was guiding her with an open hand, instead of misdirecting her, and, forcing herself upright, Caton tried to find some sense of balance as she rose to her feet to follow.

Back in the kitchen, Amelia was already halfway through her work - dough rolled out on the counter, a pile of cut vegetables nearby - and Caton wondered just how long she had lain there contemplating.

"Do you want some help?" she belatedly offered.

"I've got it," Amelia returned with a smile, and Caton poured more wine into the glass she'd abandoned on the bar, taking a fortifying drink, knowing she should find an excuse to leave even as she settled next to the bar to watch Amelia.

It was amazingly efficient, Amelia's process. Though surprisingly hands-on, her cooking style was as no-nonsense as the rest of her life. Watching her distribute ingredients with more expedience than precision, it occurred to Caton that, under normal circumstances, Amelia wouldn't be doing it at all. Her life would be even more efficient, Sole taking care of her base needs while Amelia toiled away in her office or worked out downstairs or did something equally result-oriented.

Caton was the inconsistency, the poorly-fitted piece, in Amelia's life. She was the one who made Amelia do messy things, waste time, take unnecessary risks. She was wrong for Amelia, as Amelia was wrong for her. While that fact may have been clearer in the beginning, it was still every bit as true, no matter what strange things Amelia did to make Caton question her sanity.

Opening the oven, Amelia dropped the pizza onto the stone inside and set the timer, and Caton followed her path back to the bar, watching her refill her glass and take a drink. Leaning forward against the bar top, Amelia's forearms stretched across it, and Caton wondered if it was in offering, before deciding she didn't care. It was within reach, she had no desire to fight the overwhelming urge to touch Amelia, and, if she was wrong, she knew Amelia would let her know.

As her hand slid forward, Amelia looked more intrigued than put-off by the approach, and, when they met, Amelia's hand turned up to meet Caton's, tips of her fingers curling around Caton's in a tentative connection.

Letting out a nervous breath, wondering if it was what she really wanted, Caton lifted her glass to her lips. "So," she posed, with forced casualness, "what is it with you and Selene?" Taking a sip as her lips went instantly dry, she hoped to look as if whether or not Amelia chose to answer was of little concern.

Amelia's eyes dropping to their joined hands, Caton anticipated a retraction and instinctively tightened her grip, knowing it was noticeable when Amelia's eyes returned to hers in an instant. For a painful minute, Amelia said nothing, and Caton was sure any changes she noticed were only cosmetic.

"She..." Amelia finally began, shaking her head. "She has been angry at me for the past few years."

"Why?" Caton questioned carefully.

"She had some trouble at school," Amelia continued. "Some other students were harassing her. She said it was about a group project, but I don't know if it was that simple. I made the mistake of telling Jack."

Amelia sighed, regret heavy in her words. "And instead of handling it like any normal parent, he had them all expelled. After that, everyone was afraid to talk to Selene. She lost all her friends. The only people who wanted to be around her were the mean girls, so that's what she became. She doesn't like them. She doesn't want to be one of them. She doesn't want to be there. She's just doing what she has to do to survive."

"Why don't you just bring her home?" Caton asked without thought, drawing back slightly when Amelia's eyes turned almost warning. "I mean," she attempted to backpedal. "Aren't there good schools here? You want her home, I can tell you do."

Something in the line of questioning softened Amelia's features. "It's not that simple," she said in a way Caton knew was meant to end the conversation.

"You're her mother." Still, Caton couldn't stop.

"It's not that simple," Amelia repeated, hand slipping from Caton's, and Caton wasn't sure if she had shattered the intimacy or if it was fake from the start.

Pouring more wine into her half-empty glass, Amelia walked to the oven, glancing at the timer with a grim expression and leaning back against the counter when there was no excuse to busy herself. "So, what are your brothers like?"

Not expecting the conversation to continue, Caton had to give the question some consideration. "A menace for most of my youth," she replied, succeeding in putting a fleeting grin on Amelia's lips. "Now, they're pretty okay."

"They're older than you?"

"Yeah." Caton nodded. "Bryan is a teacher. He's married with one son. And Elliott is a radio producer with an ex-wife and two sons."

"Three nephews," Amelia said, almost wistfully.

"How about you?" Caton was grateful for the seemingly straightforward subject. "Do you have any brothers and sisters?"

"I did," Amelia replied, eyes casting downward, and a lump dropped into Caton's chest, slowing the tempo of her heartbeat. Apparently, with Amelia, no subject was straightforward. "I had a sister."

Swallowing, Caton knew she shouldn't. The ground around Amelia was always so hazardous, just waiting to crack, which was probably why Amelia always stepped back when Caton stepped forward. Since Amelia had opened the subject, though, Caton risked a hesitant step.

"What happened to her?"

"She was born with defective lungs," Amelia stated matter-of-factly. "She died when she was five-months-old."

"How old were you?"

"Six," Amelia responded, finally glancing up, any feelings about the topic masked, as always, beneath the long curtain of her eyelashes.

"I'm sorry," Caton breathed.

"It happens," Amelia said, casually accepting her own pain, and turned to the oven at the beeping of the timer to go about business as usual. In the past, Caton would have been certain Amelia didn't feel anything. Knowing she did, though, Caton only wished she could tell how deeply, or understand why Amelia was so quick to dismiss her feelings.

Burdened by the loss Amelia refused to feel for herself, she startled when Amelia appeared by the bar with a pizza carrier and two plates. "Can you carry those." She nodded toward the glasses of water on the counter that had appeared as if by magic.

"Sure," Caton returned automatically, grabbing them and trailing Amelia from the room.

Pressing the button on the panel inside the basement door, Amelia led Caton to her old floor of exile and refuge. Passing by the gym, Caton followed Amelia into the small, misfit room at the back corner that had no place in such an ornate palace.

Sliding the pizza onto the table, Amelia sat at one end of the standard, mid-priced sofa and pulled slices onto the plates, and Caton sat at a distance, setting the glasses on the table and taking the food offered to her. Afraid of dredging up more painful subjects unexpectedly, she was afraid to say anything, and so was Amelia, apparently, because the silence descended heavily and the room felt too small for both of them.

"Do you want some of my peppers?" Amelia asked out of the silence, and it sounded like some kind of bizarre peace offering. "Um..." She gave an uneasy laugh as Caton looked to her, motioning to her plate. "My mama, she uh… whatever she was making, she would just toss things on, or dish it out as it came. Like pabellon criollo or paella. She always said, when you were eating with the right people, it didn't matter who got what, because you could… you know, you could trade."

Not sure if she was seduced more by the story, or the sudden appearance of Amelia's native language, Caton felt suddenly more and less at ease with Amelia. Holding her plate out, she watched Amelia drop the peppers onto it, before taking her choice of items from Caton's pieces and popping a mushroom into her mouth with a smile.

After that, conversation came more easily, though Caton let Amelia guide it, and Amelia guided it to the most impersonal of topics. Safe, the discussion was also circular, leading them nowhere, and Caton was never quite able to tell if Amelia's laughter in all the right places was genuine or the well-placed response of a woman who knew how to charm her way through anything.

It wasn't until they collected the wine from the kitchen and returned to the couch, legs leisurely intertwined between them, that Caton relaxed enough to forget why she had stopped asking questions. Coaxed into comfort by the warmth of the alcohol and the intimate feel of Amelia's foot moving against her hip, her curiosity got the better of her. Amelia was like an unsolved riddle. Without asking questions, she could spend a lifetime trying to decode her, and they didn't have a lifetime. They had two months.

"How did you end up here? With Jack?" she questioned, and, even to her, the second half of the query sounded unmistakably spiteful.

The only rise the question got out of Amelia was at eyebrow level, and, clearing her throat, Amelia glanced away. "I know you think this is my world," she motioned absently to the empty air. "But it isn't. I actually grew up poor. Really poor." The words were softer.

The declaration came as such a shock, Caton paused with her glass halfway to her lips, and the rim bisected Amelia, leaving her half real before Caton and half reflection. When she had thrown out the accusation that Amelia married for money, it was more of an "adding a few extra millions to the riches" statement than a "moving up in the caste" statement. Realizing the words had to have been more of a barb than she'd intended – or maybe she did intend it at the time – Caton lowered her glass without taking a drink.

"As soon as I could work, I started taking jobs to help my family," Amelia went on without prompting. "I had gotten this great job at a resort on Trinidad for the summer. Jack had come to Venezuela for some sort of business venture, and he was visiting the island. He stayed at the resort where I worked. And he was Jack. He decided what he wanted, and he got it."

Nodding numbly, Caton wished it was answer enough, that the rest didn't matter. At last taking the drink, she was unnerved by how much it did. "How?" she pressed.

Though Amelia didn't balk at the question, she did pause long enough that Caton worried whatever she said would be a made-up tale, another purified version of the truth.

"He was there for a week," Amelia began haltingly. "He asked to take me out. He took me to all the nicest places, ones I could never afford. He treated me like a queen. He elevated me above my position. He did everything right for a nineteen-year-old with no real experience."

Nodding again in response, Caton wasn't sure she actually wanted Amelia to continue. Swallowing what remained in her glass to temper the feeling of inadequacy that reared up out of nowhere, she cast an agitated glare toward the empty wine bottle.

"At the end of the week, Jack asked me to marry him," Amelia went on at the small, disingenuous prompt. "I told him my family was in Venezuela, and he took me there to meet them. He was charming to my family. He was generous. He changed their lives immediately. My parents thought he was a gift."

It was no wonder, Caton acknowledged, realizing she had posed the question more out of active comparison than idle curiosity. "What did you think?" she questioned, a glutton for punishment of her own making.

"I thought he was insane," Amelia replied. "He'd known me for a week and said he loved me. But," she acknowledged more slowly, "I also thought he was impetuous and romantic."

"Of course." Caton forced a hollow laugh. "Why wouldn't you?"

Amelia's hand landing on her shin, warmth penetrating her pant leg and sinking into her skin, Caton glanced up, and, meeting Amelia's gaze, for once so open, she lost her ability to be flippant.

"He was always calculating, Caton," Amelia stated quietly. "I was never a wife to him. I was an acquisition. It wasn't generosity. It was a dowry. Of course, that became clearer over time. It was harder to see then. He didn't want to marry his equal, because he knew he would have one more person telling him what to do. He married me, because he thought I wouldn't complain. He thought I would be grateful. And, for the most part, I haven't and I am."

Caton wasn't sure what she expected to hear, but it certainly wasn't that level of disclosure. Awash with sudden guilt, she acknowledged it was exactly what she had hoped Amelia would say, that there was nothing real between she and her husband. Listening to the revelation of the facts as Amelia saw them, though, she realized she didn't want that to be Amelia's story after all. Jack may not have deserved Amelia, past or present, but Amelia deserved more than years of his, or anyone's, indifference.

"Were you in love with him?" Caton asked, no longer sure how she wanted Amelia to respond.

It was a difficult question to ask, but Caton didn't expect it to be a difficult question to answer. Amelia's surprise melting into uncertainty, her gaze drifted off. "No," she finally whispered, and it sounded more like a sudden realization than an age-old fact. "I thought I would fall in love with him. He was so good to me at first. I didn't know he didn't want to be loved. He wanted to be respected, admired, followed, but not loved. You can't love a tyrant. But, as things are turning out," Amelia continued a beat later, eyes losing focus as they stared across the room, "maybe I never could have loved him anyway."

Not quite an admission, it was close enough to speed Caton's heart, going to her head faster than the wine, Amelia's touch, or any of the other surprises over the past few hours. Like everything else, it could easily be illusion, so she chose to ignore the sensation. She also suspected

Amelia would regret most of the conversation when she didn't have half a bottle of wine coursing through her.

"You have to understand," Amelia's eyes returned to Caton's, near plea in them. "It's not all bad. I am not the only one Jack elevated above her surroundings. He brought my parents to the U.S. for the first time. They've traveled here since. They live in a villa with my family. They have plenty to eat. They have good health. They have a view of the ocean. They don't have to worry. And I can visit them whenever I want. I don't know," she shrugged helplessly. "Maybe we all wanted to believe in the miracle."

Unable to produce even fake amusement at the notion of Jack as a savior, Caton's jaw tensed, disquieted but the entire narrative, but one part lingering more than any other. "You are more than Jack's equal," she declared, throat tight against all the accusations she wanted to hurl at Jack, at the hatred she felt toward him, growing even in his absence. "You are better than him."

Amelia smiled half-heartedly, unconvinced, and Caton bit back any further exposition. She had pushed enough for one night, had gotten more than she ever expected, knew more than she really wanted to know, and didn't know what else to say. By the way Amelia's hand moved inside her pant leg to gently massage the back of her calf, Caton thought maybe Amelia didn't want her to say anything.

The feel of Amelia's leg moving beneath her came an instant before Amelia's toes pressed against the seam of Caton's pants, and Caton's eyes fell closed on a gasp. Another distraction, it was effective just the same. Instinctively, Caton shifted forward as Amelia's foot pressed into her, resulting in a collision that forced a moan over her lips, and when she opened her eyes, gazing across the short distance, the smile on Amelia's face was pure wickedness. "Think I can make you orgasm from here?"

"I'm certain you can," Caton replied, no doubt Amelia could make her climax hands- and mouth-free in less time than it should have taken anyone, sans a magician.

Just as Caton acknowledged the fact, though, Amelia abandoned her opportunity to prove it. Retracting the foot, she flipped to her knees, crawling across the cushions to hover over Caton, smile fading into something less-easily identified. As Amelia's lips descended on hers, Caton slid down on the sofa, pulling Amelia with her, and, at the press of Amelia's hips between her legs, she ripped her mouth from Amelia's on a hiss. Smirking, Amelia seemed just as content to prove her talents in close proximity.

The conceit was genuine, and it wasn't. Amelia knew the areas in which she had talents, how alluring she was to people, but, beneath all that, Caton saw the woman who was honestly unaware of her true worth. So much of their early time together she had spent thinking Amelia needed humbled, only to discover humbling was the last thing Amelia needed.

Sharp trill of the phone jolting them both, Amelia thrust closer, and Caton grasped the back of the sofa with a helpless whimper. "You should get that," she gasped.

"I don't have to," Amelia responded, eyes never leaving Caton's as the press of her body turned more deliberate.

"You should see who it is, at least," Caton stated breathlessly, not sure if she was trying to excuse Amelia or save herself. "It's late. What if it's important?"

With reluctance, Amelia pulled back, eyes scanning Caton's face for signs of subterfuge, and Caton smiled, not sure what she was trying to avoid exactly, but almost relieved when Amelia disentangled herself and walked the few steps to the phone. When Amelia grabbed it with haste, though, she worried she had unintentionally wished Amelia bad luck.

"Selene?" Amelia answered, voice edging on worry. "Are you okay? Why are you up so early?" Glancing toward the clock, she finally sighed in relief. "Yes, of course we can talk."

On her feet before Amelia could turn apologetically, Caton pulled her shoes on and grabbed her bag, smiling as she moved silently toward the door. A hand on her wrist stopping her, she was drawn back toward Amelia. Noting the expression of disappointment on Amelia's face, Caton thought it safest to attribute it to too much wine and unfulfilled arousal.

"Honey, could you hold on for a second?" Amelia said into the phone. Pressing the receiver against her shoulder, she took the small step that carried her into Caton, her thumb moving over the skin at Caton's wrist dangerously hypnotic. "Are you okay to drive?" she asked.

"I'm fine." Caton nodded.

"Are you sure? I can get you a car."

"I'm fine," Caton assured her. "I can walk a straight line, find my nose with my finger. I'm good."

"Okay," Amelia smiled, voice barely a whisper. "I'll see you tomorrow."

Nodding in response, Caton could do nothing but respond when Amelia's mouth brushed hers, too weak to tamp her own feelings, which rose up unexpectedly to take a choking hold on her. Pulling away with as much poise as she could muster, she turned from the claustrophobic intimacy of Amelia's presence, the room, and the house, wondering as she escaped through the front door why in the hell she hadn't done it hours ago.

34

Waking to the dull throbbing and thickly-coated palate of too much wine and too little sense, Caton forced herself out of bed and plodded to the kitchen to hydrate. Gulping lukewarm tap water, the memory of the night before spilled over her in a cacophony of sensations, both pleasant and unnerving. She had woken with more insight into Amelia than she had come to expect, but Amelia would have to wake up too, and Caton could only control one of their reactions.

After making it through her morning routine on resolve alone, Caton found everything as expected at the Halston Palace - Sole alone in the kitchen and Amelia in hiding. Not in the kitchen, not in her office, Amelia's absence was exactly the consequence Caton feared. As much as she had given in to the allure of confidences shared, she knew Amelia would regret her loose tongue come morning.

In the time it took for her to drop her bag on her temporary desk and turn on the computer, footsteps in the hallway drew Caton's gaze to the door of her office, where Amelia appeared an instant later in white silk pajamas and the same slippers from the night before. All her expensive, tailored clothes and perfect hair days, and Amelia had never looked as insanely beautiful as she did half-awake and disheveled.

"Good morning," Amelia said, the hint of doubt in her tone belying her casual appearance.

"Good morning," Caton uttered, heart clenching in prophetic anguish.

"About last night..." Amelia began, stepping into the room, head bowed demurely, and Caton awaited the fallout.

Forget everything that happened.

Don't ask me anything else.

Take your stuff and go.

There were a slew of possible endings to the introduction, each worse than the last, and Caton had anticipated them all throughout the morning. Perhaps most disturbing was the fact that any one of them might provide a less painful conclusion to their doomed liaison than what might lie ahead.

"I'm sorry." Amelia's declaration was among the last things Caton expected to hear. "That Selene called." She seemed to think further explanation was needed. "I mean, I'm not sorry she called. But I'm sorry you left."

Maybe it was the unexpected declaration, the strange informality of Amelia stumbling directly out of bed and into her presence; maybe it was the fact that there was no detectable gimmick behind the declaration; or maybe Caton just wanted to believe it, because the possibility that it was sincere was too tempting to resist.

"Me too," she confessed in turn.

Amelia's slow smile of response melted Caton on the spot, fusing her feet to the floor, so she couldn't run even if she had the inclination. A rush of steps carrying her forward, Amelia took Caton's face in her hands, the light scent of cinnamon infusing the last breath between them before Amelia's lips met hers with gentle urgency.

It was the same feeling with which Amelia had made her entrance, not sudden or surprising, more like a continuation of the night before, embers left smoldering all night, waiting to be fanned back to life. Knees giving out under the sudden onslaught, Caton clutched Amelia's hips for support, as, pulling back just enough to be torturous, Amelia's eyes moved over her face, a dark swirl of unexpressed thoughts.

When Amelia's warm hand trailed her arm to wrap around her hand, and Amelia took her first leisurely step backward, Caton followed without resistance. She knew where they were going, where they always seemed to end up. "I thought we had work," she appealed to her own willpower.

"It can wait," Amelia quashed it in an instant. "I can't."

Two doors down, the guest bedroom welcomed them like a sanctuary dedicated to a single purpose - her communion with Amelia. Caton knew it was a dangerous path to enlightenment, that there would be consequence. She was a pagan in a Christian world. Eventually, the inquisition would come.

Pushing the door closed at her back, she watched Amelia slide open the buttons on her nightshirt until she could slip the fabric from her shoulders - a goddess revealed - and knew it didn't matter. The woman who once seemed to thrive on domination and vengeance appeared humble and benevolent before her. Caton couldn't unlearn the truth, she couldn't unknow the real Amelia. Until they tied her atop the pyre, she would be a true believer.

Disturbed by the realization, she drifted away, chest fluttering anxiously as she stopped at the chair by the wall and fumbled at the hem of her shirt. Jerking it over her head, she draped it over the back of the chair, the tidiness of the action doing nothing to clear up the chaotic screeching inside her head.

It blared so loud, and Amelia's approach came so quiet, Caton didn't know she was there until soft breasts yielded against her upper back and Amelia's hands crossed over her stomach, pulling Caton against her. Moaning at the unexpected contact, at the feelings it never failed to elicit, Caton knew she had been, and would continue to be, a willing sacrifice, no matter what Amelia proved herself to be next.

Lips opening against Caton's shoulder, Amelia's tongue laved a spot with comfort before her teeth dug in with seductive brutality, dropping Caton's head forward on a sound that was half moan and half sigh. Feeling Amelia's hands on her back, her sides, her hips, she barely registered her clothing falling away until the pieces were lying on the floor around her. If she wasn't careful, Caton knew she could be subjected to the same fate - picked apart and scattered before she knew what was happening.

Amelia's hands cupped her breasts, lips softening against Caton's skin to move across her shoulders and down her upper back, savagery giving way to such care Caton thought she would dissolve on the spot. Reaching back, her fingers found the bare skin of Amelia's hip as Amelia's tongue flicked at her shoulder blade, and she couldn't endure the languid pace.

Turning in Amelia's arms, she wound her fingers into the hair at Amelia's shoulders, yanking with enough force to make Amelia groan before swallowing the sound with hungry lips. Each voracious kiss was met with equal response, and Caton tripped over her own feet as she was turned and propelled backward without warning.

Falling onto the bed, she reached for Amelia with greedy hands, and Amelia urged her backward. Heeding the command and rebelling against it at the same time, Caton directed Amelia's lips back to her own, impeding their progress as they scrambled onto the bed in a flurry of want so overwhelming, it was the only driving force in the room.

Amelia's knee was insistent between Caton's thighs, separating them with bruising force, but the hand that slipped between them, feathering against over-sensitized flesh, eased all pain. Pushing toward the seeking fingers, Caton knew she was begging. Silently, but undeniably. Shameless efforts rewarded by Amelia's hand pushing deeply into her, intense and invasive, she was beyond pride.

If not for the overwhelming need to respond to Amelia's touch in turn, she would have surrendered completely.

Hand skimming along Amelia's side, it wedged between their bodies, and Caton exhaled in relief when her fingers met the silken heat of Amelia's desire. Her breath mingling with Amelia's muffled moan, it formed an intimate duet as her fingers thrust inside Amelia.

Mouth. Thighs. Fingers. Stomach. There was nowhere Amelia wasn't, and there was nothing Caton wanted more than to be consumed completely by her. Lost to the feel of Amelia against her, to the thrumming intensity of her own body under Amelia's control, to the pulsing point ahead, Caton rushed to the precipice, floating at the edge for only an instant before giving in.

Wrenched from reality, head floating, she was hyperaware. Amelia's face was smooth softness against her cheek. Amelia's leg was solid strength between her thighs. She could smell the sweat on Amelia's skin and hear Amelia's quiet gasps turn to whimpers, before easing into silence as Amelia tensed and succumbed beneath her hands.

Tremors leaping between them, Amelia fell on top of her in a display that Caton was certain looked more graceful than it felt. The sensation of skin on skin sent an aftershock through her, and Caton fought the reflexive urge to push Amelia away, to create a safe distance in which she had control over her own body, her mind, and her erratically-firing nerves.

When her hands did finally move, though, it wasn't to relocate Amelia off of her, but to pull her more firmly against her. Nestled against her hip, Amelia's top half sprawled over Caton, caging her in, as her head tucked into the hollow of Caton's neck.

Stillness fell and lingered, contentment fitted to the moment, but not to the circumstances surrounding it. She was an idiot for letting it come to this, Caton knew, the real affair, the emotional entanglement, but, lying there with Amelia pressed against her, chill settling on her skin as the occasional creak of the house echoed loudly against the quiet, she knew that's exactly what it had become. At what point they stopped being two people fucking and became these two people, she couldn't say, but she also couldn't deny.

"So..." Amelia's voice was rough. "Jack will be gone next weekend."

Flinching slightly at the mention, Caton's sudden tension dissipated just as quickly as Amelia's hand moved upward from her hip, dancing along her rib cage, fingertip sneaking up to circle her nipple.

"He goes on an annual retreat with three college friends." The words blew across Caton's skin. "At least, that's where he says he is, and it may be the only thing he's ever told me I actually believe."

Amelia's finger still moving, Caton's body arched into the touch. Absently, she hoped she wasn't expected to verbally respond.

"I was thinking, we could spend the weekend together." Amelia's fingernail scraped across her hard nipple, and Caton sucked in a breath in response. "It doesn't have to be here. I could come to your place, or we could go somewhere else." Amelia's deep inhalation pressed against

Caton's side before Amelia released it on a sigh. "It doesn't matter where."

'Yes,' Caton thought instantly, roping in the response before it could leave her lips, not sure if she was responding to the suggestion or to Amelia's touch. Either way, she wanted it, time with Amelia, more than stolen moments, often so fleeting she couldn't be sure they had happened at all.

The logical part of her, though, the part that retained the flicker of sanity she had left, knew it was wrong. Things were already too complicated. She was already too wrapped up. There were certain paths of no return, she'd taken most of them, and this had all the markings of one.

Amelia's hand stilled suddenly, moving to rest on her rib cage, and Caton's mind unfogged somewhat.

"Unless, of course, you're busy." The hard edge was just barely evident in Amelia's voice. If it hadn't been for the unusual serenity leading up to it, Caton may not have even noticed. "With Laura, maybe."

Caton wasn't sure if it was a jab or a question, but it provided a good excuse either way. Real or a figment of Amelia's imagination, Laura was a perfect obstacle between them, a barrier impeding their way. When Amelia's weight grew heavier against her, though, tension palpable throughout her body, Caton couldn't let her believe it.

"I'm not," she uttered, hand running up and down the crackling bones of Amelia's spine, her fanatical worship leaving her weak and obedient. "Laura's not really around anymore."

When Amelia became worryingly still at the statement, Caton wasn't sure the truth was what Amelia wanted after all.

Finally shifting, Amelia cautiously raised her head, almost as if she was afraid to look at her. "Since when?" she questioned quietly, eyes searching Caton's face for truths Caton couldn't bring herself to reveal.

Shaking her head in response, Caton's eyes darted away, returning to Amelia's as Amelia shifted above her. Her gaze met Amelia's for only an instant before Amelia's lips were on hers, bold and possessive, and whatever answer Caton might have given was rendered suddenly insignificant.

35

Caton never agreed to spend the weekend with Amelia, but she never refused, and at some point it was just understood. Just as the change in their relationship was understood. And that sex was always an option before that. And that Amelia could come to Caton whenever and wherever the mood struck her before that, and Caton would give into her every time. They had spent the entirety of their unusual courtship doing without discussion. At the point they had reached, words seemed superfluous.

At the point they had reached, a weekend with Amelia should have seemed routine.

Amelia had a sixth sense about Jack that Caton could only assume came from years of marriage to a lying husband who never bothered to call. She knew when Jack would be late, which was most nights. She knew how late Jack would be. Those nights, Caton stayed, sometimes at Amelia's request, sometimes because she couldn't bring herself to leave, and, between the two, they had tallied many hours together under the palace roof.

She knew she shouldn't give in to either of their desires, she knew with every hour she was digging herself deeper. But, in the silence of the house, when Sole left them alone and Amelia did speak, quietly and in halting phrases, still holding back, but giving more each time, Caton also knew she would plummet willingly into a black hole with Amelia with no concern for what awaited her on the other side. So, despite how it should have felt, pulling through the gates of the palace Friday morning was anything but routine. Racked with both giddy anticipation and utter dread, it was practically schizophrenic.

The balance tilted somewhat when Caton pulled up behind the sports car in the driveway, readied for departure, but not departed, and realized Jack was still inside. For a moment, she entertained the notion of driving off, coming back when he was gone, or waiting in the car for him to leave. Either would send up red flags, but maybe that was exactly what she should have been doing, fanning smoke signals, tapping out Morse code. She was in over her head. Maybe someone would come to her rescue.

Or maybe that was as much a fantasy as her relationship with Amelia seemed at times.

With a sigh, Caton threw open her door, well aware that, if there was going to be a rescue, she would be doing her own saving.

Sneaking into the house with as little indication of her arrival as possible, Caton glanced toward the stairs. Nothing but silence met her, heavier than usual, so she went to the one place where she could always count on finding a friendly face.

"Good morning," Sole greeted as she passed through the doorway to the kitchen.

"Good morning," Caton returned, moving to the bar. "Is Amelia upstairs?"

"Yes. She's with Jack." Sole kept her tone neutral, setting coffee onto the counter without asking, and Caton took the middle seat at the bar as usual. She could tell by feel that someone had switched the positions of the stools, and realized she was getting far too used to certain aspects of her current situation.

Dragging the cup closer, she glanced at the clock, wondering how long it would take Jack to leave. His presence alone was stifling, putting her uncomfortably on edge, which was more her doing than his. It was, after all, his house.

Minutes later, sounds at the doorway carried Jack into the room, and Caton tried to maintain her composure. "Hello there, Caton," Jack said, smile almost passive.

"Hello," Caton replied, looking past him to Amelia, whose lips spread into the same bewitching smile that made every bad choice seem worth making.

"Is everything ready?" Jack asked Sole, and Caton dragged her eyes from Amelia, returning them to her coffee, which she deemed the safest place to keep them until Jack was gone.

"Right here." Sole pushed some boxes on the counter toward him, and Jack grabbed the stack in one hand as he turned to Amelia.

"I have to get on the road," he declared, oddly chipper. "I said I'd be there by lunch."

"Drive safe," Amelia said, her concern sounding strangely sincere.

"Sometimes I think you really do love me," Jack grinned, wrapping his free arm around his wife's waist and planting a kiss solidly on her lips.

With a rush of something she refused to give name, Caton realized she had failed to keep her eyes trained on her target, and turned back to the bar. Hands curling around the cup, she clutched with such force her knuckles went white and the ceramic cried for mercy. It was a split second, an absolute contradiction to the way in which they normally interacted, but, for that split second, Amelia and Jack looked very much like a happily married couple.

"I'll be back Monday," Jack said to no response. Caton suspected he was often given the final word in his household.

The lull that followed Jack's departure was a perfect calm, and Caton felt like a lone soul drowning in a vast, still ocean, cries for help lost to the hypnotic serenity of the breaking surf.

Amelia's footsteps were nearly drowned out by the quiet, but her presence was suffocating as she insinuated herself into Caton's personal space as if it was part of her lordly domain. "Good morning," she said, the hand sliding onto Caton's back as likely to push her under as to save her.

When she tensed at the touch against her will, the hand stilled at once. "What's wrong?" Amelia questioned softly.

Biting her lip, Caton stared at her hands with curiosity. Though she could feel the heat settling in on her palms, branding them red, they felt detached at the same time. As if the pain belonged to someone else.

"Caton," Amelia softly commanded, and Caton looked to her. Bitterness like an aftertaste on her tongue, she knew it had to show. Oddly enough, the corners of Amelia's lips jumped up at the sight, as if there was something humorous or pleasant about the situation. "Are you..." Amelia started and paused, moving closer like a territorial hunter. "Are you jealous?"

Sometimes Caton didn't know how she kept anything from Amelia, when the woman always seemed to read her without effort or permission. Turning away, the muscle in her jaw ticked almost painfully. "Of course not," she uttered. "I have no right to be jealous."

If anything, she should feel guilty. She was the one sitting in Jack's house, wishing his marriage all kinds of ill will, readying herself to spend the weekend with his wife.

"You have a right." Amelia eliminated the space left between them, hand skimming across the bar top to slide the mug from Caton's hands. "You just have no reason."

Caton's resistance was half-hearted at best when Amelia's fingers, extra warm from the mug, rose to her chin and guided her eyes around to meet her reassuring gaze. Hands sliding onto Caton's cheeks, Amelia kissed her in a way that was undeniably persuasive, and Caton admitted her weakness. Even if Amelia was lying to her, even if every word that left her lips was fabrication, she would only ever believe what Amelia wanted her to believe.

Pulling back, Amelia seemed satisfied with her efforts. "Now, come upstairs," she ordered. "I need you." And she walked off without waiting for reply.

Watching her disappear through the doorway, Caton turned back to the bar, pretending for a moment she had the will not to follow, and, glancing up with a smile, Sole pretended to believe her.

She didn't know why it was so surprising that Amelia needed her for work. It was why she had been hired, after all. When she got to the landing of the second floor and Amelia called her into her office, though, Caton approached the desk with confusion.

"I have to make some calls," Amelia explained, moving behind Caton and slipping a hand around her hip, fingertips resting in a particularly distracting spot as she waved toward a folder on her desk with the other. "There's a lot of stuff in here. Just see what you can do with it. It's all pretty self-explanatory." Breath pouring over Caton's ear, Amelia's teeth nipped so hard it stung. "And we'll both hurry, because the sooner we get done, the sooner we can..."

Amelia left the statement hanging and when she pulled away without warning, Caton couldn't stop the groan of frustration that leaked from her lips. Watching Amelia sit down across the desk, she was pacified somewhat by Amelia's smile, but not so much that she didn't feel the imbalance of power. Things had changed, but only so much. Amelia still got to say where and when and for how long, and Caton still had to heed her commands.

"And if I don't want to do anything?" she asked more out of curiosity than defiance.

Setting forward in her chair, hands folding almost primly in front of her, Amelia's smile faded into a good-natured smirk. "Then, I guess you can go play with Sole. Innocently," Amelia emphasized. "And I'll come find you when I'm done."

Smile easing across her lips, it occurred to Caton that Amelia might let her get away with more than she had ever attempted. She wondered what would happen if she made her own demands, cleared Amelia's work away in one destructive swipe and took Amelia on the same desk where she had chosen to demonstrate her sexual prowess on so many occasions.

Amelia could see it, Caton's urge to exert some authority. She could tell by the way Amelia's eyes trailed over her, waiting for her to make a move. So, Caton did. Picking up the folder from the corner of Amelia's desk, she glanced into Amelia's smoldering gaze before heading for the door.

"Caton." Amelia's rasp tickled down her spine, and anticipation thrummed through Caton's body as she turned back. "I was just trying to help him so he would be gone before you got here."

Not even close to what she expected to hear, Caton lurched at the abrupt change in subject, embarrassed at her obvious need for reassurance, and even more so that Amelia's words made her feel better. "You don't have to explain," she uttered.

"I know," Amelia declared, smile warming her gaze.

The hand could save her or push her under, Caton reminded herself, weakly returning Amelia's smile before escaping the confines of her office. She could feel Amelia's eyes trail her from the room, ever-vigilant, and, sinking into the high-end office chair next door, could swear she felt Amelia's gaze through the wall.

36

For someone who had work to do, Amelia made more than her share of appearances. Every twenty minutes, it seemed, she sauntered in with a remark that was somehow lascivious and classy at the same time, much like Amelia herself - wicked, unorthodox fantasy wrapped in veiled illusion.

Suggestive repartee disrupted only by intentional full-body brushes made to seem accidental, it was punishment, Caton knew, payback for what she had thought but hadn't done. She may have joined Amelia's game, but Amelia wasn't going to relinquish her title without demonstrating her mastery.

When Amelia made her appearance around lunchtime, Caton had accomplished exactly nothing, save the admittedly impressive feat of not coming completely unraveled. Of course, that was exactly what Amelia wanted, Caton was certain, as Amelia stepped up behind her, pressing against her back as the copier flashed light onto the table in front of them.

"Are you hungry?" she asked, and nowhere in the simple question was there any inference to actual food.

Pushing off the table, Caton whirled on her so fast, Amelia startled back a step. Catching her before she could retreat, Caton yanked Amelia against her, watching Amelia's expression melt in relief and knew Amelia had done as much damage to herself as she had to her target. "You fucking know I am," Caton whispered, and Amelia's light laugh turned to a groan as she crushed their lips together.

"Hold on," Amelia tried to slip free as Caton dragged her lips along a delicately-curved jawline, and Caton's frustration only amplified when Amelia seemed amused by it. "I'll be right back," she promised. "Just wait here."

With an aggrieved sigh, Caton released Amelia against her will, and Amelia sashayed toward the door. Turning back, she tossed Caton a look that was both alluring and cruel as she disappeared around the wall, and Caton waited only a second before following Amelia to the doorway. Leaning against the frame, she watched Amelia climb the last of the stairs to the third floor.

Each second ticking slowly by as she awaited her return, Caton started to wonder if it was a new game they were playing. Hide-and-seek. Whether it was or not, little did Amelia know if she hid too long, Caton was going to come seeking.

Reappearing at the top of the stairs a few minutes later, Amelia was halfway down before she noticed she had an audience. The realization putting a smile on her face, and more swagger in her step, she reached the second-floor landing with a flourish. "Still want me?" she questioned.

It was so cocky, Caton wished she could leave Amelia standing there for even a prolonged moment, but, knowing Amelia's arrogance ran only skin-deep, she pushed off the doorframe as if she'd been handed the keys to the universe. Maybe she had, she considered, arms closing around Amelia again, the same delirious elation she always felt when she was close to Amelia permeating every fiber of her body. Unwise, dangerous even, and utterly irresistible.

Her kiss open and honest, Amelia's body was more resistant than usual, hands on Caton's sides keeping her from coming too close. If not for their steady progress in the direction of the bedroom, Caton might have feared the distance.

Careful steps carrying them through the door and over to the bed, Caton's hands moved to the button at Amelia's waist with single-minded intent, and when Amelia dislodged them with a genuinely hard slap, Caton did pull back in question.

Amelia's smile never faded, though, the sultry upturn of her lips pairing with a slow shake of her head that warned Caton against further attempts. Movements deliberate, she held Caton's arms to her sides in unspoken command, before releasing them to slide her hands inward, cupping Caton's breasts for an instant and moving down to the hem of her shirt, tugging with enough force that all Caton could do was lift her arms and let Amelia strip the garment over her head.

Tossing it carelessly aside, Amelia's warm fingertips returned to Caton's skin, running the length of her spine. Lips playing at an exposed collarbone, they dragged lower to close over one hard nipple through silken fabric. Arching into the sensation, Caton was obedient as Amelia unhooked her bra and tossed it somewhere in the vicinity of her shirt, and was rewarded by the return of Amelia's mouth, her tongue circling the same nipple that grew impossibly erect in response. Hands clenching at her sides, Caton fought the urge to touch for only a moment, at last raising an uncertain hand to Amelia's shoulder. When Amelia didn't admonish her, she raised her other hand to Amelia's opposite shoulder, bracing herself against whatever Amelia would do next.

Expeditiously relieved of the rest of her clothing, Caton let Amelia guide her to the bed, and Amelia pulled the covers back almost primly before settling Caton on the edge and tossing an overstuffed pillow to the floor.

It was with near worship that Amelia sunk to her knees before her and pressed Caton's legs apart. Eyes holding Caton's, Amelia's arms curled beneath her thighs, surprisingly gentle. Then, Amelia wrenched Caton forward and Amelia's mouth was on her, giving Caton no chance to prepare, to think, to breathe, and, arms giving out, Caton fell to her back in a graceless display.

Hot and focused, Amelia's tongue circled her clit, dipping lower to tease inside Caton before moving upward again. Fingers digging at the sheet on either side of her, Caton lost all clarity and control. Aggressively responding to Amelia's attack, her body controlled her. Arching into Amelia, every part of her submitted to Amelia's will. Frantic mutterings falling from her lips that might have been curse or prayer, her body knew no ego or dignity. It knew only Amelia and the peak toward which it was rapidly ascending.

Amelia had never claimed to be merciful, though, and she showed Caton no mercy. She prolonged on purpose, and Caton's body suffered her merriment. Shaking with every barely-there brush of Amelia's tongue, Caton strove toward something Amelia kept promising and retracting, aching for more.

Minutes grew longer. The properties of space altered around them. Caton felt so close and so far at the same time. It was a diabolical skill, Amelia's ability to hold Caton right at the edge, while preventing her from jumping in.

Then, Amelia stopped as suddenly as she'd started, and Caton wondered if this was her true punishment. Amelia had all the power, they both knew it, and Caton had rebelled, briefly and unsuccessfully, but still she had, and she would pay for it. Eyes clenched shut tight, she felt tears leak from them to slide down her temples. Left as she was, she was overloaded with Amelia's influence. Without Amelia releasing her, she would never get her body back.

"Amelia, God... Baby, please..." Caton felt her lips form the words, but they made little sense.

Barely conscious of Amelia's movement, Caton focused solely on survival, until Amelia's fingers feathered down her sternum and between her ribs. Shuddering under the caress, Caton lurched into the touch as it dipped between her legs.

"Shhh," Amelia breathed, hand retreating with haste.

Frenzied, needy, Caton exhaled a sob, certain she would die without Amelia's touch, before Amelia's skin grazed her inner thighs and she was filled so unexpectedly, in such an unaccustomed fashion, her eyes snapped wide. Mouth parting on a gasp, she watched Amelia's mischievous gaze warp into a satisfied expression as her body adjusted to the alien invasion.

"Not a prude, right?" Amelia reaffirmed.

Using what little strength she could find, Caton pushed onto an elbow, looking down at the accoutrement at Amelia's hips with shock and amusement, overshadowed only by her painfully acute arousal. "That's cold," she shakily replied, though it was also effective and extraordinarily well-planned, she had to admit.

Smirk growing, Amelia rolled her hips, burying the silicon deeper, forcing Caton's eyes to flutter and her arm to quake beneath her. "Sorry," she uttered, but didn't sound the least bit, and certainly wasn't acting it. "I trust it'll warm up quickly."

At the mesmerizing sparkle in dark eyes, Caton gave herself over to Amelia's inherent powers of persuasion. She never would have expected it, but Amelia had consistently proven that Caton shouldn't expect or discount anything. Sinking to her back, she moved one foot to the edge of the bed in casual consent. Not that Amelia ever needed or awaited her permission. Caton couldn't remember consenting to anything that wasn't already in progress. Not that she had ever shown herself less than willing to meet Amelia's every inclination.

Permission granted, Amelia pulled out slowly, an intentionally torturous reprieve, and Caton clutched at the wrinkled sheet as Amelia thrust into her with enough vigor to force Caton's eyes closed and a harsh exhalation past her lips. Then again. And again. Until Caton forgot that there was anything between them that didn't belong, and every sensation became an extension of Amelia.

Everything was an extension of Amelia.

"Do you like that?" The question came from close by, and Caton opened her eyes to find Amelia only inches away, hovering over her, tormentor and guardian.

"I can..." Amelia thrust, smile widening her lips. "Take it or leave it."

"Well, I guess, right now you're gonna take it," Amelia surmised, and it was the truth entire. Now, future, past, here, there, nowhere, Caton would take anything Amelia offered and always want more.

When Amelia thrust again, harder, deeper, Caton found the reserves to push up from the mattress. Meeting Amelia halfway, their teeth knocked, but they still pushed closer, tongues tangling, until the pain melded into the pleasure, one glorious sensation with no end and no beginning.

Uneven exhalations fell from Caton's lips as she gave up the fight and fell back to the mattress. Eyes half-open, she watched Amelia raise her fingers to her mouth, sucking them between her lips, the vision almost as effective as the touch it foreshadowed. When that hand moved between their bodies, determined fingers finding their target, Caton returned instantly to the place she had stalled before Amelia's surprise interlude.

With one expert stroke, Amelia carried her over the edge into such immediate euphoria, Caton cried out. Rising from the bed in an involuntary arch, she was seized by a series of aftershocks, drawn from her one after the other by the finesse of Amelia's fingers, playing her like her damn piano.

Body finally twitching in response to the touch, Amelia withdrew her hand and carefully extricated the implement she had so enthusiastically buried into Caton a short time before.

Forcing her eyes to open, Caton saw another grin of satisfaction pass over Amelia's face before she walked to the foot of the bed, curving around the end of it, and started peeling away her clothing with haste.

Rolling to her stomach with some effort, Caton had to crawl across the mattress to see beyond the tall footboard. Settling her head on her crossed arms, she determined it worth the effort as she watched the black straps slide down Amelia's perfect legs, laughing at the muted thump the sex toy made when it hit the floor.

Amelia's eyes shooting over in surprise, her smile turned sheepish. "I just wanted to see what it was like," she stated quietly.

"And?" Caton asked as Amelia returned to her, a light sheen of perspiration polishing her flawless skin.

"Overrated." Amelia shrugged.

"Where are you reading these ratings?" Caton countered, and Amelia laughed as she climbed onto the bed. Swiveling to lay against Caton's side, her warm hand falling to the small of Caton's back, she pressed a kiss against Caton's shoulder.

Feeling the immediate upsurge of the other thing, the thing that wasn't just sex, Caton fought the swell. It was these moments, Amelia's needless, impetuous affection, which threatened to undo her.

"Should I have asked?" Amelia questioned, propping her head on her free hand.

Fleetingly, Caton wondered once again what she wouldn't let Amelia do to her, with or without asking, and again came up with nothing. "Oh, where would the fun have been in that?" she returned.

"So, I didn't hurt you?" Amelia asked carefully, and Caton saw a flicker of doubt. It was the first time Amelia hadn't looked entirely confident all day.

"You didn't hurt me," she breathed.

Desire battling lethargy, she was moved by the dominant force, lifting her head from its comfortable position to meet Amelia's lips, which moved against hers in a gentle caress.

Amelia's hand swept down her back, making every invisible hair along the length of Caton's spine stand at attention. When it breached the swell of Caton's hip, skating inward, Caton pulled away, casting a disbelieving look at Amelia, but Amelia only smiled as her touch trailed between Caton's thighs, determined fingers moving over hypersensitive flesh.

"Better?" Amelia asked when Caton gave into the soft play of Amelia's hand, despite the spasms that rocked her body with each fleeting touch.

"Better," she sighed.

When Amelia kissed her again, just a tease of lips and tongue, Caton felt some strength return. Pressing a strong shoulder, she flattened Amelia against the mattress, ambushing her with a kiss that demanded more, delighting when Amelia whimpered and squirmed beneath her.

Trying to drink her fill, Caton realized she had no limit. She could spend a lifetime at Amelia's lips and still feel starved for their taste.

At last pushing away, it was Amelia who clung, and Caton struggled against her possessive embrace to get upright. Edging her knee beneath Amelia's thigh, she palmed a smooth hip, turning Amelia enough to maneuver closer, and heard the anticipatory hitch of Amelia's breath.

Hand slipping between them, Caton sighed at the slick heat coating her fingers as she parted anxious flesh, angling in until her clit brushed against Amelia's and the atmosphere ceased to exist in an instant. Though she could hear Amelia's breath rush from her body, Caton was the one who felt deprived of oxygen. Letting her hand trail to Amelia's abdomen, she tried to acclimate to the heady air as their warmth combined and Amelia throbbed against her.

Not quite adapted, Caton figured she never would be, and Amelia's head pressed back into the mattress, beads of sweat forming rapidly between her breasts, shimmering like jewels in the sunlight that filtered through the gauzy curtains, as she moved against her.

"Do you like that?" Caton parroted Amelia's arrogance with admitted difficulty.

"God, yes," Amelia breathed.

Heat permeating every inch, sweat ran down Caton's back as she felt herself rising again, and could feel Amelia rise with her. Faster, with more intent, Caton urged them toward the apex, shifting as Amelia's hips arched from the bed, her hand reaching out for Caton. Catching it with her own, Caton threaded her fingers through Amelia's as the current passed between them, heart stopping and mind going blank as sensation overwhelmed them both.

Released from its clutches moments later, Caton slumped in exhaustion, gulping at the air as liquid fire oozed from her body. Beneath her, Amelia was unnaturally still. Eyes closed, she looked more serene than Caton had ever seen her. As Caton tried to disentangle them, though, Amelia's hand wrenched from Caton's to clamp onto her knee.

"Don't," Amelia breathlessly commanded, eyes flying open to hold Caton in place. "Don't move. Not yet."

So, Caton didn't move. She stayed as Amelia wanted her, catered to Amelia's desire, until Amelia at last tugged on her wrist to pull her down beside her. Hand smoothing across Amelia's waist, Caton could feel the tremors moving through the muscles beneath her fingertips as she watched Amelia's eyes drift closed. She wondered how much of this was a first for Amelia, as so much of it was for her. Amelia was the first to have such undeniable power over her, to make her want to risk everything for each fleeting moment. She was the first to make Caton feel the other thing, the thing she dare not give name, which was both illuminating and terrifying.

When Amelia opened her eyes, dark orbs locking on Caton's, Caton bit her tongue, afraid of what she might say, afraid of what Amelia might say. Casting her eyes away, she looked for something to fill the silence before either of them had a chance to say anything that might come back to haunt them.

"You're wealthy, right?" she finally managed. "Like stupid rich?"

When her gaze returned to Amelia's, a crinkle of confusion disturbed the contented look on Amelia's face. "I guess you could say that," she returned.

"You should hire some people to sit right over there." Caton tossed her head in the direction of the chairs alongside the room's bay window.

"Exhibitionist now?" Amelia asked.

"Not really." Caton shook her head. "But somebody should really rate that."

The throaty laugh that poured from Amelia's lips was both reward and punishment. Amelia was so beautiful happy, it was cruel. Because any happiness Amelia had with Caton could only be temporary, and every smile Amelia gave her was one closer to the last.

37

If there was anything at which Jack was truly an expert, it was upholding a reputation. His life depended on it. From a young age, he had been taught the secrets of the trade - how to put on a public face, how to build a brand, and how to keep his secrets secret. There were some things, though, best shared, and he waited all year to talk about his true exploits with the only two people in the world who wanted to hear and protected the details.

The afternoon with Lyle and Tony had been civilized, lunch at the country club and eighteen holes amongst company in which discretion was necessary. Walking into their usual dive, though, twenty miles down the road and off-the-beaten-path, the need for respectability was gone. It was another world, one where Jack didn't have to calculate every action and watch every word.

"Hey, guys. Welcome back." The scraggly old man who tended the place looked almost as rundown as the walls and the wood furniture bought second-hand twenty years ago.

"Hey, Matty," Tony answered, reaching across the bar to shake the man's hand.

"Stocked up just for you guys," Matty responded, pulling three Dos Equis from the cooler and popping the caps before sliding the bottles across the bar. "Nice to see you again. I'll start you a tab."

That was it. No questions. No observations. Just a welcome back and a beer. Sometimes, Jack did envy the little people. Nodding in acknowledgment, he grabbed one cold bottle and followed Tony and

Lyle toward the booth in the back with its duct-taped seat and bent table edging.

At a two-top along the way, a woman in a dress that tried too hard nursed a beer that looked long-warm and barely-tasted. Much like the woman herself. Jack didn't remember seeing her in there before, and, at second glance, it occurred to him she may have just reached legal drinking status.

"Hey, Sweetheart," Lyle said as they passed. "How you doing tonight?"

"Okay." The young woman gave Lyle a smile that was proof positive he would have her back at the lodge before the weekend was over.

Sliding into the booth, Tony glanced past Lyle to raise his glass to the woman as well. "You going to save some of that for us?" he asked.

"Like you guys need it," Lyle returned. "You've got the new babysitter, and Jack's got that secretary."

"This is like a record for you, isn't it?" Tony came at him too. "You fallin' in love or somethin', Jack?"

Laughing off the insult, Jack took a pull from the bottle and placed it on the table, looking around the dilapidated old joint and wondering how much longer it could stay standing. "I'm just not bored," he answered with a leisurely stretch. "This girl, she will do anything, and I do mean anything, to keep her job."

Watching jealousy flash in the eyes of both his friends, Jack withheld his grin. It wasn't all about one-upmanship. These men were the only two people who knew most of Jack's secrets, the only two people whose secrets Jack would never use against them. That meant something. But it didn't hurt knowing that, of the three of them, he had the life that inspired the most envy.

"Well, if you're not using her, I'd be happy to come fuck your wife for you."

Letting the grin slip free, Jack took the statement as verification. Tony always did have a thing for Amelia. Probably always would.

"I can fuck my own wife, thanks," he returned, leaving it at that.

Watching Tony take a long drink, he knew the man was seething, despite his poker face, and let him stew in it. Tony didn't need to know

Jack couldn't remember the last time he'd had sex with Amelia, that in recent years she had become so cold and rigid, it was like screwing a mannequin. If the woman had any emotion left in her, she wasn't wasting it on him, which made Jack's life considerably easier, but fucking her a drag.

Tony's gaze trailing off, he stared at something across the bar. Another woman of interest, Jack was certain, until Tony turned back with an inquisitive look. "Is he with you?" Tony asked, tilting his bottle toward the front of the bar.

Unease spreading before he even looked over his shoulder, Jack lost all humor at the familiar figure, sitting erect in a chair, eyes open and watchful upon him. Turning back toward Tony and Lyle, he offered no explanation as he slid from the bar stool, grabbing his bottle, the cold glass against his palm doing little to diminish the prickly feeling of irritation that settled in.

Seemingly unmoved by Jack's approach, Marcus Slater downed the contents of his glass and thumped it back to the tabletop.

"Can I buy you another drink?" Jack asked.

"No," Slater responded with a humorless laugh, the sharp eyes locking on Jack filled with palpable animosity. "I have no idea where that money came from."

"You act as if you know exactly where it came from." Jack joined Slater in his joyless amusement, grinning spitefully as he tried to see through the veil of authority and figure out the man's real game. He had been through it all before, the accusations, the audits of his work, the close-calls, but he couldn't recall anyone from the past who looked at him with such sincere resentment.

He probably didn't get paid enough, Jack surmised. It must have been a real ball-breaker to collect a pittance while following around a man who made more money when he slept than Slater would make in a lifetime of putting his life on the line. Jack could change that, offer the man a jaw-dropping salary and benefits beyond his wildest imagination. One never could tell with titled do-gooders, though. They were just as likely to add a charge of bribery as to do the smart thing. There was a special kind of ignorance in taking the moral high-road when all the rewards lined the road with the money.

"I take your calls," Jack stated quietly. "I put up with the visits of your agency peons, going through everything, looking for a pot of non-existent gold at the end of some imaginary rainbow. But this is harassment."

"This is a public bar," Slater replied, and, civility shriveling instantly, Jack laughed as he dropped onto the table's vacant stool.

"I don't know what you think you have on me," he uttered. "But you don't have anything. My business practices, they may be just this side of legal, but they are this side. I have a very good team who sees to it."

"Are you sure about that?" Slater asked with such calm, Jack felt the foreign sensation of fear move through his system and pin him to his seat. "That's the thing about toeing the line, isn't it? You never know when you might accidentally..." Slater paused to click his tongue, fingers on the tabletop demonstrating his point. "Step over."

When Jack could think of nothing to say in his defense, Slater stood, looking even bigger than he had at the club. The dimly lit room turned him into a massive beast of a man and hardly the type one would want to tangle with in a bar fight. "This really doesn't seem like your kind of place," Slater said, sniffing the air. "Guess you never really can tell about a person. I hear you breakfast at the diner in town, and Bob makes a great quiche. I can't wait to try it. And I would love to have a word with your friends."

With a nod toward the back table, Slater turned for the door, disappearing through it without a backward glance, and Jack jumped up from the stool, grasping at the table in irritation when his legs felt less than sturdy. Teetering on the edge, Slater's glass looked as if it might hang on, as if it might have a chance against Jack's wrong move, before finally giving into gravity and meeting its untimely end on the termite-infested hardwood.

38

The sound of Amelia's heartbeat was steady in Caton's ear, each thump an individual reminder as to why she shouldn't be there. Not like this. Not when she couldn't separate the *this* from the *that*. If she could just have sex with Amelia, spending a day in bed with her would be a matter of recreation. Since she couldn't, spending a day in bed with Amelia was a sure sign of voluntary madness.

All day, they had barely moved, rising only when Sole knocked to tell them she was going to the guesthouse and remind them to eat something. When she cracked the door open, everything remained where it had fallen, including Caton and Amelia, but Sole did her usual believable job of pretending not to see a thing.

Even after heeding Sole's advice, and cleaning up the evidence of their afternoon tryst, they returned to the bed, evening unfolding in a series of peaks and valleys, until all light faded beyond the curtains and they surrendered to the tranquility of the empty house.

Lying in the darkness, Caton was sure Amelia had fallen asleep beneath her, so the quietly inquisitive voice was startling in the quiet. "Where'd you get your name?"

Eyes drifting open, Caton watched the rumpled sheet rise and fall at Amelia's chest. "It's my grandmother's maiden name."

"Mmm," Amelia returned lazily, hand sweeping up Caton's back to brand a warm imprint on her exposed shoulder. "That's nice. I was named after Amelia Earhardt."

"Really," Caton replied casually, more statement than question. If she'd learned anything over the past days, it was that the less Amelia was pushed for information, the more she volunteered.

"My dad was obsessed with her when he was little," Amelia said. "And when I was too really. He was a bigger feminist than any woman I've ever known. He always said we should be running the world, because men were llevándolo a la cagadero."

The soft timbre of Amelia's voice rolling down her back, Caton shivered. It was still rare that Amelia used her native language, but, when she did, it was its own brand of foreplay.

"What does that mean?"

"Taking it to the crapper," Amelia replied, laughter rumbling through her chest.

Apparently, it didn't even matter what she was actually saying.

"He was sick," Amelia whispered, and Caton stilled instantly, hand on Amelia's side ceasing its movement. "My papa," Amelia clarified. "He couldn't work, because he was sick. That's why things were so hard for us."

Afraid to say anything, for fear that Amelia would stop talking, Caton gave into her desire to know Amelia more, to understand her, when Amelia stopped talking anyway. "What was wrong with him?" she asked, clutching softly to Amelia's side, anticipating Amelia closing up on her.

"He worked in the mines when he was young," Amelia surprised her by answering. "They didn't have any real regulations. With all the smoke and the grit and the chemicals he was breathing, he was an old man by the time he was thirty. He wanted to work, but he couldn't. His body was weak. He could barely walk across the room without losing his breath. And at night when he would try to sleep, he would cough and it was… it was this horrible sound."

When Amelia paused long, Caton moved her hand to Amelia's arm, stroking softly over delicate skin, silently encouraging her to go on.

"When I was thirteen," Amelia's voice grew more halting, heavy breaths falling in the spaces between phrases. "He borrowed a gun from one of his friends. But his hands shook too much, so the bullet only grazed his head and he ended up with this scar that cuts across his scalp where hair won't grow. We call it his crop circle."

When Amelia laughed lightly, it was genuine, but so were the tears Caton could hear in her voice. Lifting her head in the darkness, she found the trail on Amelia's face and wiped the drops away with her fingertips, pushing up further in the bed to press her lips to Amelia's temple.

"My mama, she was so angry," Amelia said, and Caton risked keeping her head up, eyes on Amelia's face as she went on. "I had never seen her angry like that. She told him things would be all right, that we would make it, that we would endure whatever came at us, but we would never get over that. After that," Amelia's tone lightened, the weight of the past easing up on her slightly. "He was different. His body, it was still broken, but his spirit, it wasn't. He just needed to be reminded, I guess, that we didn't need him to make everything okay for us. We just needed him there."

Hand moving over Amelia's skin, Caton didn't realize where it was headed until she felt the steady beat of Amelia's heart beneath her fingertips.

"Should we head to your place?" Amelia changed the subject, fingers closing around Caton's where they rested against her chest as her gaze moved to the night beyond the window.

When Amelia's eyes returned to Caton, they were as clear and filled with wonder as a starry night. Sinking quickly into brown depths, Caton tried to find sense in getting up and getting dressed when she could stay in the warmth of Amelia's arms without interruption.

"I'm fine where I am," she responded. "If you're okay."

"Yes," Amelia murmured, hand rising to gently tuck the loose hair behind Caton's ear, before moving in gentle caress down her cheek. "I'm fine where you are too."

The skipping of her heart ensuring Caton she hadn't misheard, she chose to take the declaration as a slip of the tongue. Knowing better than to try to respond to it, she dropped her head back to Amelia's chest. It was exactly the kind of thing she didn't need Amelia saying, exactly the kind of thing that could lead her to make even more bad decisions.

Closed off and hostile, Amelia was still enticing. Open and gracious, she was dangerously irresistible - an Eden laden with land mines. And Caton knew, if she kept pressing onward, something was bound to explode.

Caton woke from a nightmare into a dream, though they felt like one and the same.

In sleep, she had been on the rack, wrists and ankles shackled as she was pulled slowly in opposite directions. Awake, the vice was Amelia, holding her in place with nothing but a light hand on her abdomen that had settled there as they slept.

Shades neglected the night before, the room was too bright as Caton let her head fall to the side to take in Amelia's serene features. Sun pouring over her face, she looked ethereal, and the thought alone made Caton want to slip out of the bed and run.

Glancing at her clothes, neatly piled on a chair by the window, she wondered if she could escape without waking Amelia. That would certainly send a message, a message she had needed to send for a while. Eyes trailing back to Amelia, though, she lacked the power to go anywhere. Amelia sleeping in sunlight was utter perfection, and Caton wanted nothing more than to wake up to it the next morning, all mornings after be damned.

Captivated by the spell of dark silken hair, the scattered, barely-there freckles, the long lashes resting against Amelia's cheeks, offset by the few lines that appeared by her eyes when she truly relaxed, for several long minutes Caton couldn't move. Then, she couldn't resist.

Gently plucking Amelia's sleep-heavy hand from her stomach, she lowered it to the mattress between them, encouraged when Amelia didn't seem to register the change. Covers blocking most of her view, Caton reached cautiously across the mattress, smiling when her fingers found skin.

Traveling the soft plane of Amelia's torso, they climbed the slope of Amelia's breast, brushing a nipple that firmed at her touch. Amelia's breaths growing quicker, shallower, her eyes remained still beneath their closed lids. Caton wondered what she was dreaming, wondered if she could alter Amelia's dreams.

Hand trailing the muscles of Amelia's side, she edged closer, and Amelia took a deep breath, expelling it slowly. Eyes trained on Amelia's face, still showing no indication she'd woken, Caton eased the covers back with her elbow, sliding lower until she could close her lips around the tight nipple. The instantaneous arch of Amelia's body was pure reflex, and Caton felt a rush of power as she closed her arm around Amelia, hand sliding up Amelia's upper back to rest between her shoulder blades.

She could tell when Amelia woke, could feel the intentional straining to get closer. The same hand that found Caton in sleep moved to cradle the back of her head, urging her on, and Caton flicked the nipple with her tongue, drawing a moan from Amelia.

"Caton." Amelia's fingers worked into her hair, nails scratching against her scalp.

Following the curve of Amelia's breast to the top of her rib cage, Caton's tongue dipped into the soft space beneath hard bone, hand leisurely trailing down Amelia's body.

"...doing back here?" Sole's voice wrenched Caton from nirvana. Head whipping toward the closed door, she half-expected to find Sole in the room with them.

"Things didn't turn out as planned." Jack's voice was a far crueler surprise.

Ice melting down Caton's back, her gaze shifted to the speaker beside the door.

"I'm sorry," Sole returned convincingly, her voice surprisingly calm. "Let me get you some breakfast."

"I should take this upstairs," Jack stated, and Amelia stroked a hand across Caton's shoulder in an attempt to ease her burgeoning panic.

When she looked to Amelia, the hand moved inward, thumb brushing Caton's cheek, and, though she sighed, Amelia didn't look particularly worried.

"Leave that until later," Sole distracted. "Come on. It's all ready."

When the conversation ceased and there were no footsteps in the hallway, Caton assumed Jack had taken the bait. Amelia looked up at her, disappointment and annoyance playing at her features, and Caton knew she no longer had to worry about escaping the rest of the weekend.

Reality had just kicked her out of it.

39

Caton wanted to slip out the window like a common burglar. It took some convincing to assure her Jack would be occupied and would never see her walking out the front door. Even then, she was in a state of panic, as if Jack finding her there on a Saturday morning was the worst thing that could possibly happen.

Amelia wasn't sure how Jack would react to the discovery that Caton had spent the night, even if he knew exactly how Caton had spent her night, but she suspected he wouldn't care beyond the ego-crippling fact she had gotten in somewhere he couldn't. Of course, the same could be said for Caton. She had certainly unlocked passageways into Amelia Jack had never found or explored. Realizing the revelation of their relationship would actually be a double blow to Jack's manhood almost made it worth telling him.

If only Caton weren't so afraid.

At the front door, Amelia actually had to catch Caton's arm and hold it with some force to keep her from bolting without a goodbye the instant she reached it. "Caton," she demanded, and desperate green eyes swung her way, though they were more focused on what might be coming from behind her than they were on Amelia. "I'm sorry."

It didn't come near capturing the extent of what she felt, the intense disappointment, the longing to have her stay, but it was all she had time to say.

Caton said nothing in return. Eyes dropping away from Amelia's, she looked more ashamed than anything as she eased her arm out of Amelia's grasp and slipped out the door into the cold morning. Watching her rush down the stairs, Amelia pushed the door shut against the biting wind, the parting expression on Caton's face leaving her disquieted.

Caton's panic, Amelia could handle. Caton's regret, she couldn't.

Listening for the quiet roar of Caton's departure, Amelia knew when she didn't hear it that Caton was over-thinking things. Smiling at the fact she at least knew Caton well enough to make such an assessment, she walked to the living room window, pulling the curtain aside and finding no sign of Caton anywhere. With a small shake of her head, she wondered where exactly Caton had hidden herself.

Knowing Caton would freeze out there before giving them away, Amelia took a deep, steadying breath and headed for the kitchen, rounding the corner to find Jack at the bar, forking eggs into his mouth, newspaper folded on the counter by his plate as if he passed many a Saturday morning that way.

"What are you doing back here?" she asked by way of greeting, and the look Jack sent her way said he expected nothing more, despite them parting on good terms.

"My plans changed," he said, and went back to his paper.

"Good morning," Sole greeted, looking apologetic, as if she could have somehow prevented Jack's return and the subsequent ruining of Amelia's weekend.

"Morning," Amelia uttered, feeling the "good" part particularly unfitting.

"Is Caton here?" Jack asked absently, and Amelia engaged her substantial training to keep her expression neutral.

"Why would she be?"

"Her car is in the driveway," Jack said.

"Is it?" Amelia returned with little interest.

"I believe Caton had car trouble," Sole interjected, and Jack glanced up at her.

The explanation seemed to appease him, even if the excuse left Amelia feeling decidedly hollow.

"I'm not surprised," Jack tossed out unnecessarily, before digging back into his food.

Returning her gaze to Sole, Amelia managed to execute her casual routine flawlessly. "Sole, could you please handle that errand I asked you to run?"

Looking understandably confused, Sole knew better than to ask the obvious question out loud, and Amelia slid her eyes toward the front room, hoping Sole would read her mind.

"Of course," Sole replied at last, amused nod indicating she at least somewhat understood, as she turned at once to shut off the burner and put a lid over the pan on the stove. Perfect as always in following the request, she left with just enough haste to make the task seem important, and just enough leisure to make it seem less important than it was.

"Thank you," Amelia whispered as Sole passed, and Sole reached out to squeeze her arm on her way from the kitchen.

Alone with her husband, the last place she wanted to be at that moment, Amelia went to the cabinet, pulling out a glass and filling it at the refrigerator.

"You should have some of this," Jack declared, his civility forced and empty. "I assume it was made for you."

"Why are you home, Jack?" Amelia questioned, turning toward him and lifting the glass to her lips. The water soothing her parched throat, it did little to ease the deeper withering.

"I can't just want to spend time with my lovely wife?" Jack baited her.

Humorless laugh flowing past her lips, Amelia crossed her free arm over her chest. "Why are you home?" she questioned again.

"It's nothing for you to worry about," Jack returned dismissively.

"Then there is something for me to worry about," Amelia reasoned. It was hardly the first time she had dealt with secrecy and bizarre behavior that went beyond Jack's usual lies. "What aren't you telling me?"

"What aren't you telling me?" Jack countered instantly.

Studying him for a moment, Amelia realized he didn't know. Not everything. Coming home to her sleeping in late, to a breakfast too big for one cooking on the stove, and Caton's car in the driveway, Jack still wasn't convinced of the obvious.

"As much as possible, Jack," Amelia finally declared.

Laughing at the response, caring little so long as Amelia stopped asking questions, Jack went back to eating without concern. Whatever it was that brought him home, he wouldn't tell her by choice. That was part of the deal. Jack never told her anything. The closest he'd ever come to any sort of revelation was a few years before, when he staggered home one night and thought he was going to use the last vestiges of his sex drive on her at three a.m.

After shoving him off and climbing out of bed, Amelia had listened to him raving like a madman about busybodies and moralists, before she finally got her wits back enough to ask him if they were going to be forcibly ejected from their lives.

"Relax," Jack had slurred, head dropping to the bed. "If anything happens, just grab the gnarly bitch and Vespasian her to Antigua."

It wasn't until Jack came downstairs the next morning, looking like a man suffering a hangover he didn't know how to handle, that Amelia realized he wasn't merely drunk, but high on something he wouldn't soon use again. He didn't even remember his homecoming the night before, and, from the way his car was parked in the middle of the lawn, was lucky he hadn't tarnished his carefully-tended reputation forever in one ill-advised evening.

Jack also didn't remember saying anything to Amelia, and Amelia certainly never told him, so he had no idea Amelia knew anything, and Amelia had no real idea what she knew.

Well aware she would never get any truths from Jack sober, not sure she even wanted to hear his truth, she headed for the door.

"I think I'll invite my parents over for dinner tonight," Jack announced suddenly, and, though it sounded like the thoughtful whim of a good son, Amelia knew she was being punished for a crime Jack couldn't even name. "Call Sole and tell her to pick up something nice to make for them while she's out."

Pausing just long enough to listen to the full command, Amelia turned through the doorway, knowing her retreat was only temporary. She could escape the conversation that was going nowhere as usual, she could even escape her role for hours at a time, but she couldn't escape her own life.

40

Caton wished she was an idiot, that it hadn't even occurred to her that if her car, which was blatantly sitting in the driveway, vanished suddenly upon Jack's arrival, it would tell a clear story. A story she didn't particularly want nor need Jack to know.

Of course, freezing to death amidst the clump of miniature pine trees next to the gate, just yards from salvation, would also tell a story.

Peering longingly through the branches, Caton wondered if she should risk it. Maybe she could just get in her car and drive off, and nothing would ever be said.

Or maybe it would ruin everything.

And Jack's unexpected return had already ruined enough.

Scoffing derisively, she realized how rich it was for her to cast herself as the victim, when, if anything, she was one of the bad guys. The early symptoms of delirium setting in, she considered simply dropping down in the snow and allowing nature to take its course. The way her teeth clattered together, her body convulsing for all the wrong reasons, she trusted it wouldn't take long, especially if she cast her coat and scarf aside in forfeit.

It was the sound of a car starting up, distant but not distant enough, that jostled Caton out of her self-pity. On instant alert, she stepped further back into the trees, watching the bend of the driveway as if her doom would come curving around it. When neither Reaper nor car appeared right away, Caton shifted forward just enough to watch a sedan roll from behind the house, moving ever-so-slowly, as if searching for something. Her, she realized, when she recognized the car as Sole's. Showing herself with caution, she watched the car pull to the edge of the driveway and roll to a stop, and Sole leaned over to open the door for her.

"Get in."

With no other option, Caton did as she was ordered, sinking into the seat and pulling the door closed before accepting the blast of hot air from the vents with open palms.

"Are you all right?" Sole asked, easing the car forward until the gate began to open.

"Did Jack ask why my car was here?" Caton countered.

"Yes," Sole answered.

Releasing an aggravated exhalation, Caton wondered if loathing herself would somehow stop her from doing what she was doing. She didn't know why it would. It hadn't brought out the better parts of her so far.

"I told him you had car trouble," Sole added, and Caton numbly nodded. So, getting in her purportedly "troubled" car and driving off may well have ruined everything, or at least destroyed one bad alibi.

"What in the hell am I doing?" she asked no one, which Sole seemed to realize, because she didn't answer. Moments later, silence of the car pressing in on them, Caton felt her mouth open and heard mumbled words she meant to only think. "I am fucking up everything."

"For whom?" Sole did question that, and Caton met her sidelong glance before turning back to the dash.

"For everyone," Caton uttered. "Amelia, you, me... Jesus Christ, I was hiding in the fucking trees."

Small, nervous laugh escaping her, Sole waved at a neighbor walking his dog, and Caton slumped in the seat, trying to make herself invisible.

"You didn't have to do that," Sole said. "Amelia would have come up with some explanation."

"I don't want to be fucking explained!" Caton's vehemence surprised even her. Hand thrusting into the car's dash with a thud that pulled Sole's eyes from the road, it was followed by a rush of pain that made

Caton instantly nauseous. "Sorry," she uttered, realizing she was not only distracting, but it wasn't her car she was attempting to destroy.

"It's okay."

"It's not okay," Caton countered, sinking further into the seat and dropping her head into her hand, roots of a headache already sprouting. "None of this is okay."

That wasn't Sole's fault. Or her car's. And the fact that Caton was complaining like a brat didn't strip away the truth in what she was saying. She was the only one at fault, and the only one who could stop herself from continuing down the dangerous path she felt compelled to travel. She was like a crack needlepointer, embarking on a design far beyond her expertise, too invested in the pretty picture to admit defeat.

That picture was getting uglier every day, though, new snarls piling on top of each other, and, recognizing that there was no attractive end in sight, she attempted to blink back the tears that formed in vain. "I have to end this," she breathed.

"Is that what you want?" Sole asked instantly.

Of course it wasn't what she wanted. She wanted Amelia. She had given into the attraction, then the seduction, then the illusion that it was more than it could ever be, knowing the entire time it was a short ride on a doomed expressway.

"I want to do the right thing," Caton murmured. If she said it enough, maybe she could make it true.

"How do you know this isn't the right thing?" Sole questioned.

That, in a single, impossible question, was the problem. Morality, duty, decency, Caton was certain of nothing anymore. Inside, an infernal battle was raging between logic and heart. She wondered if it would burn her alive, slowly cauterize her from the inside out. Feeling the warring factions rising up, rushing each other with no regard for casualties, Caton shrugged her shoulders against the building tension. "You should let me out," she warned Sole. "Because I really want to tear the hell out of your car."

"Go ahead," Sole returned gently. "It's only a car."

The overly-compassionate response wasn't what Caton had coming, but, combined with the sympathetic smile Sole cast her way, it was enough to call a temporary cease-fire within Caton. Instead of clawing at the car's interior, she dropped her head back against the seat, eyes fixated on the passing scenery.

When her phone rang in her bag, she knew who it was without looking, and Sole knew too. Caton could feel the other woman's anxious gaze on her as she resisted the temptation to answer. Fingertips going white where she clutched her bag, she waited for the ringing to stop. When it finally did, returning the interior of the car to relative silence, Caton could breathe again. One battle won, though she knew it was only the first of many.

41

It was more than punishment. It was hell. They were her personal hell.
There wasn't a single form of torture Amelia could imagine that would
be greater torment than an eternity in the presence of Jack's parents.

"So, Jack tells me you have an assistant," Victoria uttered. It was
almost pleasant, her demeanor, like a snake curling around a body in
temporary embrace before it squeezed the life out of a person.

It was the same every time. Amelia tried to be ignored. She tried to be
polite and silent, letting the conversation happen without her. But that
was boring for them. These people were hunters. They needed a target.
So, they drew her in against her will, hoping she would give them a
reason to shoot her.

"Did he?" Amelia returned.

"We saw the car in the driveway," Victoria added.

"Not paying her much, I see," Jack Sr. joked, and Jack and his mother
laughed along at Caton's expense. The have-nots, they were such comedic
fodder for the haves. As an ambassador for the poor in their luxury
world, Amelia had learned that lesson quickly.

Saying nothing in Caton's defense, knowing it would only lead to
grander insults, Amelia took a drink, bitterly swallowing as she looked
toward the doorway. It was always the same, and, yet, it was different.
Normally, Victoria and Jack Sr. were the major nuisance of any given day
in which she had to endure them. Tonight, they were just one more
thing plucking at Amelia's thin nerves. Jack's interruption had been the
first, and, since she left, Caton wouldn't take her calls. Amelia had tried

her half a dozen times, before deciding she wasn't going to behave desperately. It wasn't her fault Jack returned, it was the last thing she wanted, so if Caton chose to blame her, if she chose to be unfair and juvenile, Amelia wasn't going to keep trying.

Mostly because she didn't have her phone, and these weren't the kind of people who allowed one to excuse herself from a meal. They expected their prey to stick around to face their taunts and flying bullets.

Returning her eyes to her uneaten food, Amelia realized her in-laws were waiting for her to say something. She never knew with them when they actually expected response, or when they were just running commentary on her life. "Jack brought her here." Amelia hoped the truth would be the end of it.

"Yes," Jack said with a boastful grin. "Amelia was a little overwhelmed with the duties of both fundraising and being a beautiful wife." If anyone else had said it, Amelia might have thought it a compliment.

"Hmm," Victoria hummed. "Well, I guess some people are just more capable than others."

Amelia was amazed, as usual, at the way the woman delivered her insults as if she was making a passing reference to the weather. She wasn't the only one thinking it, they all thought it, but this was one of the many rules in their world. Only a woman could attack another woman. If a man did it, it just looked uncouth.

"How's Selene?" Jack Sr. changed the subject, and Amelia was grateful to sink back into invisibility.

"She's back at school," Jack responded. "She's doing well."

Fighting her urge to scoff in response, Amelia wondered how Jack made such an assured declaration. Not once since Selene left home had he actually picked up the phone to call his daughter.

"That's good. I noticed she was a little clingy at Christmas," Victoria declared, eyes sliding to Amelia in silent blame. "I thought she'd grown out of that. You are encouraging her to make her own way, aren't you?"

"Of course I am," Amelia stated, hand tightening on her glass.

"Our children can't simply be reflections of us." Victoria doled out her parenting advice in the same way she delivered her insults.

Glancing at Jack and Jack Sr., sitting across the table from each other, exact same mannerisms, exact same beliefs, same fields of business, same infidelities, Amelia might have laughed if she cared enough to truly engage. Of course, it wasn't that they didn't want Selene to be a reflection. They just didn't want Selene to reflect off her.

Taking another drink, she was saved from the repercussions of the sharp response on her tongue by Sole walking into the dining room to clear their plates. Reaching Amelia's, Sole cast her a worried look that Amelia avoided before taking the uneaten food away. "Could I get anyone dessert?" she dutifully asked.

"Not now," Jack's father answered for everyone, waving Amelia's only ally from the room. "I have a few investors who are looking for a project, Jacky," he continued once Sole was gone. "I'm going to tell them to invest with you."

Amelia's relief at having the focus pulled from her and the people she cared about was eradicated by the long delay in Jack's response. Taking a drink, Jack swallowed with effort, returning his glass slowly to the table. "We're not really in need of investors right now," he finally replied, hand going to his chin and rubbing the five o'clock shadow there. It was his tell, the too-common gesture paired with every well-crafted lie. "I think we'll need them more in a few months. If you could hold them off, I'll be able to use them when I need them."

Their way of talking about people as if they were cash cows was unsurpassed, but Amelia was accustomed to that. It was the composed answer, initial hesitation disguised with the prolonged drink, that gave Jack's bluff away. Though his response was completely transparent, as usual, his parents pretended they couldn't see through it.

"I'll explain to them that you're in transition," Jack Sr. returned. "That you'll have more lucrative opportunities for them down the road."

As Jack nodded his appreciation, Amelia felt the injustice swirl warmly amidst her slight intoxication. They had no problem going after her, Selene, Caton, for being overwhelmed, affectionate, middle-class, but Jack off-handedly admitted he'd gotten his company into some kind of serious trouble and it didn't even warrant a question.

"We can always use their donations in our charity work," Amelia interjected, knowing too well she shouldn't. It would come to no good end, but, as far as she could see, there was no good end in sight for a day that had started with such promise.

"I think these people actually want to make money," Jack laughed. "They're looking for an investment."

"It's an investment in the future," Amelia countered with her usual line of persuasion, and the smile with which she always delivered it. "Isn't that what we tell all our donors? I'm sure they would be happy to invest in the future." When she glanced over to include Jack Jr. in her pitch, he looked at her with unconcealed contempt that she would dare challenge his son.

"Okay, that's enough," Jack stated, not even bothering to play, smile fading as he wiped the cloth napkin across his lips.

"I don't understand," Amelia returned sweetly. "Why wouldn't you want their money? If you can't use it, you can put it toward the charity work, which helps build the company's reputation."

"I'm not looking to build reputation right now," Jack declared.

"I thought you were always looking to build reputation," Amelia countered.

"We will talk about it another day." Jack's voice rose just enough to satisfy Amelia's immature desire to ruin his night as he had ruined hers.

"The needs of these people don't wait, Jack." Amelia's smile faded.

"What people are those, dear?" Victoria's voice cut through the smog that had formed between them, odious and unbreathable. "Your family?"

Flinching as if it was an actual bullet Victoria had sent her way, Amelia swallowed the bile that rose into her throat, a searing mix of wine and stomach acid. Turning her gaze to Victoria's smug expression, she barely contained the urge to lunge across the table and tackle the bitch to the floor. The fact that she had never broken a glass and stabbed her mother-in-law in the jugular might have been Amelia's only remaining shot at Heaven.

All that talk about Selene becoming her own person, and they still ended up right back here. Amelia challenged Jack, and, when it looked as if Jack wasn't outright winning, Victoria rushed in to rescue him like he was a three-year-old on a playground.

Amelia knew better than to engage in a battle of wills when it was three-to-one, but she had lost herself for a moment, rebellion fueled by too much wine on an empty stomach, by having to endure some of the most vile human beings on the planet, and by Caton, who wouldn't take her fucking calls.

Pushing up from her chair, she didn't glance back, letting them, and knowing very well they would, call her what they wanted when she left the room. She remembered the first time like it was yesterday. When she had arrived in the States with Jack, and he had taken her to his parents grand estate, she had felt like a queen. Then, she'd gone to the gilded bathroom and returned just as Jack's mother was calling her his Moabite bride in such a way that she really should have just said 'savage' and spared everyone the translation.

Then, there was the wedding, that glorious, glamorous affair, when they lavished her parents with clothes and expensive haircuts and spa treatments. At the time, she was naïve enough to believe it generosity. It would take her years to see it for what it was, a necessary concession to make them more presentable, because the Halstons couldn't be embarrassed on a day that invited public scrutiny. Appearance was everything, and her parents had to look the part.

As Amelia rounded the corner into the kitchen, Sole turned from her dinner at the bar. "Are you okay?" she asked, though she didn't have to ask to know the answer.

"Where's my phone?" Amelia demanded.

Sliding it from the bar top beside her, Sole handed it to Amelia. Having given it to Sole with the instruction to let her know if Caton called, it was infuriating to ask for it back.

Moving toward the French doors, Amelia heard Sole jump up behind her. "It's cold," Sole said. "Let me get you a coat."

"I'm fine," Amelia tossed over her shoulder, wrenching back the lock and pulling the door open.

The frigid air biting into her exposed skin at once, the physical punishment was almost relief in the wake of the other pains she'd been made to endure. Closing the door behind her, Amelia marched through the snow that remained on the ground, cold flakes flicking onto the backs of her legs as she made her way from a house that had never been refuge. Dialing Caton, she waited, once more, for the phone to go to voice mail, angrily ending the call when it did and immediately calling again, prepared to repeat the pattern as many times as it took.

She couldn't say what she was thinking to Jack or Jack's parents, to her supposed society friends, to her repeat donors, or even to Sole or Selene most of the time, but, with Caton, she could be honest. She could tell her exactly what she thought about her avoidance. She could unleash on Caton the reaming she deserved for ignoring her all day.

"Hey," Caton's voice softly answered as Amelia was getting ready to end the call and try again.

Eyes closing at the sound, Amelia missed her cue. Instead of rupturing from her in a torrent, the anger abated, and she felt dizzy. She felt cold. She wasn't angry, she realized, not at Caton. She was hurt. She was confused. She was everything she had learned not to be.

"I'm sorry I didn't pick up," Caton stated carefully. "I… couldn't find my phone."

That was a lie too, Amelia knew, but at least it was a lie told for her sake, meant to make her feel better instead of worse. She wanted to ask why Caton would lie to her at all, why she didn't want to talk to her. She wanted to ask Caton to come back and take her away from it all. For a night. Two nights. For the rest of her life.

"I'm sorry that Jack came home." Amelia could get no further than the same apology from before.

"Maybe it's better this way," Caton returned.

That hurt too. Not just that Caton would say it out loud. That she would even think it.

Agreement would have been the highest form of self-preservation, the simplest, least messy path, but, gaze trailing to the house, the soft light from the kitchen appearing more cold and uninviting than the dark, snow-covered landscape around her, Amelia didn't have the strength to pretend.

"No," she said simply.

The only response from Caton came in the form of a deep, drawn-out sigh, which sounded perfectly harmonious to Amelia's ear, because she felt exactly the same way.

42

Though it sounded the same monotonous tone she woke to every morning, the alarm echoed like a warning. Pressing it off on automatic, Caton knew she needed to get up, to leave, to flee the city even, but she made it only as far as sitting before losing all motivation.

It was only two months, she tried to remind herself. Two months until her contract was up, until her assignment was fulfilled, until she was freed from Amelia and the overwhelming pains and pleasures that went with her.

She had used the same self-talk to power through the monotony of the storage room, Jack's come-ons and Amelia's animosity. *It's only temporary, Caton. The end is in sight.* Once a point on the horizon that looked like freedom, though, the end had become a looming threat, and, with no consolation awaiting her on the other side of it, Caton simply couldn't find the point in rising.

At some point, her phone rang. She didn't know how long she had been sitting there as it trilled its annoying blast into the room, and, clock right beside her on the bedside table, she couldn't find the desire to look.

It rang again sometime after. And again sometime after that. When the ringing finally stopped altogether, Caton wasn't sure if the caller had given up, or if her phone had used up the last dregs of its battery she hadn't bothered to charge the night before.

Knees pulled to her chest, cheek resting against one bony point, time moved fast and slow, and she made no guesses as to how much of it had passed between the last weak ring and the knock that came at the door, loud and emphatic. With no noticeable break between the first thunderous assault and the next, Caton pressed her ear tighter to her knee, hand rising to cover her other ear in protest.

At last, the racket ceased, the eye of the storm, Caton discovered, as a crash made her jump from her skin.

"Caton?" Amelia's voice was almost unrecognizable, and it occurred to Caton she had never heard Amelia truly panicked.

An unrecognizable thunk followed, before Caton's bedroom door opened and Amelia appeared breathlessly in the doorway. Concern mingling with annoyance when she saw Caton sitting there in perfect exterior condition, Amelia blew out a short breath. "Why in the hell didn't you answer the door?"

"I didn't feel like it," Caton returned, watching confusion bordering on doubt pass over Amelia's features. The receptive response of her body to Amelia's presence reminding her she was in the most dangerous possible position, she slid from the bed, glancing down at her relative nudity with alarm, and reached for her pajama pants.

"Are you okay?" Amelia questioned.

"Why wouldn't I be?" Caton countered, pulling the pants over her hips and casting an anxious glance toward the door at Amelia's back.

Only one way out, and no fortified place to hide, she attempted to skirt around Amelia. When Amelia reached out, Caton shrugged her off, but the touch on her arm lingered as she continued into the main room, her gaze going instantly to the ajar door, knob hanging on by a single screw, the fire extinguisher from the glass case in the hall abandoned in her entryway.

Just one more mess to clean up.

Back turned, she filled a glass at the faucet and tried to think of something she could say or do to put an immediate end to the ongoing tug-of-war she had jumped into with the naive belief she was going to be an adroit player, only to discover she was the rope.

It wouldn't take much. Amelia had exposed herself far more sensitive to certain types of criticisms than Caton would have ever expected her to be. The right words, and Caton trusted she could turn Amelia off for good. All she had to do was find the right button to push.

The thought alone made the glass tremble in her hand, and she placed it carefully on the counter, knowing it was the right thing to do, even if they both got hurt in the process. Spinning to look for a point of weakness in Amelia before she lost her nerve, she stepped back when Amelia was right there, so close Caton wasn't sure how she made her approach without detection.

"Don't," Amelia uttered.

Prescient pain swirling in the dark eyes locked on her own, Caton had the disconcerting feeling Amelia could read her thoughts. "Don't what?" she tried to play it off.

"Just don't," Amelia's voice further softened until it became more plea than command.

Shadows playing across the contours of Amelia's face, Caton yearned toward her, to give into her, to fix everything. But she didn't have the power to fix everything. She didn't have the power to fix anything. Arms folding behind her, she dug her fingers into her forearms, locking them together, the closest thing she had to restraints.

Fighting her own desire, she longed to go back to a time of ignorance, when her undeniable attraction to Amelia bred nothing but contempt, when Amelia had no redeeming qualities, aside from her captivating charm and beauty. And she longed to go forward to a time of enlightenment, when she could fully understand why a woman with so much to offer kept it hidden behind a curtain of detachment and deceit.

She couldn't do it. Even if it was right. Even if it made sense. She couldn't hone in on a vulnerability and exploit it, not now that she knew Amelia had so many she kept locked away, how carefully she guarded them. But things couldn't go on as they were either. Rack or rope, something had to give, or Caton would come apart, fray at the sinew until there was nothing left holding her together.

"I can't do this," she quietly stated, all attempts at outward blame turning inward where they belonged.

Amelia shifted, and before Caton could think to move, Amelia's body was flush against her, altering her intentions. "Yes, you can," Amelia whispered. "You can."

Amelia didn't know what she was asking, what she encouraged, and Caton didn't know how much she wanted talked back into what she had tried so hard to talk herself out of until Amelia managed it in two words. Hands going to Amelia's face, she brought their lips together, realizing in an instant she had been depriving herself. She couldn't control what she wanted to burn freely, even if it ended up consuming her. The taste of Amelia going instantly to her head, she pulled away, head oddly tingly as she dropped it to Amelia's shoulder, nose teased by the familiar scent that somehow calmed and aroused her at once.

"I need you." Amelia's whispered words were so quiet, Caton wasn't sure if they were a statement, a prayer, or a figment of her imagination.

Regardless, they were a lie. Amelia didn't need anyone. But Caton didn't need to be needed. Knowing Amelia wanted her, at least enough to come busting through her door like a lunatic, was more than enough.

When Amelia kissed her again, Caton didn't care if it was imagined or wrong or foolish. She had been nothing but foolish, and as much agony as it had brought her, it had brought her ten times the ecstasy. With Amelia's body pressed softly against her, Amelia's hand on the back of her head holding her close as her tongue worked magic in Caton's mouth, ecstasy always felt only a heartbeat away.

The knock at the door was so soft, Caton thought she had imagined that too, until Amelia pulled back and glanced toward the doorway, eyes registering only a fleeting trace of shock, before her face settled into the same determined charisma she faked so well.

"Excuse me." The voice called Caton's eyes to the door, and she went board-straight as she registered the uniform of the police officer standing inside her apartment. "Is everything okay here?"

Amelia's hands retreating from her body, Caton felt exposed in their absence. Glancing down, she reaffirmed that she was, in fact, wearing clothes.

"Yes, Officer," Amelia responded. "I'm so sorry. This is Caton. She lives here, and, as you can see, she's fine."

"A neighbor called in a disturbance," the officer explained, glancing from the fire extinguisher at his feet to the broken door knob.

"Yes." Amelia smiled her winningest smile. "Sorry about that."

"Miss." The officer addressed Caton directly. "Are you all right?"

"Yes, I'm fine," Caton managed, despite the extreme discomfort that snuck up the back of her neck to set it aflame.

"I'm just going to take a look around," the officer said, and Amelia gestured with an open palm, as if she could grant entrance to Caton's place.

"Hello," Amelia greeted someone in the hallway to no verbal response, and Caton assumed there was a partner she couldn't see.

Why not add spectacle for the neighbors to the mix, she thought, cracking her neck as she watched the first officer disappear into her bedroom, wondering what he might determine about her character from the clutter scattered about the room. If he made any snap judgments, he kept them to himself as he came back through the door.

"The neighbor thought you were breaking in," he explained, as he passed back by Amelia.

'Probably because she was,' Caton responded in her head, a small smile intruding upon her grim mood.

"I was worried," Amelia admitted, and the smile widened against Caton's will.

"Next time, call the super," the officer advised.

"Good advice," Amelia returned, though Amelia and the officer both seemed to know that, should there be a next time, Amelia would handle it exactly the same way.

"Have a nice day." The officer sounded surprisingly sincere as he walked out, despite the inconvenience of being called to a scene without a crime. At least, none that he could detect.

"You too," Amelia returned. "Thank you."

Though Amelia managed to return the door to its proper position, it refused to stay closed. Improvising, she rolled the fire extinguisher against it with her foot, standing back to admire her handiwork when it held the door temporarily shut. Abashed grin playing at her lips, she glanced over at Caton and looked so adorably culpable, Caton could do nothing but laugh.

Not long after finding herself back in Amelia's arms, Caton found herself back in bed.

Amelia insisted she eat, so they had to wait for takeout. Then, she insisted she pay to fix the door, so they had to wait for the repairman. By then, it was late evening and the sun was starting to set as Caton returned from her shower to find Amelia kicking her shoes off and pushing her jeans down her legs. Watching the last of Amelia's clothing join the rest, Caton trailed her to the bed, offering no resistance when Amelia's hands went to the towel tucked at her chest and eased it apart.

Worn terrycloth falling to the floor, the instantaneous sensation as her bare skin pressed against Amelia's shook Caton to her core. As Amelia's eyes searched her face, she could tell she was looking for something in particular, and it showed, Caton was certain, every thought and emotion written clearly on her face for Amelia to read and exploit.

Caton didn't realize she had ceased to breathe until Amelia moved to push down the blankets. Sucking in a desperate, pained breath, she let Amelia pull her down to the mattress, giving in to the feel of Amelia's slightly chilled skin warming rapidly against her own.

Amelia's hands on her were the same, but different. Slow and without desperation, it was as if they had all the time in the world. Which, Caton well knew, was painfully untrue.

Still, when Amelia kissed her, Caton kissed back. When Amelia dropped her lips to her neck, Caton tilted her head back, offering more. When Amelia's fingers entered her, Caton let herself be consumed. And, when Amelia's breaths grew wanton in her ear, Caton wanted nothing more than to satisfy the anguished desire, to give Amelia everything she wanted or needed.

Falling atop Amelia, exhausted, but not quite content, as Amelia's body shuddered beneath her, Caton trembled as Amelia's arms closed around her, holding her closer, tighter, as if she would never let go.

Waking some time later, Caton could feel the lateness of the hour. Shifting to see beyond the rise of Amelia's body, she looked at the clock, sighing at the rules of their lives. "Amelia," she uttered, shaking Amelia's shoulder firmly enough to rouse her. "It's late."

Eyes sleepily parting, it took Amelia a moment to process the information. "Then go back to sleep," she husked at last.

Gaze going once again to the clock, Caton was certain Amelia didn't understand. "Don't you need to go home?"

"No," Amelia uttered, appearing perfectly coherent as her fingers ran up Caton's spine in the darkness, where the tension vibrated just beneath her skin. "Just go back to sleep, Caton."

Lifting her head with some effort, Amelia pressed a soft, fleeting kiss to her lips and turned onto her side, tugging Caton's arm around her and falling almost instantly back to sleep.

Uncertainty weighing, Caton watched another minute tick by, before molding herself against the smooth back, lips coming to rest against the addictive skin of Amelia's shoulder. Breathing in, she was soothed by the familiar scent, by the curve of Amelia's body, and by a feeling so overpowering, she couldn't give it name.

43

Caton didn't try to fool herself again. What Amelia wanted, Amelia would get. Whether it was a quasi-date at her favorite restaurant or impromptu sleepovers. If Amelia asked, Caton said "yes" instinctively. It was the only thing she ever wanted to say to her. Thinking had done nothing but fill her head with torment, while leading to no constructive action. It was easier, she had discovered, to simply do.

So, when Jack was invited to a gallery showing for the daughter of a business acquaintance and Amelia was sent in as emissary, allowing Jack to make a good impression without actually having to give up his own time, Caton agreed to accompany her without thought.

Heeding the cocktail attire dress code with flair, Amelia was, as usual, the most stunning woman in the room. No one failed to notice her. Though, as far as Caton could tell, Amelia failed to notice anyone, save for her. Every time she looked up, Amelia's eyes were on her, slinking down her in such a way that Caton's body positively thrummed without a single touch.

"Excuse me, Amelia." A woman insinuated herself into Amelia's attention half an hour after they'd arrived, and Amelia put on her public face, the one that smiled without ever really smiling. "Would you come talk to Mr. Johnson for a moment? He wants to ask about Jack."

"Yes, of course." Amelia glanced apologetically at Caton, though Caton wasn't sure if it was because she was about to be abandoned or for the mention of her husband. "I'll be right back."

As she moved away, the chill on Caton's skin indicated just how close Amelia had been standing, how warm Amelia's hand had been on her back, and Caton shivered without her presence. Eyeing the bar at once, she made her way to it, ordering up the only courage in the room with a twist.

"Is she as much of a bitch as Jack says?"

The voice as unwelcome as the question, Caton's insides curled in response. Refusing to look back, she failed to spare herself the confrontation when Jenna swung into view, a smug look on her overly made up face.

"Oh... you're friends," Jenna stated with some amusement, eyes moving over Caton's tight expression, and Caton returned her gaze to the bar, hoping the bartender was doing more tending than listening. "More than friends?" Jenna added, waiting for a response Caton didn't provide.

"Shouldn't you be off somewhere fucking Jack?" she muttered instead, wondering how in the hell Jenna deduced her relationship with Amelia in the time they had been at the gallery, when she hadn't even noticed Jenna amongst the minglers.

"Does he know?" Jenna countered.

"No, why?" Caton glanced at her with distaste. "Are you going to tell him?"

"It would help build trust," Jenna returned casually, and a muscle twitched in Caton's jaw as she tried to decide whether it was worth the fallout to tell Jenna exactly what she thought of her.

"Caton." At any other time, Amelia's voice may well have alleviated the tension, the hand that slid across Caton's lower back may been comforting, but the way Jenna followed the touch with such amused fascination made it feel unsavory.

Glancing to Amelia, Caton watched her eye Jenna with an oddly neutral expression. "What do you want?" she asked.

"Just saying hello," Jenna lied. "We did work together. Lovely dress, by the way."

"Go away," Amelia responded, and though she did so with a disbelieving scoff, Jenna did as she was told.

Potential repercussions smacking her square in the face, Caton felt sick as Amelia moved in front of her, hand sliding from her back to her side.

"What's wrong?" Amelia asked in concern. "Did she say something?"

Raising her eyes to Amelia's, Caton felt short of breath, and wondered if one could develop asthma in her thirties within twenty seconds. "She knows."

Her own gaze rising with more interest than concern, Amelia glanced in the direction of Jenna's departure. "How?" she asked.

"Apparently, it's obvious," Caton returned, and Amelia looked between them, taking in the lack of space, the way her hand rested against Caton's hip leaving little to the imagination, though she made no effort to pull away. "So, now what?" Caton asked, realizing as she asked that she was terrified of how Amelia might answer.

"I don't know," Amelia returned at last, reaching back to pluck a glass of champagne from the bar and taking a sip. "Do you want to look at the rest of the art?"

Laugh disjointed as it poured unexpectedly over her lips, Caton enunciated, "Jenna knows."

"I heard you," Amelia returned.

"That doesn't bother you?" Caton asked. Her own heart pounding rapidly in her chest, she felt an inordinate amount of fear, as if they had been caught together in the trap of a serial killer. "You don't think she'll tell Jack?"

"I don't know what she'll do." Amelia shook her head. "Whatever she does, though, there's nothing we can do about it."

They could stop, Caton's mind supplied instantly, make sure when Jack went looking, there would be nothing for him to find. Meeting Amelia's eyes, though, she couldn't even suggest it, and was more relieved than she should have been when Amelia didn't state the obvious solution either.

"So, do you want to look at the rest of the art?" Amelia asked again, head tilting toward an adjoining gallery.

"Yeah, whatever," Caton shrugged helplessly, not sure what else to do. Grabbing the harder spirits the bartender had left on the bar for her, she put half the drink away as she let Amelia lead her across the room. Not seeing Jenna anywhere as they passed through the cluster of rich people, Caton couldn't shake the knowledge she was there.

Passing through the curtain Amelia held apart for her, Caton was given respite from the eyes and ears of strangers and foes alike, as the dissonant hum of too many people talking at once faded into the background.

"There's no one back here," she declared.

"I know," Amelia replied from behind her.

"Are we supposed to be back here?" Caton questioned, glancing around the hushed space. The dim light of the gallery casting ominously upon each work, the sculptures looked like monsters lurking in the shadows.

"I got permission," Amelia replied. "I wouldn't want the police to show up again." Arms closing around Caton's waist, she took a step that carried her gently into Caton's back. "You look amazing," she whispered, lips pressing to the exposed skin at Caton's neck.

The majority of her acquiescing instantly, one stubborn part of Caton rebelled in fear. "No, Amelia." The words sounded foreign together as Caton pushed at the arms at her waist, whirling to hold them at bay.

"Really?" Amelia returned, trying and failing to keep a smile from appearing.

Of course, Amelia knew she didn't mean it. Not wholeheartedly. Or, at the very least, couldn't sustain it. She was far too aware of Caton's weakness, far too aware that she was Caton's weakness.

"I tell you that Jack's... whatever the fuck she is to him... knows we're sleeping together, and you think that's a good time to provide videographic evidence." Caton gestured into the darkness.

Even knowing there had to be cameras everywhere, it was a ridiculous argument. The storage room at the Halston Palace also had its closed circuit, and that hadn't stopped her from letting Amelia have her way. Realizing she had no basis for the argument, Caton dropped her hand helplessly.

"I wasn't planning to ravage you on the marble floor," Amelia said in a tone that almost made Caton wish that was exactly Amelia's intent.

"Because you've never done anything like that before," she returned, not sure if she was scolding Amelia or trying to tempt her.

Sliding her hand from Caton's loose grasp without effort, Amelia palmed her hip, pulling Caton closer. "I just wanted to be alone with you," she replied. "Just for a minute."

Hands falling to Amelia's arms as they closed around her again, Caton didn't pretend that she wanted anything other than to lose herself in the embrace. Jenna's presence had been disquieting, though, and it lingered, tainting the moment between them.

"Amelia, I..." Caton started without forethought, no idea where she might end up.

"Shhh," Amelia breathed at once, moving in to capture Caton's lips in a kiss that was meant to make her forget everything else.

For a while, it did.

44

If she was going to get caught with her hand in the cookie jar, Amelia was going to consume as many calories as she could first. Meeting Caton's rational, but dismal, concern that Jack would find out about them with the suggestion that, if Jack was going to find out anyway, she may as well spend the night, Amelia effectively put her own worries to bed.

The first night she had stayed at Caton's, Jack asked where she'd been, but, as someone who knew the answer better than anyone, he didn't need to push. As expected, he was relatively unconcerned, which was only fitting. Though, it was undoubtedly less fairness and more prudence that guided his lack of response. If there was one thing Amelia knew without a doubt, it was that, if the hammer came down, it would do so on Jack's terms, when it was of the most use to him. It wouldn't be while Amelia was playing diplomat at his public appearances or pulling together his business associate's fundraiser in a pinch because the company the man hired "fucked the nugget," per his colorful explanation.

Finalizing the menu with the dessert shop's owner, Amelia thanked the woman and stepped outside, glancing toward the print shop where Sole was taking care of last-minute changes. Seeing Sole nowhere, she made her way to the nearby bench, the unseasonably mild day feeling even warmer as she sank into the sun and pulled her book from her purse, reveling in a moment when she had no other option but to relax and wait.

She wasn't even three paragraphs in before footsteps approached, and she glanced up, curiosity turning to vigilance as she watched a large man she didn't recognize loom nearer. Heeding to caution, Amelia glanced around, noting the man loading bags into his car in the parking lot and the woman piling books into the display window of the bookstore five feet away.

"Amelia?" the man questioned, though he seemed to know well who she was, and Amelia went on alert.

"Yes," she said carefully, walking the fine line between not giving the stranger too much in case he was a threat and being polite in case they had met in the past and she simply didn't remember.

"I'm Marcus Slater," he stated. "I'm with the Business Regulatory Commission. I need to ask you a few questions."

Not sure if she should feel more or less at ease, Amelia dropped her eyes to her book, thoughts swimming too rapidly to pull them into coherence. "All right," she uttered, knowing there was little choice in the matter, and moved her bookmark back into place with a deliberate movement that afforded her the opportunity to take a breath, before sliding the book back into her purse and giving the man her full attention.

When Slater settled into the open space beside her, the bench bowed slightly and Amelia put her hand on the green metal slats to steady herself.

"You handle a lot of fundraising for your husband, don't you?" he asked.

"That depends," Amelia returned haltingly. "Who do you think my husband is?"

"I know who your husband is, Mrs. Halston," Slater returned, and Amelia tempered her reaction as any hope of mistaken identity was extinguished by Slater's unrelenting gaze.

"Yes," Amelia acknowledged. "I do"

"Do you handle the finances?"

Question leaving little room for interpretation, a silent sigh raised Amelia's shoulders. "No," she returned. "I create a budget and the company cuts the checks."

"So, if someone were to add things or take things away from the statements, you would never know?" Slater inferred.

"No."

The answer seemed to line up with Slater's expectations. Nodding, he glanced up, finding something of interest in the sky behind Amelia's head, watching it for a moment before he dropped his eyes back down to her. "Has anyone ever asked you for anything unusual when you're doing all this fundraising?"

Laughing lightly, Amelia shifted on the bench, hoping it appeared more physical than mental discomfort. "They're fundraisers," she returned. "They are nothing but unusual. Ridiculous ice sculptures, sexual party favors, thirty-two-dollar-a-gallon coffee. That's the game."

"Yeah, of course," Slater responded reasonably. "But no one has ever asked you to do anything illegal?"

The specific question more about her than about Jack, Amelia wondered who was truly Slater's target. Over the years, she had been asked for everything, from cocaine to underage prostitutes to snuff films. It was always easiest to play off such requests as jokes, because there was nothing she could do about the predilections of others, and she preferred not to think about what people would do when they could get away with it. Those who could afford the best attorneys played considerably faster and looser with the law. Slater had to know that.

Amelia had never obtained anything, though, other than disgust with humanity, in regards to those requests, and she knew better than to be baited into lying. "Why are you asking this?" she countered instead.

"Just looking into a few things," Slater declared.

"You're looking into Jack?" Amelia asked.

"Do you think there's a reason I should be?"

Opening her mouth to respond, Amelia didn't know what to say. She was hardly the person to defend the finer points of Jack's character when she was one of the few people who ever saw his truest lows. Looking up at footsteps considerably lighter than the ones that had brought Slater into her presence, she was grateful to see Sole arriving just in time.

"Is everything okay?" Sole asked, concern showing clearly on her face.

"Everything's fine," Slater responded before Amelia could, sparing Sole a passing glance before returning his observant gaze to Amelia. "Listen, I'm not saying your husband is or isn't in trouble, but if you notice anything strange or think he might be in over his head, you give me a call." Holding out his card, Slater's jaw tightened when Amelia didn't take it, and he placed it on the bench between them as he stood. "Have a good day."

Watching Slater walk off without swagger or satisfaction, the meeting felt uncommonly low-key. Amelia had answered her share of questions about Jack, those of hotshot young agents looking to make their names and move up the ranks at unforeseen paces, only to fail miserably and end up looking even more like rookies.

Marcus Slater was far from a gung-ho novice. Each line on his face was probably carved there by a criminal he'd put away at great expense to himself, and his face was nothing but lines. He was a veteran, he was clearly intent on Jack, and, picking the card up from the bench beside her, the paper dry and dull between her fingers, Amelia assumed there was good reason.

Back at the house, Amelia climbed the stairs slowly, each step resonating in her head. She had realized in the car what was different about Slater. In the past, the agents she'd dealt with had always seemed desperate for her answers, pushing and prodding to get her to slip up, to give them something they could use.

Slater, he didn't seem to need her at all. It was more like she was supplementary. It would have been nice for him to have her on board, but she wasn't required to navigate. Which meant Slater already had direction. With or without her.

Dropping heavily into her chair, Amelia fished Slater's card from her purse, looking at the no-nonsense text and wondering what kind of trouble Jack had gotten them all into.

"Hey." The warm voice pulled her back into the present, and Amelia looked up to find Caton drifting into her office like a warm breeze on a bitterly cold day. "I finalized the guest list, and confirmed you can get the tables you want. Apparently, they're heavier, so there's an extra delivery charge." Raising her head with an easy smile, it faltered instantly on her face. "What's wrong?"

"Nothing." Amelia shook her head.

"Amelia, I can tell something is wrong," Caton declared, stepping forward to drop the papers in her hand onto the corner of Amelia's desk, before continuing around it to lean next to Amelia, close enough that Amelia got dizzy from the swift change in her mood.

Feeling Caton's concerned gaze from above, she slid open the desk drawer and tucked Slater's card into a stack of less-interesting business cards she hoped would conceal its true purpose. "I just had a conversation I wasn't expecting while I was out," Amelia admitted. "With an agent from the BRC."

Glancing up, she was just in time to see the surprise on Caton's face transition into concern. "What did he say?"

"He was asking questions about Jack," Amelia recounted. "About what I do. About the money. The usual."

Watching Caton work her lip between her teeth, it occurred to Amelia not everyone had extensive experience with federal investigators, and it probably sounded far more frightening than it ever ended up being in the end.

"And what did you say?" Caton asked.

"I didn't." Amelia shrugged. "I don't know anything. I'm sure it's nothing," she tried to convince them both. "What were you saying?"

Looking around blankly, as if she couldn't remember why she had entered, Caton's gaze finally landed on the papers on the desk. "Oh," she recovered. "Just that we're good to go on everything."

"Good," Amelia said. "Now we can pass the whole mess off and it can go back to being someone else's problem."

Though she delivered the words with her most dazzling smile, Caton didn't buy the stage show. Her eyes sliding downward, they saw right through Amelia's act, before at last returning to Amelia's. "He upset you," Caton stated gently.

Heart slowing, body dulled, Amelia dropped the pretense at once. "No." She shook her head. "This isn't my first investigation. Jack never tells me anything, and he always gets out of it." Pausing on the point of revelation, she remembered she didn't have to keep things from Caton, that she didn't want to keep things from Caton. "Sometimes," she went on quietly. "I just wish I knew what was going on in my own life."

When Caton's gaze fell away, Amelia realized how she sounded. The last thing she wanted from Caton was her pity, especially when Caton offered so many better things.

"But," Amelia stated, spinning her chair in Caton's direction, hand sliding up the flexed muscle of Caton's thigh. "I don't have to know right now."

Well aware of what she was doing, Caton still allowed Amelia to divert her attention. Her hands dropping to the armrests of Amelia's chair, she dipped down until Amelia could reach her lips. Tasting the faint traces of coconut, Amelia smiled in earnest, wondering what treat Caton had helped herself to while they were out.

Easing away, Caton moved one hand to the top button of Amelia's shirt to gingerly flick it open. Another button undone, and Amelia couldn't remember why she was trying to sidetrack Caton in the first place. Slowly, Caton worked the remaining buttons apart, hand slipping between the sides of Amelia's shirt to tease down her stomach, coaxing Amelia's body instantly back to life.

"I swear," Caton murmured, voice a caress on Amelia's senses. "Sometimes, I can barely stand to look at you. You are so fucking unreal."

Hand at Amelia's abdomen turning over, Caton's soft, warm knuckles traced the pattern her fingertips had drawn, and when Caton looked up, her awe was evident, sincere, and Amelia fell into her, lips converging on Caton's, every neuron rushing to the single point where their mouths met.

Within seconds, Amelia was relieved of the rest of her clothes, doing her part to help without registering it. Knee crooking over Caton's shoulder, her foot found leverage on the desk, her hand in Caton's hair, as Caton relieved her of all residual tension.

Like this, nothing else mattered. Together, all the ill-fitted pieces clicked into place, and everything else became the distraction. They were right. It was the world around them that was wrong. With all Amelia didn't know, that was the one thing she knew without question. In her office, in the middle of the afternoon, she unraveled, willingly, letting Caton take her apart, knowing then that Caton would expose the deepest depths of her. It was only a matter of time.

45

With every passing moment, she wanted Caton more. It was a frightening truth she couldn't deny. Waking the next morning, though, in the empty, sterile bedroom she shared with her husband, Amelia wanted Caton most of all.

She had felt the dip of the mattress when Jack came in late and crawled into bed across from her, and again when he got up. In the next room, she listened to him getting ready, marching robotically through his morning routine, and, at the sound of him in his dressing room, the familiar scuff of the brush buffing day-old marks from the toe of his shoe, Amelia climbed out of the bed and pulled her robe on.

Jack looked up as she entered, with little expectation of having a civilized conversation, and returned to what he was doing without greeting, the rhythm of brush-on-leather filling the empty space.

There had always been misfirings, had always been something lacking, but it hadn't always been quite so vacant between them. There was a time when Amelia held out hope she would be able to create a cautious friendship with her husband, but Jack didn't want friends either. This was what Jack wanted, a partnership that was a hollow stand-in for something real. Watching him look for imperfections in the toe of a shoe that looked perfectly fine to her, she almost felt sorry for him.

"Do you know a Mr. Slater?" she asked, knowing from the way Jack paused mid-brush, his movements less fluid as he returned to the task, that he at least knew the name.

"I've talked to him," Jack returned. "How do you know him?"

"I talked to him too," Amelia answered. "Yesterday."

Stopping instantly, Jack spun the brush in his hand, a nervous habit Amelia was certain he didn't know he had, as he looked up. His gaze moving freely over her, Amelia pulled the robe tighter at her waist, feeling inappropriately exposed.

"He came here?" Jack asked.

"No." Amelia shook her head. "I was out running errands. I assume he followed me."

Eyes trained on her, Amelia could tell Jack wasn't seeing her. Finally nodding, there wasn't an iota of surprise in his expression. "What did you talk about?"

"He asked me about the charity work," Amelia returned carefully. "The finances."

"You don't know anything about that," Jack rushed to say, as if she needed a reminder.

"Yes," Amelia stated, defenses pricking up at the condescending tone she had no reason to accept. "That's what I told him."

"Did he say anything else?" Jack questioned.

"No," Amelia responded.

With a sigh, Jack dropped his brush back into the holder on the side of the bench and slipped his shoe on. "I'll take care of it," he said, glancing dismissively up at her, and Amelia left at the cue, knowing there was nothing left to be said between them.

She had no desire to investigate. She told Jack what she knew, well aware Jack would give her nothing in return, and she wasn't going to concern herself with what she had no power to change.

It was wise in theory. In reality, the investigation came to her.

First, the man came to check the wiring, and Amelia longed to be naive enough not to recognize the code. Caton showed up as he was sweeping the house for bugs, and Amelia felt hatred flare up at Jack when she shrugged and lied "Old house" in response to Caton's query about the man's presence.

Then, Jack, who had behaved as he normally did, perfectly in control of the situation, when she told him, grew erratic in his near-routineness.

He would come home on time, sometimes early, he would leave late some mornings, and Amelia and Caton were caught in the crossfire, never sure when he might walk in, never safe in a moment.

Though Jack seemed strangely indifferent to what was happening on the bottom floors, leaving Caton alone for once and spending the time he was there up in his office, Caton was still standoffish, and Amelia felt abandoned amidst Jack's insanity, even when Caton was in the same room.

A few days into Jack's new routine, Amelia followed Caton home, unable to stand the distance between them that seemed to flourish under Jack's influence. It was the first restful night she'd had since Jack lost his sense, but when she returned to the house the next morning, Jack was waiting for her.

"I need you home now," he ordered, no real explanation, and Amelia knew she was being made to pay, once again, for his bad behavior. Still, all she could do was follow the command, unaware of how much the auxiliary life she had established with Caton had been holding her together until it was ripped from her without warning.

Jack was the unexpected snag, but it was Amelia who began to unravel at the seams.

"I need you to plan a dinner party." Jack marched into Amelia's office one night without warning, after his unexpected, overbearing presence had already caused Caton to leave early and to flinch when Amelia kissed her goodbye at the door, her eyes casting anxiously around as if Jack was omnipotent.

"For when?" Amelia responded dutifully, despite being precariously on edge, knowing she was partly responsible for Caton's distance, since she hadn't exactly put her foot down against the new order of things.

"Tomorrow night," Jack replied.

"Tomorrow night?" Amelia finally looked up at him.

"It doesn't have to be a big deal," Jack stated. "It's just for a couple of guys from the law firm. Just make it look good, so it looks like it's been planned for a while."

Standing inside the doorway of her office, Jack looked more authoritative than human, and Amelia wondered for a fleeting moment if he was always that way, if he delivered his commands at Halston & Company with the same demanding tone he delivered them to her. Or if the people Jack paid for their services got some courtesy she didn't.

"So, you need to talk to your lawyers without it looking like you're talking to your lawyers," she surmised. "What's going on, Jack?"

"You know." He threw his hand into the air, as if he was at the mercy of the investigators and had as little a clue as to what they were looking for as she did.

"No," Amelia countered, getting up and moving around her desk, approaching Jack with scrutiny. "I don't know, because you have been investigated before, and you have never acted this way. Why is it different this time?"

"It isn't," Jack argued.

"Did you do something?" Amelia went to the heart of the matter.

"No," Jack scoffed.

"Then why are you panicking?"

"I'm not panicking." Jack attempted a laugh, but it did nothing more than distort his face into something completely unknown to Amelia. And she thought she was familiar with all of Jack's faces. "But things can slip through the cracks."

"Not if you're well inside the law," Amelia responded, out on a limb, distance to the ground unknown.

When Jack glanced back at the open office door, she expected him to abandon the conversation, to let her know in his usual way that he didn't have to tell her anything. It was surprise when he took a step back to the door and pushed it closed, lowering his voice warningly. "I am inside the law. How far is none of your concern."

"Then where I spend my nights is none of your concern," Amelia argued for the only thing she truly needed.

"Jesus fucking Christ," Jack spit. "I should have left you in Venezuela."

"Fuck you, Jack," Amelia shot back, and when his hand flew up before her, Amelia flinched on instinct.

The anticipated strike remaining undelivered, Amelia cautiously raised her head, white hot anger spreading down her neck, despite the fact that Jack looked more nervous than angry as his hand fell limply to his side.

"Give me a reason," she encouraged.

An excuse was more like it.

She knew well Jack's limits, knew she had been pressing at them for weeks. But Jack knew her limits too. He knew what she would and wouldn't live with - it was part of their detente developed over years of arguments and narrow misses - and just how close he had come to crossing a firm line showed in his slack face.

Moving away from her, Jack looked as weak as Amelia had ever seen him. "Would you please just take care of this for me?" he asked with surprisingly sincere contrition. "I'm sorry."

"Fine," Amelia returned, finally finding a leg to stand on. "I will do it tonight, but then I have to get out of here. I don't know what's going on, but I can't stand this."

Though he appeared loath to accept those terms, business instincts kicking in, Jack seemed to realize his interests were best served by negotiating. "Fine," he said. "Set everything up with Sole, and you can go wherever you want."

Pulling the door open, Jack left with no way near the enthusiasm with which he had entered, and Amelia thought about following him out the door, grabbing what she could and just going. She knew she wouldn't make it far, though. In the hallway or on the stairs or in the foyer, she would come to her senses. They had negotiated a treaty and she would hold up her end. First, she would do what Jack needed done, and only then would she do what she wanted.

46

Social courtesy dictated warning someone before showing up at her door first thing in the morning. Knowing it would be easier for Caton to say no to her on the phone, though, and that saying no would be Caton's first impulse, Amelia opted to ignore propriety.

When Caton answered, fully-dressed and obviously confused, Amelia almost hoped she took some convincing. Apparently, being with Caton in vertical bursts with one eye on the door, after having leisurely afternoons in which to indulge in her, was like walking out of the rainforest and into the Sahara.

"Amelia, what are you doing here?" Caton asked, but, thoughts already halfway in Caton's bed, Amelia was slow to comprehend.

"Come away with me," she said at last, watching Caton's eyes widen in premature refusal. "Just for a few days."

"Where?" Caton tempered the reaction to ask.

"It's a surprise," Amelia smiled, recognizing Caton's subsequent hesitation as an attempt to find a reason she shouldn't, knowing she wouldn't have to search far to find a whole arsenal. "Please," she added.

"Come in," Caton sighed in apparent defeat. Pushing the door closed, she stood unmoving for a moment, a near statue, before finally turning to face Amelia. "Where does Jack think you are?"

"He knows where I'm going," Amelia responded, wishing Caton could leave Jack out of the conversation where he belonged. "He may know you're going. I don't care."

Gaze sinking through Amelia's skin, Caton looked as if she was scanning and interpreting data only she could see. "Is that what this is about?" she asked, X-ray eyes moving away. "Sticking it to your husband?"

"Is that what you think?" Amelia couldn't find the strength to be truly offended by the accusation.

"I don't know what to think," Caton replied, one finger pressing into the skin above her eye, as if trying to massage her own thoughts away.

Closing the distance that Caton had made sure to keep, Amelia eased her hand over Caton's hip, feeling her own anxiety dissipate, wondering why Caton could never just let things happen. "I think you do know what to think," she responded.

When Caton's hand moved to her wrist, for an instant, there was the equal chance she would tell Amelia she had to leave or give in. "Let me grab some things," she said at last, and, with a relieved sigh, Amelia let her temporarily go.

The notion that Caton might want a moment alone, some illusion of privacy, did occur to her, but it didn't stop Amelia from shrugging her coat off and throwing it over the back of the couch to follow Caton into her bedroom.

"Will we be inside or outside?" Caton asked as she entered, and Amelia smiled, not entirely sure until that moment Caton wasn't still looking for a way out.

"Mostly inside," Amelia responded, imagining what act of God it would take to budge her from the warm refuge of Caton's body once she got back to it.

"Casual, I assume," Caton coaxed, pulling open the door of her closet.

"You don't have to wear anything if you don't want to," Amelia returned, and Caton paused in the doorway, glancing back with a slight smile she couldn't suppress.

Returning to the bed a moment later with a duffel bag in one hand and a handful of clothes in the other, she tossed them to the bed and slipped out of her pants without warning. Drawn by the sight, Amelia was behind Caton before she even registered she was moving. Hands sliding around Caton's waist, they dipped lower to caress exposed skin so warm Amelia wasn't sure how she hadn't frozen to death before Caton came into her life. The familiar scent of Caton's shampoo winding around her, Amelia pressed her lips to Caton's shoulder just above the neckline of her shirt.

"Stop." Caton's hands covered Amelia's, and she made an effort to put distance between them. Trapped between the edge of the bed and Amelia, she had no place to go.

"Why?" Amelia breathed.

"Because we'll never leave," Caton said. It was the only good reason she could have given, and, reluctantly, Amelia backed away, acute desire trumped by the desire to have uninterrupted time with Caton, to have her, for once, truly to herself.

Without interruption, Caton was changed and packed in a few minutes, turning to Amelia with a hesitant smile, as if she knew she shouldn't be happy, but felt it anyway.

Amelia had looked tired when she appeared at the door. It was only when she asked Caton to drive, though, programming the address of a destination into the built-in GPS before promptly falling asleep in the passenger seat, that Caton realized the toll Jack's sudden reemergence as a prevailing force in both their lives had taken on Amelia.

The display showed more miles to their destination than Caton was expecting, and Amelia slept through most of them, waking with a contrite smile and an apology when Caton stopped for coffee, only to fall back asleep ten miles down the road with her hand in Caton's and her own coffee going cold in the console beside her.

Aside from north, Caton had no idea where they were going, but she was still surprised when she drove beyond the cities into forestland, and even more so when the robotic voice at last told her to make a left into a drive she couldn't see until she was right on top of it. Slowing Amelia's SUV to a crawl, she turned onto the gravel path, bumping deeper and deeper into a tunnel of trees until the real world disappeared from the rearview mirror and they appeared to be heading straight to nowhere.

Waking at the turbulent ride, Amelia sat upright in her seat, shoulders stretching back as she glanced over at Caton. "Sorry," she said again.

"It's all right," Caton assured her, half-expecting Amelia to tell her she'd made a wrong turn. Then, the cabin came into view, nestled against the lake behind it like the focal point of a painting. Of course, it would be utter perfection, Caton thought. No idea where she was going, and yet she knew it would be a dream when she got there.

Despite the fact she had driven the miles herself, and was aware how far north they were, the cold still shocked Caton's system as she climbed out of the car. Teeth chattering, she wrapped her arms around herself to no avail.

"It's warmer inside, I promise." Amelia climbed out of the passenger's seat and grabbed her bag from the back. Grabbing her own bag, Caton threw it over her shoulder, hurrying behind Amelia to the door.

Despite the frigid temperature, the key slid into the lock without effort, and a blast of warm air hit Caton as Amelia pushed the door open. Guiding her into the small vestibule, Amelia closed it, before turning to unlock the interior door into the cabin. If the place could reasonably be called that. Everything top of the line and nothing out of place, it was more like a miniature palace. The temperature set and a fresh bouquet of flowers on the kitchen table were evidence someone had been there before them.

Of course they had. Amelia had a life where people took care of things for her, in which, even if nothing else was right, her needs and desires were met with style.

"This is..." Caton worked past the lump that formed in her throat at the thought. "Impressive."

"It serves its purpose," Amelia conceded.

"What purpose is that?" Caton turned to face Amelia, straps of her bag clutched so hard her hand ached.

"Escape," Amelia responded, taking a deep breath, the stress of the past few days visibly leaking from her as she exhaled. "This is my own private getaway."

"So, Jack doesn't come here?" Caton couldn't stop the question, but it didn't seem to bother Amelia.

"Occasionally," she responded. "He's used it in the past to meet with people on business, to host parties. He doesn't come just to be here, though. This isn't exactly his scene."

"But it's yours?" Caton asked.

"Does that surprise you?" Amelia countered, and Caton had no logical answer. Sometimes, she felt as if everything was a surprise with Amelia, as if she would never fully know her, but since she expected surprise, nothing surprised her anymore. Seeming to realize Caton wasn't going to respond to the question, Amelia glanced around, looking oddly fitted to her surroundings. "This is the only place on Earth that feels more mine than his."

The admission struck Caton as desperately sad, but, having seen her shake off far deeper pain with the casualness of a paper cut, it wasn't all that surprising when Amelia dropped her bag to the table and approached with a smile. "Come on," she said, sliding the straps of Caton's bag from her hand. "You have to see the view."

"Does that mean I have to go back outside?" Caton returned warily.

"Yes," Amelia responded matter-of-factly, setting the bag next to hers and taking Caton by the hand.

Soaring into exposed beams, stone fireplace dominating one wall, the living room of the cabin made the kitchen look practical. The wood chest Amelia stopped at was antique, the kind bought at auction for thousands of dollars. Nothing like the antiques of the real world, which were really just hand-me-downs by another name.

Propping the lid, Amelia pulled a blanket from inside and shook it out, wrapping it around Caton's shoulders with a smile Caton couldn't resist, before grabbing one for herself and beckoning Caton toward the glass doors.

Following Amelia onto the porch, the brutal temperature compelled Caton to turn back, even as the masterpiece of nature held her spellbound. The frozen lake before them was a spectacle, marked by places where the wind picked up the water and froze it so quickly, the liquid turned to sculpture. The trees around it hung heavy with icicles, branches so thickly encased even those that couldn't bear the weight wouldn't break free until spring.

It was exquisite carnage, sheer destruction masquerading as perfect beauty.

Mesmerized as she was by the sight, Caton still saw the small smile that played at Amelia's lips as she turned toward her, always too aware of Amelia not to notice. "Okay," Amelia said. "Now we can go in."

"No." Caton shook her head. "Not yet."

Wordlessly agreeing, Amelia slid behind her, parting her blanket to pull Caton inside. With Amelia pressed against her, cocooned in the layers of fleece, Caton grew so warm, she was surprised the icicles on the overhang didn't dissolve into puddles, heat emanating outward to melt the art of the lake.

It was a contradiction she never could have seen coming. Five months before, Caton was convinced Amelia was as cold and uninviting as the frozen landscape, but, just like the lake before her, there was a whole world, warm and alive, hiding beneath the surface.

Settling into Amelia's arms, feeling the steady rhythm of Amelia's heart beating against her back, Caton tried not to get lost in the fantasy of an impossible future. She tried to remember things were not as they felt, but as they were. Amelia had made a commitment, so had she, and neither of them was to each other.

47

Caton was painfully aware of each passing minute, not just of their time alone together, but of time in general. Every clock in the cabin grabbed her attention and held it, a mocking reminder that her tenure with Amelia was rapidly coming to a close.

They had left the cabin only once to go to a diner in a nearby town, where the pie was nearly as good as Amelia's salivating description. With their idle mornings and afternoons in bed that stretched into evenings, the minutes should have slowly ticked by, but the hours had passed in a whirlwind. Caton watched the last of them burn down in the fireplace, flames leaping and crackling, and despite the distance, swore she could feel them licking at her skin, just waiting to burn.

"Something wrong?" Amelia asked, hand trailing Caton's shoulder as she curved around the arm of the sofa, eliciting a visceral response Caton wished could be tempered through will alone.

"No," she lied, not sure whether she was sparing Amelia or herself.

"Tired?" Amelia asked, folding one knee beneath her as she settled next to Caton on the sofa.

"A little."

"We should start back early. It's supposed to snow," Amelia replied, and she sounded distant, even as her arm stretched across the back of the sofa, fingers toying with Caton's hair where it rested against her shoulder, a tenuous connection broken easily when Caton nodded her response.

Caton tried to remember why there was good reason in that, why they had to go back. Though there were many that should have been convincing, in the end it was only the fact that, while the cabin may have felt more like Amelia's, it was legally Jack's that forced Caton's concession. Given the option, she might have chosen to stow away with Amelia for the rest of her life.

False smile flashing briefly before she gave up the act, Caton rolled toward Amelia, fingers stroking along a sculpted jawline as their lips met. With gentle pressure on the back of her head, Amelia drew her closer, taking over, as she so often did, much to Caton's surprising pleasure. From the beginning, before Caton even understood what the hell was happening between them, Amelia always seemed so certain in what she wanted, and there were times when it felt as if Amelia's conviction was all they really had.

"Let's go to bed," Amelia whispered, rising to push the glass doors closed in front of the fire before Caton could deny her. Turning back as Caton made it to her feet, Amelia's gaze was withdrawn, obscured by thoughts Caton couldn't read.

When Amelia took her hand, though, to lead her down the hallway, Caton put one foot in front of the other, following where Amelia led with full awareness, until Amelia flipped the switch to turn the light off, sending them into temporary blindness.

Hand grasping tighter to Amelia's, Caton extended the other until her fingertips brushed the wall, assuring her the world remained unchanged around them, whether she wanted it to or not.

The firelight from the living room flicked after them, relenting at the bedroom door, and, feeling the doorframe against her palm, Caton let go of the last vestiges of solidity and let Amelia lead her into the pitch, air puckering her skin as Amelia turned suddenly to yank her shirt over her head without warning and drop it somewhere in the darkness.

It was by feel alone that they sent the rest of their clothing to the floor and climbed into the slight chill of the oversized bed. Reaching out for Amelia in the darkness, Caton sighed against the warm lips that found her own, arching closer to the body that sought hers, sinking into their combined warmth. Thigh settling between Amelia's, Amelia's ankle wrapped encouragingly around her calf, fingernails scratching down Caton's back as she moved against her, digging in until Caton felt welts rise in their wake, not wholly painful, but entirely possessive, as if Amelia knew it was all slipping through her hands.

Each kiss a beat too long, the darkness heavy around them, Caton felt faint as she pulled back to feel Amelia's broken breaths against her cheek. Eyes finally adjusting, she could see Amelia beneath her, but only just, like a mirage or a ghost, and couldn't decide how much was real and how much was recent memory, seared forever on her consciousness.

Closing her eyes, Caton gave in to the pull of Amelia's body, lips drawn to intimately familiar places, the dip below Amelia's sternum, the hard line of her collarbone, the yielding hollow above. Further up, Caton's teeth sank into Amelia's shoulder, mouth pulling at tender flesh until it grew hot against her tongue and Amelia canted up from the bed, hands scrabbling at Caton in pain or need.

Relinquishing the spot, Caton edged downward, until Amelia halted her progress, hands on either side of Caton's face urging her back up. Lips crushing together, it turned into a contest until Amelia suddenly wrenched away, cheek brushing against Caton's as ragged breaths fell over Caton's ear. "Touch me now," Amelia demanded. Or pleaded. From her mouth, the two so often sounded alike.

"I am touching you," Caton made the effort to tease, to prolong, but her hand obeyed instantly, a restrained moan leaking past her lips at how accessible she found Amelia, at how Amelia bucked against her, flesh so hot it burned Caton's skin. Over the last few days of her life, Caton had taken every opportunity to explore Amelia's body at her leisure, had found every secret Amelia's bones and muscles and skin could possibly hold, but nothing had proven more gratifying than the moments when Amelia simply wouldn't wait.

Arching into her touch, Amelia let out a relieved sigh as it moved inside her and lay back against the pillows, her covetous embrace dragging Caton down with her. Fingertips grazing Caton's jaw to clutch at her neck, Amelia tugged Caton's mouth to hers, body grasping at Caton's hand, beckoning her deeper.

Retreat met with a whimper, Caton smiled against Amelia's pouting lips as she increased the touch, hand sinking surprisingly effortlessly into Amelia's warmth.

"Caton," Amelia breathed, and there was no mistaking it was plea. Nor denying the exquisite throe of pleasure that rippled from where Amelia's lips brushed hers to the soles of Caton's feet. From the beginning, Amelia seemed so certain in what she wanted, and had hardly been shy about it, but Caton still craved the reminders that there were times when she was the thing Amelia wanted the most.

Retreating again, Caton gave Amelia more, deeper, watching Amelia's head tilt back against the pillow, a series of gasps and senseless babble pouring from her lips that Caton drank in like nectar on the air.

Amelia's arms slackening around her, Caton's lips were free to trail down the column of Amelia's throat, to taste the sheen of sweat beading on Amelia's chest, to pull a firm nipple into her mouth, causing Amelia's body to jerk beneath her, as if the extra sensation might wrench her apart.

Lingering, then moving on, Amelia's hands alternately clutching and resting against her shoulders, Caton rediscovered every small scar, every ridge of Amelia's ribs, the toned stomach muscles strained taut in exertion, and Amelia's belly button, which was of infinite interest to her.

She knew she needed to indulge, to memorize, to savor every fleeting moment that remained, but Amelia's leg crooked beside her, heel digging into the mattress at Caton's side, and her hand buried itself in Caton's hair as climax overtook her. Forever, it seemed to shudder violently through Amelia's body, then ended far too quickly. Resting her head against Amelia's hip, Caton felt the final pulses clutch at her hand, before Amelia was pulling at her, drawing her upward, and she was forced to extricate herself, despite the gentle resistance that tempted her to stay.

Amelia's breathing came rough and uneven, as she pulled Caton's lips to hers, last strong breaths sacrificed to the kiss. Finally fully depleted, Amelia let her head fall back again, eyes slowly opening, and Caton swallowed thickly at the intent gleaming against the darkness. Touch coming from nowhere, and everywhere, Amelia's fingers thrust into her without warning, and Caton caught herself on the mattress, hands sliding against the sheet on either side of Amelia, a quiet curse leaking from her lips as her eyes fell closed. Pressing them open again, she watched the satisfaction stretch across Amelia's face.

Hand firm against her shoulder, Amelia pushed her up, and Caton sat shakily back onto her knees, the warmth radiating off Amelia's thigh heightening the feel of Amelia's fingers driving deeper. The blankets shook free from her shoulders, exposing them both, but meeting each thrust of Amelia's hand, Caton felt no cold.

At the brush of Amelia's thumb against her clit, she was set free. Hands clutching at the pile of blankets behind her, she arched into the ecstasy, Amelia's fingers sinking deeper into her, her free hand alighting on Caton's chest to stroke down her skin, fingertips brushing against a willing nipple, sending new shockwaves after the old, until it felt like there was nothing left to expel, as if she had been utterly and expertly picked clean.

Weakness chasing euphoria, Caton dropped forward, landing at Amelia's side, bodies just touching. Using her last surge of energy to press her lips to the perfect curve of Amelia's shoulder, she let her head fall to the pillow as Amelia situated the covers back around them, clutching Amelia's hand when it reached out for her in the darkness.

It was muted footsteps on the hardwood floor that pulled Caton from sleep in the middle of the night. Blinking into awareness, she watched Amelia's graceful silhouette vanish through the doorway, knowing Amelia had tried and failed not to wake her. Distantly, a phone hummed and ceased, and Caton closed her eyes, dozing in the resumed silence.

Waking again, the bedroom felt colder. She didn't how long Amelia had been gone, but it felt like too long. Rolling to the edge of the bed, Caton reached in vain for her clothes on the floor, finally giving up the pursuit and pulling the quilt around her.

Halfway down the hall, she picked up on the quiet sounds, following them to the living room, where the fireplace doors once again stood open. Soft light dancing against the fabric of her silk robe where she stood before the flames, Amelia held a small stack of papers to the fire, letting the edges ignite before dropping them atop the faux logs. Watching the pages crinkle into ash, the relief Caton felt at finding Amelia turned to nausea, despite not knowing exactly what she was seeing.

Turning to grab more papers from the pile on the sofa, Amelia jumped at Caton's unexpected presence. "I didn't mean to wake you," she said quietly, hand going to her heart. She looked lost for a moment, as if she couldn't remember where she was, before remembering the slightly larger stack of papers in her hand and turning back to the fireplace, the flames inside rising dangerously high as Amelia sent them to a fiery end.

"What are you doing?" Caton asked, the smoke on the air seeping into her voice.

"Destroying evidence, I imagine," Amelia responded, her tone as nonchalant as her actions, as, rotating back to the sofa, she plucked more papers from the pile.

"What?" Caton questioned disbelievingly, drifting forward to look at the pile at Amelia's back, even as Amelia sacrificed the papers in her hand to the blazing fire.

"Jack said to empty the drawers in the desk and burn everything," Amelia answered. "I don't know why else he would tell me to do that."

"Well, what the hell are they?" Caton found her emotion, looking to the pile again. Numbers and text trailing across the pages, there was nothing instantly identifiable, explicitly incriminating.

"I don't know," Amelia replied, reaching back again.

Fetch and destroy. Fetch and destroy. Amelia was a disassembly line of one, dismantling the faulty goods someone else had built.

"So, you're just doing it?" Caton questioned, staring at the side of Amelia's face, scarcely recognizing her.

"Jack told me to," Amelia stated, the subservient response sending a chill down Caton's spine. Of all the excuses Amelia might have given, Jack's word as law was the last she expected to ever hear from her.

The papers in Amelia's hands floating into the fire, she turned again.

"Stop!" Caton shouted, rushing forward to grab the stack from Amelia's hands, hearing the papers rip between them. Amelia was barely surprised at the attack. She barely reacted at all. "What is wrong with you?"

"Nothing's wrong with me," she returned, face finally showing a trace of confusion, as if Caton's actions were the ones that should be questioned.

Disturbed laughter rising in her throat, Caton looked harder at Amelia, trying to see the woman she knew, or even the woman Amelia had pretended to be before she knew who she really was, beneath the stranger who stood before her.

"Jack asks you to go to an event so he doesn't have to, he tells his friends to send you their problems, he treats you like you're his secretary, and now he calls you in the middle of the night and tells you to burn papers, and you just do it?" She didn't realize how much Amelia's total compliance with Jack's demands bothered her until the words were flowing without censorship, and, for a moment, Caton was sure Amelia felt something, if only a trace. It flashed in her eyes, instant and brief. Then the curtain fell once more, hiding the Amelia she knew behind the one she would never know.

"I have to," Amelia responded far too calmly, rotating back to the fire like some perfectly-aligned gear in a machine.

Papers in her hands tossed back toward the sofa, Caton grasped the silk at Amelia's chest, jerking Amelia around to look at her, eyes searching desperately for a flicker of anything other than apathy. "Jesus Christ, Amelia," she sputtered. "Listen to yourself. You are a fucking slave!"

In an instant, all the emotion Amelia had refused to show appeared in a torrent. "Maybe I am," she declared, voice shaking as distressed brown eyes met Caton's. "But there are worse forms of slavery."

Shoving Caton off, she grabbed the entire pile of papers and whirled to the fireplace, and Caton surged forward, quilt slipping from her shoulder and dangling precariously as she wrested them from Amelia's grasp. Battle lost, Amelia tried to retreat, and Caton let the pages fall to the floor, holding the quilt around her with one hand and reaching out for the only thing she truly cared about with the other.

"Let go," Amelia uttered as Caton's fingertips closed around her arm.

310

"No," Caton replied instantly.

"Let go," Amelia said again. When she glanced back all anger was gone, replaced with pain so unfiltered it seized Caton's chest and made each breath a struggle.

"No," Caton whispered, grip softening as she stepped closer.

"What do you want, Caton?" Amelia questioned helplessly, a solitary tear escaping the corner of her eye to roll unchecked down her face.

"I want to understand." She felt as if she was begging.

"You can't understand!" Amelia's sudden vehemence surprised her, and Caton took a reflexive step back. "You think having two parents who have to work comfortable jobs is a struggle." The perverse amusement that appeared on Amelia's face vanished in a scoff. "You don't know what poverty looks like. I had friends who were prostituted by their own fathers. I saw kids sold for five-hundred dollars to strangers on the street!"

Face clenching with rage and memory, Amelia's eyes were unforgiving, and Caton's gaze fell to the vein stretched so tight in Amelia's neck, she feared it would snap.

"People offered my parents money for me," Amelia's voice dropped to a whisper, but seemed somehow more forceful, pushing thoughts into Caton's head she didn't want to think. "All the time. And they needed it." Stepping into her space, Amelia forced Caton's eyes back to her own. "We all needed it. My father wasn't just sick. He was dying. And my mother, she barely made enough for us to eat once a day. Even when I was old enough to work, it was never enough. We were *suffering*."

Each syllable its own blow, it was more than just a word. Caton could feel it, the hunger and the desperation, echoing in Amelia's voice. Teeth clenching until her jaw ached, the pain and sorrow and fear rose inside of her, but she knew it wasn't her own. It was Amelia's. Amelia was inside of her. Amelia had been for far too long.

"They wanted me to leave." Amelia's voice further depleted, more tears surfacing to streak down her face. "But they kept me safe when parents around us were using their kids like currency, and I was not going to just leave them there to die. Jack..." She broke off in a pained laugh, wiping her fingers beneath her eyes as she shook her head. "He *was* a godsend for us. He has given us everything. He bought my parents their home. They are royalty there now. He got the best doctors. He saved my dad's life. And I…" Amelia trembled violently, a deep-rooted fear seizing her, and Caton realized she would never know fear the way Amelia had known it. "It could have ended up so much worse for me."

In the unnatural silence that followed, Caton felt the shock fully set in. Palm registering the only warmth that seemed to remain in the room, she realized she still held Amelia's arm and gripped it tighter, but Amelia still slipped away from her, dropping wearily to the sofa.

Insides aching, as if she was the one who had been hollowed out, Caton watched the firelight flicker against Amelia's hair, wishing their path was straighter, that she could have seen around the bend and taken the turn with greater care. Amelia kept the thorns in her life so well hidden, Caton never knew she was pushing Amelia into a patch of brier until Amelia was already cut and bleeding. With no clue as to how to tend Amelia's wounds, she could do nothing but sink to her knees before Amelia, hoping for atonement.

One hand reaching hesitantly through the opening in the quilt, she was terrified of inflicting more damage. Only second to that was the fear Amelia would refuse her, Caton discovered when Amelia shifted away from her touch.

"Don't." Amelia turned away, body folding in more tightly on itself. She looked as if she wanted to cease to exist, to disappear into the sofa, and Caton could scarcely recognize the telltale signs of shame, strikingly out of place on the confident, enthralling woman she…

She loved.

Releasing the quilt, Caton slid both hands onto Amelia's thighs, clutching tightly enough that Amelia couldn't break free, barely registering the fabric as it slipped from her shoulders and left her completely exposed.

"Amelia, please," she breathed when Amelia refused to look at her. "I'm sorry." It encompassed everything. She was sorry for pushing Amelia, for breaking her, for ruining the achingly short time they had left. Mostly, though, Caton was sorry for Amelia's past, for what she had witnessed, for what she had been made to endure, for the pain she carried with such stoicism and grace no one would ever know from looking at her how heavy its weight. "I am so sorry, Baby."

Releasing a pained breath, tears falling unchecked, Amelia at last met her gaze, eyes churning with anguish Caton felt through every fiber of her being. "I am doing what I have to do," Amelia declared.

"I know." Caton pressed upward, body molding against Amelia's knees, fingers closing around her hips.

Suddenly, she knew far too much. Suddenly, all Amelia's contradictions made perfect sense. Suddenly, she knew her feelings weren't illusion, something her body and mind invented, but she couldn't possibly feel. The last wall falling before her, Caton felt her heart pounding within the debris as Amelia at last leaned closer, reaching behind her to pull the quilt up, wrapping it around Caton's shoulders and clutching the fabric tightly at her chest.

"I can't leave him," Amelia stated, eyes pleading for forgiveness as they met Caton's again. It was a rather final statement on a conversation they hadn't even started, and Caton shut her eyes against the truth.

It was instinct to pull away, to separate herself from Amelia before the pain became even more unbearable. Hands sliding from Amelia's knees, she tried to rise, but Amelia reached for her, hands cupping Caton's face, fingertips warm and welcome against Caton's wishes. "I want to," Amelia declared. "But I can't."

Caton believed that was true too, and it made it harder to just let go, to let Amelia grieve on her own. If any heartache was ever truly shared, this one belonged to both of them. Arms wrapping around Amelia of their own accord, she felt Amelia break down against her shoulder, Amelia's hands clutching at the quilt to pull her closer.

It was fascinating, the difference, and disturbing. All the times they had held her, Caton's arms had never been able to feel that Amelia was so fragile. Now, it was all they could feel, the vulnerability that lay hidden beneath the sturdy facade.

Amelia was a porcelain doll inside a suit of armor. As indestructible as she appeared, she was designed to shatter.

48

The late-night interruption set them back in waking, though Caton didn't actually sleep. Curved around Amelia all night, she picked up on every tremor and sigh that moved through Amelia's body, but still felt as if it had all been a dream.

Home wasn't tempting for either of them. It was clear in the way they lingered beneath the covers, Amelia's murmured complaints about the cold justifying the delay, then over breakfast and the view outside, before finally locking the door on the fantasy and heading back to their reality.

With the late start, darkness had long fallen by the time they pulled up in front of Caton's apartment, and, eyes open but aching, Caton was glad Amelia had gotten more sleep than she did.

Easing the car into park, Amelia glanced over, smile gentle and sincere, despite everything. "Thank you for coming with me," she said.

"Thank you for asking me," Caton returned. It felt unnaturally casual. All day, they had found things to talk about, without broaching any of the subjects that lingered from the night before. They wouldn't broach them, Caton knew, not again. She had gotten everything Amelia had to give, and rehashing would be both painful and pointless. "So," she uttered, latching onto the inside of her jaw, grinding up words she wanted to say, but never would. "I'll see you on Monday?"

Smile fading on Amelia's lips, she looked away, taking the question like a barb, though Caton didn't intend for it to sting. "How about tomorrow?" Amelia returned, glancing back over at her. "Can I come over?"

For once, there was no sense of entitlement, or mere decorum, in the question. Amelia was actually requesting permission.

Withholding her question as to how Amelia would clear her absence with Jack, Caton fought back a shiver at how tight Jack's hold truly was on the reigns, how he could jerk Amelia back at any moment. Feeling a surge of hatred toward him, she put forth substantial effort to suppress it, assuming Amelia wouldn't ask if she didn't have a way. "Yes," she whispered weakly.

Whatever Amelia wanted. Whatever she asked.

Trace of her smile returning, Amelia reached across the space between them, hand closing warmly around Caton's wrist, and leaned in, stopping halfway, as if testing how far Caton was willing to go to meet her.

Caton had to wonder herself. She'd always thought she knew her limits, but Amelia had an expert way of reshaping her boundaries. At the very least, she would always go halfway, and she did, lips opening against Amelia's to taste her soft exhalation, nagging feeling of desolation setting in before she even pulled away. She knew the more time she spent with Amelia, the harder it would be in the end, but she never expected to be spoiled by three days.

"Be careful getting home," Caton whispered, releasing Amelia before she lost the will to do so, and climbing out of the car to grab her bag from the backseat.

Rushing to the door, she wriggled the key into the lock, which was no way near as forgiving of the cold weather as the locks at the cabin, and let herself in, barely able to make out Amelia's shadow through the tinted glass as the door swung slowly shut at her back.

Inside her apartment, Caton couldn't recall the steps that carried her there. Dropping her bag and shrugging her coat off, she heard distant thumps as each hit the floor. Her eyes bouncing around the mismatched space, she wanted to destroy everything they landed on, and it occurred to her just how much she needed sleep. And to get away for real. And to go back in time.

Of course, given the chance to undo, she would undo all the wrong things. Logic said Amelia was her greatest mistake, but Amelia was the only mistake that had been worth making.

Treading the shortest path to the liquor cabinet, Caton yanked it open, eyes catching on the bottle of Absinthe, sparkling like a diamond amidst coal. Hand around the neck, she twisted the cap off with a satisfying crack, vaguely remembering her friend's warning not to drink it straight, which she promptly ignored to take a shot's worth straight out of the bottle.

It didn't hurt real good. It just hurt, searing its way down her throat and dropping fire into her stomach, doing damage she was sure would take time to heal. At least it would heal, though, which was more than she could say about the other pains she'd brought upon her life.

Taking another drink, Caton's eyes teared as the magic of the potion was lost on her and she still remembered everything. The burn working its way back up and outward, she exploded, contents of the bottle splashing down her back as she raised it above her head and smashed it in the sink, eyes closing on instinct as splinters of glass and liquid pierced her clothes and skin.

She had no right to feel anything. She had done what she had done, knowing exactly what she was getting into and all the reasons she shouldn't. Amelia had been born into suffering. Caton had facilitated her own. In so many ways.

Anger turning to nausea, she abandoned the mess in the kitchen, tracking broken glass through the living room and bathroom, where she flipped on the light, recoiling at her own reflection.

The woman who stared back at her was a haunting version of herself, pale and unrecognizable. On her cheek, a trickle of blood formed like a tear beneath one eye, a clear crystal of glass embedded above it. Without thought, Caton yanked the shard free and blood streaked rapidly down the phantom woman's cheek. Fingers rising to her face, she watched the blood in the mirror smear.

All of a sudden, she could feel it, the pain. Not the cut. Not the alcohol. The real pain, the one that had throbbed dully in wait all night and day, and sharpened to a blade in an instant. Breath stolen from her chest, Caton struggled to take in air, but the air tasted toxic, like lies and regret. She tried to hold herself up, but her legs went suddenly numb. Hands grasping at the sink, she fell to her knees, bowed by a sensation that gripped her in icy fingers, squeezing unrelentingly. She would suffocate, she realized, on her own bad decisions.

Or maybe that was only wishful thinking.

When breath finally broke through, it was on a sob, life returning in a torrent of tears that Caton couldn't stop. Releasing the sink, she crashed against the wall, sliding down until there was no further to fall. She wished she didn't, but she knew all too well how she had gotten herself there. She simply couldn't fathom how she was ever going to get back up.

49

Hours later, Caton woke in the same position in which she had landed. Hissing at the glass that had embedded in her palm, she stared down at the shards that glittered against her jeans like a bad bedazzle job.

Closing her eyes again, she waited, imagined time rolling backward, choices unmade, life less complicated. When she opened them, the pain and the glass remained, and time continued to tick inevitably forward, so Caton had no choice but to keep moving along with it.

Over the next hour, her penitence was to follow her path of destruction back to its origin on her knees, retrieving the fragments left behind in her wake. Picking the floor clean and disposing of the broken bottle, she returned to the bathroom to wash the last splinters of glass from her skin and hair, until finally it was as if nothing had happened.

When Amelia appeared at her door the following afternoon, Caton bore no markers that anything was wrong, save for the angry red line across her cheek, too prominent to go unnoticed. Amelia's eyes flashed concern as her fingers traced the broken skin with care, and Caton sold the half-truth that she dropped a bottle with a self-effacing shrug, kissing Amelia before she had time to think about it.

The night sped by them. As did the next morning.

One week ticked away.

Two weeks.

Jack's worry dissolved, temporary insanity cured by the belief that everything was within his control, mind eased by his own sense of superiority, and he returned to normal, late nights and indifference, which freed Caton and Amelia to return to normal too.

All thoughts of work forgotten, they spent their days in the bedroom - their bedroom - and Caton tried to comprehend how she had let herself become so deeply ingrained in a world she was committed to leave.

On the first day of her final week at the Halston Palace, Amelia didn't ask Caton to stay. She attacked her as the day was coming to a close, all but dragging her down the hall and taking possession of her without permission or resistance.

Lying with Amelia curled against her side, contentment fractured by her own discord, Caton stared at the window, watching darkness fall with a weighty feeling of dread, knowing she should be pushing Amelia away with conviction, not knowing how.

"Caton," Amelia husked, and the sound sunk into Caton's skin, an instant reminder of how weak Amelia made her.

"Yeah?" she roughly returned.

"I don't want you to leave."

Heart thudding one heavy beat before coming to a stop, Caton knew Amelia had to feel it.

"Do you want to leave?" Amelia softly questioned, and Caton's heart started beating again, pausing out of time, like the notes of some strange cadence.

When Amelia lifted her head to gaze up at her, expression open, almost innocent, a whisper of concern edging in at the corners of her eyes, Caton felt the sudden need to rethink everything she had already rethought. It was a vicious loop in her head, the knowing and not knowing what she was doing, the certainty overtaken by the uncertainty, only to rally once more.

"Do you?" Amelia prodded, giving her no time to fully consider.

"No," Caton admitted before she could come up with a safer lie.

Smile spreading across Amelia's lips, relief evident in every relaxed line on her face, Caton felt it all crumbling. Everything she had planned, everything she had done, all she needed to do, was fracturing under the sheer radiance of Amelia's smile.

"I'm going to tell Jack to extend your contract," Amelia uttered. "Indefinitely."

Seeing Amelia content, happy even, Caton felt happiness reach out for her too, trying to seduce her. Almost placated, almost grateful, she knew her feelings were polluted. Realizing how close she was to agreeing to Amelia's terms, to settling for an unsatisfactory half-life just to be with her, Caton was suddenly so angry at herself, she had reserves to spare.

"Until you no longer require my services?" she returned, and the hopeful expression on Amelia's face sharpened with a wince.

"That is not what I meant," she said.

"Really?" Caton countered, giving into the resentment, relying on it to carry her through. "Because that is exactly how it sounded."

Shrugging her arm out from under Amelia, she scooted to the edge of the bed, her back to Amelia to keep from seeing her, to keep from giving in, as she fished her clothes from the floor and pulled them on, movements simultaneously jerky and mechanical. Every bend was contempt. Every raise of her arms was punctuated with anger. She needed to be angry. She couldn't afford to feel anything else. Anything else and she would give in, she would do exactly what Amelia wanted and ruin everything.

"Caton?" Amelia was unsurprisingly dumbfounded, her hand alighting on Caton's back as she sat up in the bed behind her.

The gentle touch was like a knifepoint, threatening to fell Caton once and for all. It barely made contact, and all Caton wanted was to turn back, to crawl into Amelia's arms and accept whatever terms came with having her. If it was truly an option, she would have, she knew she would have, but it wasn't an option. It never had been.

Standing to pull her pants over her hips, Caton fastened them as she turned to face Amelia, who held the sheet against her chest like a shield, otherwise completely vulnerable, eyes wide in distress.

Caton thought she would have something to say, that she could come up with something final, but meeting Amelia's worried gaze, she couldn't say anything. It was better to just leave, to get away from the proposal that was too tempting, before she changed her mind.

With an unavoidably quick lunge, though, Amelia caught her wrist, pulling Caton back around as she tried to go. "Caton, please... talk to me."

"What's there to talk about?" Caton asked. Eyes glazing, she refused to see what was right in front of her, refused to feel Amelia's fingers like solace on her skin.

"Everything," Amelia returned. "I want you to... I just..." She shook her head, and it was unnatural, watching Amelia struggle to find the right words to persuade. Most of the time, they seemed to live on the tip of her tongue, just waiting to be of use to her. "I just want you," Amelia found them at last, and it was everything Caton feared she might say.

Dissolving instantly, surrendering to Amelia's touch, to the tears that welled in her eyes, to the honesty, Caton couldn't remember why, but she knew she had to fight. If she didn't do it now, she would never do it. She would end up treading water, the rising and falling tides of Amelia dictating her every move.

"No, you don't," she countered. "You don't just want me. You want it all. You want this..." She gestured to the luxurious appointments of the room and the house beyond. "And this." Watching her hand gesture between them, Caton couldn't feel the motion at all. "And you will want whatever comes along next that you think you have the right to."

Words insincere and ruthless, Amelia took them as she should, as an insult and a lie. "I wasn't looking for anything to come along." Her concern turned to defense. "You walked through my door."

"Do you think I don't know what this has been?" Caton returned before Amelia could find more logic she wanted to believe. "You were bored and I was a new plaything for you. That will get old, Amelia. It always does." When Amelia's mouth began to open in protest, Caton went on in a desperate rush, knowing how likely it was the next words from Amelia's mouth would be the ones that convinced her to stay. "People like you, you collect people like me. You keep us as long as you want and release us when we're all used up. You are just like your husband."

Words fading to a whisper, Caton knew at once she had gone too far. She could see it in the stricken look on Amelia's face, in the dulling of her eyes, in the pain that seemed to ooze from every pore before she turned away, looking set adrift in the big bed.

Caton wanted to take it back, to change tactics, but time refused to roll backward. It was better that she couldn't, she knew, because nothing could have possibly been more effective. Amelia wouldn't even look at her, and Caton knew it would take only a look to bring her to her knees.

Realizing she wasn't going to get any further objections from Amelia, she turned for the door, letting the resentment carry her through it without a backward glance. Halfway down the stairs, the tears started falling, and Caton knew she had officially done her worst. For months, she had made very few moves that could be considered morally right, but it was the first time she felt like a villain.

50

When things went beyond their limits, they tended to limp across the finish line.

So was their fate.

They barely spoke. They never touched. Amelia was rarely in her office. She was rarely even home. Caton's worst, it seemed, was also her best, and she spent the last days of her contract merely existing in Amelia's space, as if Amelia thought it was what she wanted.

It should have been what Caton wanted.

Her last day, Amelia stayed at the palace, present, but not social. Caton was uncomfortably aware of her, and, taking the deep breath that had to get her through the rest of her life at afternoon's close, she went to meet the end next door in Amelia's office.

"I'm leaving." She meant to announce the fact at the door, but it came out little more than a whisper. Too afraid to walk in, Caton was even more afraid to walk away, so she stood in the doorway, a physical testament to her indecision.

Staring unflinchingly at her, stony facade expertly in place, Amelia didn't move either. "Am I going to see you again?" she asked.

It was the first sign things weren't irreparable, that the rock hadn't reformed throughout Amelia, and Caton's fingers curled around the strap of her bag in painful reminder of what she needed to do. "I don't think that's a very good idea, do you?" she returned. "You can't leave your husband, and I'll never be happy being someone's mistress."

Seeming to anticipate the answer, Amelia's face showed nothing as she at last got up. Slow steps carrying her closer, Caton worried she wouldn't be able to resist Amelia without the buffer of space.

"Here's the rest of your money," Amelia said quietly, maintaining a respectable distance between them. "I asked Jack to throw in a little extra. You've been a big help to me."

Eyes clouded as she slipped the check from Amelia's hand, Caton thought she couldn't read, and frowned as she realized she was reading the number just fine. It was far beyond a little extra. It was more than double what they had agreed upon, as if she was being paid for services she didn't have to render.

For her affection.

For her silence.

Eyes rising to Amelia, Caton's instant indignation faltered as she met her steady dark gaze. There was another explanation, it occurred to her, that Amelia wanted to make sure she would be okay, because their feelings went both ways and this was as hard for Amelia as it was for her.

The notion making the check feel even more like blood money in her hands, Caton thrust it back out to Amelia. "I don't want it," she uttered.

"Take it, Caton," Amelia whispered, stony facade cracking as she stepped closer, and Caton knew she couldn't be around when it crumbled.

"I don't want it," she repeated, shoving the check into Amelia's hand.

Spinning around, she escaped Amelia's office, the palace, and its fortifications, not stopping until she was far enough away that it was further to go back than it was to move forward.

Pulling into the deserted end of a parking lot, she threw the car into park and latched onto the steering wheel, screaming until her throat was raw and she choked on the tears streaming down her face. Head falling to the steering wheel, she felt the imprint of the manufacturer's emblem against her cheek.

Phone ringing next to her, Caton dove to the passenger's seat, fumbling in the depths of her bag, hoping for another chance to go back, to undo. Everything she said to Amelia was a lie, and she would admit it. She didn't want money. She didn't want any of it. The only thing she wanted, she had left standing in that office, as perfect and in control of herself as ever. Caton would tell Amelia that. She would confess everything, if only she had the chance.

The phone vibrating in her hand as she pulled it from her bag, she glared at the name on the screen. Not Amelia, it wasn't anyone Caton wanted to hear from at that moment, or ever again.

Mr. Superhero-Ambitions was so adamant he was going to change the world, and he had. He changed her world.

He ruined her fucking life.

51

With nothing else to do, Amelia had returned to her desk chair and looked out into her office. As usual, everything was in its place, an exquisite home in perfect order. Nothing in her life had changed at all, and nothing remained the same.

Staring into the empty space, she felt tears run down her cheeks, dripping into her silk blouse to turn cold against her chest. It wasn't supposed to be this way. She thought she knew what she was doing. She had gotten so adept at calculating her emotions, at avoiding things that added up to pain. Apparently, there was no accounting for unfamiliar equations for which she had no formula.

"Amelia?" Sole started carefully, stepping into Amelia's office as evening darkened beyond the windows.

"I'm fine, Sole," Amelia returned instantly, making no move to get up or conceal anything. There was no need. Sole knew how to keep a secret. "You can go."

Though it was meant to be an order, Sole took it as a suggestion, moving forward to sit in a chair across from Amelia's desk. Watching her sink into the seat, Amelia stared at her without saying a word. There was nothing to say. They both knew Amelia would get over it, as she had gotten over so much more. It was just going to take longer and hurt more acutely until the scar hardened.

"You should wash your face," Sole advised at last. "Let me make you something to eat."

"I'm not hungry," Amelia replied instantly, cringing at the self-pity in her voice.

"That doesn't matter," Sole declared. "You still have to live."

Far from a brimstone-and-fire testimony about the sanctity of life, it was a sad statement on Amelia's singular purpose in life, to survive so that others would not suffer. Sole knew her story. To some extent, she shared it. Sole too had people who depended upon her willingness to be servant or slave, and, in the end, they both took their orders from the same master. It was enough of a reminder to pull Amelia from the chair and insist Sole take her leave for the night, which Sole finally did to great protest.

A few hours later, when exhaustion set in, Amelia went to her bedroom. The air inside, always set to Goldilocks-perfection, puckered her skin, and the bed was like a tundra, sprawling and uninviting. As tired as she was, she couldn't sleep, but she didn't think either. Mind going pleasantly blank, body turning liquid against the sheets, if there was one thing Amelia knew how to do well, it was simply exist.

Still awake when Jack came in, she didn't need to look at the clock to know it was a ridiculous hour, and he was at his usual volume, quiet enough to pretend he didn't want to wake her, loud enough to remind her that a man of his position didn't have to be quiet in his own home.

When he climbed into the bed beside her, the expanse wide enough for two bodies between them, Jack still felt too close. His presence in her bed disturbed Amelia's fragile neutral state. Despite years of experience lying unfeelingly across the bed from him, the immense room felt suddenly too small.

Rising too quickly, Amelia felt light-headed as she reached for her robe, pulling it on against the chill as she moved for the door.

"Where are you going?" Jack asked from the darkness.

"Away," Amelia paused to answer, before fleeing any further questions.

Down the staircase, she turned at the end of the banister, no idea where she was going until she landed in the guest bedroom, in the bed she had shared with Caton. There, sleep was just as elusive, but memory was pervasive. Sounds. Tastes. Phantom caresses that haunted Amelia's skin. Caton was gone, but she was still present, more real than anything within Amelia's reach.

A few more nights, she tried the master bedroom. Tried. Even when she slept, though, Amelia woke when Jack came in, slipping out of the bed to the guest room without question, tossing fitfully against the ghosts that lived there, recent, but still firmly in the past.

Caton had made that clear.

After that, she stopped bothering with the trip to the third floor, unconcerned with anything she had left behind there. Mysteriously, though, clean clothes and personal items appeared for her as she needed them, Sole's efforts making everything look almost normal.

Amused the first morning, Jack's curiosity increased in agitation as the days passed. When Amelia came down from her bedroom a week after she had staked her claim to it, it was late in the morning, but Jack was still there, waiting tensely at the bar for her. Not knowing what to make of it, Amelia didn't put too much effort into deciphering Jack's behavior. She had angered him plenty of times over the years, but she had never done anything to make him mad enough to fight on her schedule.

"Why are you still here?" she asked, breezing past him to the coffee, shaking her head at Sole when she moved to take over the trivial task.

"What is going on with you?" Jack returned.

"What do you mean?" Amelia turned to lean against the counter, the familiarity of arguing with her husband strangely calming.

"Why the fuck are you sleeping in the guest room?" Jack demanded.

"Why do you care where I sleep, Jack?" Amelia reasonably asked, intrigue her first real feeling in days.

Watching Jack's jaw grow tight, Amelia felt no fear, nor pleasure. She felt nothing for or about him, and there wasn't a thing either of them could say that was going to change that.

"There is a lot of shit going on, Amelia. You know that," Jack responded. "This is not the time for you to fall apart on me."

"Do I look like I'm falling apart?" Amelia countered, eyes dipping to her perfectly tidy state. Inside, she might have been ravaged - empty, raw and bleeding - but she knew she was the only one who could see it. "Put me out in public, and I will be the perfect shining star for Halston & Company, I assure you."

"Things need to be very normal right now," Jack gritted through his teeth. "I can't have you pulling away from me. It looks bad."

"To whom?" Amelia tossed off. "Sole's not going to tell anyone."

Pausing at Amelia's side, Sole clearly didn't expect, nor want, to be acknowledged.

"Could you leave us alone, please?" Jack requested, glancing her way, and Sole followed the order with relief, eyes meeting Amelia's in sympathy or frustration as she crossed in front of her to disappear through the dining room door.

Left alone with Jack, Amelia's gaze returned to him, and she watched the arrogant judgment she knew so well appear on his face, her composed state coming to an abrupt end at the sight alone.

"How was Caton, Amelia?" Jack asked. "As you know, I've wondered myself many times."

Casual animosity sharpening to a deadly point in an instant, Amelia clutched the cup in her hand, feeling the burn of hot liquid through porcelain. "Don't," she uttered.

"I'll bet she's a firecracker. Warm and enthusiastic," Jack went on with perverse glee. "How did she taste?"

Glancing to the window, Amelia tried to escape, to be anywhere else, to ignore him and his attempts to provoke her. In all their years together, Jack had rarely gone for the kill, happy to let his mommy do it for him, putting Amelia back in her place like a parent tidying her toddler's room. Not that Amelia often needed reminding of her position. She knew well the lines they wanted to hear. It was a rare misstep that she went off-script.

"Indescribable, huh?" Jack couldn't help himself. "Is that it? Do you miss Caton's taste?"

For Jack to come at her, he must have felt truly threatened, Amelia realized, though the knowledge did nothing to ease the churning rage in her stomach.

"Jesus Christ, Amelia," Jack laughed. "I've fucked dozens of women and have had no problems with forming attachments. You fuck one and think your world is coming to an end?"

Script burned in protest, Amelia improvised, hurling her cup at him, coming surprisingly close for an aimless throw. Jack dodged the cup with an inch to spare, and it smashed against the French doors, falling to the floor in a hundred pieces. Easing back upright, Jack wiped his hand across his face, red streaks cutting down his cheek and neck where the coffee burned, and all traces of humor left his face.

"I. Am not. You," Amelia stated, and the words were more shock to him than the physical attack.

Jack needed to be admired, and Amelia had always allowed him to believe he was, that fitting into his world, being like his kind, was something she had striven to achieve and struggled every day to maintain. The idea that she wanted to be nothing like him, or his fucking mother, rendered him momentarily speechless.

"I am going to a hotel for a few days," Jack finally stated, sliding off the bar stool and letting out a slow breath as he met Amelia's eyes. "I have enough to deal with right now without your shit. Get your head on straight. You are my wife, you are going to stay my wife, and, when I get back, you're going to be a better one."

Piece said, Jack departed the conversation, and, with no argument against it, Amelia let him go.

Jack was right. When he came back, she would be better. She would put on a happy face, and do exactly as he said.

As she always had.

As was required of her.

There was simply too much at stake for her to do anything else.

52

It wasn't exoneration. It was reprieve. Like the stay of an execution.

When Jack came back, Amelia would return to their life, to their bedroom. She would lie beside him, providing the consistency he liked, and feign whatever emotion each moment demanded of her.

Until then, she was free to live as she wanted.

Climbing into the bed in the guest room, Amelia curled up with Caton's memory and the maudlin sentimentality of a drink too many. The instant her head touched the pillow, it seemed, she was waking to a sound, distant, yet somehow close, as if it came from outside the house or out of her dreams.

Slightly more conscious, the next sound was closer and clearer. Brain fogged with sleep, body lethargic, Amelia's first reaction was panic. Eyes jumping to the ceiling, she sat up, clutching the covers against her chest, her anxiety slowly subsiding as she remembered she didn't live alone and the only people who had the code to the alarm system were those who had a right to be there.

There was really no need for her to stir at all. Recognizing the distinctive creak of the bad floorboard in Jack's office, though, Amelia knew the only reason he would return in the middle of the night was if he was up to something he shouldn't be or checking to see whether she had fallen back in line yet. Either possibility infuriating her, she threw the covers back and got out of bed.

The hardwood cold against her bare feet as she climbed to the third floor, Amelia's steps slowed when she saw nothing but darkness above.

There was no reason for Jack not to turn on the light, no logical reason for him not to have come by daylight. Still, Amelia bypassed the open door of the master bedroom to turn toward his office, hesitating for only a moment when a narrow beam of light appeared in the hallway outside the door and vanished just as quickly.

It was in the interest of safety to retreat, she knew, to hide behind the fortified door of the master suite with the phone and gun inside, but her feet continued to move anyway, carrying her forward to the wall outside Jack's office, and, as she peered around the door frame, Amelia felt only a hint of the fear she thought she should feel.

The beam of light rushing up to meet her from inside, it blinded Amelia to everything but the black clothing of the intruder, who went rigid at her sudden presence. It was exactly what she expected, exactly the outcome to which each clue had pointed. She had walked straight into danger for a reason she couldn't quite explain. Standing face-to-face with it, though, Amelia's survival instincts kicked in. Foot slamming against the doorframe as she turned, she thought she heard her name, but it was lost to the rush of blood through her ears, to the pounding of her heart in both her chest and her head.

Clearing the bedroom door, she didn't hear the intruder behind her before the arms closed around her waist. Struggling against their hold, Amelia fell forward, pain radiating through her knees as she pulled the intruder with her to the floor. A scream ripping from her throat as she kicked out, she felt her heel smash into the shadowed face, rewarded by the pained grunt as her attacker reeled backward.

She didn't have the fight left in her to win, though, and as Amelia rolled to get up, the attacker lurched forward again, hands pushing her to the floor, pinning her in place as a shockingly warm body pressed against her back. She had always known Jack could get rid of her, that, if he really wanted to, he would make her disappear. She never expected it to be so intimate, the last moments of death, to find such gentle embrace in the violence.

"Amelia, it's me," the intruder panted in her ear. "It's me."

In the instant it took to reconcile the voice with the sensation of her, Amelia stopped struggling. Then, she struggled harder, pushing the weight off with a determined elbow and crawling out from beneath it. Turning to face the small patch of Caton she could see between the low-pulled black cap and turtleneck, residual fear and shock amplified her voice. "Caton? What the fuck are you doing here?"

Darkness deep around them, Amelia could scarcely see Caton's flinch, but the blood appeared vibrant as Caton wiped the trickle at the corner of her mouth before moving her gloved hand up to catch the steady stream from her nose. At the realization that Caton wasn't going to answer her, Amelia glanced back down the hall, piecing together bits of memory from before the threat of danger stole her ability to think. "What were you doing in Jack's office?"

Caton's eyes flashing upward, they met Amelia's fleetingly, before Caton dropped her gaze again. Watching her stare at the floor for more than a reasonable amount of time, Amelia pushed to her feet, brushing herself off as if Sole would allow the weekly cleaning crew to leave a speck of dust behind on the floor. "Fine, don't tell me," she uttered, managing to sound relatively normal, despite Caton's appearance at her home in the middle of the night and the pulsing feeling in her body that hadn't gone away, despite knowing there was no threat.

Able to see more clearly as Caton rose from the floor, Amelia felt an unwarranted pang of guilt as blood gushed again from Caton's nose at the movement. Raising the black glove, Caton stemmed the flow with the back of her hand. Even in the weak light, she looked overly-tired, like she hadn't slept in days.

Hand falling away, Caton sniffed, her gaze stroking down Amelia's body as she took a tentative step forward. Against every instinct she had, Amelia forced a step back, grabbing the post at the foot of the bed like a crutch. When Caton's sigh filled the empty space between them, Amelia resisted the urge to let her close the distance.

"Amelia." Caton shook her head. Roughness gone, she sounded the same, and, lured by the comfort, Amelia's fingers tightened on the post to hold her in place. "Jack is not a good man."

"Yes, I know," Amelia responded tersely. "What does that have to do with anything?"

As Caton's gaze dragged away, Amelia could see her teeth working against the inside of her lower lip, the nervous habit excruciatingly familiar, as Caton contemplated whether or not to answer the question. Finally pulling off the gloves and yanking the black cap from her head, Caton ran her fingers through her hair, trying to tame it. "The man you talked to on the street..." She posed it like a question.

"The investigator?" Amelia returned, and Caton nodded.

"He has been looking into Jack for a long time. What Jack's doing... Amelia, Jack is doing some really reprehensible things."

"Like what?" Amelia asked, not knowing if she wanted the answer. What she knew about Jack had always been enough to know she didn't want to know what he did in business. Caton, though, Caton owed her an explanation, and if that was part of it, so be it.

"It doesn't matter," Caton said in a rush, head jerking from side to side. "But Slater knows Jack is walking a very narrow line between what's legal and what isn't. Jack knows how to stay within the law. But people are going to come here tomorrow. They are looking for something, and they are going to find it."

"I don't understand," Amelia replied, looking around the room for something that made sense, but finding only more questions. "If Jack is within the law, then how..." It was Caton's falling gaze, the sudden hunch of her shoulders that gave her away, and, breaking off, Amelia looked back down the hallway, realization dawning painfully on her as her gaze lingered at the door of Jack's office. "You're planting evidence?"

Caton said nothing. She didn't need to say anything.

"So, Jack walks a line," Amelia uttered. "But you cross right over it? How does that make you better than him?"

"It doesn't," Caton responded instantly. "This isn't about me."

Arms crossing before her, Caton tried to look resolute, but looked every bit a martyr. Not sure whether she should be furious or inspired, Amelia settled on being rational. Suddenly, it was about Caton, and the fact she had planted herself firmly in the line of fire for a reason she wouldn't explain.

"Jack's lawyers cost two-thousand dollars an hour, Caton. Do you really think they are not going to know you planted evidence? Jesus Christ. It's on video."

"The cameras are off," Caton quietly returned, and, once again, Amelia felt as if Caton had grabbed her by the arm and spun her in circles. Trying to find a way off the fast-moving wheel, the whole room seemed to move.

"How did you..." she started.

"I watched." Caton shrugged. "I know the codes. I know the passwords."

Words sinking in, Amelia thought back to all the times she had to have entered them without feeling the need to watch her back in Caton's presence and lost her breath. "You used me."

"I wasn't using you," Caton rushed to assert. "I didn't ask for this kind of access. Jack invited me in. He gave me access. To the files, to the codes."

"To me?"

"I was not using you," Caton stated again, each word crisp, as if perfect enunciation would make Amelia believe them. "If anything, you made this harder."

"Well, I am so sorry," Amelia countered mockingly, but she couldn't get sufficient anger behind it. Aside from utter confusion, the only feelings that seemed real were the ones that threatened to hurt more, and she shut them down as they arose, turning herself off to Caton a piece at a time.

"I didn't want this job," Caton tried to explain herself. "I wasn't going to take it. But when Jenna told me what Jack had done -"

"Jenna?" The name was like a grenade dropped on the conversation, and Amelia felt too stunned to run for cover. "You're working with Jenna? That's why you were worried about her finding out. It wasn't about me. You were worried about it messing up your little set-up."

"That is not true," Caton replied, and her remorse, at least, was real. Not that it mattered, for all the comfort it brought. "Jack has to be stopped, Amelia," she went on. "You think I am using you? He has used you."

"What has he done?"

"Amelia." Caton attempted to dissuade her from the line of questioning.

"What has he done?" Amelia asked again, and, seeming to realize it was the way things were going to go, Caton gave a near-imperceptible nod, fingers tearing at the cap in her hands as if they might pick it completely apart.

"Jack uses the charities to make millions," she answered. "Then, he leaves them to go bankrupt. He charges them for everything. He distributes to his friends, to his friends' friends. The charities get thousands, if that."

"That's impossible," Amelia uttered, the hairs on the back of her neck standing on end as a chill moved down it. "I have collected hundreds of millions of dollars for him."

"You don't see the paperwork," Caton responded. "Why do you think he wants you to handle all this? You look good. You look honest. He's stealing from the pockets of the most needy, the dying, the suffering, and you help him do it."

"I didn't know!" Amelia shouted, the burden of guilt settling in before she'd even fully decided if what Caton was telling her was true.

"I know you didn't," Caton returned gently. "I thought you must, but..." She exhaled heavily, a sad smile canting her lips. "You were so proud. You thought you were helping so many people. But Jack takes, Amelia. He doesn't give. You, above everyone else, should know that."

Amelia wanted to reject the allegation, to take Caton's word with skepticism. If Caton had rushed to use it as excuse, she might have been able to do so. She knew it was true, though, by how much Caton clearly didn't want to tell her. And she knew Caton was right, Jack wasn't exactly the charitable type. It never had made much sense.

Swiveling around the bed post, Amelia sank weakly to the edge of the mattress, tears coming to her eyes and turning the gray room darker. "What else?" she asked.

When Caton took too long in answering, Amelia glanced back, watching Caton step closer to the foot of the bed, testing their boundaries. Amelia let her, wanting her closer, wanting her further away.

Wanting her not to have come, so she didn't have to start readjusting to her life all over again.

"He..." Caton tried, voice fading into nothingness. "He does a lot of business with less-than-upstanding associates."

"What does that mean?" Amelia prodded.

Caton huffed, as if she had the right to be exasperated by the interrogation when she had just broken into someone else's home. When her eyes returned to Amelia, though, her head shaking in warning, Amelia knew Caton wasn't keeping the details to herself for her own sake. "It's bad business," she whispered.

"Like what?" Amelia asked, knowing she should let it go, Caton's lack of response fueling her foreboding. "Like what, Caton?"

Such utter torment flashed across Caton's face that fear chased sympathy through Amelia's gut. She wondered what exactly Caton knew, how long she had known it, and if Caton's extreme unease around Jack wasn't based solely on the obvious, but supplemented by a truth from which Caton was clearly trying to protect her.

Realizing she didn't need Caton for answers, Amelia pushed herself up, moving back through the doorway and down the hall before Caton could make a move to stop her. Caton was right there next to her, though, by the time Amelia flipped on the light in Jack's office to discover the contents of the shelves out of place, a wood box she had seen many times, but had never given any real thought, sitting in the middle of the huge oak desk.

"What is this?" she questioned, moving around Jack's desk, barricading herself from temptation, before looking up and grimacing at Caton's face, which was already turning a deep shade of purple she was going to have a hard time explaining.

Visibly drained by the question, Caton leaned tiredly against the doorframe. "There was a man arrested in Sao Paulo about a year ago. He told Slater he exchanges tokens with his associates when they complete a deal. Like souvenirs. He claims he gave that box to Jack after they did some business in Panama."

"What kind of business?" Amelia asked, and Caton returned instantly to her intentional silence, eyes pleading with Amelia to let it go. Pulling at once at the lid of the box, Amelia discovered there was a trick to it and felt along the edges for a way in. "How do I open it?"

Staring unceasingly at her, Caton refused to provide answers, and Amelia fumbled with the box, a breath away from smashing it on the floor when she finally found a piece that gave. Sliding it free, the lid popped instantly open, and Amelia pulled it up to find the box empty. When she glanced to Caton in confusion, she knew she was in the right place by the concern that remained on Caton's face, and, finger running over the inside of the box, she felt the lining give way.

"Amelia, don't please," Caton pleaded as Amelia pressed her finger against the wood cutout that lay beneath the lining, feeling it too come free.

"Is this what you put here?" she asked, pulling the tightly folded paper from the hidden compartment and glancing up with satisfaction as she unfolded it. When Caton again refused to answer, Amelia turned her attention to the evidence in her hand. Nothing more than a list of names and dates, it was more disturbing than illuminating. "Miguel Almeida, Marina Carvalho, Yasmin Costa." Each name further tightened her throat. "What is this?" Glancing up, she watched Caton's eyes flutter downward, truth concealed as she stared at the floor. "What is this?" she asked more forcefully. "If you don't tell me, Caton, I will only think worse."

"You can't think worse." The reply came in a pained whisper, and tears formed instantly in Amelia's eyes as Caton looked up at her, gaze so sympathetic, Amelia knew what she would say next. Pushing off the door, Caton took tentative steps to the edge of the desk, close enough to touch. "Those are people who have gone missing over the past two years in Brazil," she explained softly, haltingly. "The man who was arrested admitted to kidnapping or buying each of them, transporting them to Eastern Europe and selling them. He claims Jack is his bankroll, that Jack covers the expenses and splits the profits."

Head already shaking, Amelia didn't want to hear any more, and needed to hear it. "Go on," she prompted when Caton was too decent to continue.

338

"According to Slater, this man is not Jack's only partner. The companies Jack works with in South America, Central America, the Middle East, Africa, Eastern Europe, Russia, they are all fronts. They look like legitimate businesses, but they make their money trafficking. That has been Jack's only truly successful business venture. It's probably how he met you." Caton's tone turned impossibly gentle. "It's probably why he was there."

"No," Amelia heard her own voice, felt her head shake more emphatically. "Jack is a bastard, but he isn't... I would know."

Collapse imminent, she watched Caton come another step closer, wishing Caton would give her more. Too numb to seek comfort, Amelia would give into it if it was offered.

When it wasn't, she felt too tired to hold herself up. Hands on the edge of Jack's desk, she dropped to her knees, handles of the drawers digging into her back as she turned to lean back against the wood. Anyone else and she could have chosen not to accept it, but, if there was one thing she believed without doubt, it was that Caton would never tell her this if she wasn't convinced herself.

"You think one piece of evidence is going to convict him?" Amelia questioned, voice tight and thick in her throat. "That is not going to happen."

"Probably not," Caton acknowledged. "But it's enough for them to make the connection. They already have his partner, and, when they investigate, they're going to find out about Jack's meetings with his lawyers, about his changes in behavior, about the money he's moved."

Nodding numbly, Amelia finally felt the tears on her face and absently wondered how long they'd been falling. "You're making him hang himself."

"He already has," Caton said, and Amelia closed her eyes, not sure what she felt. If she felt anything.

Then, suddenly, Caton moved, dropping down before her, one hand on the corner of Jack's desk inches from Amelia's shoulder, and a tremor of warmth moved through Amelia's body. Following Caton's free hand as it reached out to her and stopped, she willed Caton to just touch her and take away the pain.

"But..." Caton turned the approach into a weak gesture. "If they find nothing when they serve the warrant, it will be over."

"What?" Amelia uttered.

"Slater is not going to get another chance," Caton continued in a rush. "He put his career on the line. He has been quietly after Jack for a long time. He knows if he goes after him now and he finds nothing, he will be discredited. That's why I'm here." Caton seemed to be appealing to Amelia, though Amelia wasn't sure what Caton wanted from her anymore. "I put that there weeks ago." Caton gestured to the box above Amelia's head. "I came to get it back."

"Why?" Amelia shook her head. "Isn't this what you want? To see Jack hang?"

"Not anymore."

The response striking her as insanely bizarre, helpless laughter burst from Amelia's throat. "Why? Suddenly you can't do that to him?"

"I can do it to him." Caton was so hard and unforgiving, the laughter died on Amelia's lips. Then, eyes roaming Amelia's face, Caton's gaze softened, her voice fading to a murmur. "I can't do it to you. Apparently." Leaning in, she cast shadow over Amelia as her hand finally closed around a bare calf. "Even if Jack isn't convicted, Slater is going to do whatever he can to make Jack's life hell. They will take everything. You will lose everything."

Amelia didn't want to feel it, the surge of longing that battered her fragile defenses. Longing for a different life, for a return to ignorance, but mostly for Caton, who was too near to let her shatter in peace and too distant to catch her. For days, she had been wishing her life with Jack to a close. Jack always did tell her to be careful what she wished for, because she just might get it. Not once had she ever mistaken her husband for the greatest man in the world, but it had honestly never occurred to her he might be one of the worst.

When she felt Caton's hand move away, as if she just realized she was touching Amelia, Amelia no longer felt weak. Just alone. Pulling herself up, she could feel Caton rise beside her, and watched her move back to the edge of the desk, putting some distance between them. She could tell Caton was just waiting for the command, to get rid of the evidence, to untangle the web they had weaved together and hand Amelia her life back as it was before. As if that was possible.

"When are they coming?" Amelia asked, folding the paper and sliding it back into the hidden compartment, before pressing the wood piece back into place and smoothing the felt atop it.

"First thing in the morning," Caton replied.

Eyes rising to Caton, Amelia saw concern and remorse and something she didn't want to see. She was furious, she realized with sudden tension. More than she had ever been. More than she would ever be. She'd had years to get used to Jack's lies. She'd expected different from Caton.

"Put everything back the way you found it," she ordered. "Then, you should go."

"Amelia..." Caton began to protest.

"Put it back," Amelia snapped, and Caton did as she was directed, returning the box to its place on the shelf and positioning the other trinkets around it. Watching them fall into place, Amelia wondered if they too were souvenirs.

Task complete, Caton turned from the shelves, and Amelia prepared herself for Caton's departure, for the burden of silence that would fall in her absence. When Caton took a step, though, it was in entreaty, not retreat. Watching her close in, Amelia didn't back down, but she couldn't submit. As angry as she was, though, when Caton's arm closed around her and Caton's lips captured hers, it was impossible for Amelia to remain detached. Hands clutching at Caton's shoulders, she tried desperately to hang onto the one feeling that remained good, despite everything she knew.

Breaking away, Caton leaned her head against Amelia's. "Amelia, I..." she breathed, and Amelia anticipated the next words on her lips, knowing she would forgive Caton any and all trespasses against her if she said them.

Caton couldn't forgive herself, though. Hands abandoning Amelia to the cold room, she exhaled a last uneven breath and dropped Amelia's gaze, as if she had no right to be looking at her. "I am so sorry," she whispered, hastening to the door and disappearing beyond it.

The first few footsteps down the hall were clear, but the sound of Caton's departure quickly faded into the creaks of the house, as if she was never really there.

53

The vibration against the nightstand woke Marcus Slater from a dead sleep, sending him reaching for a gun he didn't have on him. Lifting his head with a grunt when he realized where he was, he reached for the offending device, squinting at the identifier on the screen, and realized he should use more logical aliases if he was going to have to decipher them mid-sleep.

"Caton," he answered gruffly. "It's the middle of the night."

"I know what time it is," she returned in a way that forewarned a drawn-out conversation.

Groaning beneath his breath, Slater regretted anew ever leaning on the woman to help him. Half the time she spent mourning people she'd never met. The other half she spent vacillating between utter conviction and deep doubt as to whether she was doing the right thing. Caton was conceivably the worst inside man who had ever existed. She was also his last and best chance at making Jack Halston pay for the crimes he committed without conscience, which was why he had devoted so much time in the past months to talking her down, despite the fact that, when he'd taken his career aptitude test in high school, therapist came in dead last as a career choice.

"Caton, I have a busy morning," he reminded her calmly. "I'll call you tomorrow afternoon."

"Don't hang up," Caton uttered.

"Fuck, seriously," Slater sighed. "Unless you have something important -"

"Shut up and listen to me." The firm command surprised him into silence. "When you get to the Halston house tomorrow, you are going to find what you want, but I need you to fix this. You need to take some money, make it disappear."

"I can't do that," Slater returned, wiping the sleep from eyes in an effort to wake his brain.

"Really?" Caton's voice was unnaturally stern. "I am certain you can."

"I'm not taking that risk," he clarified. Reaching for his cigarettes on the nightstand, Slater crushed the carton in his hand upon finding it empty.

"All the other risks you've taken, and you won't take one more?" Caton questioned in disbelief.

"So, you want paid now?" Slater asked, scrubbing his hand over his face, realizing for the millionth time everyone truly was alike, no matter how they seemed at the outset. He had paid so many "good" people to help him take down bad people, he could scarcely see the line anymore. "I thought you were in it for the greater good."

"Fuck," Caton uttered. "It isn't for me. They are going to lose everything. Amelia... and Jack's daughter. They didn't do anything wrong. They don't deserve this."

"Way of the world," Slater replied. "You should know who you're getting into bed with."

"Goddammit!" Caton screamed. "I have done everything you asked me to do! Do this for me!"

"I can't," he snapped, frustration getting the better of him.

"Then I'm going to come clean," Caton threatened.

The words like a bucket of ice water dumped on him, Slater sprung up in the bed, fully awake in an instant. "What the fuck, Caton?" he returned. "You do realize you'll go to jail, right?"

"I don't care." Caton sounded so calm, he felt his career and life slipping through his hands. "If Amelia goes down, I'm going down and I am taking you with me."

"Don't be an idiot," Slater hissed. Ever since Jenna told him, he had been waiting for this particular snag to come into play. "I know you have feelings for this woman, but it doesn't change what Jack Halston has done," he argued. "It doesn't change the fact that he is a despicable human being who will keep getting away with whatever he can get away with for as long as he can. Is that what you want, to save this one woman and let a thousand other people suffer the consequences?"

He wasn't sure it would matter. It had always been enough to convince her in the past, but Caton had never sounded as certain in anything she was saying.

"Please," Caton pleaded, the sudden change in tone reviving Slater's intermittent belief that she was a single screw away from being completely unhinged. "Please. Give her something."

There was more. He could hear it. Jenna told him Caton was sleeping with Jack's wife, but clearly she saw only the partial truth. He'd had a lifetime of listening for what people didn't say, and there was so much Caton wasn't saying, he could write a book about it.

Still, it didn't change the stakes. Even with a live wire like Caton in play, everything had gone as planned. Hours away from the fruits of his years of tedious labor, he couldn't risk a dumb mistake.

"I can't," he said again, and could only hope Caton would come to understand.

"Then go to hell," Caton responded, and Slater sat listening to the dead line.

It sounded like the prelude to his own demise.

54

The house was a fucking exhibit, starting with the wife who answered the door in slacks and a sweater, looking far too impeccable for such an early hour. A year of his salary probably wouldn't have paid for a single vase on display, but at least the money he did have he'd earned through his own blood, sweat and tears, and not by spilling those of others.

From the foyer, his team spread out, and Slater went through the act, asking if Jack was home, though he knew well where Jack had been staying the past few days, asking if Jack had an office as if he didn't know it was two stories above at the front corner of the house.

The wife nodded, instructing the housekeeper to call Jack and their lawyer, before leading him up the stairs. Standing inside the doorway of Jack's office, she looked as uncomfortable as expected, and Slater told her she could wait downstairs. Not seeming to know what else to do with herself, she opted to stay where she was, drawn, he assumed, to the only person in her house she had seen before.

He could certainly see what made Caton so gallant, suspecting Jack's wife elicited that response in many people, making them willing to fall on their swords on her behalf. Normally, having a beautiful woman who didn't want to leave his side would have been a perk, but it did make his job more difficult.

Eyes going to the wood box, Slater was eager to get at it, worried that Caton had carried through on her threat, that she had somehow undone what she had done, destroying any chance they had of ever putting Halston away for his many sins that were somehow only borderline crimes. He knew he couldn't hit the jackpot on the first spin, though, so he opened the drawers of the desk, poking around for evidence he had no expectation of finding.

That part of the show over, he turned to the cabinet behind him, feigning surprise at the scuff marks on the wall. Setting his feet, Slater dragged the heavy piece of furniture forward, revealing the wall safe behind it.

"No chance you know the code, is there?" he asked, glancing back, and when Jack's wife shook her head, he stepped past her into the hallway. "I need the safe drill and evidence bags," he called to the techs in the master bedroom, before moving casually back into the office.

The safe, he knew was there. Its contents, however, remained a mystery. He doubted there would be anything incriminating inside. If Jack were that sloppy, he would have already been in jail. Still, it wasn't a good show until something got broken.

Shuffling back to the desk, Slater moved some papers around on top of it, before giving in to his need to make sure Caton hadn't ruined everything. Skirting over the items on the shelf, he picked up the box, hoping it looked natural, and pulled uselessly at the lid. Top holding firm as expected, he reached for the key piece, bypassing it when he realized he looked like he knew what he was doing.

"Any idea how you open this?" he asked, and the wife shook her head.

Arms crossing over her chest, her gaze dropped away, and she appeared to have little interest in his performance. Without an audience, Slater felt no need to prolong it, and he slipped the wood key from its position to pull up the lid. Inside, the felt corner bent upward like a pull tab, and he pulled it back as the tech came through the door with the requested tools. Withholding his relief at seeing the paper lodged inside, Slater no longer trusted it, and he unfolded the worn note to ensure its contents.

Jack's crimes against humanity staring back at him, it was an ugly thing, and it was a beautiful thing. Exactly as Mateo Vega described it to him, it was almost as if it had been real from the start.

He could hardly call it a gift, Slater's ability to know what people wanted, to have such deep understanding of the roots of their behavior, but it did come in useful. He knew Mateo was looking for a way to take some time off his sentence, to end up with a few years in the sun at the end of his life, and Mateo knew Slater was looking to put an end to Jack Halston.

Once Mateo told him about the box, it was easy to lead him to a little more.

For weeks, Slater made his regular trips to Panama, questioning Mateo about his exploits, and Mateo had pushed Jack as mastermind, begging for a chance to help build a case against him. When Mateo insisted they would find the box at Jack's house, that he would be willing to testify against Jack if he could be bumped to a prison with a smaller population and get a few years shaved off his sentence, Slater listened, but held back the important question.

He knew they had to build trust first, that they needed to know each other inside out before he dared ask.

"How do you think we're going to link that box to you? Even if we find it, Jack can say it came from anywhere."

Mateo looked so unsure at the question, Slater thought it had all been a waste of time, that Mateo wasn't as smart as his years of not getting caught indicated. Then, Mateo nodded, realization dawning as he looked up at Slater in collaboration. "There's a list of the names in there," he said. "I put it in there as a little surprise for Jack to find, but he's never mentioned it, so I doubt he ever has."

"A list of your victims, you mean?" Slater took the opportunity to remind Mateo what those names really were, and the rapport between them actually worked to put a fleeting look of remorse on Mateo's face.

"Yeah," he responded. "A list of our victims." And, though they both knew it was a lie, it was all the lie Slater needed.

That list in his hand, Slater had to hand it to Caton. She might have regretted it, but she did a perfect plant job.

"Hmm," he grunted.

"What is it?" the tech asked.

Glancing up, Slater watched the wife come to attention. Maybe it was good to have her around. No talk of planted evidence if she was standing right there when he found it.

"Nothin'," Slater said, folding the paper back up and returning it to its compartment. Dropping the lid closed, he handed the box and its missing key to the tech. "Bag everything," he ordered, knowing the tech would know what to do and the less his own hands were in the mix, the better.

Watching the planted evidence, the only evidence they would find, walk out the door, Slater wanted to make the rest look good. Starting in with the safe drill, it took only seconds to pop the door, and he found a world of perfect order inside. Estate papers bound together, a few personal files in a neat stack. At the back were several expensive jewelry items that likely belonged to the woman standing at his back, but, to her credit, she said nothing as Slater began to drop them into the clear plastic bags as potential evidence.

Pulling the last item from the safe, a stark contrast to the diamonds and rubies that came before it, Slater thought it was possibly the ugliest locket he had ever seen. Pinkish toned with an ivory face, twisted and poorly carved, it was supposed to be a Cameo, he assumed, but had to be a knockoff.

"Wait." The wife stepped forward suddenly from the doorway, eyes on the necklace as he went to bag it, a flash of life showing in them for the first time. "That was my grandmother's," she whispered. "Jack said it had been lost."

Glancing down at the ugly piece in his hand, it made considerably more sense amongst the riches. Jack would never buy and keep something so hideous, but Slater could definitely buy him hiding it just to be a prick. "It has to go into evidence," he said.

With an accepting nod, the wife faded back into her position against the wall. Body slack, she looked suddenly defeated, as if he could take everything of financial value and it meant little to her, but losing something so sentimental was a crushing blow she couldn't endure.

Mind again going to Caton, to her insistence that Jack's family didn't deserve what Jack had coming to him, Slater reluctantly acknowledged that, if nothing else, he owed her. She had, after all, only threatened to renege. In the end, she had done what she promised.

Prying the locket open, he was surprised at the old black-and-whites inside, a couple in their mid-thirties, smiling happily into the camera. "Your grandparents?" he asked, and Jack's wife nodded, attempting a smile even as her world collapsed around her.

At his approach, she straightened a little, trying to stand tall despite the circumstances, and Slater glanced past her out the door, before pulling her hand up and dropping the locket into it. "They'll never know it was here," he said quietly, feeling justified in the overstep when her eyes filled with grateful tears.

"Thank you," she breathed, dropping her gaze to the locket for an instant, before easing the old chain over her head and tucking it beneath her sweater.

The heirloom seemed to return an iota of strength to her, and Slater hoped it would be enough to appease Caton, that she would somehow know. He finally had Jack, and he couldn't stand the thought of losing him just because he'd scorned the wrong woman.

55

Caton had never thought of herself as the kind of person who would run home. If a single thing in her life were going right, maybe she wouldn't have, but demonstrating a mastery of self-destruction she didn't know she possessed, she had managed to fuck up her personal life, professional life, and sanity all within a few months, a feat that, from an alternative perspective, might well have been impressive.

Before she could tuck her proverbial tail between her legs and make her escape, though, she was forced to watch things fall apart from inside. Slater was insistent that she return to her old job to avoid raising suspicion, and, surprisingly enough, Jack kept his word, putting her back in her old position, even taking the time out of his overextended schedule to rehire her himself, despite the authorities banging down his door.

Settling across the desk from him, Caton considered the possibility it might be an interrogation, that Jack suspected her part in his downfall. As it turned out, he wanted only to drop veiled references, thanking her for keeping his wife "occupied" and for "taking care of Amelia's needs". Perfect world on the verge of collapse, he apparently needed to gloat to the one person he thought he had bested.

"Well, someone had to." Caton had smiled calmly, refusing to give him further insight. He thought he knew everything, but Jack had no idea how much she had lost. Since Amelia's worth had never been appraised in a dollar amount, Jack wouldn't have understood her losses if Caton did try to explain.

A few people stayed at Halston & Company, but those who could ran, and Caton was certainly the only person walking back in. In the weeks she was forced to wait it out at the office, she watched her coworkers pack up their desks and move on, trying to distance themselves from the Halston brand as expediently as possible. Agencies refused to send temps to replace them. Senior executives cashed out their stock options while they still had some value.

Caton had never imagined how fast a company could fall when there were public investors. Soon enough, it looked more suspicious for her to stay than for her to leave, and she was relieved of her final duty in the takedown of Jack Halston.

"We all fall down," Jenna had declared, appearing in her cubicle as Caton was tossing the few personal items she'd brought for show into her bag.

"Shut up, Jenna," Caton returned instantly.

Fairly or not, she still placed a large chunk of the blame upon Jenna's shoulders. If Jenna had just let it go, if she had just let Caton walk away from Jack's office without interference, instead of jumping into the elevator with her and explaining the very sick truth that she was getting close to Jack for the sole purpose of seeing him fry, then Caton never would have had to destroy Amelia's illusions. She never would have given herself over so completely to a woman she was going to be forced to live her life without.

Scoffing, Jenna insinuated herself further into Caton's cubicle. "I just came to say goodbye," she stated, as if it was a grand gesture.

"Why?" Caton had asked her, finally glancing back. "Do we like each other now?"

Though she looked put-off by the question, Jenna seemingly came to the same conclusion as Caton. They would forever guard some of each other's deepest secrets, but there was really nothing more than a felony between them.

"No," Jenna acknowledged. "I suppose we don't." It was hardly civil, but the honesty was a welcome change, and it served as Caton's parting thought from Halston & Company and Chicago in general.

A few days later, she was settled into her temporary pity job from a friend of her father and the break in rent for the studio above her cousin's garage, and it felt utterly unnatural to be back in such mundanity.

Sighing, she turned from the desk, spreading files across the counter space behind her, reminding herself that she had better get used to it. Never again would she take a commission from a below-the-law agent or enter into a relationship that had no chance of lasting. The quotidian was her life. She would adjust to its realities and embrace the tedium.

"You go undercover for the BRC and this is what you get in return?" the voice uttered behind her, low tone meant for secrecy, but succeeding in sending a shiver of desire racing down Caton's back.

The ancient base creaking with her weight as she turned the faded desk chair, she expected to find nothing. It wouldn't be the first time she'd heard Amelia's voice when she wasn't there, though it usually came at night in the darkness of her pathetic living quarters before she self-pitied herself to sleep.

Eyes locking on intimately familiar brown, Caton fell instantly into their depths. It was only as she was gasping at the air seconds later that she realized she had forgotten to breathe.

"It wasn't exactly an authorized mission," she whispered, not trusting that her eyes weren't deceiving her, not trusting her legs to get up and find out. "How are you?" she asked, in case she wasn't hallucinating.

Shrugging as if she didn't know, or as if the answer didn't matter, Amelia tilted her head, gaze dark and circumspect, slightly longer hair brushing past her shoulder. "How are you?" she asked in return.

Dragging her eyes from Amelia's, Caton glanced around the office with a forced laugh, relieved Amelia was still there when she returned her gaze. Forcing her body to stand, she moved around the old, chipped desk on unsteady legs, gravitating toward Amelia. Desperate to touch her, she was terrified Amelia might dissolve on contact. "How did you find me?"

"You're not exactly hidden," Amelia responded. "And I can be very persuasive."

All the ways in which Amelia was incomparably persuasive inundating her at once, Caton reached out for support, finding the corner of the desk and leaning heavily on it. There were so many things she needed to say, things she had meant to say, but they jumbled together in her head, making every thought nonsensical.

"Is Selene okay?" She finally found a question that seemed fitting.

"She's good," Amelia responded. "She's been home for a while."

"I'm glad." Caton felt an iota of real relief.

"So is she," Amelia returned.

"And your parents?"

"Living up their golden years," Amelia responded, a small smile playing at her mouth. "They still have no desire to move here. It's too cold. Or so they say."

"They're still in their home?" Caton questioned.

"For now," Amelia answered. "And," she interrupted as Caton opened her mouth again. "Sole is also fine, before you ask."

Caton was going to, mostly because she knew no other way to fill the awkward silence that yawned between them, wide and trap-filled. Line of questioning shut down, she could think of nothing else to say. All the slow steps she and Amelia had taken toward each other, and it was as if they had made no progress at all.

"I've been living in the guesthouse." Amelia spared them continued silence. "Sole moved into a bedroom in the house. Jack let me, which means he knows I know and he knows he's guilty. You understand, I wanted to take you at your word, Caton, but you hadn't given me a lot of reason."

Gaze lowering to the floor, Caton felt prepared and unprepared for the statement. Her eyes tearing, she swallowed against the urge to break down and cry, to grovel, to beg forgiveness. "I'm surprised he lets you leave the house," she uttered.

"Jack is being very accommodating actually," Amelia replied. "He has something to fear now. That's a new concept for him."

Caton imagined. She doubted Jack had ever had to fear anything.

"They don't have much, though." Amelia continued on a sigh, and Caton wasn't sure if it was relief or disappointment. "That's what Jack's lawyers said. Apparently, part of the evidence was lost in transit. They have the box, but not the list. Just the sworn testimony of a bunch of agents who saw it. Which is a relief, I guess, since my fingerprints were all over it."

"I knew Slater was going to..." Caton started, before realizing she was probably only further incriminating herself in Amelia's eyes. "I knew it was never going to make it into evidence. I never would have left it if I thought it could hurt you."

Amelia's gaze unblinking upon her, it provided no insight, and Caton wasn't sure if Amelia believed her or not. It was almost a relief when Amelia finally glanced away to inspect the items on the desk. "Jack's lawyers also said, if he does get convicted, which I seriously doubt, it will take decades. They can appeal until the end of his life if that's what it takes. They can keep Jack from his business, thank God, but they're not going to take anything, not for a while."

"Good," Caton uttered. "That's good." It was hardly a win-win. Jack keeping his luxurious life wasn't at all what he deserved, but if it meant Amelia didn't have to suffer along with him, she would take it. "I hope you can be happy."

"I can't stay with him," Amelia surprised her by saying, and Caton looked up, her gaze falling to Amelia's mouth as it moved again. "Not knowing what he's done."

The announcement everything Caton had been hoping to hear, it was rendered meaningless by her own misdeeds. What Jack had done was done. What she had done was done. She couldn't take it back, and she couldn't expect Amelia to forgive it. She didn't even dare hope Amelia could.

"You said that I was using you," Amelia stated, and, eyes closing, Caton felt the squeeze of regret, like a tourniquet around her. The hypocritical words had haunted her since the moment they left her lips, but somehow they were more haunting from Amelia's.

"I said that you were using me," Amelia continued.

Feeling the shift in the room, Caton's eyes opened and she watched Amelia come closer until Amelia's body poured over her like liquid, no air left between them, her lips hovering torturously out of reach.

"Is that what we were doing, Caton?" she questioned, tongue sliding slowly across her lip, hand rising between them to tug gently at the platinum and diamond pendant in the hollow of Caton's throat. "Were we using each other?"

Warm breath blowing over her, dark eyes pinning her in place, Caton's head swam, heart lurching forward before her body could catch up. She knew she didn't deserve it, to feel Amelia, to have her, but she wanted it anyway. Swallowing Amelia's harsh exhalation as their lips met, she waited for the feel of Amelia's hands against her shoulders, shoving her away with all the force she deserved.

When Amelia's body pressed into her instead, the warm hands against her lower back dragging her closer, Caton wound her fingers into dark hair and gave in. It was her answer. Both of their answers. Wrong as it should have been after everything that had happened, it was no less right, and, deserved or not, she could feel Amelia's forgiveness wash over her. With something else, something unspoken that was there every time they touched.

Senses overloaded, it took Caton a moment to register there was something that didn't belong. The realization didn't dissuade her from the haven of Amelia's lips, though, until she heard the voice, well-known and jarring in the moment. "I am so sorry. I'll just…" it broke off, and, pulling away from Amelia, Caton felt like a thirteen-year-old who just got caught making out in her bedroom for the first time.

"Mom," she said, watching her mother turn back in the doorway, cheeks flaming pink, but otherwise surprisingly composed. "It's okay."

Glancing back to Amelia, Caton wondered if it actually was okay. Amelia appeared more anxious than her mother, nervous in a way Caton had never seen her. Whether due to the surprise or the sudden introduction, she wasn't sure. Amelia looked so intriguingly human, though, it was hard for Caton to pull her eyes away to return them to her waiting parent. "This is Amelia," she said, and Amelia's usual assurance fell into place as she turned to face the unexpected visitor.

Her mom's eyes widening and narrowing in no uncertain way, Caton knew she had made a huge mistake. When she told her mother everything that happened, save the parts that made her a felon, her mother rushed to condemn Amelia, placing all the blame on Amelia's shoulders for corrupting her decent daughter and turning her into the kind of girl who would have an affair with a married woman. No matter how much Caton tried to assure her she was no victim, her mother still chose to view her as the helpless lamb to Amelia's worldlier wolf. Maybe she hadn't tried hard enough to exonerate Amelia. At the time, she never expected the two to meet.

"Hmm," her mother said shortly, eyeing Amelia with open disdain that Amelia didn't deserve.

"Reese, right?" Amelia recovered from her shock with aplomb. "I've heard so much about you."

Expert grace carrying her forward, she offered her hand, which Caton watched her mother rudely refuse, wondering how in the hell she was going to fix it. Before she had even a working idea, Amelia pulled out the same winning style Caton had seen her drop on rich people to strip them of their money, now put to the task of raising the value on herself. "And clearly you've heard about me," she continued. "And don't think very highly of me. I can't blame you. I didn't think very highly of myself for a long time."

Recognizing the admission as more than a line, Caton sent her mother a stern glare and a telepathic message to play nice. She really didn't want to get into a fight in the middle of her office in the middle of a workday, but she wasn't about to let her mother treat Amelia like a miscreant either.

"But I am in love with your daughter," Amelia proclaimed, and, gaze snapping back to Amelia, Caton forgot all about her thoughts of civil war. "I want to be with her. I think that gives us common ground, don't you?"

Though she watched the lips on Amelia's profile move in time with the words, Caton still wasn't convinced she had heard them.

"I guess it does." Her mother sounded equally stunned.

"Good," Amelia returned simply, gaze drifting to Caton, and, seized by it, Caton felt as spellbound as ever.

"I'll just leave that here for you," her mother said, and Caton assumed there was something being left as her mom started out the door again, then changed her mind just inside it. "Do you want to come to dinner?" she asked, and Amelia's gaze abandoned Caton to swing back toward the door.

"I would love that." Amelia's smile was sincere. "I do have my daughter with me, so I would like to bring her, if that's okay."

"Daughter?" Caton's mom sounded overwhelmed. Weren't they all? "That's right," she uttered. "Caton said something about that. Of course... Seven, Caton?"

Only somewhat aware that she was being addressed, Caton nodded, not realizing her mother had left until Amelia turned to her again, a smugly satisfied smile on her face. The expression faded slightly as Caton brushed past her to the door, shutting it with a light slam, and turned to grab Amelia by the expensive fabric of her shirt, crushing their lips together so Amelia stumbled back into the desk.

Lips reluctantly breaking from Amelia's, Caton searched dark eyes. She didn't dare hope. Yet, hoping was all she could seem to do. "Was that true?" she questioned breathlessly. "Or are you just using those expert skills at telling people what they want to hear?"

Smile returning, more honest than before, Amelia's hand stroked down Caton's cheek, eyes trailing its path until it came to rest at the base of Caton's neck. "What do you think?"

Caton didn't have to think. She could see it, not flagrant or theatrical, but stripped bare in Amelia's gaze. Stepping back into the comfort of Amelia's body, she could feel it wrap around her.

"It won't be the same, you know," Amelia warned, hands on Caton's hips easing her closer. "We're going to be like Dan and Reese, working to make ends meet for the rest of our lives. Plus, there's Selene, and, as you know, she can be challenging. It may be hard."

Not sure if Amelia was trying to counsel her or remind herself, the notion of such a life with Amelia brought Caton nothing but relief. "I told you I'm not proud."

Grin flashing briefly, Amelia's usual swagger faltered just enough to be noticeable. "Does that mean you're in?" she questioned, swallowing the anxiety that appeared to chase the question up her throat.

Laughing brokenly at how senselessly she was in, Caton slid her hands beneath the dark fall of Amelia's hair, earning a look of indulgence from Amelia that eased away any lingering doubts. "I'm pretty sure I was in the day I followed you down to that fucking basement," she confessed.

A brilliant smile spreading across her face, Amelia wrapped her arms around Caton's waist to pull her closer, and, for the first time since Amelia walked into the office, Caton was convinced what she held in her hands was real.

56

Considering the trajectory of their relationship, landing at dinner with Caton's parents and Selene was surreal in its domesticity. Amelia could tell she had her work cut out for her when it came to raising Caton's mother's opinion of her, but Reese and Selene were like kindred spirits.

Selene had never spent any real time in a house like the one Caton grew up in, so pragmatic and homey, and she was fascinated with everything, from the thirty-year-old dining room table to Caton's dad's record player. Dan was more than happy to show off the relic of a bygone era, educating Selene on girl groups of the 60s as he thumbed through his substantial vinyl collection.

The squalor that surrounded Amelia's childhood was no more than family mythos to her daughter. Selene was accustomed to the perks of affluence, without even realizing it, and it was a relief to see how she took to a world of less privilege.

She made herself so at home that Caton's parents invited her to stay, and Selene enthusiastically sought her permission, though Amelia suspected there was some strategy involved on all their parts and wondered just how obvious it had been to Dan and Reese that she couldn't wait to get her hands and lips on their daughter.

Braced on one arm, Amelia pulled Caton's hips in tighter, feeling the pulse of Caton against her as they climaxed together, a culmination that wasn't worth the time spent apart, but did take the edge off the prior months. The modern furnishings of the hotel room disappearing around them, time ceased, until panting and depleted she fell atop Caton, hearing the breath expel from Caton's body in a rush. Hands tightening against her skin, they drew her closer, and, head resting against Caton's shoulder, Amelia felt a heart pounding between them, though she couldn't tell whose.

With nowhere else to be, and no fear of intrusion, they remained as they fell. Everything the same. Everything different. All the times before, any potential future felt heavily burdened by forces beyond them. Lying there, the road stretched open before them, their route entirely within their control. That was the path down which Amelia's thoughts were wandering, at least.

No matter how intimately entangled, though, in silence she couldn't know Caton's mind, and it was jarring to suddenly pass Caton going the opposite direction.

"I could come back with you," Caton stated quietly. "Things could go back to the way they were."

Words an arctic blast against her over-heated skin, Amelia raised her head, but, Caton's face cast mostly in shadow, she couldn't see beyond the statement itself. "Why would we do that?" she asked carefully.

"Because it worked." Caton's shrug brushed against Amelia's chest.

"You said you would never be happy being someone's mistress," she whispered.

"I lied," Caton returned instantly.

There was some honesty to it, Amelia could hear it, but it wasn't wholly sincere. Wondering why Caton was promoting a life with restrictions neither of them wanted, she braced herself on her forearm, settling in for debate.

"I don't want to be with him," Amelia declared, though she thought she'd made the fact clear.

"You wouldn't be with him," Caton returned. "You would be with me. You said he's being accommodating. Who knows, maybe he'll even let me move into the guesthouse with you."

Said in jest, there was a touch of wistfulness to the hypothetical suggestion that Amelia couldn't ignore. "Is that what you want?" she asked, and the real truth was in the hesitation, in the way Caton's eyes trailed past her shoulder to the gap in the curtains. The light streaming through them finally illuminating Caton's entire face, Amelia could see the incongruity between what she felt and what she said.

"I don't want anyone to suffer," Caton admitted.

"Caton…" Amelia hoped to derail the train of thought before it could pick up momentum.

"If we go back," Caton's gaze returned to Amelia's, "you can have everything."

"I don't need everything," Amelia insisted, but the remainder of her argument was cut short by Caton's hand on her cheek, compelling her into silence.

"I want you to have everything," Caton whispered.

The admission hovering between them, Amelia had never felt more deserving, and had also never been more sure there was only one thing she needed that wasn't hers through biology.

If Caton's concerns began and ended with the privilege she would be giving up, though, they might easily be assuaged. Glancing in the vague direction of her purse, unable to make it out in the darkness, Amelia didn't particularly want to rise, but she knew the moment of courage was fleeting, as every moment before it had been. If she didn't do it immediately, she might never do it. Then, they would never know.

Determination already wavering, she slid off Caton, pulling Caton's hands from her hips when they tried to keep her in place. "I'm coming right back," she promised, dropping a kiss against Caton's lips before throwing the covers off and meeting the chilled room head on.

Finding the zipper of the purse in the darkness, Amelia scavenged the interior until her hand closed around the silver compact buried in her makeup bag. Flicking the clasp open, the locket inside it fell into her hand.

"What is that?" Caton asked, gaze following Amelia back to the bed, and, with a shiver, Amelia turned the light on and climbed back beneath the covers.

"Maybe nothing," she answered. "Maybe everything we don't already have."

Eyes shifting to Caton, she knew it wasn't a deal breaker. Whatever happened, they would figure it out, they would make do, and Amelia's faith in that fueled her nerve. Popping the locket open, she glanced down at the black-and-white photos, seeing only what lie beneath.

"Who are they?" Caton questioned, hair tickling Amelia's bicep as she slid closer.

"No clue," Amelia replied, grinning as she recalled the look on Marcus Slater's face when he'd opened it, his naive acceptance that the strangers inside were her grandparents. Though, it was admittedly unexpected. Until that moment, Slater had seemed all but gullible. "But your Agent Slater believed it belonged to me."

"He let you keep it?" Caton asked.

"Well, look at it?" Amelia countered. "Wouldn't you?"

Watching the small grin slide over Caton's face, Amelia was seized by the desire to put possibilities aside and focus on the one thing of which she had no doubts. All the deliberate fitness choices she had made in her life, and she had never truly known how much energy she possessed until Caton had provided her a worthwhile place to exhaust it.

"Then why did you want it?" Caton's breast brushed against Amelia's forearm as she shifted again, and Amelia tried to keep her thoughts on the subject at hand.

In lieu of response, she pressed her thumb against the edge of a photo, watching it pop free and flutter to the mattress along with the slip of paper behind it. Plucking the paper from the sheet, she held it up before them, staring at the string of numbers. "If I were to make an educated guess, it would be that this is a nameless bank account in Antigua."

"Those still exist?" Caton questioned doubtfully.

"For the general public, or for people like Jack?" Amelia returned.

"Good point," Caton conceded, staring at the paper with the same combination of mistrust and curiosity with which Amelia had regarded it since it came into her possession.

"He has it memorized, I'm certain," Amelia went on. "But Jack is frozen. He can't make a move without them seeing it."

"So, what are you going to do with it?"

Eyes scanning Caton's features, Amelia wasn't sure she should do anything. For the first time in months, maybe even years, she was exactly where she wanted to be, Caton was exactly where she wanted her, and anything that jeopardized that seemed unnecessarily risky.

Then again, maybe she was just trying to psyche herself out of it for the hundredth time.

"There is only one photo of Jack and I up at the house," Amelia answered slowly.

"I know," Caton uttered. "I've ignored it on many occasions."

"The picture frame says 'Antigua'."

"So?" Caton replied.

"So, I've never been to Antigua," Amelia uttered, already reaching across Caton to pull the phone on the bedside table closer. "Under that photo, I found another number."

Hitting the button for the speaker phone, she began pressing the digits before she could again talk herself out of it, reminding herself it was, after all, only a phone call. Midway through, Caton's teeth scraped across her nipple and Amelia nearly lost her place. Glancing down with a look meant to be scolding, Amelia assumed it came off as encouraging when Caton smiled and sucked the nipple into her mouth.

Mind bent on one desire, body on another, Amelia entered the remainder of the numbers before she lost her nerve, hesitating on the last one long enough that Caton ceased what she was doing to grab her hand. "Are you sure about this?" she questioned.

"There's only one way to find out," Amelia responded, gently caressing Caton's palm with her thumb when a touch of fear entered her eyes, before breaking free to enter the final number.

Ridiculously tense, Amelia considered the worst that could logically happen. It wasn't like a swat team was going to swoop down on them for dialing a random island number. She didn't think. Still, when the line picked up, she stopped herself just short of hanging up.

The voice that came on was automated, offering no indication as to where or what they had reached, just a request for her to enter a valid number. With a shaking hand, Amelia did as instructed, knowing she had managed to input the numbers correctly when the automated voice requested a password.

Taking a deep breath, she knew she had only one shot. As far as she knew, Jack had only made the one mistake he didn't know about, the only mistake he wouldn't have known to clean up. "Vespasian," she stated clearly.

In the next instant, the line went silent, and Amelia was sure she had figured everything wrong, that Jack's intoxicated ramblings had been nothing more than that, and all that she had gotten out of Marcus Slater was the ungodliest piece of jewelry ever crafted.

"Yes. How may I help you?" A heavily-accented voice interrupted her runaway musings, and Amelia startled back to reality.

"I need my account balance," she rushed into her predetermined script, cringing at how anxious she sounded.

"Yes, ma'am," the young man didn't seem to notice. "Your current balance is sixteen million, three-hundred and forty-two thousand, one-hundred and eleven dollars."

Despite the fact that she had spent her entire adult life dealing with such staggering wealth, the number still jolted her and Amelia's thoughts scattered. Feeling Caton move beneath her, she glanced down, the shock in bright green eyes somehow quashing her own, so that, wisely or foolishly, she felt invincible.

"My financial information was seized three months ago." She found her footing, and a flourish of typing at the other end of the line indicated the news was taken with as much importance as she anticipated.

"I see no activity on the account since then," the man responded. "Would you like to cash out or move the funds to another account?"

Not knowing what either of those things entailed, and with no clue as to what to do with that kind of cash in hand, Amelia told him to move the money, telling him the line was secure enough when he asked if she was on a secure line, and crawling back out of bed to grab the notepad and pen from the corner desk when he wanted to give her a new account number.

Relative to the warmth of the bed and Caton's body, the air was biting as Amelia stopped by the nightstand and lifted the phone's receiver from its cradle. She could feel the sting on her skin, but felt strangely warm at the same time, a heady combination of power and Caton's eyes, which had followed her every move.

The mystery voice on the other end of the line gave her the new account number, requested a new password, and told her to call back when she was ready to collect her funds. Thanking him automatically, the civility sounded unsuited to the situation and she wondered if she had given herself away.

"You are very welcome, Ma'am," the man responded without pause. "Thank you for calling."

Replying to his goodbye with her own, Amelia watched her hand drop the phone back into its cradle and sank down on the bed next to Caton, feeling Caton press tightly against her back. The welcome sensation made it feel more like a dream, and Amelia worried the entire day had been nothing but a long, incredible hallucination.

When Caton reached out for her, though, hand curving around her hip, Amelia had experienced both the fantasy and reality enough to distinguish the touch as real. "Okay," she breathed. "The money is gone as far as anyone else can see. It's ours."

Holding the note pad up by her shoulder, her hand tingled as she turned to look at Caton. Meeting eyes shiny and curious in the dim light, she worried what those eyes saw.

"I don't want it all," she quickly declared. "I just want enough. To live on. To take care of Selene. To make sure my parents are okay. To keep Sole. The rest, we can give back, we should give back. You can help me with that, right?" She knew she was rambling, but Caton's nod encouraged her to go on. "I just want enough," she reiterated. "I think I've earned that."

It was too much to want. She had Caton, and she had Selene, and that was more than many people had. Maybe she had no right to more.

"So do I," Caton responded, looking strangely relieved as her warm palm caressed the chilled skin of Amelia's back.

"But I don't need it." Amelia wanted to make the point clear. "If you don't want to deal with the money, I can tear this up right now and it just disappears forever."

Peeling the paper from the notepad, ready to make it go away at Caton's command, Amelia stopped only when Caton grabbed her hands. "Maybe we should hang onto it," Caton suggested.

Grin pulling at her lips, Amelia tossed the notepad onto the nightstand, interest in everything else diminishing as she shifted closer to Caton.

"We could keep just a little extra," she tempted. Finger trailing down Caton's chest, she dragged the covers out of the way, delighting at how she could still make Caton tremble with the simplest of touches. "Enough that we can go wherever we want, do whatever we want. Would that make us horrible people?"

God knew there were those amongst the "charitable" donors she'd dealt with over the years who deserved to have their money stolen, and, with her hands on the money, the charities would get more back than they would ever have gotten from Jack. Maybe she'd even start her own charity, take the skills she had unknowingly used to make Jack richer and put them to good use.

"No," Caton replied, but when she reached out to stop Amelia's hand, her expression was far grimmer than Amelia would have liked. "Are you sure about this, Amelia?" she questioned, and Amelia felt her happiness hanging by a thread. "This is your chance to start over. You could have a new life. No past entanglements. No one you feel like you can't trust."

Watching the shadows fall across Caton's face, Amelia wondered how many times she would have to forgive Caton before Caton forgave herself. "Or I can trust you," she stated. "I can trust you, can't I, Caton?

Though she looked slightly pained by the question, Caton nodded, and Amelia believed her, as senseless and risky as it might be.

"Aren't you angry?" Caton asked.

Over the past months, Amelia had unleashed so many internal tirades at Caton she'd lost track of them. Caton had been candid when she wanted to be, leading Amelia to the erroneous belief she had no secrets, only for Amelia to be reminded that everyone had secrets and one could only know someone to the extent the person wanted to be known.

Gaze breaking from Caton's to sweep down her body, where she had found so many pleasures - and more - Amelia knew it was worth the risk.

Lifting the covers, she slid down next to Caton. There was truth there, at least.

"I have spent my entire adult life doing what I thought I needed to do and resenting it," she responded. "Now, I want what I want. I don't want to be angry."

Skin caressing skin, it occurred to Amelia it was as much a matter of need as desire. All the money in the world, and she couldn't imagine living without the look in Caton's eyes, the way Caton's body strove to make contact, the feel of Caton's lips against her throat before they trailed across her jaw to meet her own. With Caton, she could live without the money. She wasn't sure she wanted to endure life the other way around.

When Caton's lips broke from hers and her head fell back to the pillow, Amelia could barely see her. Hair tumbling around her shoulders, it hung like a curtain, casting them both into darkness, until, hands rising to Amelia's face, Caton pushed it back and let the light in.

Epilogue

The gentle lull of the string quartet trickled through the ballroom, vibrating Amelia's sinew as she watched the red marker tick another notch higher on the fundraising thermometer.

Goosebumps breaking out without warning, she expected a sense of relief, some indication things had changed. But she didn't expect it be so intensely visceral. Didn't anticipate the sort of intimate euphoria that seized her amidst the crowd, rippling in delirious waves, making her wish she were alone. Well, not alone exactly.

Scanning the crowd for Caton, Amelia found her holding court with a group of attendees, amongst them Victor Pasquale, owner of a chain of independent hotels throughout the American Southwest. Clearly arguing with Pasquale over something, Caton did so with the hint of a smile, and everyone standing around them smiled as they watched her, waiting to see how the debate would come out.

For Amelia, there was no question. Pasquale would give a little more, dig a little deeper into his plentiful fortune.

They always did.

Amelia was good at this.

Caton was better.

And it was mesmerizing to watch her.

At first, Caton had trouble finding her footing. She was like a hybrid, half butterfly, half chameleon, emerging uneasily into this aristocratic, often pompous world. In that way, she reminded Amelia much of herself many years before.

Then, Caton realized she had enchanting colors and could change them quite readily. While Amelia had always felt she had only one real asset to her advantage, or perhaps a few closely intertwined, Caton's gifts were broader. She could attract a donor with an enigmatic smile, but once she had them in her clutches, she annihilated them with shrewd debate.

Caton thought she had no use for her extensive education, beyond her deeper, somewhat cynical view of the world, but philosophy proved rather useful in fundraising it turned out. If one could make a person explain why they were stopping at one number for a donation, she could often encourage them out of more.

Caton could at least.

Why would a person donate $1,000 when the average tuition in the schools they supported cost $180? Wouldn't it make more sense to give only $80 more and cover six whole children instead of five and only the upper torso of one?

Often, it did make more sense to the donor the way Caton explained it. Often, it made more sense to cover the education of ten children instead of six, or however many children attended a particular village school, and the money ticked higher and higher on the donation boards like rising tides of good karma.

Tonight, $73,000 had passed by in a blip, a far cry from the $625,000 at the thermometer's apex, but the only number that truly mattered to Amelia tonight. Already, they were at $96,000. Now, $103.

Hearing Victor Pasquale's sudden roar of laughter, Amelia had no doubt Caton was vying for a truly lofty donation. And no doubt she would get it. It also meant Caton wasn't watching the board. Caton hadn't noticed the $73,000 come and go, hadn't felt the same surge of exhilaration, of freedom, and Amelia was somewhat deflated as the moment passed with only her to recognize it.

Small sigh slipping past her lips – both childish and selfish, Caton was off doing truly meaningful things – Amelia moved toward the bar, trying not to drag her feet and eyeing the pre-poured red on a tray waiting to be circulated, but considering ordering something with a little more punch.

"Two glasses of champagne, please." Caton's voice came almost immediately at her back, its soft husk a whisper upon Amelia's neck. "And don't leave any space. Don't worry. The boss won't mind."

Bartender going about her task, Amelia turned, finding herself in the soft confinement of Caton's arms, one hand on her hip sending sparks through her lower half as the other at her waist infused her with strength.

"I hear you're a self-made woman." The words rose like a hymn, soft but inherently powerful, and another shiver seized Amelia as she slipped her own arms around Caton's shoulders. "Every dollar earned. Not a penny unaccounted for."

It was all Amelia had wanted, to put the money back. The money Jack made her swindle out of thousands of people to put towards God only knew what ends. She hadn't been a part of it, not with any real knowledge. But she had certainly contributed unknowingly. She had taken in millions, tens of millions, hundreds of millions of dollars in donations she thought were being used for good things. Now, it was hard to believe even Jack's charitable endeavors were at all charitable. It was hard to believe they were even just fake displays for public consumption. Once the foundation had the money in its coffers, who knew what they actually did with it? Amelia didn't want to know.

"Not completely self-made." Hands sliding onto Caton's neck, she drew Caton's lips to her own, sighing at the taste of her, so familiar now, but exhilarating in a whole new way.

She *had* done it. Finally. The thought escaped on a moan as Caton's hands smoothed across her lower back to draw her closer. She had put the money back. But she had hardly done it alone. Caton had been there the whole time. Selene. Sole, in her new role as their foundation's executive assistant. They had all done it together.

It took time, putting those millions of dollars of dirty money back into the world in positive ways. A lot of time. More time than Amelia would have liked. She wouldn't say she was antsy… exactly… but the closer they got to bringing in the agreed upon figure and redistributing it, the closer they got to being out from under the onus of Jack's sins, the slower time seemed to move.

How long had she been waiting for this? Two years? Five?

More than five, Amelia could admit to herself in the safety of Caton's embrace. Since the night they first kissed, since she went to Caton's apartment and Caton's lips touched her own this way, she knew. Knew why she had followed Caton across the city like a stalker. Knew no one else would ever feel the same.

She felt the same way now, in a way, as though she was tripping through a minefield, everything almost too alive around them. Not as uncertain in her footsteps, but still on edge. What if Caton rejected her now?

What if she didn't?

Caton pulling suddenly away, the breath fell from Amelia's lips and she staggered weakly against her, not sure when she lost her sense of time or balance.

"Aiming for a real spectacle here, aren't you?" Caton softly panted, and it was like a trigger phrase, a command, the urge to pull Caton down and ravage her against the floor achingly strong.

"I didn't feel you pulling away."

"That's because I wasn't."

Caton's murmur was a bow across her spine, and gooseflesh broke out once more, traveling along Amelia's vertebrae, tickling around her to spread across her chest. Looking for something to quash her rapidly rising arousal, she remembered the bar and glanced to find their champagne poured and waiting for them.

"Thank you." She noticed the bright pink of the bartender's cheeks as she reached for a glass, handing it to Caton before picking up the other. Then, free hand on Caton's lower back, Amelia moved them so quickly through the room she could actually feel the wind against her bare arms.

"Gee. I wonder if anyone knows what we're heading off to do."

Amelia could see Caton's smirk from the corner of her eye, but she didn't care. She felt alive – terrified - and strangely possessive. Possessive because she wanted Caton all to herself. Strange because she had spent nearly two decades with a man who was always cheating with someone and had never really cared. Let the people think what they wanted to think. As long as they all knew Caton was hers, and she had no intention of sharing her, they could imagine until their hearts' content.

"You do know your daughter is somewhere in this room, right? We've probably scarred her for life."

"She's a grown woman. She can handle it."

Even saying it aloud, it was nearly impossible to believe, but the fact was Selene *was* grown, working for the foundation part-time and halfway through undergrad at the University of Miami.

It had surprised Amelia when Selene said she actually wanted to go to college. She had so often grumbled about it, that it was just another boarding school they were shipping her off to. But Jack always talked about Princeton and Harvard, the sorts of schools he thought his child should be seen to attend. A pedigree he could buy that reflected more on him than it did on Selene.

It wasn't that Selene didn't want to go to college, Amelia realized, not long after they left Chicago. It was that she didn't want to go to a college of Jack's choosing. She felt burdened by her father, as they had all felt burdened by him in some way, and was happier out from under his reign. Much happier. In a way Amelia had never quite seen her. All those years, Amelia felt as though she was doing the right thing, giving Selene her best possible life, opportunities she never had. Now, she carried some guilt for keeping her there for so long.

Still, things were better now, and Amelia didn't just think, she absolutely knew, Selene *was* somewhere in that crowd… cheering her on.

A moment later, standing outside the doors of the ballroom, guests abandoned inside, Amelia fumbled for Caton's hand, pulling her toward the elevator.

"You know, a restroom stall would be less likely to spontaneously open." She could still hear the smirk in Caton's voice. "And less likely to have someone watching our every move."

"I'm taking you somewhere." Pressing the up arrow with some conviction, Amelia glanced to Caton, her own smirk faltering at the intensity in Caton's eyes, the smoldering rays that threatened to melt her to the plush, designer carpet.

"If this doesn't turn into an 80's love song and you don't say 'Heaven' next, I am going to be terribly disappointed." *Smolder, smolder.*

"Time will tell." Amelia forced nonchalance and forced her eyes away, knowing if she didn't she would lose the plot completely and do exactly what Caton's expression suggested she should. But the mirrored elevator doors only reflected Caton's proximity back at her, as if she could forget for a moment she was there, and taking a small sip of champagne to cool her palate, she watched Caton's smirk grow as she moved nearer, her breast brushing the back of Amelia's arm in a casual assault.

The arrival of the elevator a second later was like a godsend, and, it blissfully, came up empty. Theirs was the only event in the building tonight. Amelia had made good and sure of it by renting out the entire place. The only people they could encounter were their own guests or security. But, hopefully, everyone else was well occupied and they would have the run of the other floors to themselves.

"Antsy?"

As soon as the doors closed, Caton slid closer again, her free hand gliding across Amelia's stomach, her lips pressing to the skin just below Amelia's jaw.

"Oh, you know. Just trying to get to Heaven faster," Caton murmured against her skin, and Amelia surrendered. Gave in. Just a little. Turning her head, she met Caton's gaze, before letting her eyes fall to the soft, sinful smile on Caton's lips, and was surprised by how calm she actually felt. Highly aroused, yes, but she had no trouble sorting out her priorities.

"You should try to be a good girl then."

Turning back toward the doors, she heard Caton's broken laughter beside her. Half scoffing, half bemusement, it was the throaty sound Caton always made when she was sincerely irritated, but too humored to be angry.

It was also one of Amelia's favorite sounds in the entire world, and thoroughly tested her resolve to be good herself.

Caton wasn't wrong. This elevator being monitored by security right at this very moment was almost a given. But that wasn't even a factor. Amelia couldn't say there wasn't still some appeal in Caton's attentions, in giving into them, in turning into Caton and pressing her back against the elevator wall. In knocking the wind out of her and sending two glasses of champagne careening to the floor in a messy splash of liquid sugar. It wasn't like they couldn't afford to pay the cleaning bill.

But she could endure. For the sake of more important things.

It wasn't much longer before the doors of the elevator slid open, and Amelia was delighted to see the small vestibule empty, instead of a waiting audience. Though, glancing to the windows, it was impossible to know if there was anyone outside them, guests who already knew the secret of this building or had gone off exploring on their own. The overhead lights, soft as they were, glared off the glass, so they couldn't see anything beyond. But Amelia knew at least *what* was out there, and led Caton to the door, pulling it open and nudging her through it.

Just outside, Caton came to an abrupt, unanticipated stop, lips falling softly open on a gasp, any lingering irritation she felt dissipating in the sultry night air.

Good, Amelia thought even as her own impatience grew, her hand on the small of Caton's back encouraging her to move forward. *Good*.

Plenty of buildings in the city boasted rooftop gardens, but few of them used the natural climate so well to their advantage. Around them, palm fronds stood as tall as they were, birds of paradise reaching their soft beaks out to guide the way along the boarded walk, soft blue lights dotting the branches of the ficuses between. And, beyond that, the city, a vibrant mishmash of shape and color reaching up into an indigo sky.

Watching the tops of the buildings grow as they moved closer to the roof's parapet, Amelia inhaled the ocean air as the lush heat warmed her skin.

They hadn't gone back to Chicago for long. It could be said they never really returned there at all. They did so in body, only long enough for Amelia and Selene to get those few things that truly mattered to them and pack them in a storage container to be shipped to their new home. It was strange to see how little there was in a house so big. Especially for Amelia. She knew it was never really her home, her world, but she hadn't grasped until then just how little she existed in her old life, how much she was just another thing kept in a grand palace with no purpose and even less significance.

That first year, they had stayed in Ohio, in a house on the shore of Lake Erie, not far from Caton's parents. It was a test almost, to see if it held, or if both she and Caton were just that happy to be out from under Jack. At first, Caton even kept her tiny apartment over her cousin's garage. Then, one day Caton woke at the house and just never left. Or, perhaps, Amelia didn't allow her to leave. By then, Chicago felt like another world, another lifetime, completely unreal. It was as if she and Caton had met under far different circumstances. Better circumstances. As if she had always had Caton. Or as if she had nothing before her.

"This is incredible." Glancing her way, Caton's eyes glowed impossibly green against the greenery at her back, even in the blue-tinged lights, and the past evaporated once more, drifting away like a nightmare that couldn't be forgotten, but had lost all power over them.

"I thought that you would like it," Amelia husked, taking a sip of her champagne to soothe her suddenly parched throat. Though, she didn't know how it was dry in the press of humidity, and it did less to fortify her unsteady hands.

In the end, they had chosen Miami for its equidistance. It was Caton who first suggested it. As close as they could get to Venezuela without leaving the country, it seemed a fair compromise. *Plus, the weather*, Caton offered with a vixenish smile.

"Jungle fantasy?" Caton asked her now, and Amelia felt the laughter rumble in her throat.

"Something like that," she said, instantly more at ease.

And happy. Almost too happy. It was like an illusion, at first. Not entirely real. How could it be? She was so used to her life feeling like a chore, every day spent looking for pleasure in a world which had none. Now, every day carried some small delight. Even the worst of them had laughter. Wonder.

And she kept waiting for the spell to break.

But it wasn't breaking.

Even now, eyes drawn by Caton's long, slow sigh, Amelia felt entranced, seduced, as Caton raised her glass to her lips in an almost teasing gesture, as if waiting for Amelia to make whatever move she was planning to make.

So, Amelia did.

Taking a step forward, she laid her hand over Caton's hand that held the glass, pressing a kiss to Caton's champagne-cooled and sweetened lips, and stole her drink as she pulled away.

"Hey," Caton half-heartedly protested, but it worked as Amelia expected. As she walked off, Caton trailed after her. Hearing her footsteps fall against the garden path, Amelia listened with rising alertness. Like prey being stalked by a predator. Only with every intention of being caught.

Some steps later, they emerged into the jewel of the garden, a small grass-carpeted clearing where the density of palm fronds and trickle of water as it poured over the edges of a stone fountain nearly drowned out the sounds and lights of the city completely.

Leaving the boarded path for soft grass, Amelia went to the table carved from a repurposed tree stump that sat between two benches and put down their glasses, turning to find Caton already at the side of the fountain, fingertips playing in the water where it ran over the edge, small smile curving her lips.

It was a perfect moment. A perfect vision.

Caton had no idea how perfect she made it.

And she had no idea how long Amelia had searched for this place. Well, how long Selene and Sole had searched. They truly were troopers in the process, doing all of the legwork when it would look too suspicious for Amelia to do it herself. Between the two of them, they had to have been to at least three dozen venues, sending back pictures, patient as saints when nothing was quite good enough.

"Well…" Caton glancing suddenly up at her, it distracted Amelia from the warm thought that the two women she was closest to before Caton had been only too happy to oblige her fanciful whims. It was almost as if they were as fond of Caton as she was. Well, hopefully, not quite as fond. "Are you going to stand there all night, or are you going to come over here and kiss me?"

Thrill of the question moving through her, more of a whisper than the scream it would once have been, Amelia felt the smile that softened her lips as her heels sank into soft grass.

A few steps more and she kicked the shoes away, feeling the formality of the evening seep out of her. All pretense. All worry. And, taking her cue, Caton did the same, looking absolutely delighted and relieved as she did.

By the time Caton was against her, settling close like it was reflex or an autonomic function, the calm and thrill pressed together until Amelia was in a state she only ever seemed to reach in Caton's presence – perfect harmony.

"I like this." Caton slipped one bare foot over the top of Amelia's, the smile on her lips so soft and sincere, it was impossible not to kiss. So, Amelia pressed her lips to Caton's slightly upturned ones, breathing in the warmth of Caton's breath as their lips gently parted.

How long they stayed like that, mouths meeting in the moonlight, there was no cause to track, but it was long enough it went to Amelia's head and most of the rest of her. Pulling back on a slow exhale, she let her forehead fall to Caton's. But when she opened her eyes Caton's gaze was so close and so intent she was afraid she couldn't resist it. Pressing a kiss to Caton's cheek, her jaw, her throat, she slid down her body, hands gliding against the silky fabric of Caton's dress until she felt the grass beneath her knees.

"You are going to stain the hell out of that dress."

"Shame." Shrugging it off, Amelia took one bare foot in her hand, pressing a kiss to its top, before straightening back up to full kneel, palms skimming the backs of Caton's calves, dragging the fabric of Caton's dress along with them.

"I could look at you like this forever."

Caton's hair tumbling somewhat recklessly about her face, she looked different than she did in the harsh light of the ballroom and the oppressive presence of strangers. Like an angel in the soft blue lights off the trees, somehow entirely put together and coming disheveled at the same time.

"Half-naked on a rooftop?"

"Yes," Amelia acknowledged with a laugh.

"You'll probably get sore after a while."

"Probably." Amelia laughed again.

It came so naturally to her now.

It was something she never could have imagined at the start, how much they would one day laugh together. Once upon a time, it was such an unimaginable thing, that laughter could ever be something they would have. Now, it was their everyday. How they had made it from such a hopeless situation to being together here on this rooftop was still difficult to fathom. And, suddenly overwhelmed, Amelia dropped her head to Caton's thigh, torn between saying even more cheesy things and doing something entirely inappropriate given how many people could just fancy a stroll and happen upon them.

"Amelia… Baby… are you okay?" Delicate fingertips combing through her hair, that was impossible too. The casual affection, mildly tinged with concern. Caton's voice so incredibly gentle. The hand in her hair so soothing. How had she lived without it for so long?

Nodding, Amelia lifted her head, blinking back tears and breathing out a choppy breath. "I'm fine. I think… I think I'm just nervous." She realized with another near laugh.

"About what?"

"I don't know exactly." She couldn't say that she expected it, or that she had any right to such feelings. How many strangers had she beguiled over the years? How many dates with groups of patrons had she gone on with nary a drop of perspiration? Now, the person she knew she had, the only person she wanted, and she felt as if her soul was about to depart from her body, float off in a quivering miasma of anxiety.

"Hm." Caton exhaled a soft sound, her knees giving a slight bend, and before Amelia knew what was happening, they were kneeling eye to eye.

Gasp of protest escaping her, Amelia tried belatedly to press Caton back up. This wasn't how things were supposed to go. They weren't supposed to be on the same level. She was trying to be reverent. Couldn't Caton see she was trying to be reverent?!

"Maybe this will help."

Small, shiny object suddenly in Caton's fingers, it glinted off the blue lights in the trees, and Amelia felt her soul return to her with a heavy thud. As if she had leapt from a great height and landed sooner than expected. Mouth falling slightly agape, she stared at the ring - small and glittering - in Caton's hand, without comprehending or being able to form a single thought.

"No." When her brain finally shook free, she wondered how it had happened, how she had managed to completely lose control of this moment. "I'm proposing to you."

"Well, that may be… but you're not doing it before I get to," Caton stated matter of factly. "I mean, don't get me wrong. This…" Gaze going to the dangling blue in the trees, her eyes sparkled in their glow, as the sound of the water trickling over the edges of the fountain filled the momentary silence. "Is incredible. I appreciate all of the effort. But I bought mine first."

"How do you…" Amelia began to ask, but realized Caton must have a reason for making such a bold proclamation and altered the question. "When?"

"As soon as we got here."

Response ripping a small huff out of her, Amelia nearly tossed forward. Well, there it was. And that would, in fact, be well before she bought her ring, which had only been three months before when it finally felt as if this tangled mess might actually be conquerable.

"But then why…?"

But she knew why. Of course, she knew. She had been so strange at the start, afraid of saying all the things she really wanted to say. Afraid of feeling the things she couldn't help but already feel. So, she had tried to compensate. Had tried to be casual and non-clingy. Even as Caton moved into the house in Ohio. Even as they packed their things into joint boxes to move states away. Afraid if she held too tightly to Caton, she would only end up pushing her away.

Afraid, deep down, Caton really wanted to go. That she would realize what they were dealing with and that she didn't have to deal with any of it. Realize Amelia came with an entire cargo load of baggage, and it was heavy.

Caton had probably bought the ring to calm her ass down.

"You were worried about the money." Caton shrugged weakly. "You called it blood money, and you weren't wrong. So, it never really felt like the right time."

Then, of course, there was that.

But that was all done now. They had replaced those ill-gotten gains with fairly reaped ones and had done a lot of good in the process. Amelia was certain they could never do enough to counteract all the bad Jack did, but they couldn't live under the onus of him forever. Their own karma was clean.

"But Selene and Sole…" Hand going to Caton's shoulder, Amelia felt a little as if she might pass out and took a moment to draw a full breath.

"They knew," Caton said. "Why do you think they gave me a heads up? They know what's fair."

"Of course, they do." If Selene and Sole knew Caton meant to propose to her, of course they were going to warn her when Amelia tried to usurp her big moment.

But there was more to Caton's story too. And that was that part that kept bounding back in Amelia's brain. She had given Caton so many outs, had held the door open with the tip of her boot just in case Caton ever wanted to go. Part of her almost wished Caton *would* go, would take off and find some easier life, so she could stop feeling so guilty about dragging her into such chaos.

"You were never going anywhere." Looking to Caton now, Amelia was exceedingly grateful she hadn't.

"I was never going anywhere," Caton returned "Still not. I mean, as long as you want me."

As long as… God, what a stupid fucking thing to say.

Taking Caton's face in her hands, Amelia captured her lips, tasting the salt from her own tears.

As long as you want me. How could she not want her? From the moment Caton walked into her kitchen, she was a ticking timebomb, an explosive destined to detonate in Amelia's carefully constructed world. And when she did, she blew everything to pieces until Amelia didn't know how to want anything else.

"You know, you're making it really hard to hold onto this thing," Caton murmured against her lips, and, pulling away, Amelia glanced down at the ring. So small. So simple. They had more money than they knew what to do with, Caton had access to all of it if she wanted, and she picked a ring she could have bought working at any office job. Simply put, it couldn't have been more perfect.

"You can always put it here." Swallowing, Amelia held out her hand, trying to stop the flow of tears to no avail, and the smile that came to Caton's face was pure light as she raised the hand to her lips, fluttering a kiss over the knuckle of Amelia's ring finger and slipped the ring on.